Dup.

BIG LIES

in a

SMALL TOWN

ALSO BY DIANE CHAMBERLAIN

BIG LIES

in a

SMALL TOWN

Diane Chamberlain

ST. MARTIN'S PRESS
NEW YORK

First published in the United States by St. Martin's Press, an imprint of St. Martin's Publishing Group

BIG LIES IN A SMALL TOWN. Copyright © 2019 by Diane Chamberlain. All rights reserved. Printed in the United States of America. For information, address St. Martin's Publishing Group, 120 Broadway, New York, NY 10271.

www.stmartins.com

The Library of Congress Cataloging-in-Publication Data is available upon request.

ISBN 978-1-250-08733-1 (hardcover)
ISBN 978-1-250-08735-5 (ebook)
ISBN 978-1-250-27052-8 (international, sold outside
the U.S. subject to rights availability)

Our books may be purchased in bulk for promotional, educational, or business use. Please contact your local bookseller or the Macmillan Corporate and Premium Sales Department at 1-800-221-7945, extension 5442, or by email at MacmillanSpecialMarkets@macmillan.com.

First Edition: January 2020

10 9 8 7 6 5 4 3 2 1

For my stepdaughters,
Brittany Walls, Alana Glaves, and Caitlin Campbell,
each an artist in her own right

BIG LIES

in a

SMALL TOWN

PROLOGUE

———— ✦ ————

Edenton, North Carolina
March 23, 1940

The children knew it was finally spring, so although the air still held the nip of winter and the grass and weeds crunched beneath their feet, they ran through the field and woods, yipping with the anticipation of warmer weather. The two boys and their little sister headed for the creek, drawn to water, as they always were. The girl, only three and not as sure-footed as her brothers, tripped over something and landed face-first in the cold water of the creek. Her big brother picked her up before she could start howling, cuddling her close against his thin jacket, a hand-me-down from one cousin or another. He looked down to see what she'd stumbled over and leaped back, dropping his sister to the earth. Grabbing his younger brother's arm, he pointed. It was a man, lying there, his rumpled clothes sopping wet and his face as white and waxy as the candles their mama kept around the house for when the electric went out, which was every other day, it seemed.

The younger boy backed away. "He alive?" he whispered.

The little girl got to her feet and started moving toward the man, but her older brother grabbed her arm and held her back.

"Uh-uh," he said. "He dead as a doornail. And look"—he pointed—"his head all caved in."

"Let's git outta here!" the younger boy said, turning to run back the way they'd come, and his brother was quick to follow, holding their sister beneath his arm like a football. He knew they wouldn't tell. Wouldn't say nothing to their mama or no one. Because though they were young, one thing they'd already learned. Colored boy found with a dead white body? That didn't look good to nobody.

Chapter 1

———✦———

MORGAN

North Carolina Correctional Facility for Women
Raleigh, North Carolina
June 8, 2018

This hallway always felt cold to me, no matter the time of year. Cinder-block walls, a linoleum floor that squeaked beneath my prison-issue shoes. You wouldn't know what season it was from this hallway. Wouldn't know it was June outside, that things were blooming and summer was on its way. It was on its way for those outside, anyway. I was facing my second summer inside these cinder-block walls and tried not to think about it.

"Who's here?" I asked the guard walking by my side. I never had visitors. I'd given up expecting one of my parents to show up, and that was fine with me. My father came once after I'd been here a couple of weeks, but he was already wasted, although it wasn't yet noon, and all he did was yell. Then he cried those sloppy drunk tears that always embarrassed me.

My mother hadn't come at all. My arrest held a mirror up to their flaws and now they were as finished with me as I was with them.

"Dunno who it is, Blondie," the guard said. She was new and I didn't know her name and couldn't read the name tag hanging around her neck, but she'd obviously already learned my prison nickname. And while she might have been new to the NCCFW, I could tell she wasn't new to prison work. She moved too easily down this hallway, and the burned-out, bored, bitter look in her dark eyes gave her away.

I headed for the door to the visiting room, but the guard grabbed my arm.

"Uh-uh," she said. "Not that way. S'posed to take you in here today." She turned me in the direction of the private visiting room, and I was instantly on guard. Why the private room? Couldn't be good news.

I walked into the small room to find two women sitting at one side of a table. Both of them were somewhere between forty and fifty. No prison uniforms. They were dressed for business in suits, one navy, the other tan. They looked up at me, unsmiling, their dark-skinned faces unreadable. I kept my gaze on them as I sat down at the other side of the table. Did they see the anxiety in my eyes? I'd learned to trust no one in this place.

"What's this about?" I asked.

The woman in the tan suit sat forward, manicured hands folded neatly on the table. "My name is Lisa Williams," she said. She had a pin on her lapel in the shape of a house, and she reminded me a little of Michelle Obama. Shoulder-length hair. Perfectly shaped eyebrows. But she didn't have Michelle Obama's ready smile. This woman's expression was somewhere between boredom and apprehension. "And this is Andrea Fuller. She's an attorney."

Andrea Fuller nodded at me. She was older than I'd thought. Fifty-something. Maybe even sixty. She wore her hair in a short, no-nonsense Afro sprinkled with gray. Her lipstick was a deep red.

I shook my head. "I don't understand," I said, looking from one woman to the other. "Why did you want to see me?"

"Andrea and I are here to offer you a way out of this place," the woman named Lisa said. Her gaze darted to my lacy tattoo where it peeked out from beneath the short sleeve of my pale blue prison shirt. I'd designed the intricate tattoo myself—black lace crisscrossed with strings of tiny pearls and chandelier jewelry. Lisa lifted her gaze to mine again. "As of next week, you've served your minimum sentence. One year, right?" she asked.

I half nodded, waiting. Yes, I'd served my one-year minimum, but the maximum was three years, and from everything I'd been told, I wasn't going anywhere for a long time.

"We . . . Andrea and I . . . have been working on getting you released," Lisa said.

I stared at her blankly. "Why?" I asked. "You don't even know me." I knew there was some sort of program where law students tried to free prisoners who had been wrongly imprisoned, but I was the only person who seemed to think my imprisonment had been a mistake.

Andrea Fuller cleared her throat and spoke for the first time. "We've made the case that you're uniquely qualified for some work Lisa would like you to do. Your release depends on your willingness to do that work and—"

"In a timely fashion," Lisa interrupted.

"Yes, there's a deadline for the completion of the work," Andrea said. "And of course you'll be under the supervision of a parole officer during that time, and you'll also be paying restitution to the family of the girl you injured—the Maxwell family, and—"

"Wait." I held up my hand. I was surprised to see that my fingers trembled and I dropped my hand to my lap. "Please slow down," I said. "I'm not following you at all." I was overwhelmed by the way the two women hopped around in their conversation. What work was I uniquely qualified to do? I'd worked in the laundry here at the prison, learning to fold sheets into perfect squares, and I'd washed dishes in hot chlorine-scented water until my eyes stung. They were the only unique qualifications I could think of.

Lisa lifted her own hands, palms forward, to stop the conversation. "It's like this," she said, her gaze steady on me. "Do you know who Jesse Jameson Williams was?"

Everyone knew who Jesse Jameson Williams was. The name instantly transported me to one of the rooms in the National Gallery in Washington, D.C. Four years ago now. No, five. I'd been seventeen on a high school trip. My classmates had been ready to leave the museum, but I'd wanted to stay, smitten by the contemporary art, so I hid in the restroom while my class headed out of the building. I didn't know or care where they were going. I knew I'd get in trouble, but I would deal with that later. So I was alone when I saw my first Jesse Jameson Williams. The painting quite literally stole my breath, and I lowered myself to the sole bench in the gallery to study it. *The Look*, it was called. It was a tall painting, six feet at least, and quite narrow. A man and woman dressed in black evening clothes stood back-to-back against a glittery silver background, their bodies so close it was impossible to separate his black jacket from her black dress. They were both brown skinned, though the woman was several shades darker than the man. His eyes were downcast, as if the man were trying to look behind himself at the woman, but her eyes were wide open, looking out at the viewer—at me—as though she wasn't quite sure she wanted to be in the painting at all. As though she might be saying, *Help me*. When I could breathe again, I searched the walls for more of Jesse Jameson Williams's work and found several pieces. Then, in the museum shop, I paged through a coffee table book of his paintings, wishing I could afford its seventy-five-dollar price tag.

"He's one of my favorite artists," I answered Lisa.

"Ah." For the first time, Lisa smiled, or nearly so, anyway. "That's very good to hear, because he has a lot to do with my proposal."

"I don't understand," I said again. "He's dead, isn't he?" I'd read about his death in the paper in the prison library. He'd been ninety-five and had certainly led a productive life, yet I'd still felt a wave of loss wash over me when I read the news.

"He died in January," Lisa said, then added, "Jesse Williams was my father."

"Really!" I sat up straighter.

"For the last twenty-five years of his life, he dedicated himself to helping young artists," Lisa said.

I nodded. I'd read about his charitable work.

"Artists he thought had promise but were having a hard time with school or family or maybe just heading down the wrong path."

Was she talking about me? Could Jesse Williams have seen my work someplace and thought there was something promising in it, something that my professors had missed? "I remember reading about some teenaged boy he helped a few years ago," I said. "I don't know where I—"

"It could have been any number of boys." Lisa waved an impatient hand through the air. "He'd focus on one young man—or young woman—at a time. Make sure they had the money and support necessary to get the education they needed. He'd show their work or do whatever he saw fit to give them a boost." She cocked her head. "He was a very generous man, but also a manipulative one," she said.

"What do you mean?" I asked.

"Shortly before he died, he became interested in *you*," Lisa said. "You were going to be his next project."

"Me?" I frowned. "I never even met him. And I'm white." I lifted a strand of my straight, pale blond hair as if to prove my point. "Aren't all the people he helped African American?"

Lisa shook her head. "Most, but definitely not all," she said with a shrug. "And to be frank, I have no idea why he zeroed in on you. He often helped North Carolina artists, so that's one reason—you're from Cary, right?— but there are plenty of others he could have chosen. Why you were on his Good Samaritan radar is anyone's guess."

This made no sense. "Isn't anything he had planned for me . . . or for anyone . . . didn't his plans die with him?"

"I wish," Lisa said. She smoothed a strand of her Michelle Obama hair behind her ear with a tired gesture. "My father's still controlling things from the grave." She glanced at Andrea with a shake of her head, while I waited, hands clutched together in my lap, not sure I liked this woman. "I lived with him," Lisa continued. "I was his main caretaker and he was getting very feeble. He knew he was nearing the end and he met with his lawyer"—she nodded toward Andrea—"and updated his will. He was in the process of building a gallery in Edenton. An art gallery to feature his paintings and those of some other artists as well as some student work."

"Oh," I said, still puzzled. "Did he want to put one of my pieces in it?" Maybe that was it. Had he somehow heard about me and wanted to give my career—such as it was—a boost through exposure in his gallery? Ridiculous. How would he have heard about me? I couldn't picture any of my professors at UNC singing my praises. And what on earth would I put in his gallery? My mind zigzagged through my paintings, all of them at my parents' house . . . unless my parents had gotten rid of them, which wouldn't have surprised me.

"Nothing that simple," Lisa said. "He wanted you to restore an old 1940s mural, and he stipulated that the gallery can't be opened until the restored mural is in place in the foyer. And the date of the gallery opening is August fifth."

This had to be a mistake. They had to be looking for someone else, and I felt my chance at freedom slipping away. Restore a *mural*? In two months? First, I had no experience in art conservation, and second, I'd worked on exactly one mural in my nearly three years in college and that had been a simple four-by-eight-foot abstract I'd painted with another student my freshman year. "Are you sure he meant me?" I asked.

"Definitely."

"Why does he . . . why would he think I'm 'uniquely qualified' to do this?" I asked, remembering the phrase. "How did he even know I exist?"

"Who knows?" Lisa said, obviously annoyed by her father's eccentricities. "All I know is you're now my problem."

I bristled at her attitude, but kept my mouth shut. If the two of them could actually help me get out of here, I couldn't afford to alienate them.

"I suppose he thought you were qualified by virtue of your art education," Andrea said. "You *were* an art major, correct?"

I nodded. I'd been an art major, yes, but that had nothing to do with restoration. Restoration required an entirely different set of skills from the creation of art. Plus, I hadn't been the most dedicated student that last year. I'd let myself get sucked in by Trey instead of my studies. He'd absorbed my time and energy. I'd been nauseatingly smitten, drawn in by his attention and the future we were planning together. He'd told me about his late grandmother's engagement ring, hinting that it would soon be mine. I'd thought he was so wonderful. Pre-law. Sweet. Amazing to look at. I'd been a fool. But I knew better than to say anything about lack of qualifications to these two women when they were talking about getting me out of here.

"So . . . where's this mural?" I asked.

"In Edenton. You'd have to live in Edenton," Lisa said. "With me. My house—my father's house, actually—is big. We won't be tripping over each other."

I could barely believe my ears. I'd not only get out of prison but I'd live in Jesse Jameson Williams's house? I felt the unexpected threat of tears. Oh God, how I needed to get out of here! In the last miserable year, I'd been bruised, cut, and battered. I'd learned to fight back, yes, but that was not who I was. I was no brawler. My fellow inmates mocked me for my youth, my slender build, my platinum hair. I lived in a state of perpetual fear. Even in my cell, I felt unsafe. My cellmate was a woman who didn't talk. Literally. I'd never heard a word from her mouth, but her expression carried disdain. I barely slept, one eye open, expecting to have my throat slit with a stolen knife sometime during the night.

And then there were the nightmares about Emily Maxwell, but I supposed I would bring them with me no matter where I went.

"You'll work on the mural in the gallery, which is only partially built at this point," Lisa interrupted my thoughts. "There's plenty of room in the foyer. That's where my father wanted it displayed."

"It's not painted on a wall?"

"No, it's on canvas and it was never . . . hung, or whatever you call it."

"Installed," Andrea said.

"Right," Lisa said. "It was never installed."

"Who painted it?"

"A woman named Anna Dale," Lisa said. "It's one of those Depression-era murals. You know how, during the Depression, the government hired artists to paint murals for public buildings?"

I nodded, though my knowledge of those WPA-type programs was sketchy at best.

"This mural was supposed to be for the Edenton Post Office. But Anna Dale went crazy or something—I can't remember exactly what my father told me. She lost her mind while she was working on it, thus the finished product was never installed. My father's owned it for decades and he wants—wanted—to hang it in the foyer of the gallery. And he said it has to be in place by the date the gallery opens."

"August fifth," Andrea said in case I hadn't heard the date the first time. I most definitely had.

"That's not even two months from now," I said.

Lisa let out a long, anxious-sounding breath. "Exactly," she said. "Which is why you need to start on it immediately."

"What kind of shape is it in?" I asked.

Lisa shrugged. "I haven't actually seen it. It's been rolled up in a corner of my father's studio closet all these years—it's a massive thing—and I don't know what condition it's in. It must be salvageable, though, if he expected you to fix it."

I tried to imagine what nearly seventy years would do to a huge canvas stuffed in a closet. What Lisa needed was a professional restoration company, not a novice artist. But what *I* needed was my freedom.

"Would I be paid?" I looked at Andrea. "If I have to pay restitution to—"

"My father left fifty thousand for the project," Lisa interrupted.

"For the whole gallery?"

"No," Lisa said. "For *you*. For you to restore the mural. Fifty K, plus another several thousand for any supplies you need."

Fifty thousand dollars? Incredible. Even if I'd gotten my degree, I doubted I could have found a job that would pay me that much in a year's time, much less for two months' work. Two months' work I had no idea how to do. I tried to keep my self-doubt from showing on my face. *Uniquely qualified?* Not hardly.

"This is your 'get out of jail free' card, Morgan." Andrea leaned forward, her red lips forming the words slowly and clearly. "If you hold up your end of the bargain—finishing your work—*quality* work—on the mural by the fifth of August—you'll be out on parole and will never have to set foot in this place again. If I were you, I'd start reading up on restoration."

I looked toward the doorway of the small room. I imagined walking through it and down the hallway to the front entrance and freedom. I imagined twirling in circles outside, my arms stretched wide to take in the fresh air. I didn't think I'd ever be completely free of this place, though. I'd always carry my prison with me. I felt that imaginary prison closing around me even as I sat there, even as I imagined walking out the front door.

Still, I would rather an imaginary prison than this hideous real one.

"I'll do it," I said finally, sitting back.

How I would do it, I had no idea.

Chapter 2

---※·※---

ANNA

December 4, 1939
Edenton, North Carolina

From the United States Treasury Department, Section of Fine Arts
Special 48-States Mural Competition
November 27, 1939
Dear Miss Anna Dale,

The Section of Fine Arts is pleased to inform you that you are one
of the winning artists in the 48-States Mural Competition. Your sketch
for the proposed mural to adorn the Bordentown, New Jersey, Post
Office received many positive comments from the judges. Unfor-
tunately, a different artist has been awarded the Bordentown Post
Office, but the judges were sufficiently impressed with your work that
they would like you to undertake the creation of the mural for the post
office in Edenton, North Carolina. This will require that you send us
a sketch for the Edenton assignment as soon as possible. Once you

receive the Section's approval on the sketch, you can begin the actual work on the (full size) cartoon and, finally, the mural itself. The size of the Edenton mural will be 12' by 6'. The project is to be completed by June 3, 1940.

It is suggested that artists become familiar with the geographic area surrounding their assigned post office and make a special effort to select appropriate subject matter. The following subjects are suggested: Local History, Local Industries, Local Flora and Fauna, and Local Pursuits. Since the location of Edenton, North Carolina, was not your first choice and you are therefore most likely not familiar with the town, it is strongly suggested you make a visit there as soon as possible.

The payment for the mural will be $720, one third payable on the approval of your sketch, one third payable on the approval of your cartoon, one third payable upon installation of the final mural. Out of this amount, you will pay for your supplies, models if needed, any travel, and all costs related to the installation of the mural.

Sincerely,

Edward Rowan, Art Administrator, Section of Fine Arts

Anna arrived in Edenton for her planned three-day visit late on the afternoon of December 4. She could have taken the overnight train, but at the last minute she decided to drive. The '32 navy blue Ford V8 still held her mother's scent—the spicy patchouli fragrance of the Tabu perfume she'd loved—and Anna needed that comfort as she set out on this new, very adult venture. Her first paying job. Her first time away from home. Her first everything, really.

The car skidded on a patch of ice as she turned onto Broad Street in the fading sunlight, and for a moment she was certain her introduction to the town would consist of slamming into a row of parked cars, but she managed to get the Ford under control. As soon as she did, she found herself behind a cart drawn by a horse, or perhaps a mule. She couldn't get a good look at the animal and wasn't sure she'd know one from the other anyway. She didn't see many of either in her hometown of Plainfield, New Jersey.

She slowed down, thinking she should get a good look at the little town that would be the subject of her mural. When she'd viewed Edenton in the atlas, it had been a watery-looking place, nothing more than a speck surrounded by a bay and a river. Even on the map, it had looked strangely foreign to her, and she'd closed the atlas with a worried sigh.

She hadn't expected to win the competition, and the timing could not have been worse. She'd just buried her mother. Her best friend. The one person in the world whose love and nurturing Anna could always count on. But she couldn't turn down work, not with jobs so impossible to find. Not when her mother was no longer around to bring in the sewing money that had paid for their food and expenses. No, she needed to be grateful for this opportunity, even if it meant she had to travel more than four hundred miles to "become familiar with the geographic area" she was to immortalize in the mural.

She'd never had any yearning to travel south of the Mason-Dixon line, and she was glad she'd only be here for a few days. The South seemed so backward to her. Segregated schools and ridiculous laws about keeping colored and white apart on buses and at water fountains and in restrooms. She'd had a few colored classmates at Plainfield High School and she'd counted a couple of the girls as friends. They'd been on the basketball team and in glee club together.

"You're looking at Plainfield through rose-colored glasses," her mother would have said. Even in Plainfield, those colored girls Anna thought of as her friends couldn't go into certain shops or restaurants with her, and one of them told her they had to sit in the balcony at the Paramount Theater. The roller rink had a "colored night" set aside for them each week and they—as well as Anna's Jewish friends—were unwelcome at the country club. But still, everyone knew it was worse in the South. They actually *lynched* Negroes in the south.

She'd considered simply doing her research for the mural in the Plainfield Public Library, knowing the drive to Edenton would take her two full days, but she'd read and reread the letter from the Section of Fine Arts that advised her to visit the little town. Her mother would have told her to do the job properly. Anna imagined her saying "be grateful for the work, sweetheart, and embrace the challenge." Her friends who had graduated with her from the Van Emburgh School of Art in Plainfield were still hunting for jobs that simply didn't exist, with the economy the way it was. Many of them had also tried to win the Section of Fine Arts competition and Anna knew how lucky she was to have been given the honor. She would do everything she could to make the Section glad they put their trust in her.

A few days before she died, her mother had given Anna a journal. The book of blank pages was bound in velvety-soft brown leather, the cover fastened together with a simple gold lock and key. So beautiful. Her mother had known then that it would be the last gift she would ever give her daughter, but Anna hadn't known. It angered her when she realized the truth, and she didn't want to feel that emotion toward her mother. In a fit of rage, she'd tossed the journal in the kitchen trash can, but she dug it out again, cleaned it off, and now it was packed in her suitcase. She wouldn't throw away anything connected to her mother again. She needed to hold on to it all.

She also had her mother's camera with her. Anna had choked up as she sat at the kitchen table winding a new roll of film into the Kodak Retina. She pictured her mother's hands doing the same task over the years . . . although when Anna thought about it, she realized many months had passed since her mother had picked up the camera. Photography had been her passion. It brought in no money, but had given her great pleasure during her "lively spells." The doctor called them "manic episodes" but Anna preferred her own term. The lively spells were always a relief to Anna when they followed the days—sometimes the weeks—when her mother could barely get out of bed. The lively spells came without warning, often with behavior that was impossible to predict. She'd awaken Anna early to inform her she was skipping school, and they'd take the bus to New York where they'd race through museum after museum or roller-skate through Central Park. One time, when Anna was about twelve, they slipped in the rear door of Carnegie Hall, found a couple of empty box seats, and watched an orchestra perform. It wasn't the music Anna remembered from that day. It was the sheer joy of sitting next to her mother, leaning her head against her shoulder, feeling her wired energy. Knowing that, for as long as the lively spell lasted, their days would be joy-filled.

When the good spells came during the spring, as they often did, one of her mother's favorite activities was to walk at a brisk clip through Plainfield's neighborhoods, carrying her camera, snapping pictures of people's gardens. She adored flowers and she'd walk up the driveways of strangers to reach window boxes overflowing with geraniums, even ducking behind the houses to capture backyard gardens filled with roses and hydrangeas and peach-colored daylilies. As far as Anna knew, no one ever badgered her mother about the intrusions. Maybe people had thought of her as a bit of a kook. Or perhaps they'd felt sorry for her, a woman widowed young with a daughter to raise. Or maybe they knew the truth—Mrs. Dale was not a well woman—and they kindly let her be.

Anna fended for herself when her mother's spirits were low. She'd cook for both of them, although her mother ate almost nothing during those times. She'd clean the house and do the laundry. She did it all with patience, with love, waiting out the melancholia. There was one terrible time when Aunt Alice dragged Anna's mother to a psychiatrist who insisted she be hospitalized. For two long months, Anna, then fourteen, lived with her aunt and uncle, angry at them both for putting her mother in that terrible place. When her mother was finally released, there were gaps in her memory, precious moments the hospital seemed to have stolen from her, and Anna vowed she would never let anyone lock her away again. She tried to keep her mother's low moods a secret from her aunt after that, making light of them, riding them out. Perhaps, though, she'd made a mistake this last time. Perhaps this last time, her mother had needed more help than Anna had been able to give her. She tried not to think about that. She'd simply been waiting for the lively spell to return. She'd lived with her mother long enough to know that, in time, the smiling, happy mother she adored would come back, full of crazy ideas that would leave both of them giggling with wonder.

"Never be afraid to try something new, Anna," her mother would say.

That's what Anna was doing now, wasn't it? Driving for two whole days through unfamiliar territory, landing in a tiny town where she didn't know a soul. From somewhere in the heavens, her mother was applauding.

⇒▸•◂

The letter from the Section of Fine Arts had arrived with a list of the winners of all forty-eight states. Anna had felt embarrassed and intimidated when she looked at that list. The contest had been anonymous, which she assumed was the only reason she'd been able to win. Still, many of the other winners were famous artists. There was So and So, from New York City, president of the League of Artists, studied in Europe, experienced muralist, had one-man exhibitions in New York and Los Angeles, and on and on. Winner after winner had accolade after accolade. And then there was Anna: *Anna Dale. Plainfield, New Jersey. Born 1918. Graduate of Van Emburgh School of Art.* And that was it. She thought the panel of judges must have been stunned into silence when they opened her envelope to discover the inexperienced girl they'd selected. She had to keep reminding herself that they'd legitimately picked *her*, fair and square, and she remembered what Mrs. Van Emburgh had whispered in her ear when she handed Anna her graduation certificate: "You are a standout, Anna," she'd said. "You have a future in the art world." Her words still sent a shiver up Anna's spine. She'd told no one about them, not wanting to appear conceited, but she clung tight to the compliment now that she'd won the competition. Now that she was, so completely, on her own.

She had to come up with a whole new idea for a sketch very quickly, and the thought overwhelmed her. The concept for her Bordentown sketch had come to her easily. Clara Barton had founded the first free public school in Bordentown, so Anna had painted her ringing the school bell outside a little redbrick schoolhouse with lines of children walking and skipping to the school. She was proud of the way she captured the swish of the girls' skirts and the energy of the boys. Too bad she wouldn't be able to paint that mural now. The memory of her eager, happy production of that sketch, before everything changed, seemed to be from another lifetime.

She *did* have an idea for the Edenton mural, though. In the Plainfield library, the librarian pointed her toward the American Guide Series' book on North Carolina. In it, she read about the "Edenton Tea Party," an eighteenth-century women's movement in which fifty-one women signed a petition to boycott all English products. She thought that might make an intriguing mural and wouldn't be too challenging to paint. The idea seemed so simple to her at first that she thought she might not even have to travel to Edenton to do her research, but then she realized she actually *wanted* this trip. She needed to get away for a few days. She needed an escape from the sadness in the little house where she expected to see her mother every time she walked into another room.

King Street. She spotted the sign and turned left to see a big brick block of a building. The Hotel Joseph Hewes. It would be her home while she was in this town she knew as well as she knew Jupiter or Saturn. She drove into the parking lot, heart pounding, hands sticky on the steering wheel, wondering what the next few days would hold.

Chapter 3

———— ✦ ————

MORGAN

June 13, 2018

I blinked against the bright sunlight as I walked with Lisa toward the silver sedan in the prison parking lot. The only words Lisa had said to me so far were "do you have everything?" and the two of us were quiet as we left the building. I breathed in the sweet air of freedom, but my stomach was full of knots. I held my chin high, though. Put on the tough-girl look I'd perfected inside. *I'm not afraid of anything,* I told myself . . . though the truth was, I was undeniably intimidated by the woman at my side. Lisa was Jesse Jameson Williams's daughter, which was enough to intimidate anyone, but it was more than that. I couldn't read her. Her brittle silence, for starters. What was that about? Her upright carriage and no-nonsense speed walk as she headed toward the car while checking her phone every two seconds. Her unsmiling, clenched-teeth expression. Anger bubbled just below the surface in this woman, I thought, and I didn't like the fact that she held all the cards for my future.

I hadn't anticipated the unease I felt getting into a car. It had been a bit more than a year since I'd been in any sort of vehicle, and my fingers froze on the outside handle of the car door. Lisa was already in the driver's seat by the time I managed to pull myself together enough to open the door. Even then, I stood there holding the plastic bag of my very few belongings at my side, the muscles in my legs locked in paralysis.

"Come on, get in," Lisa called.

I climbed into the car and sat down on the leather seat, dropping the bag of belongings at my feet. I pulled the door closed, then buckled the seat belt with fingers that felt ice-cold despite the warm spring weather.

Lisa stuck her phone in the holder on the dashboard, then started the car, still not speaking. Of course, I wasn't speaking, either. I wanted to say *thank you for doing this,* but that would make me sound more vulnerable than I wanted to appear. I felt so strange, like I was attempting to step back into the person I used to be. For the first time in a year, I was wearing my small silver hoop earrings, the silver stud in my nostril, and my old blue sleeveless shirt. Not that I'd selected the shirt from my closet; I'd been wearing it the day I got locked up, so that was all I had with me. Still, I was glad I had on this particular shirt, not only because the day was warm, but because I wanted Lisa to see my tattoo in its entirety. The intricacy of the lacy design. It was the only thing I had with me to illustrate that I had any artistic talent. But Lisa said nothing about it.

Why was this woman wound so tight? Did she resent the fact that I was a criminal she'd been forced to spring from jail? Or that she was conservatively dressed and groomed within an inch of her life—I could smell jasmine-scented perfume in the air—while I sat there in my torn-at-the-knee jeans with a tattoo on my arm? Or that some of the money Lisa stood to inherit was going into my pocket? Or maybe that I was white on top of it all? I had no idea. All I knew at that moment was that Lisa was too close to the car in front of us while driving sixty-five miles per hour. You were supposed to allow a car length for every ten miles per hour. I remembered the rule from driver's ed, though I'd probably never followed it myself. But that was before. Now I had to fight the urge to press an imaginary brake on the floor to slow Lisa down. *This is the new Morgan,* I thought sadly to myself. *The Morgan afraid of the outside world.*

We'd ridden ten minutes in silence before Lisa finally spoke.

"The government never fully paid the artist—Anna Dale—for the mural, so after she went crazy—or whatever happened—it essentially became my father's property to do with as he pleased," she said. "But since the gallery is a gift to the community, your work on the mural becomes a sort of community service." She glanced at me, and the smallest of smiles lifted the corners of her lips. "So says Andrea."

The rationale seemed quite a stretch and I waited for her to continue, unsure of her point. "I understand," I said when it was clear Lisa had nothing more to say on the subject. "But why did the mural end up with your father?"

She shrugged. "No idea," she said. "He didn't leave me much in the way of details. I'm just following his orders."

I kept my gaze riveted on the brake lights of the car in front of us.

"You have to meet with the parole officer within three days," Lisa added.

"I know." My responsibilities had been drilled into my head. "Is it possible . . . I can get an advance on my pay?"

Lisa looked at me sharply.

"I need clothes for the outside," I said. "I mean, for . . . I just need clothes. I don't have any with me except what I have on. And I'll need a phone."

"Could your family send you your clothes?"

"My parents and I aren't talking."

"Do they know you're out? Would that make a difference?" Lisa's phone rang and she looked at it. Pressed a button to stop the call. "I mean, would they talk to you now?" she continued.

I hadn't called them. What was the point? If I'd learned anything at all those AA meetings I'd attended this past year, it was that I needed to cut toxic people out of my life.

"No, it wouldn't make a difference," I said.

Lisa didn't respond and we drove in silence for a few more minutes. Then she made a call using the speaker on her phone. Something about a house. A contract. She was a real estate agent, I realized, and the little house pin on her lapel suddenly made sense. As she spoke into the phone, Lisa's voice was higher, friendlier, more upbeat. A completely different person. When she hung up, she glanced at me. "Yes, you can have an advance," she said. "You *are* going to need a phone. We need to be in touch all the time, and you're going to need a laptop computer for restoration research, I'm sure. So I'll advance you four thousand. Get what you need."

"Thanks," I said.

We were on Route 64 now and I watched the speedometer creep past eighty. I tried to shift my thinking to the absolute insanity that I was now out of prison because of Jesse Jameson Williams. Just the idea of him having known my name sent a thrill through me, though I still couldn't help but feel he'd had me confused with another Morgan Christopher. Yet what was the likelihood there was another young artist—some young black artist, maybe—with my name in North Carolina? I wished I knew how he'd learned about me. It wasn't like I'd been a top student. If my lifelong passion for art had been enough, I would have been a star, but my desire to create hadn't been enough. One of my not-so-tactful professors told me I was in the top of the pack when it came to effort, but the "bottom of the middle of the pack" when it came to talent. "Talent can't be taught," he told me. He'd crushed me with those words. I'd thought of dropping out then, but art was all I'd ever cared about. Trey told me to tough it out. "He's an asshole," he said about my professor. "Your work is awesome." Trey always had a way of building me up when I was down, but he wasn't an artist, so what did he know? And then the accident happened and I'd landed in prison, and that pretty much made the "drop out/don't drop out" decision for me.

"What did you mean about the artist going crazy?" I asked Lisa. "What does that mean, exactly? Schizophrenia? Psychosis? Things were different back then. Maybe she'd just been depressed and was never able to get treatment for it." I thought I knew something about going crazy. Sometimes in the past year, I'd felt insanity creeping in. Paranoia in my case, but that had been based in reality. There'd been women in the prison out to get me.

Lisa kept her eyes on the road and shrugged almost imperceptibly. "I don't know," she said. "My father told me that about her one time and I didn't think to ask him anything more. I'd never seen the mural, so I didn't really care, but I think he was obsessed with it." She looked in her rearview mirror and put on her blinker to change lanes. "Whatever was wrong with the artist, it was enough to prevent her from turning the mural over to the post office and getting paid, so it must have been pretty serious."

"What's the subject of the mural?" I asked, trying to focus on conversation to keep my mind off the road.

"I think just things related to the town," Lisa said. "To Edenton. Most of the old murals were like that. We'll see it soon enough, anyway." She didn't sound all that invested in the mural, and I guessed it was just a means to an end for her. Something she had to take care of to get the gallery up and running.

"So . . . you said there would be other artists' work displayed in the gallery?" I asked.

Lisa nodded. "There'll be a permanent collection of my father's work, then a room for a few other well-known artists he had in his collection, many of them his good friends. That will change every few months. Then a rotating display of the work of the young artists he's helped over the years and that work will be for sale." Her voice had grown tight. "There's just too much to be done before we can open the doors."

"Is this your background, too?" I asked. "Art?" Lisa didn't strike me as an artist. She looked more like the *patron* of an artist, if anything. Someone who could afford the awesomely tailored suit she was wearing and the diamond tennis bracelet that glittered at her wrist.

"I'm a Realtor," she said. "I have no artistic talent . . . or interest . . .

whatsoever, except with regard to the historical architecture of the houses I sell."

"Oh," I said. "Why did Jesse Williams—I mean, your father—put you in charge of the gallery, then?"

Lisa didn't answer right away and I thought I might have stepped over a line with the question. But she finally spoke. "I'm his only child, so I'm it." She let out a sigh. "I knew the gallery was in the works when he died, of course, but I had no idea he was going to dump it all in my lap." She glanced at me. "Don't get me wrong," she said. "I loved my father—I *adored* him—and I want to do this for him, but he gave me an impossible deadline and threw you into the mix . . ." She shook her head. "I still have my real estate business to run. I have clients to deal with. This is a busy time of year for me."

"He must've thought you could pull it off," I said.

Lisa sighed again. Then she reached for the radio, pressed a few buttons, and a podcast began to play. Something about mortgages, and I guessed we were done with our conversation, such as it was.

> ⊱•⊰

If anyone had asked me to guess what sort of house Jesse Jameson Williams had lived in, I would have pictured a Frank Lloyd Wright contemporary hugging a hillside. And I would have been wrong. Lisa pulled into the long driveway of a huge, two-story Victorian with double-tiered porches decorated with elaborate white railings. The whole front of the house looked like it was covered in white lace, and a garden, alive with color, stretched the entire width of the house.

"This was Jesse's house?" I asked, surprised.

"The De Claire house," Lisa said as we got out of her car. "A man named Byron De Claire was the first owner when it was built in 1880. My parents bought it in 1980."

I followed Lisa to the front door and into the house, which showed its age only in the Victorian architecture. As Lisa turned off the elaborate-looking security system, I peered into the rooms I could see from where I stood. The foyer, living room, and parlor were painted in muted pastels: seafoam, and lavender, and blue-tinged gray. Artwork adorned every wall, and while Lisa talked on her phone inside the front door, I moved from painting to painting in the huge foyer, almost afraid to breathe near them. I recalled reading somewhere that one of Jesse Williams's paintings went for ten million dollars at an auction, and here I was, surrounded by several of them at one time. Most of the work was his, but I spotted two of Romare Bearden's collages and a huge painting by Judith Shipley of young girls sitting in a field of daisies. I quickly searched the Shipley for the iris the artist always hid in her paintings, a tribute to her mother by the same name, but with all those daisies, I soon gave up and turned my attention to one of the Bearden collages instead. It was full of African-American musicians, mainly guitarists, standing against a vivid red background. I felt a thrill of excitement that I was close enough to these original paintings to touch. Maybe I wasn't much of an artist, but I would always love art itself.

"Come in the kitchen," Lisa said, getting off her call.

I followed her into the spacious white-and-stainless-steel kitchen.

"Didn't Jesse Williams—didn't your father—live in New York most of his life?" I asked.

"Not most, but for many years." Lisa opened the wide, double-door refrigerator and handed me a bottle of water, then unscrewed the cap of another for herself. "And he lived in France before that," she said, leaning against the white-and-gray marble-topped counter. "He was in France during the war and just stayed. He met his first wife there. That lasted fifteen years or so, and after his divorce, he moved to New York and married my mother. She was much younger. It looked like they weren't going to have children, but then I came along." Lisa took a long drink from her water bottle. "She was thirty-nine and he was nearly fifty. He felt the family pull then and wanted to move back to Edenton. Back to his roots. I was seven. He had a name by then, and Edenton wanted to claim him." She set her bottle down and began rifling through a manila file folder on the island. "Even so," she continued, "they had to buy this place for cash. No one would have given a black man a loan for a house in this neighborhood back then. It's hard enough now," she added under her breath in a mutter. She pulled a sheaf of paper from the folder. "I want to read you this part of his will," she said, holding up the paper.

I nodded, and Lisa began to read.

"'My plans for the foyer of the gallery: In the closet of my studio'—his studio is back there, and it's a mess." Lisa pointed through the kitchen window, and I could see a good-size white cottage in the rear of the yard. "'In the closet of my studio,'" Lisa continued, "'you will find a large rolled canvas. This was painted in 1940 as part of a government-sponsored competition for post office murals by a young woman named Anna Dale. Anna completed the mural but became unwell before it could be installed in the post office, and it has been in my possession in one way or another since that time. The mural is to be the focal point of the foyer in the new gallery. Of course, it needs to be restored and that work is to be done by a young lady named Morgan Christopher, who has completed nearly three years as a fine arts major at UNC in Chapel Hill but is currently serving time in the women's prison in Raleigh.'"

I felt my stomach flip. He definitely had the right Morgan Christopher.

"'She has a one-year-minimum prison sentence,'" Lisa continued, "'and when that is up in June of 2018, Lisa will hire legal counsel to free Ms. Christopher to have her restore the mural. The work will be done in the gallery itself. At no time will the mural leave Edenton, so Lisa will make arrangements for Ms. Christopher to live in town while she works. I will leave a sum of fifty thousand dollars as compensation for the work, along with another ten thousand for any supplies and expert advice Ms. Christopher might need.'" Lisa looked up from the page. "He goes on to say how the mural should be displayed, the lighting, et cetera." She began reading again. "He says, 'To the best of my memory, there are no tears in the mural nor is there adhesive on the back that will need to be removed, since it never made it to the post office wall. I am confident, therefore, that despite Morgan

Christopher's lack of restoration experience, she will complete this project in time for the gallery opening on August 5, 2018. That opening date, with the fully restored mural in place, is firm, and my other bequests are contingent on the restored mural being in the gallery on that date.'"

Upon reading that last sentence, Lisa shook her head with what looked like a mixture of exhaustion and annoyance. "Unbelievable," she said, more to herself than to me.

"Wow," I said, overwhelmed. "What does he mean by the other bequests?"

Lisa waved the question away. "They have nothing to do with you." Her phone rang and she checked the screen, rolled her eyes, and hit a button to stop the ringing. "Follow me," she said, setting the papers back on the island.

I followed her out of the kitchen and through the lavender dining room and into a large, brightly lit sunroom. A full-size bed was at one end of the room, a recliner and dresser at the other.

"My father had this sunroom converted into his bedroom so he wouldn't have to use the stairs, and I haven't gotten around to converting it back, so it'll be your room while you're here. His things have been cleared out and I got rid of the hospital bed and had this full-sized brought in."

The space was so sun-filled, so unlike what I'd experienced in the last year that I felt my throat tighten with gratitude at the thought of making this room my own.

"The upstairs is mine," Lisa said, "so off-limits to you. We'll share the kitchen, but I don't expect either of us to be here much except to sleep. You're going to be practically living in the gallery, and I have more than enough work to keep me busy. We'll take care of our own meals. The housekeeper comes on Wednesdays and she's here most of the day." She gave me a stern look. "Absolutely no drugs in this house," she said. "I know you had a problem and I—"

"Not with drugs." I felt defensive. "I never—"

"I keep wine in the kitchen," Lisa interrupted me. "Is that going to be an issue for you?"

"No. I don't drink. Not anymore. And I never drank wine, anyway. Only beer."

Lisa gave a laugh that sank my spirits. "Hard to drink in prison, I suppose," she said.

"I'm done," I insisted. I would never drink again. Not ever.

Lisa looked at me as though unsure whether to believe me or not. "Fine," she said finally. "If it becomes a problem for you, let me know and I'll keep the wine in my room. I can move a minifridge in—"

"It won't be a problem." I felt my cheeks burning. I wished she'd stop talking about it.

"No smoking in the house."

"I don't smoke."

"All right, then." Lisa gestured toward the hall. "The bathroom's right down the hall by the kitchen. Freshen up and let's go see your mural."

Chapter 4

———◆◆◆———

ANNA

December 5, 1939

Anna wondered if it was rude to write in her journal while eating breakfast in the big hotel restaurant but decided not to worry about it. The hotel guests were not the people she needed to impress. So, in between bites of soft-boiled eggs and sausage—which came in a flat patty instead of the links she was accustomed to—she jotted down her thoughts. Grits were also on the menu. She'd heard of them but had no idea what they were, and after seeing them on another diner's plate, she decided to pass. The accents flowed around her like syrup, easy and affable and unfamiliar. She supposed she would sound just as strange to her fellow diners.

Most of the people in the restaurant were men, and she felt their eyes on her. Was it the journal? Her hair? Maybe she should have gotten a more suitable hairdo before heading here to Edenton, but she'd been wearing her nearly black hair in a bob with bangs for so long that she wouldn't recognize herself without it. Perhaps she wouldn't fit in with this style here, but she was her mother's daughter: when had she ever cared about fitting in?

She *had* given in to the realization that she'd best wear a dress on this trip. After spending the last three years in pants while attending art school, she'd nearly forgotten what stockings and garter belts felt like, so getting dressed in her hotel room this morning had been an ordeal. But she needed to make a good impression in Edenton, so she'd left her pants at home. Her mother probably would have told her, *Oh for heaven's sake, Anna, wear the pants! Just be yourself!* But her mother was no longer around to advise her one way or another, and Anna decided on playing it safe.

Looking up from her journal, she saw a man staring at her from a nearby table, making her feel both attractive and vulnerable. When she accidentally caught his eye, he nodded at her, not unkindly, but his scrutiny made her nervous and she shut and locked her journal and focused on her food for the rest of her meal.

⸺⁂⸺

She decided to walk rather than drive through Edenton as she explored the town. The sky was a brilliant blue that belied the cold air and the slivers of ice still on the road from some recent storm. She left the hotel bundled up in the long beige woolen coat that had been her mother's, along with her favorite red velvet halo hat and gloves. She had a target in mind—the post office where her mural would hang—but she thought she should see a bit more of Edenton before heading there.

Next door to the hotel stood a redbrick courthouse that she thought might look stunning in a mural. She was drawn to red, always. She snapped a couple of pictures of it before crossing a long expanse of grassy parkland, walking toward the waterfront. Near the water's edge stood three Revolutionary War cannons, all pointing out to sea. The nearby houses were enormous and looked well cared for, despite the financial difficulties most people had faced during the last decade. She took a few more pictures, then turned in the direction of Broad Street and was disappointed by the unsightly waterfront. Winter-barren fish shacks, along with an ice plant, a blacksmith shop, and sheds filled with lumber nearly blocked the view of the rough gray water. The buzz of saws filled the air, and she suddenly felt the weight of the sadness that had dogged her since her mother's death. She needed to get away from the depressing waterfront. Quickly, she turned around and headed back toward downtown. There was nothing on the waterfront she could use in a painting. Maybe the Tea Party ladies would have to carry the entire weight of her mural. Which was the real Edenton? she wondered. The gritty-looking harbor or the elegant houses? How could she capture the true feeling of a place so unfamiliar to her?

She drew the collar of her coat closer to her throat as she walked the few blocks to the post office, passing dozens of businesses along Broad Street: department stores, barbershops, drugstores, a hardware store, a grocery store, a filling station, a bank. The street bustled with people. The town was not as quiet as she'd first thought, and every single person she passed—*every* single one of them, man, woman, and child—nodded a greeting to her as she walked by, which made her forget about the unappealing waterfront and lifted her mood. That would not happen if a stranger walked down Front Street in Plainfield, she thought.

She took a picture of the local theater as she passed it. The theater's name stood out in huge letters above the roof: TAYLOR. The marquee announced that *Dancing Co-ed* with Lana Turner was playing. Her mother would have loved to see that film. *Why, Mom?* she thought, biting her lip. *Why did you do it when there were still things you were looking forward to?* Turning her back on the theater, she continued her walk.

The post office stood across the street from an Episcopal church and graveyard. The small brick building looked quite new. Its four front windows were topped by smart striped awnings, and slender pillars flanked the front doors. A flag flew from a pole on the roof. Inside, Anna felt a jolt of excitement when she spotted the wall where her mural would be installed. The bare space was above the door to the postmaster's office and she instantly realized that she could divide one large canvas into three images if she chose to. Three images connected to one another by style, but reflecting three different elements of the town—whatever they might turn out to be. She stood there for several minutes, snapping pictures of the space, oblivious to anything else going on behind her in the small post office.

"Can I help you?"

She turned at the sound of a male voice and spotted the clerk behind the counter eyeing her curiously. Two customers, both women, were also gazing at her, and she wondered if she looked quite silly standing there in the middle of the room, taking pictures of a blank wall. She felt very much the stranger, then, but she smiled and they smiled back.

"I'm looking for the postmaster," she said. "Is he in?"

"Just knock on that door." The clerk gestured to the door in front of her. She knocked and was immediately invited inside.

The man behind the desk was almost exactly what she'd imagined. He was a string bean of a man—middle-aged and very tall. He had a graying brown mustache that matched his graying brown hair. He had on metal-rimmed glasses and he smoked a pipe, a fragrant curlicue of smoke rising toward the ceiling. The only surprise was his remarkably bushy eyebrows. On his desk was a nameplate: Clayton Arndt.

"Mr. Arndt?" Anna inquired. "I'm Anna Dale. I'm here to do a little research into the—"

"Why, you're the artist!" he exclaimed, rising to his feet. It took her a moment to understand what he'd said. It sounded like *Wah, yaw tha ahtis!* He looked slightly stunned. "I must say, you are not at *all* what I expected," he said, motioning to the chair in front of his desk. "Sit, young lady. Sit."

She lowered herself into the chair. "What did you expect?" she asked.

He took his own seat again. "Well, when we learned we were getting a mural, of course we expected a male artist. That's understandable, isn't it?" He looked apologetic, his big eyebrows rising halfway up his forehead. "Most artists are men. Women have little time for those pursuits, what with taking care of the home, right?"

"Well, I don't yet have a home to take care of," Anna said, blocking the memory of the small house she and her mother had shared for all of Anna's life. She thought about adding that she hoped to always be an artist, domestic responsibilities or not, but figured it was best to keep her mouth shut on that matter. She didn't yet know who she was dealing with.

"But then we got word that the artist's name is Anna Dale . . . right?" He tapped his pipe on the ashtray on his desk, then set it aside.

"Yes." She smiled. "That's me."

"So, we got over the surprise of you being a female, but now I see you're barely out of grammar school! You're just a girl." There was unabashed disappointment in his voice. "I'm sure you're up to all the work this will entail, though, right?" He liked to end his sentences with the word "right." Or *raht*. That much was clear.

She would not let this man cow her. She remembered Mrs. Van Emburgh's whispered words to her at her graduation. "I'm twenty-two," she said, holding her head high. "And I recently graduated from the Van Emburgh School of Art in Plainfield, New Jersey."

"And there's another thing." Mr. Arndt folded his slender hands on his desk and looked perturbed. "When the Section of Fine Arts let us know our artist was from New Jersey, I wrote to them and said, 'I believe this might be a mistake.' I was afraid they were throwin' you to the wolves. I'm sure those boys up in Washington, D.C., think you're a talented artist who will do a fine job on a mural, but I'm concerned you'll have a hard time gettin' a real feel for Edenton and the folks here, what with you being from New Jersey, right?"

She wasn't at all sure what he was asking or if he was asking her anything at all. "I plan to do my best," she said gamely.

"Well, they said you were selected fair and square, so we'll make it work, right?"

"Of course." She shifted in the chair, hoping to take some control over this meeting. "And who is 'we'?" she asked.

"The folks who run this town," he said. "The movers and shakers. Our

Mayor Sykes. Then there's the editor of our paper, the *Chowan Herald*. Our various business leaders and myself, of course."

"I see." She realized she'd been mispronouncing "Chowan," the county Edenton was in, if only in her head. It was *Cho-WAN*. She would have to remember that. What else was she getting wrong? "Well," she said. "I'm going to do my best to give Edenton a mural it can be proud of."

"I'd like to see your sketch," he said. He looked toward her hands where they rested in her lap as though she might have the thirty-six-by-eighteen-inch sketch hidden away inside her coat. "Do you have it with you?"

"I don't have a sketch yet," she admitted, then told him about winning the competition based on her sketch of Bordentown, New Jersey.

"So you have no sketch at all for an Edenton mural?" He sounded aghast, his eyebrows crawling up his forehead toward his hairline again. "Do you have an idea, at least?"

"That's why I'm here," she said, trying to reassure him with a calm voice, although her stomach tightened with anxiety. "I want to learn about Edenton to get a subject—or subjects—for the mural. Perhaps I could meet with . . . the movers and shakers, as you call them? I need to learn what's near and dear to an Edentonian's heart."

"A fine idea." He nodded, finally looking a bit more relaxed. "I can set somethin' up for next week."

"I'm afraid I'm only here for two more nights," she said. "Is it possible to get together with them sooner?"

He hesitated, looking thoughtful, then nodded again. "I'll make some calls," he said. He picked up a pencil from his desk but did nothing with it other than tap it on his blotter. "There's somethin' you should know," he said, eyeing her from beneath those unruly brows.

"Yes?"

"An Edenton artist by the name Martin Drapple—a fella everyone knows—he was born and raised here, as was his daddy. Anyway, he also sent in a sketch to the Forty-eight-States Contest. Understand?" He looked at her to see if she was following him. She was. "No one will think it's very fair some young girl from New Jersey won when Martin has lived here his whole life, right?" he said. "Martin's a fine artist, too. Near everyone has a Martin Drapple painting hangin' somewhere in their house. Everyone expected him to win." He let out a small chuckle. "'Specially him," he added.

"Oh." She had no idea what to do with this information. What was she going to be up against in this town? If everyone in Edenton had one of this man's paintings, though, he most likely didn't need the income from the mural. It sounded as though he had plenty of work to do. Anna, on the other hand, would be flat broke if not for the small amount of money her mother had left her. "Well," she said, "the judges didn't know he was from Edenton or that I was from New Jersey." She wanted to sound strong without being argumentative. "They judged the entries on the merits of the design."

"Yes, I do understand that," Mr. Arndt said. "I only worry that it's goin' to put you in an awkward position and I wanted to give you fair warnin', right?" He got to his feet in a signal that the meeting was over. "It just doesn't seem fair to Martin."

He stopped talking and she wondered if he expected her to resign right then and there and turn the assignment over to this Martin Drapple fellow. "Perhaps not," she said, getting to her feet. "But the decision wasn't mine to make."

"No, I know that, and if the gov'ment says you're our mural artist, why then I can promise you we'll do our level best to cooperate with you."

She thanked him, then left the post office and began walking back to the hotel, playing the meeting with Mr. Arndt over and over in her mind. She'd started the day with a sense of promise and optimism. After meeting the postmaster, she was not so sure. By the time she reached her hotel, though, she had her confidence back. She would do a stellar job on the mural and ignore any petty concerns about her being a female, or a Yankee, or any of the other complaints they might have against her. She would give this little town nothing to complain about.

Chapter 5

———— ❦ ————

MORGAN

June 13, 2018

I hadn't really noticed the town when we drove through it earlier, but now, on the drive with Lisa to the gallery, I took it in. In front of a sunny, clean, touristy-looking waterfront, Lisa made a right turn onto Broad Street and drove past one shop after another in a small, picturesque downtown. The buildings looked old, some of them beautiful and unique, and all well maintained. This was not a dying downtown, like so many others, I thought. There was even an old-timey-looking movie theater with its name, "Taylor," in a playful script above the roof, but no movie titles were on the marquee.

"Is that building still a theater?" I asked, pointing toward it.

"Under renovation," Lisa said. "It's supposed to reopen in a few weeks."

I continued observing the stores as we drove past. "Is there a computer store here?" I asked doubtfully. This wasn't big-box territory. "And a phone store?"

Lisa took her eyes from the road to glance at the shops we passed. "You can get a phone here, but you'll have to order your computer online," she said.

"Okay." I hadn't felt a cell phone in my hand in over a year. It would be so good to reconnect to the world, although to be honest, I wasn't sure who I'd connect with. I'd have nothing in common with my old friends now. And I sure wasn't going to call Trey. He'd have finished with his first year of law school at Georgetown. Anger bubbled up inside me and I shook my head as if I could tamp it down that way. It was probably just as well I wouldn't be living near anyone from my old life.

"I know you're not allowed to have a driver's license while you're on parole," Lisa said, "so you'll either have to walk to the gallery—it's less than a mile—or ride with me when I go in." She made a couple of turns, then pulled into a small unpaved parking lot next to an unpainted, un-shingled contemporary structure, totally out of place to my eyes after riding through blocks of eighteenth- and nineteenth-century houses and churches.

"This is the gallery?" I asked.

"It is indeed." Lisa turned off the ignition. "My father had to fight to build it here, even though it's outside the historic district where there are rules about what you can and can't build. You can see it doesn't fit in." She chuckled, the first time I'd heard any true levity in her voice. "Or rather," Lisa added, "you can see it stands out, which I'm sure was his intent. You can also see it needs a hell of a lot of work before August fifth."

We got out of the car and walked to the huge glass front door, which stood wide open, a fact that apparently annoyed Lisa.

"We just got the place air-conditioned," she said. "The guys aren't used to shutting this door yet."

We stepped into a large, bare, high-ceilinged room. One wall was al-most entirely made of glass, and the building smelled of wood and paint. The other walls were white, and a silvery-gray tiled floor was in place, but the spacious room was otherwise empty.

"This will be the foyer, obviously," Lisa said. "I had my guys hang the drywall and paint in here first thing because this is where you'll be working and I don't want them disturbing you once you start." She motioned to the area in front of us. "There'll be a counter here with information about the gallery, and volunteers will take turns manning it. And this"—she swept her arm through the air to take in the wall above the nonexistent counter—"this is where my father wants the mural."

"Wow, that's a big space," I said. "How big is the mural?"

"Twelve feet by six, I believe." Lisa looked toward the corner of the room behind us, and for the first time I noticed an enormous roll of canvas standing upright, the only thing in the otherwise empty room. "That's it," Lisa said, walking toward it. "I had the guys pull it out of the studio closet and haul it over here last week, but I didn't want them to unroll it before you were here."

I followed her across the tiled floor until we stood next to the broad, towering roll. "I'm five seven," Lisa said, "so what do you think?"

I looked toward the top of the roll, which reached a good two feet above Lisa's head. "Eight feet, at least," I said. The outside of the roll was covered in muslin. I pulled away a piece of the fabric to find the unpainted border of the canvas beneath it. I touched the canvas, gingerly, afraid it might disintegrate beneath my fingertips and steal my job and my freedom from me before I even began, but the canvas felt firm to my touch.

"Well," Lisa said with a reluctant-sounding sigh. "Might as well get a look at this thing."

I watched her disappear through an interior doorway to another part of the gallery, calling the name "Oliver." Soon she returned with three men, two of them wearing sweaty sleeveless tees and multipocketed khaki workpants, the third in a green T-shirt and jeans. They looked at me and I felt their scrutiny. The two in the workpants were about my age, the third closer to thirty. They were the first men I'd seen besides prison guards in over a year. Their presence, their earthy scent, their very existence—especially the green-eyed blond guy who, except for his man bun, looked a lot like Trey—felt intoxicating. All my nerve endings were suddenly on fire.

"You the painter?" one of them asked. He was as dark skinned as Lisa and wore dreadlocks pulled together into a long plait down his back.

"Yes," I said.

"Morgan is the art restorer," Lisa corrected him. Hearing the falsehood out loud made me wince. "Morgan, this is Wyatt." Lisa nodded to the guy with the dreadlocks. She looked at the phone that seemed perpetually glued to her hand, but kept talking. "Wyatt's head of construction," she said. "And this is Adam, second in command." She pointed toward the blond guy, whose left arm, shoulder to wrist, was encircled by the tattoo of a snake. Not very subtle, I thought. "And this is Oliver Jones, our curator in charge of the art."

Oliver was the older of the three by eight or nine years and he held his hand out to me with a smile. "Welcome," he said. "Glad you're here." He was tall with a techie look about him. Fair skinned, his cheeks boyishly tinted with pink as though he'd just come in from the cold. Angular features and thick dark hair that swept his forehead. Behind his black horn-rimmed glasses, his eyes were so blue I wondered if he was wearing tinted contacts.

"Hi." I shook his hand, and when I let go, my gaze returned to Adam. He really did look like Trey. It wasn't just my imagination trying to torment me. He had Trey's not-too-tall, not-too-short build. Trey's broad chest. He stared at me. I was used to it. It was my hair. Shoulder length, deep bangs, naturally blond. From the time I was very small, I'd felt its power—the only power I'd had.

I pulled my gaze away from Adam, annoyed with myself for feeling any attraction to him. I should be repelled instead. I turned back to the rolled canvas. "Can I see the mural?" I asked.

"Mm," Lisa said, glancing one more time at the phone in her hand before she lowered it to her side. "Let's get that thing opened up."

The men moved as a group toward the rolled canvas.

"Better get out of the way," Wyatt said, and Lisa and I moved back toward the door.

"I've been so curious to see this thing," Oliver said as the three men tipped the rolled mural onto its side and moved it into the center of the room. He pulled a utility knife from his jeans pocket and cut the straps holding the canvas in place. Then the three of them began slowly unrolling the canvas over the floor.

"The paint's on the wrong side," Adam said as the back of the canvas was revealed.

"No," Oliver said. "Actually, whoever rolled this did it the right way. Paint side out. Covered it in muslin to protect it."

"I remember my father telling me it had originally been rolled paint side in, though," Lisa said. I glanced at her and could see that she had a death grip on her phone. She was as worried as I was about what we would find. "I don't know for how long," Lisa continued. "Hopefully it didn't do too much damage."

The men had finished unrolling the canvas, which had been wrapped around an enormous, thick, sturdy cardboard tube. Adam and Wyatt rolled the tube aside.

"It's massive," I said, overwhelmed by the sheer breadth of the canvas.

"So how do we turn it over without wrecking it?" Adam asked.

Oliver lowered himself to his haunches at one corner of the overturned mural. He touched the ragged-looking edge of the canvas. Lifted it gingerly to peer beneath. "The artist left a good eight inches of unpainted canvas on the borders." He looked up at Adam and Wyatt. "Get me an eight-foot two-by-four," he said.

Adam and Wyatt took off for the interior of the building, while Lisa walked toward the windows and began typing on her phone. Oliver turned to me. "Have you worked on one this size?" he asked.

"No," I said, trying to produce a self-confident smile. "This'll be a first." An understatement.

The men quickly returned with the long piece of wood. I watched while

Oliver laid it on one of the short ends—short being a relative term—of the canvas and tacked it into place with some device he'd pulled from his pocket. Then he got to his feet, nodded to Wyatt, and they carefully lifted the two-by-four, raising it high above their heads, while Adam and I gently unfolded the canvas from beneath it. Finally the canvas, still covered with the muslin, lay flat on the floor. Oliver stood on one side with Wyatt on the other, and the two men slowly pulled the muslin aside until the full mural was revealed.

I stared wordlessly at the grimy painting. We all did. It took thirty seconds at least before I finally said what all of us were surely thinking.

"What the *hell?*"

Chapter 6

———— ❧❦❧ ————

ANNA

December 7, 1939

Anna was the last to arrive in her hotel restaurant, although she was right on time—noon—and she had the feeling the four men—the important gentlemen of Edenton—had met early to discuss how to deal with her. She wore her dark blue dress—the one her mother had loved on her—along with her white gloves and blue pillbox hat. She thought she looked every inch the lady.

The men all stood as she approached the table, and once they were seated again, Postmaster Arndt began the introductions. Anna was nearly overcome by the scent of cigars—three of them—in addition to Mr. Arndt's pipe. The scent of tobacco was something she ordinarily enjoyed, but the air was so thick with smoke above the table that she felt as though she were looking at the men through a foggy window.

"This is our mayor," Mr. Arndt said, motioning toward the man to her left. "Sterling Sykes."

Mayor Sykes was as short as Mr. Arndt was tall. He had thinning hair, the color of which might have been blond or gray—it was impossible to tell through the haze of smoke. "Welcome to Edenton, Miss Dale," he said. "I hope you met with no problems on that long drive south?"

"None at all." She thought of mentioning how much she'd enjoyed seeing country that was new to her, but if anything, she needed to downplay her unfamiliarity with the territory. Her main problem on the journey had been that it gave her too much time to think about her mother. Too much time to wonder how she could have handled things differently. "I stayed overnight in Richmond to break up the journey," she added.

Mr. Arndt motioned to another man, this one of medium height with black, greased-back hair, a ruddy complexion, and deep bags beneath his eyes, despite the fact that he couldn't have been more than forty. "And this is the editor of the *Chowan Herald*, Billy Calhoun," Mr. Arndt said.

"How do you do," she said, thinking: *A grown man named Billy?*

"You're a pretty one," Billy said. "And don't you have the look of an avant-garde New York artist. All you need is one of them long cigarette holders, ain't that right?"

She tried not to wince at the word "ain't" spilling so easily from the mouth of a newspaperman. And avant-garde? Unconsciously, she touched her bob. She rather liked that description of herself.

"I do own one of those cigarette holders," she confessed with a smile. She did. A gift from a former beau, but she never used it. She would have felt silly.

She moved her gaze to the fourth man at the table.

"I'm Toby Fiering, manager of the cotton mill," he said. He was soft-spoken, his voice buttery and warm. Early fifties, thick gray hair, light blue eyes, and a genuine-looking smile. All in all, a handsome older man. "Why isn't a pretty girl like you married?" he asked, knocking her off balance with the question, although she'd certainly been asked it more than once. "You're not one of them divorcées, are you?"

Anna shook her head, her smile forced. "Just haven't met the right fella," she said, truthfully. "And I want to focus on being an artist."

The men observed her in silence for a long moment. Mr. Fiering finally cleared his throat. "Have you had time to see our mill and Mill Village?" he asked.

"Not yet, but I'd love to," she said. Her cheeks were getting tired from smiling. "I'm only here until Saturday, though."

"Be a shame to miss the cotton mill," Mr. Fiering said, and she thought he looked sincerely saddened by the thought.

They ordered lunch. The men all ordered roast beef sandwiches, but Anna asked for chicken soup. She couldn't imagine trying to speak at this important meeting around a mouthful of bread. The food was delivered quickly and the men dug in while she took a sip of her soup.

"I was hoping I might could have the managers of the lumber company and the Edenton Peanut Factory to join us," Mr. Arndt said, swallowing a bite of his sandwich. "But it wasn't possible on such short notice. They gave me their two cents to add to the conversation, though." He looked at Anna. "I'm supposed to tell you that we ship more than forty million pounds of peanuts a year," he said, then chuckled. "We got so much industry here in Edenton and everybody wants a piece of that mural pie, right?" A murmur of agreement went up from the men.

"I understand," Anna said. She wondered if she should take control of this meeting or if she should allow Mr. Arndt to do so. It felt very forward of her to barge in, yet she was the one who needed their guidance and she wouldn't get it by sitting mum.

"Gentlemen," she said in her most formal voice, "I so appreciate all of you taking the time to meet with me. As you know, I've been honored to be selected to paint the mural for your post office, and I'm anxious to begin on it, so I can use your valuable thoughts on what the focus should be. From what I've read, the Edenton Tea Party was an important—"

"Oh, not that tired old Tea Party again!" Mr. Fiering said, his handsome face screwed up as if his roast beef sandwich tasted rancid.

"Now, Toby," Mr. Arndt said. "Let the little lady say her piece."

She was shaken by the sudden outburst. Off on the wrong foot already.

She'd been about to take a sip of her soup, but set her spoon down. "I thought the Tea Party was something Edenton is proud of," she said.

"We're proud indeed, Miss Dale." Mayor Sykes's voice boomed so loudly that people at other tables turned to look at him. "We're very proud that our ladies stood up for our freedom. But that was a long, long time ago. There's so much more to Edenton these days, and we get a little tired of that all the time bein' the focus."

"I don't know," Mr. Arndt said, and Anna had the feeling he was going to be her ally. "When people think of Edenton, they *do* think of the Tea Party, so maybe—"

"But it's the townspeople who use the post office and I think they'd rather see the industry of the day," Toby Fiering interrupted. "The things that keep Edenton going and growing."

"Ah, I see," she said, hoping to get on everyone's good side. The image that had been taking shape in her mind of the women of Edenton signing their petition began to disintegrate. "Well, tell me what all of you *would* like to see in a mural."

"The cotton mill, front and center." Mr. Fiering set down his sandwich and made a sweeping gesture in front of his face, as though he could already picture it. "The biggest industry in the town."

"I can think of a few folks who might could argue with you there," Mr. Arndt said in his calming way. "And Rollie and Stu want to see their lumberyard and peanut factory represented, too," he continued. "And then of course, there's fishin'. We've got water all 'round us. Plus, our melons. And agriculture, right?"

Anna's fingers began to perspire around the handle of her spoon and her soup had barely been touched. "The mural is large but we don't want to overcrowd it," she said. "I think I can work in three to five scenes as the focus. One central image plus a few others."

The men were quiet for a moment. Then Billy Calhoun finally spoke up. "You know," he drawled to the mayor, "if your cousin Martin was doing this paintin' he'd know what should be in it without bein' told."

Oh, no. That Martin Drapple artist was the mayor's cousin?

The mayor raised his eyebrows with a "what can I do?" shrug. "I tried callin' the government office responsible for the mural," he said. "Can't never get through."

"You tried calling the office?" Anna asked, appalled. "To complain about me?"

"Jest don't make no sense," Billy continued as if she hadn't spoken.

"I wasn't callin' to complain," Mayor Sykes said to Anna around a mouthful of his sandwich. "I just wanted them to know why we thought my cousin Martin would be a smart choice. Nothin' to do with you specifically, dear. Just with them pickin' a stranger completely unfamiliar with Edenton. Plus, we all know Martin's got talent and experience to spare."

"Maybe it's 'cause Martin is mostly a portrait artist that he didn't git it," Billy Calhoun said. "Not exactly what they was lookin' for."

"Anyone who can paint a person as good as him would be able to paint scenes from the town," Toby Fiering argued.

"Now, boys," Mr. Arndt said. "We've been over this. Miss Dale here is goin' to be our artist and that's all there is to it. We have to make the best of it. Let's help her out here, right?"

They all turned to look at Anna, and she knew her cheeks were scarlet. They'd started burning when the mayor mentioned his telephone call to the Section of Fine Arts. Thank goodness he hadn't been able to get through! She needed an okay from the Section on her as yet nonexistent sketch. It horrified her to think the job could still be snatched away from her.

"I'm only here till Saturday," she said again, setting down her spoon and straightening her spine. "I'd like to actually see the things that are important to you. The cotton mill." She looked at Mr. Fiering. "The peanut factory. Et cetera. And I'm sure that the waterfront looks very different during fishing season, so if there are photographs of it I might look at, that would be helpful."

"I can tour you through the mill," Mr. Fiering said.

"Thank you." She nodded.

"You're right about the waterfront, little lady," Mayor Sykes piped in. "Every day during the season, we haul in thousands of herring and ship them far and wide."

"It's an industrious little town, isn't it," she said, hoping to ingratiate herself to them. She had to admit she was impressed. She'd had no idea this dot on the map was such a beehive of activity.

"So, do you paint the mural right on the post office wall?" Mayor Sykes asked.

"No, I'll paint it in New Jersey and then send it down here to be installed—attached to the wall—in the post office. I'll have to find some studio space near my home where I can work on it, and—"

"That don't make no sense." Billy Calhoun scowled. "You ought to be *here* to paint it."

"I believe he's right," said the mayor. "You're just getting a taste of Edenton these few days you're here. You go back up north and you'll lose the whole feel of the place."

"Oh, I can't stay here," she said. "I can't afford a hotel for as long as this will take."

"How long will it take?" Mr. Fiering asked.

She ticked the steps off on her fingers. "Well, first I have to decide what to paint," she said. "Then I need to make a color sketch of it and submit that to the Section—the government people who make these decisions. Once they accept it, then I need to make a cartoon from the sketch and—"

"A what?" The mayor's eyes flew open and Anna smiled. The men probably thought she was planning to make a comical mural for the post office and she could see them getting nervous.

"It's a full-sized—so twelve-by-six feet—black-and-white sketch of the mural," she said. "It's called a cartoon. I'll take a photograph of it and send that off to the Section for their approval. And once they give me the go-ahead on that, I'll begin the actual painting."

"Whole lot of steps before you can even get goin'!" Mr. Arndt sounded disappointed about the length of time it would take to have her mural up on his post office wall.

"Yes, so you see it will take several months," she said, "and I can't afford to stay here all that time."

"What about Miss Myrtle?" Mr. Arndt looked around the table at the other men.

The mayor nodded. "Good idea! I bet she'd be tickled pink to have company." He turned to Anna. "Myrtle Simms is a widow, lives across from the railroad buildin'. Her girl Pauline just tied the knot and moved out, so she has space and was talkin' about takin' in a tenant. I bet she'd be happy to take you in for no cost to you atall, but she could surely use some rent money, given that big ol' house of hers needs work."

"Oh, I couldn't do that!" Her mind raced with the idea. She couldn't stay in Edenton. She had nothing here with her, to begin with. Only two dresses, one pair of shoes, a couple of changes of underwear, and very little money. Worst of all, she had none of her painting supplies with her.

"It's a right fine idea," Billy Calhoun said.

"I'll talk to Miss Myrtle 'bout it tomorrow and call you at the hotel with what she says," Mr. Arndt said.

"I don't have anything with me," Anna said.

"Your family can send what you need down to you, can't they?" the mayor asked. "And we have stores." He smiled. "We ain't some little backwater."

I have no family, she thought, but kept her mouth shut. What was waiting for her at home in Plainfield? She had no beau. Her friends from high school and Van Emburgh were scattered to the wind. The house she'd shared with her mother felt painfully empty. She'd have to ask Aunt Alice to go to the house and pack some things for her and ship them down, but the Edenton men were right. It would be good to surround herself with the town she planned to paint.

"Is there studio space I can rent here?" she asked. "Someplace big enough for me to paint the mural? I'll need quite a bit of room."

The men fell silent, brows furrowed in thought. "I don't know no studios," Billy Calhoun said.

"Martin just paints in his attic," the mayor said.

Mr. Fiering spoke up. "What about that old abandoned warehouse out by the Carters' place? Hasn't been used in ten years, at least." He looked at Anna. "It's outside of town a ways, but not too far," he said. "You'd have your peace and quiet for workin'."

"Don't have heat," Mr. Arndt said.

"We'd have to cart in a couple of space heaters," the mayor said, then turned to her. "How 'bout we take a look at it tomorrow? Me and you? If it looks like it might work for you, and Miss Myrtle says she'd love to have you, which I can guarantee that's what she'll say, you'll stick around?"

"All right," she said, rather impulsively. "I will." And she smiled. She had the feeling she'd won these gentlemen over after all.

Chapter 7

———— ⋙•⋘ ————

MORGAN

June 13, 2018

I stared down at the mural where it lay on the tiled floor of the gallery foyer. I saw the tremendous damage—the grime and scratches and huge sections of abraded paint that nearly masked the images on the canvas. And I saw what had stunned all of us. What left us shaking our heads in confusion and sent a weird shiver up my spine.

In the center of the mural, in fairly extreme close-up, three women dressed in eighteenth-century garb sat around a small table. One of them held the shards of something—a white teapot?—in her outstretched hands.

"This is supposed to represent the Edenton Tea Party, no doubt," Lisa said. "But"—she pointed toward the skirts of the women in the painting—"this makes absolutely no sense."

Piercing the small circle of women was the front end of a motorcycle. It protruded from between their filthy skirts, its rider not visible behind the women's torsos.

"It's an Indian," Adam said. "That is so awesome." He stuffed his hands in the pockets of his khaki workpants, then looked at Lisa. "I assume they didn't have motorcycles in the seventeen hundreds?"

"The artist must've been smokin' somethin'," Wyatt said. "Who the hell painted this thing?"

"The artist's name was Anna Dale," Oliver said. He stood above the mural, arms crossed in front of his chest, a frankly delighted expression on his face. "This is fascinating, don't you think?" he asked, his gaze on me, and I nodded. "I Googled Anna Dale and read that she won the competition to paint this mural," Oliver continued, "but that was the only information I could find on her. I haven't been able to track down any other work by her, either. This style"—he motioned toward the mural—"this representational style was typical of the murals painted for government buildings back then." He chuckled. "But it looks like Anna Dale added her own unique interpretation of her subject."

My gaze had moved on. It appeared that the mural consisted of one large central section—the three women and the motorcycle—which was flanked by two smaller sections on either side. In the upper right-hand corner, an African-American woman appeared to be holding a basket of some sort, which was full of something indiscernible, thanks to the filth and abrasions. Something was wrong with the lower half of the woman's face, too. Was she clenching a stick between her teeth? Beneath her, in the lower right-hand corner of the mural, there was a row of small houses. I walked toward the other end of the mural to look at the painting's upper left-hand corner. I wasn't at all sure what I was looking at. A boat, maybe? Yes, it had to be a ship of some sort. And beneath it, in the fifth and final vignette, a white man—at least I thought his skin was white beneath the grime—stood tall, holding a log or length of wood or something like it in his hands. Five separate scenes, all of them a mess. The entire mural looked as though someone had attached it to the back of a car and dragged it facedown over earth and stones and mud for miles and miles. To me, the painting—all seventy-two square feet of it—looked utterly beyond saving.

I turned to Lisa. "Did you have any idea it was this bad, or that it had . . ." I pointed to the motorcycle. "Was that what your father meant when he told you the artist had gone crazy? Maybe he'd been referring to the motorcycle?"

Lisa slowly shook her head, her gaze riveted on the mural. "My father certainly didn't prepare me for this," she said. "I swear, that old man . . . if he wasn't already dead, I'd kill him."

"You sure you want this hanging in here?" Adam asked Lisa. "Right here in the front room where everybody starts out?"

Lisa let out a long breath. "Oh, shit, I'm not sure of anything," she said, "but my father was as clearheaded as an old man could be and his instructions couldn't have been more explicit. So it will hang in here. Once Morgan whips it into shape, that is."

I steadfastly avoided her eyes.

"I think it's sick," Wyatt said, and I knew he was using the word as a compliment. "Without the bike, it'd just be another old painting. This way, it'll be a jump-start for conversation."

"It's definitely fascinating," said Oliver. "It'll be an amazing piece of art once it's cleaned up. It'll tell some of Edenton's history, which is just what you want from one of these old post office murals. These little houses, for example." He pointed to the lower right corner. "They're the Cotton Mill Village, aren't they?" He looked at Lisa who slowly nodded.

"I guess," Lisa said, as though she hadn't yet made that connection. I wondered what the Cotton Mill Village was.

Oliver leaned as far forward as he could without stepping on the canvas. He brushed his dark hair off his forehead and squinted, as if he could summon up X-ray vision to see beneath the grime. "Look at the detail in the women's faces," he said, pointing to a less soiled area around one of the women's eyes. "Anna Dale was an excellent artist."

"If you say so," Lisa said.

"No wonder they never hung this thing in the post office," Adam said.

"That motorcycle makes absolutely no sense." Lisa shook her head.

"I'm guessing it made perfect sense to the artist," Oliver said.

Adam looked at me. "Maybe you could just paint out the Indian," he suggested.

"Are you kidding?" Oliver's eyebrows rose high above his glasses. He gestured toward the canvas. "This is obviously what the artist wanted to create. It should be restored exactly as she intended." He looked at me. "Right?" he asked.

I nodded as though I did this sort of work every day, but I couldn't quite meet Oliver's eyes. I could already tell that the curator was perceptive. I was afraid my face would give away the fact that I didn't have a clue how to fix what ailed this mural.

"There's a story here," Oliver continued. "I only wish we could know what it is." He bent over to lift one of the edges of the canvas. "Look at how ragged the edges of the canvas are," he said. "It looks like someone just hacked it from the stretcher. Why would anyone do that?"

It was only one of a hundred unanswerable questions about the mural, I thought. I tried to look beyond the damaged images to the work expected of me. The canvas reeked of mold or mildew, the scent strong enough to fill the whole room. It stung my nostrils and made my lungs burn. Filth coated the painting except for the areas where friction had simply worn the paint from the surface. There were dozens of scraped sections where there was no paint left at all. I felt Lisa turn her gaze on me.

"You'll have to finish this by August fifth," she said, quietly, so that only I could hear her. There was unmistakable worry in her voice. "Can you do it?"

Deadline or not, I didn't know how to begin. If I had a year to learn about art restoration, a year to study and practice, then maybe I stood a chance. But I couldn't let Lisa doubt me. I couldn't let her see my weakness. I wouldn't give her any reason to turn this job over to someone else and send me back to hell. I'd have to figure out how to restore this weird piece of art, and I'd have to do it quickly.

"Yes," I said, looking directly into her eyes. "Absolutely."

Chapter 8

———— ❧ ————

ANNA

December 9, 1939

Anna's very full Saturday began with moving into Myrtle Simms's large and charming old home, and she felt as though she suddenly had a grandmother. She'd never known her own grandparents, so spending time with an older, overly attentive woman was unfamiliar to her, and rather a comfort.

The Simms house stood in a row of similar good-size homes, some of which appeared to have fallen on hard times. Myrtle Simms seemed to have managed to keep the outside of her home and yard up, even if there were some signs of wear and tear inside. A bit of peeling paint here and torn wallpaper there. But all in all it was a charming home, and Anna was grateful to the men of the town for arranging her stay there.

Myrtle Simms was a compact little lady, quite short, and she greeted Anna at her front door in a yellow flowered housedress.

"Call me Miss Myrtle, dear," she said, leading Anna into a neat and clean living room with comfortable furniture and carefully displayed knickknacks on every level surface. They sat down to a snack of tea and squares of pineapple upside-down cake baked by Miss Myrtle's maid, Freda, who offered Anna a warm smile but didn't speak. Once Freda left the room, Miss Myrtle confided that the maid was mute.

"She hears fine," Miss Myrtle said, "but she's never uttered a word to me in the thirty years she's worked for me. I love her, though. She was a second mother to my daughter, growing up. We couldn't have held this house together without her."

They chatted for a while about the competition that had brought Anna to Edenton, and once they'd finished their cake, Miss Myrtle got to her feet.

"Let me show you around," she said. They headed toward the stairs, the older woman chatting the whole time. "My daughter Pauline recently got married and her husband Karl is a saint," she said. "He helps me with dripping faucets and leaky pipes. Pauline's a nurse in a doctor's office a couple of days a week, and Karl's a policeman. They live about a mile away. You'll be moving into Pauline's bedroom." They'd reached the landing and turned right. "There are two other spare bedrooms up here, but neither one has a bed." She chuckled. "One is my sewing room and the other already has a crib in it. No baby on the horizon yet, but I'm an optimist!"

They walked into a spacious bedroom, and even though it appeared that Miss Myrtle's daughter had cleared any personal possessions from the room, the wallpaper with its big magnolia flowers and the white feminine furniture made Anna feel as if she were trespassing.

"Won't Pauline mind having a stranger staying in her room?" she asked.

"Not at all," Miss Myrtle said. "I spoke to her about it yesterday evening and she was right pleased to know I'd have someone else here with me for when Freda goes home at night." She smoothed a wrinkle from the pink chenille bedspread. "I had Pauline late in life. I was forty when she was born. I'd given up on ever having a child, and then suddenly, there she was! So now I'm sixty-two years old—an old lady with rheumatism to boot—and she worries I'm going to fall or whatever and rot on the floor." She chuckled again. "When I told her about you, she came right over and packed up the last of her things to clear the room for you."

"Well, please thank her for me," Anna said

"Oh, you'll have a chance to thank her yourself," she said. "She stops over all the time. Still a mama's girl, that one."

Anna forced a smile. People had called her a "mama's girl," too. She guessed she'd never hear those words in reference to herself again.

Miss Myrtle gave her some pink sachets she'd made herself to put in the dresser drawers for when Anna's clothes arrived. Aunt Alice had responded with worry when Anna called to ask her to send her some of her clothes and art supplies.

"I don't like the idea of you being so far from home for so long," she'd said. "You're too young and you've just been through such a terrible loss." Her words made Anna wince. Aunt Alice had never come right out and said she blamed Anna for her mother's death, but how could she not? Anna certainly blamed herself.

"I'll be fine," Anna had promised her aunt, her voice filled with more certainty than she'd felt at that moment. The unknown stretched ahead of her, but she had a job and a place to stay. What more could she need? She told Aunt Alice which dresses to pack, which pants, which blouses, which shoes and stockings, which underthings, which jewelry, and finally, which art supplies, including her easel. She knew she was creating a good deal of work for her aunt, packing all that up, but Aunt Alice didn't utter a single complaint.

"As long as you're safe, Anna," she said. "That's all that matters. Do you have enough money?" As if her aunt had money to spare.

"Yes, I'm fine," she said. At least she was fine for the time being. She didn't know what she would do if her sketch wasn't accepted—how humiliating that would be—but she'd worry about that when and if it happened.

"Now tell me all about you," Miss Myrtle said once they were back in her living room, sipping tea again and eating more slivers of the pineapple upside-down cake. Anna watched Miss Myrtle put teaspoon after teaspoon of sugar in her tea until she thought the teaspoon would stand upright on its own in the cup.

She told Miss Myrtle about losing her father to pneumonia even before she'd had a chance to know him, and that she'd recently lost her mother after a brief illness. The "brief illness" was a lie, but she wasn't ready to go into detail about her mother with anyone.

"Why, you're all alone in the world!" Miss Myrtle exclaimed, her graying eyebrows pinched together above her kind eyes. "No gentleman in your life yet? You're so lovely."

Anna shook her head. "Not yet," she said. "I do have an aunt. And a couple of cousins. But I'm twenty-two, and it's time for me to make my own way."

"You must be very strong," Miss Myrtle said.

"Thank you," Anna said. She didn't feel very strong, but she was trying. She responded to more of Miss Myrtle's questions, letting the story of her life trickle from her. She talked about her mother's work as a seamstress—making the occupation sound grander and more lucrative than it had been. She described her happy childhood in Plainfield and how much she'd adored going to art school. She talked about how amazing it had been to grow up a short bus ride from New York City, and how she and her friends would spend Saturday afternoons in museums. She talked for so long that she began to feel embarrassed. Did she simply need to recite her life story out loud or was Miss Myrtle one of those people who magically drew the words from you? The term "Southern hospitality" began to make sense. Anna felt happy and content sitting there with her new landlady. Perhaps things were beginning to go her way.

They decided on rent of five dollars a month, and that would include most of her meals. They'd share the upstairs bathroom, and for ten cents, Anna could use Miss Myrtle's wringer-washer once a week.

"Now, I do have some rules," Miss Myrtle said.

"Of course." Anna smiled.

"You may have lady friends over to visit in your room or the parlor, but no gentlemen in the house without my permission," she said.

"I'm not here to socialize," Anna said, "so you don't need to worry about that."

"No drinking," Miss Myrtle said. "Are you a smoker?"

Anna nodded. "Occasionally."

The older woman sighed. "So is Pauline. I find it very nasty, but you may smoke in her—in *your*—room if you like. Just not downstairs and certainly not in the kitchen. Freda will have your head!"

"That's fine."

She told Anna about the idiosyncrasies of the plumbing and the light switches, then asked her about the mural.

"I haven't decided what to paint yet," Anna said. "It has to be something that truly represents Edenton, so I'm looking into—"

"The Tea Party, of course," Miss Myrtle said.

Anna laughed. "Well, that's what I thought, but the men I had lunch with didn't like the idea at all."

"That's because they're *men*, and *women* were behind the Tea Party," Miss Myrtle said. "I really think you must have it in any representation of Edenton. It's what we're known for." She stood up and crossed the room to a tall narrow bookcase. Pulling down a slim volume, she sat next to Anna on the settee. She paged through the book until she found a political cartoon from England that mocked the "tea party" protest, precisely because it was a movement led by women. The women looked hideous and foolish in the sketch. "And men are still mocking it," Miss Myrtle said. "We haven't come very far in some ways, I'm afraid. But it was important. It started a whole movement throughout the colonies."

Miss Myrtle's passion for the subject made Anna like her even more, but she did wish she hadn't shown her the cartoon. Now it was stuck in her head and she wasn't sure how to illustrate the Tea Party with the image of those hideous-looking women in her mind.

Miss Myrtle had a large library full of books and Anna learned that she was a college graduate. Her accent wasn't at all off-putting, although Anna wondered how her own accent sounded to her new landlady. "You don't have to tell people where you're from now, do you?" Miss Myrtle had teased after Anna's first few sentences. "All you have to do is open your mouth." But Anna liked the soft charm of Miss Myrtle's accent. Her grammar was quite perfect, and she told her how taken aback she had been while meeting with the men at lunch the day before.

"A couple of them have such poor grammar," she said. "Even the editor of the paper."

Miss Myrtle chortled at that. "Oh, honey," she said. "They know proper English. They just don't want to sound like they're above their raisin'."

"Above their raisin?" Anna frowned.

"Their *raisin'*," she said, and she spelled it out for her. "They don't want to sound hoity-toity. They want to fit in with their people. You should read one of Billy Calhoun's columns in the *Herald*. He's sharp as a tack, that one, and probably knows more big words than you and me put together."

She handed Anna a copy of the *Chowan Herald* and pointed to an article by Billy Calhoun about a tragic house fire that had taken place the week before. Anna read every word of the beautifully written piece and saw that Miss Myrtle was right. It was hard to believe the article was written by the same man she'd met at lunch. She was going to have to put her preconceived notions of the world aside while she was living in Edenton. The South was nothing like New Jersey, where what you saw was what you got, whether you wanted it or not.

That night, she went to bed in a strange room under the soft pink chenille bedspread, surrounded by magnolia wallpaper that almost seemed to glow in the dark. She felt thousands of miles from home, and the feeling wasn't bad at all. Home had felt haunted to her lately. She needed this newness. The comfort of this bed, this lovely old house, this small, sweet town. And for the first night since her mother's death, she fell asleep quickly, undisturbed by dreams.

Chapter 9

———— ✦•✦ ————

MORGAN

June 14, 2018

I barely slept during my first night in Lisa's house. Nothing echoed here and I had grown so used to echoing. No footsteps outside my cell. No clanking doors. No flushing of toilets. Although the sunroom windows were closed to keep in the air-conditioning, I could still hear the hum of cicadas in the backyard. It felt like ten years since I'd heard cicadas, the sound so beautiful to me that I felt tears roll from my eyes into my hair.

I woke up in the middle of the night after one of my miserable dreams about the accident, and it took me a few minutes to get my bearings. Those dreams were always the same: Emily Maxwell's terrified face was caught in the headlights of my car just before the horrid crunching sound of the crash. I had to turn on the night table lamp to remind myself that I was safe. My weird, silent cellmate wasn't a few feet away from me. There were no bars keeping me in the room. I was free. Sort of.

When I next opened my eyes, lemon-yellow sunlight filled the room.

I stared at the ceiling, thinking of old Jesse Jameson Williams opening his eyes to the same ceiling, morning after morning after morning. Had he lain right here in this sunny room, staring at the ceiling, when he thought to himself, *How can I help that art student Morgan Christopher? The one who so thoroughly screwed up her life? I know! I'll ask her to do the impossible, that's how!*

Oh my God. This was so ridiculous. The image of that soiled and strange mural came back to me. Filthy, stinky, bizarre, scratched up and battered and nearly bare of paint in some spots. I needed to quickly get a computer to try to figure out what to do with that thing. Setting me loose on it was so wrong. I didn't understand why Lisa was so gung-ho on following her father's deranged instructions, but whatever. It got me out of prison and if I could somehow do what needed to be done to the mural, it would keep me out.

—⦿—

Lisa was already gone when I walked into the kitchen half an hour later. She'd left a key to the front door and a card telling me how to disarm the security system, as well as a note to help myself to "whatever" and giving me directions to the Verizon store, a mile and a half away, as well as to the parole office, where I had a one forty-five appointment. She'd also left a check for two thousand dollars. *I called the bank to tell them you'd be cashing it,* she wrote. *When you get your phone, figure out what laptop you want, call me, and I'll order it for you using my credit card.* She also suggested I take an Uber to the Verizon store, but I wanted the freedom of the walk.

I locked the front door and began walking down the sidewalk from the house, stopping halfway to the street when my gaze was drawn to the concrete beneath my feet. One of the blocks of concrete contained three sets of handprints, clearly those of a man, a woman, and a child. Beneath each, a name had been carved: Jesse, Bernice, and Lisa. Sweet and whimsical. Lisa could have been no older than ten when the handprints were made. I tried to imagine my own parents taking the time or interest to create such a lasting memento of our family. Impossible.

I cashed the check without a problem at the bank on Broad Street and opened an account for myself at the same time. Then I walked to Verizon, bought a phone and earbuds, and committed my new number to memory. A new number for my new life. I plugged into my old Spotify account—the music I hadn't been able to listen to for more than a year—and I loved every second of the walk back to the house, singing along with Rihanna and Maroon 5 and Ariana Grande, feeling my freedom. Back at the house, I used the phone to figure out what computer I wanted, then called Lisa to have her order it, asking her to get overnight shipping. I was desperate to begin restoration research.

Before I'd left the gallery the day before, Oliver had talked to me about how I wanted to handle working with the mural. "Do you think you'll need a heat table?" he'd asked. "Or would you rather work on a stretcher on the wall? Wyatt and Adam'll make whatever you need. I've been working with them for a while now and they're excellent woodworkers."

I'd opted for the stretcher, having no idea what a heat table was. I was in way, way over my head.

I ordered some clothing online, then stared at the phone in my hand. Temptation. I'd lived on Instagram before everything went south. Did I dare go there? It would be like taking a drink; I'd start surfing and be unable to stop. I'd look up my old friends. I'd look up Trey. What was the point in that?

I slipped the phone in my pocket, proud of my self-control. It was nearly time to leave for the parole office, anyway. Grabbing an apple from the fruit bowl on the island, I headed out the door. It felt like a miracle, being able to walk out Lisa's—Jesse Jameson Williams's!—front door and take off down the street with no one watching my every move. My sense of freedom, though, took a hit when I pulled open the door to the parole office on Broad Street. I was not truly free. I wouldn't be free for a long time.

—≫•≪—

At one forty-seven, I took a seat next to the desk of my newly assigned parole officer. "Supervision officer," the woman called herself. Her name was Rebecca Sanders and she instantly reminded me of my mother, with her short, wavy blond hair and narrow black-framed glasses that kept sliding down her nose. I waited as she read through my file.

"So, let's see what we've got here," she said, studying the papers in front of her. "Class F felony. Driving while impaired. Aggravating factors: second DUI and serious injury by vehicle."

I took in a very long, very tired breath. "I know that's what it says," I said, "but I wasn't driving."

Rebecca slipped off her glasses to frown at me. "What do you mean?"

"I mean that my boyfriend was the one who was driving and he took off after the accident."

"So why did you end up being charged and going to prison?" She didn't believe me. I could tell. No one believed me.

I shook my head. "At this point it doesn't matter," I said, not wanting to go through it all again. "Just . . . I just wanted you to know that I didn't do it. I can't sit here and pretend that I did."

"You had an attorney, right?"

I nodded. My court-appointed attorney hadn't believed me, either. "It was just . . . at first I said I was alone in the car because I wanted to protect him. My boyfriend. He'd just gotten a scholarship to Georgetown Law and I . . . He had too much to lose. I had no idea I'd end up in prison. I thought I'd be fined, or . . . I didn't know what. I wasn't thinking clearly. It was all so . . . terrible." Sickening images flashed through my mind, and I raised a hand to my eyes as if I could block them out. "When I finally told the truth, no one believed me," I said, lowering my hand. I was so tired of explaining it all. It was pointless. I should have gone along with what was in this woman's file. Gotten it over with.

Rebecca pursed her lips. Cocked her head. "What about your previous DUI? Was your boyfriend driving then, too?" She raised her eyebrows. I supposed she was waiting for another lie.

"No, that was me," I said. "I'm not proud of it." An understatement.

"Well, if what you're saying is true about the accident, I hope you're done with your so-called boyfriend." Rebecca lifted my file in the air. "And I have to go with what I have here," she said. "That you served time for a Class F felony. And we move forward from there."

I was surprised to feel tears burn my eyes as a familiar sense of helplessness washed over me, but I looked at her squarely. "I wish you could believe me," I said. Why was this so important? Why did I need her—need *someone*—to believe me?

"I have to go with what I have," she said again. "What I *do* believe is that you're lucky to have your new lawyer." She looked down at my file. "This Andrea Fuller. The one who got you out."

What I heard behind her words was: *Most people can't afford a lawyer like yours and they end up serving their maximum sentence, and when they get out they have a record employers can't get past and they can never find a job.*

"I didn't hire her. This all just fell into my lap." I motioned to the file in her hands. "I just wanted you to know the truth about what happened."

She hesitated, her eyes tight on my face before she slipped on her glasses again. "Let's move forward," she said, returning her gaze to the file. "Supposedly you're uniquely qualified for the work you're doing in the gallery, and supposedly the work is going to improve the community. What are you doing there exactly?"

I tried to hold my head high against what I perceived to be her sarcasm. "I'm an artist," I said. "I'll be restoring a mural."

"And this will improve the community," Rebecca said. It was a statement but I heard it as more of a question.

I shrugged, trying to come up with a response that wouldn't sound argumentative. "I hope so," I said.

"Well." Rebecca lifted a clipboard from her desk and handed it to me. "I have some paperwork for you to fill out," she said. "Your supervision is for one year."

I looked down at the stack of papers attached to the clipboard. "I'll only be in Edenton a couple of months," I said.

"We'll worry about that later." Rebecca looked down at my file. "And during the time you're under supervision, you need to work twenty hours a week."

"I'll be working a lot more than that," I said.

"Fine. That's the minimum. Just so you know. And once you complete the work, you'll still be on parole until the twelve months are up."

"All right," I said. I would do whatever it took to stay out of prison. I glanced at her file. Took in a long breath. "I have a question," I said slowly. "Do you have any information on . . . Do you know how the victim of the accident is doing?" It was hard to get those words out. I shut my eyes, an involuntary reaction, as if I could block out the image of Emily Maxwell's bloody, mangled body from my memory.

"I have no idea," she said. "You haven't had any contact with her? There's nothing in your postrelease supervision preventing it."

I opened my eyes and looked down at my hands. I was afraid I was going to lose it. "I don't want to see her," I said quickly. "But I dream about her. Nightmares. I just wish I could know how she is." Emily was my age, almost to the day. When I thought about what Trey and I had done to her life . . . Sometimes I didn't think I could bear it.

"I can't help you with that," Rebecca said. She returned her attention to her paperwork. "So, here's how we work out your restitution and the payment of your court costs, et cetera," she said. She handed me a chart filled with dates and numbers and dove into a long explanation of how I could try to make up for the harm I'd done using dollars and cents. The numbers swam before my eyes.

"You were in AA while in prison?" Rebecca asked, breaking away from the chart.

"Yes."

"I'm going to require that you attend at least one meeting a week." She handed me another sheet of paper.

"I don't think I'll have time," I said. "But I'm completely over alcohol. I was never an alcoholic. I just drank when I was with—"

"You have two DUIs, Morgan. By the age of not quite twenty-one, you had two." Rebecca leaned forward again. "You crippled a young woman. Permanently. I want to hear you say it: I have a drinking problem."

I swallowed, the image of Emily rising up in my mind again.

"I sometimes used to drink too much," I said. It was the best I could do, and Rebecca seemed to give up the battle.

"That's a list of local meetings." She pointed to the paper she'd handed me. Then she gave me yet another sheet. "And here's a log for you to keep track of the meetings with spaces for the dates and locations. You need to have someone verify you were there with their phone number, and turn it in to me when we meet."

I imagined going up to a stranger and asking him or her to sign my log. "I really don't need AA now," I said. "Wouldn't you rather know I'm working hard than going to—"

"This is not negotiable, Morgan," Rebecca said. "Find a local group as soon as possible and make that connection."

I caved. "All right," I said.

"You and I will meet every couple of weeks at first and I'll be stopping by your home . . . the place you're staying or your place of employment . . . the art gallery . . . sometimes unannounced."

"That's fine."

"You may not leave Chowan County for a year."

"What about when I finish my work at the gallery?" I asked. "My work on the mural?"

"We'll talk about it then. One step at a time," she said, handing me an appointment card. "I'll see you here again in two weeks."

I nodded, then started getting to my feet.

"We're not finished," Rebecca said, and I lowered myself to the chair again.

Rebecca opened a box with what looked like one of those ankle brace-
lets that monitored people under house arrest.

"Do you know what this is?" Rebecca asked.

"Do I have to wear that?" I asked in disbelief. "I'm not under house arrest, am I?"

"It's an alcohol monitor, and yes you do need to wear it," Rebecca said.
"It goes on your ankle and reacts to your sweat. You take the smallest sip
of booze and I'll know about it even before you feel the buzz. You don't
take it off, not for showering, not for anything. I'll know if you drink and
I'll know if you tamper with it. I'll know if you try to stick a piece of plastic
wrap between it and your skin. You'll wear it for six months and then we'll
reevaluate."

I couldn't imagine being tied to that thing for six months . . . but then
I thought of Emily Maxwell. I imagined her tied to a wheelchair for life.

"All right," I said.

"You can wear pants that cover it up, if it bothers you," Rebecca said.
"Tell people it's an exercise monitor. I don't care. All I care about is that
you don't drink."

I nodded.

"You'll have an eleven P.M. curfew and I'll be checking on that occasionally. You need to attend DUI classes to get your license back. Here's a list
of where and when the classes are offered." She handed me yet one more
piece of paper. How was I going to find time for all of this? "You'll have a
random drug screen at least monthly, and—"

"I've never used drugs," I said.

"A random drug screen at least monthly," Rebecca repeated as if I hadn't
spoken.

"All right," I said, thinking it was best to nod and go along.

"Now let's talk about your risk factors," Rebecca said. "Who do you
need to stay away from to avoid temptation?"

The name "Trey" thumped inside my brain in time with my heartbeat.

"There's no one around here I need to avoid," I said. "I'm hours away from any of my old friends and I'm done with them."

"Who did you used to drink with?"

"Friends. And my boyfriend. The one who was driving that night." I looked at her as if challenging her to argue with me on that fact again.

"Have you been in touch with the boyfriend? What's his name?"

"Trey. And no."

"Whether he was driving or not, do I need to tell you to steer clear of that guy?"

I shook my head. "No, you don't," I said, and I felt my anger at Trey rise up inside me again.

—≫•≪—

The walk from the parole office to the gallery wasn't far, but I felt the monitor rubbing against my ankle with every step. It was going to take some getting used to.

No one was in the foyer of the gallery, though I could hear the buzz of saws and the pop of nail guns coming from somewhere in the rear of the building. I was alone with the mural, which seemed to have grown in size overnight. I stared down at the seventy-two square feet of dirt and abraded paint, and panic filled my chest. What a mess. I didn't even like the thing. The old-fashioned style and subject matter. The bizarre motorcycle was the only intriguing thing about it. *Jesse Williams*, I thought, *what have you gotten me into?*

I stared at the mural a while longer, already feeling time ticking away from me, growing closer minute by minute to August 5. There wasn't anything I could do with the mural until I got my new computer and learned something about restoration. Even then, I wasn't sure I'd know where to begin.

Chapter 10

———————⟶✦⟵———————

ANNA

December 11, 1939

Mid-afternoon, Mayor Sykes picked Anna up from Miss Myrtle's house in his green Chevrolet for the drive to the warehouse that he hoped would become her new studio space.

"What do you think of Miss Myrtle's?" he asked, chewing his cigar as he drove. The smoke filled the car and Anna wanted to roll down the window, but then they'd both freeze. The mayor exuded a sense of power in his strong, resonant voice. Although she remembered him being short at lunch, she hadn't realized how very fat he was. His belly strained at the buttons of his wool coat and brushed against the bottom of the steering wheel. His hair, which had seemed either blond or gray in the restaurant, was actually a mixture of the two. His entire presence was quite overwhelming to her in the small confines of the car, and she felt very young, very girlish sitting next to him. Actually, she felt quite vulnerable, an unusual feeling for her. She didn't like it.

As they chatted about Miss Myrtle's house, the weather, and the things the mayor's teenaged sons wanted for Christmas, she thought about how few men she'd truly known in her life. She'd never had a chance to know her father. Her uncle Horace, Aunt Alice's husband, was such a quiet man that she didn't feel as though she knew him at all. Then there was Mr. Prior, the sculpture teacher at Van Emburgh, who seemed to think her work was wonderful, so of course she'd liked him very much and had hardly found him intimidating. The only other male art teacher at Van Emburgh, Mr. Blaine, had been kind, serious, complimentary, and almost certainly homosexual and unthreatening.

Cigar-smoking men who took up more than their share of space were a new species to her.

After driving for a short while, Mayor Sykes pulled onto a long, narrow dirt road that led into a short tunnel of trees, at the end of which was a large, decrepit-looking, once-white warehouse partially surrounded by woods. The side of the building facing the car had a series of tall windows that Anna doubted would be enough to let in much light in that wooded setting.

"Here we are," Mayor Sykes said as he slowly drove toward the building. "No one's used this ol' warehouse in a generation or two."

Anna couldn't have said why, but she had an instantaneous fear of the building as they neared it. They weren't very far from town, yet the location felt isolated, and even before the mayor had stopped the car, she was already planning to use the excuse of poor lighting to turn down the offer of the building.

Mayor Sykes parked the car near the side door of the warehouse, and for a moment Anna wondered if she would be foolish to go into the building with him. *He's the mayor,* she reminded herself. *You're being silly.* They got out of the car, and the mayor walked her across the weedy, rutted lawn, his hand on her elbow. They entered through the unlocked side door. The scent inside was musty, a little oily and metallic, but it quickly gave way to the tobacco smell of the mayor's cigar. Anna stood still, waiting for her eyes to adjust to the interior light, and she began to notice her surroundings. For the most part, the warehouse was quite empty, save for some boards and crates scattered here and there, along with the occasional concrete block. Against one wall were three long wooden tables and a couple of chairs. The floor was a mess, littered with dirt and sawdust and who knew what else. The place was downright spooky.

"Is there a key for the door?" she asked. "I'll have supplies and other valuables in here I won't want stolen."

"Well, you might have to worry about that in New Jersey, but it won't be a problem down here." The mayor gave a self-satisfied laugh. "But sure, I can have a locksmith come and make you a key, if that'll help you rest easy."

"It would," she said.

The warehouse had not only those big windows along one side, but many skylights scattered the length of the high-beamed ceiling as well. Round pendant lights and huge black fans hung from the beams like giant bats. There were shadowy areas of the ceiling that no daylight seemed to reach and Anna shuddered, turning her gaze away from those beams. Anything could be up there.

"When the weather warms up," Mayor Sykes said, "you can open those doors over there. Let fresh air in." He gestured to the opposite side of the warehouse and for the first time Anna noticed four huge garage-type doors, far larger than the sort you'd find on a house.

"Uh-huh," she said, scrambling to think of an excuse that would let her turn down the offer of the warehouse. The windows were so filthy that the light was indeed hazy and wan as she'd predicted, although she could imagine how, once clean, they could let in enough light to work by on sunny days. Not in the morning or evening, though.

"I'm afraid I'll need more light," she said.

"I'll have some lamps brought over, along with those space heaters I promised," Mayor Sykes said.

A mouse suddenly skittered past their feet and Anna let out an involuntary screech.

"You have some company," Mayor Sykes laughed, taking her arm, as if protecting her. "That bother you?"

"Not at all," she lied, gently extracting her arm from his grasp. "It just surprised me." What else was living behind the old crates and concrete blocks in this building? There was no sign of people having used it as a place to sleep or squat. No cigarette wrappers or beer bottles. Nothing like that. Whatever was giving her the chills in the warehouse, it wasn't human.

"I'll have Benny, the custodian from my office, come sweep this out for you," Mayor Sykes said. He was standing very close to her. Although they weren't touching, she could feel the nearness of him, the heat of his body. She took a step away as if examining the grimy windows.

"Perhaps I can wash the windows," she offered, "if I can get a ladder."

"Oh, Benny'll take care of that."

"That would be wonderful," she said. She couldn't look this gift horse in the mouth. She knew the space could be made workable, as long as she could get over her discomfort about it. "Please have him—Benny—leave the tables and chairs," she said. "And I'll also need a stepladder. Where can I buy one?"

"Benny'll have to bring one for washing the windows," Mayor Sykes said, "and I'll just tell him to leave it."

They walked to the far end of the warehouse where they discovered a toilet and small sink tucked into an alcove. The mayor turned the squeaky faucet and brown water sputtered, then streamed into the sink and gradually turned clear. "Well, what do you know?" he said. "Water hasn't been turned off. You're in luck. Now we just need to get your electric back on and you're in business."

"Wonderful," she said, forcing the word past the unease in her throat. She was beginning to see the good points in the space. The shorter wall nearest the entrance was a blank slate. No door. No window. She ran her hand over the wall; it was smooth and made of wood. "This will be the perfect place to hang the stretched canvas," she said, more to herself than to Mr. Sykes.

"I would think so," he agreed.

She looked over at him. "You're very kind, thank you." She smiled at him, but found she couldn't hold his gaze for long. "I'm going to need some help," she said, turning toward the blank wall again. "Perhaps I could hire some high school students to work with me after school?"

"Want me to speak to the art teacher at Edenton High for you?"

"That would be wonderful." She was beginning to feel better about this man. He was so accommodating and generous. "Thank you for being so helpful," she said.

"We want you to enjoy your stay here in Edenton, Miss Dale," he said, and she wondered if the men she'd had lunch with had put their heads together and decided to quit talking about the artist they wished they had for the post office mural—Martin Drapple—and embrace the artist they were stuck with instead.

—⋙•⋘—

She was tired by the time she returned to Miss Myrtle's. Freda silently gave her a coconut cookie and a smile, along with a note from Miss Myrtle, telling Anna she was at her garden club, which apparently met all year long. Anna went up to her spacious room with its pink bed and sachet-scented air to write in her journal.

Tomorrow, she wrote, *Mr. Toby Fiering will take me on a tour of the cotton mill.*

She tried to imagine what that would be like, but every time her mind drifted from her writing, she was back in that shadowy warehouse once again.

Chapter 11

———— ⟡ ————

MORGAN

June 15, 2018

My new laptop was delivered at eleven that morning. I felt nervous as I set it up on the dining room table and connected to my e-mail address. I scrolled through ancient e-mail until the pain was too much for me. That mail was from another time, another world, before everything had gone to hell. There was a glut of e-mail from my former classmates at UNC about assignments and parties. Not a lot of e-mail from Trey. He'd mostly texted and all my texts were long gone with my old phone number. Just as well. The last e-mail from him read simply, *Chill, babe,* and I had no idea what it was regarding, since it had been sent before the accident, when I'd had nothing in my life I needed to chill about. I stared at his e-mail address, filling with a mixture of hurt and venom. He'd ruined my life and saved his own. Even after he realized how much trouble I was in, he did nothing to help me. Instead, he dug my grave deeper. I was tempted to e-mail him. Tell him exactly what I thought of him now. But it would be a mistake. E-mailing him—contacting any of my friends from my old life—would be a mistake I couldn't afford to make. In a moment of supreme willpower, I erased my mail. All of it. I wasn't going to live in the past. I needed to be in the here and now, and it felt good to see the empty mailbox. The blank slate.

I left my e-mail account and began researching "art restoration," quickly learning that I was in even more trouble than I'd thought. I had absolutely no business going near that mural. Restoration was no job for a novice, let alone for one person. Page after page on the restoration sites showed groups of people wearing protective gear as they worked together on a mural. Was Jesse Williams setting me up for failure for some unknown reason? Or maybe this was his approach to dealing with the kids he tried to save. Maybe he set each of them up with an impossible task and then goaded them to complete it to boost their self-esteem. Again I wondered if he had the wrong Morgan Christopher. I Googled my name on the computer, not for the first time, of course, but this time I added the word "artist" to my search. Mine was the only name that showed up. It was on Instagram, my old preprison account, when I still looked fresh faced and innocent, rather than the haunted-looking girl I saw in the mirror these days. Staring at my Instagram page, I felt myself caving. Tentatively, knowing how much it was going to hurt, I clicked on a picture of myself with my parents. I'd posted it a few years ago, why I wasn't sure. Maybe I'd wanted to pretend I had a normal life. A normal family. We'd been at the state fair, and to an outsider, we probably looked like a handsome threesome. Nice-looking father. Attractive, golden-haired mother. Blond daughter, pretty despite wearing no makeup. No one could tell the warped history of the family from this photograph, or that a short time later, the pretty daughter would be locked up. Now I saw the picture differently and it startled me. The three of us stood in front of the Ferris wheel. My father had his arm around my mother. Although it was morning, I knew he was already hammered. I could tell by the sloppy grin, by the way his hand grazed my mother's breast. My mother was probably three sheets to the wind herself, her prescription sunglasses askew. They didn't look like lowlifes, my parents. They'd both somehow managed to hang on to their computer programming jobs. *High-functioning alcoholics.* I'd learned that term in AA. I hated the way my very presence in the photograph seemed to give them credibility. Made them look like worthy parents. "You were a mistake," my mother told me once when she was blotto. "We never wanted to have kids." That had already been pretty clear to me. They'd never been there for me.

This ruminating was doing me no good.

I looked up some of my old friends' Instagram accounts, but what did I have in common with any of them now? Most of them had recently graduated, and if I hadn't screwed up, I would have graduated with them. I winced as I scrolled through their pictures. There they were, partying, laughing, without a care in the world. In bikinis at somebody's pool, bottles of beer in their hands. I'd never fit in with them again. I didn't want to. Even my best friend Robin looked like she was toasted. They'd learned zip from my experience. They probably thought that what happened to me was just shitty bad luck. I felt so alone, looking at the pictures. My boyfriend of two years—Trey—was gone. My girlfriends would no longer have a thing in common with me. My parents were worthless. I had no one.

I thrummed my fingers lightly on the keyboard. Did I dare look up Trey? In for a penny, in for a pound. Before I could stop myself, I clicked on his Instagram profile. *Oh damn.* I knew right away I shouldn't have done it. Trey stood beneath a sign that read GEORGETOWN UNIVERSITY LAW CENTER. The last year had only increased his physical beauty. That tousled blond hair. The eyes that were sometimes hazel, often green. The smile that was always there and that could melt me in two seconds. He looked so happy. So secure in his future. I realized in that moment, staring at his beautiful face, that I hated him. It was a good feeling. Almost healing, that hatred. Did Trey ever think about Emily Maxwell? Did he even know her name? I doubted it. I had the feeling only one of us had a conscience.

There was a picture of Trey with his family. The four of them stood in front of a broad, glittering Christmas tree. I remembered how they'd hunt and hunt for the perfect tree to fill the corner of their huge living room each year. Seeing his parents' smiling faces, seeing his younger sister Becky with her arm around Trey's waist, her head against his shoulder, was almost more than I could bear. I'd thought of his family as mine. The normal, happy, healthy family I'd yearned for. I'd called his mother "Mom." I'd embraced Becky as the sister I'd never had. I'd lost them when I lost everything else.

There was one more person I still wanted to search for, though the thought of actually finding her scared me: Emily Maxwell. But Google turned up only a couple of hits, all of them related to the old news articles about the accident. *Maxwell was taken to Rex Hospital, where she remains in a coma. The driver, twenty-one-year-old Morgan Christopher, was charged with driving while intoxicated.*

I pressed my fist against my mouth as I read the article. Only two people knew the truth about what happened that night. Only one of us tried to tell it.

Emily's coma lasted two months, and when she woke up, she was paralyzed. That was all I knew. All I'd been told. I was terrified to know more, and yet I needed to. I needed to know that somehow, in spite of what happened to her, she was okay. I was the sort of person who winced when I killed a fly. Who carried spiders outside instead of squashing them. I would never get over what happened to Emily Maxwell. But I could find no other information on her. No Facebook or Instagram or Twitter accounts—at least no accounts that were open to the public.

I finally left Google and returned with a vengeance to the restoration site I'd been studying. I could find no "lesson," no website that told me, step-by-step, "this is how you restore a mural." And every site I found seemed to describe different restoration methods or offer contradictory information. Restoration was not something you learned how to do on the Internet. I read until my eyes blurred and my stomach growled with hunger. By the time I shut the computer, I was more confused than ever about where to begin on the mural.

In the kitchen pantry, I found a box of Cheerios and was lifting it from the shelf when I noticed pencil markings on the pantry's doorjamb. I stepped closer. The markings were a height chart, and I bent over to see the lowest line. "Lisa, age 7." There was another mark for every age, up until she hit nineteen when I assumed she had stopped growing. I remembered seeing a similar height chart in a friend's house when I was a teenager and I felt the same envy now as I had then. This was a family that cared enough to record a child's height, a child's life passages. I was willing to bet this pantry had been painted numerous times over the last four decades, but the doorjamb with the pencil markings had been preserved. Treasured by Jesse Williams and his wife. Maybe by Lisa herself. The house suddenly felt like someone's home to me. I'd been thinking of it as more of a museum, clean and a bit sterile, filled with incredibly valuable artwork. The height chart, like the handprints in the front sidewalk, told me something different. A family had lived and loved here.

I was eating the Cheerios at the kitchen table when Lisa came in the back door. She was dressed in white capris and a button-down blue chambray shirt rather than her usual polished Realtor clothing. She looked like a different woman.

"Why aren't you at the gallery?" she asked. "You need to get cracking on the mural."

Nope, I thought. *Same woman.*

"Soon," I said. "I got my computer and I'm reading about restoration and . . . do you realize that artists really aren't the people who do it? It's a whole different set of skills, and—"

"What are you saying?" She frowned at me.

"That you need to be patient with me. I'll do it, but I don't even know how to start and—"

"You'll have to figure that out quickly," she said. "We have a deadline to meet."

I set down my spoon, annoyed. "Lisa, what's the big deal with the opening date of the gallery? So what if it opens a week late or even a month late?"

She stared at me. It was unnerving, that stare.

"Don't you want this done right?" I asked.

Lisa leaned against the counter, her body slumped, and she suddenly looked exhausted. "I have bigger fish to fry than to argue with you about this," she said. "I not only have the gallery to deal with, I have clients selling, clients buying, clients pretending to want to buy. The mural is all you have to deal with. That's it. Your only responsibility. Just seven or eight weeks of your life, and then you're a free woman with fifty thousand dollars in the bank. If it weren't for the mural and my father you'd still be in prison, all right? So get things in perspective."

"They have these big companies who do restoration," I argued, unwilling to let this topic slide. "Not one lone person who has never done anything like it before. I just don't want you to expect a perfect job when I'm working by myself, doing it for the first time, learning as I go."

"Then do an *imperfect* job," she said. "My father had to know your limitations and he still wanted you to do it. Just make it good enough to hang in the foyer. No one's going to examine it with a fine-tooth comb. It's not the *Mona Lisa*. All right?"

I worried that "imperfect" would be the kindest word anyone could find to describe my work on the mural. "Fine," I said.

Lisa glanced at her phone. "I want you at the gallery now," she said. "This afternoon. The guys are building a stretcher and you need to supervise them. You have to figure out what supplies you need so we can get them ASAP."

"Seriously, Lisa, I need to do more research before I can—"

"Research is always never-ending," she said, "and I'm not paying you to sit on your computer here in my house."

Wow, she was tough. I didn't speak, at least not out loud. Inside, I was thinking, *First of all, it's not your money. Second of all, I have no idea what I'm doing.*

"Fine," I said again. Money and freedom. That was why I was here. The mural was bizarre and my curiosity was piqued by its strangeness, but I certainly felt no attachment to it. I just wanted to figure out how to restore it well enough to be paid and stay out of prison. I'd view the mural as nothing more than a means to an end.

I carried my bowl to the sink, then picked up my purse and the laptop. "I'm on my way," I said, and I headed for the door.

Chapter 12

—⟶◦⟵—

ANNA

December 12, 1939

In the morning, Mr. Fiering gave Anna a tour of the cotton mill and the diminutive Mill Village, which consisted of neat rows of little houses for the mill workers and their families. There were a lot of children in the streets playing catch and chasing one another around. The Mill Village had a very separate feeling from the rest of Edenton, and from a few things Mr. Fiering said, Anna had the sense that the people who lived in its tiny houses were not viewed in a very welcoming light by the rest of the town.

The mill itself was quite an impressive sight. The long brick building was filled with workers and machinery and noise, and Anna felt overwhelmed by it all as she walked through it, Toby Fiering at her side. Ironically, though, it was the *outside* of the mill that she found most intriguing. Wisps of cotton were caught in the branches of the trees closest to the mill windows and Anna found the sight of them fascinating—a stunning visual she decided then and there would be in her mural along with some of the small Mill Village homes that lined the nearby streets.

After they toured the mill, Mr. Fiering dropped her off at the peanut factory, where she watched women, most of them colored, doing monotonous work on the belts that moved the peanuts from one part of the tall brick building to another. Anna liked the idea of including colored workers in the mural. She mentioned that to Miss Myrtle when she returned home from her busy day.

"Oh, honey," Miss Myrtle said, "this town couldn't survive without our colored folk! Between the housekeepers and the nannies and the fishermen and the people working the fields—why, they're the glue that holds us together. Of course they've got to be in the mural!"

Anna couldn't help but wonder why, if Miss Myrtle felt that way about Edenton's colored citizens, she made Freda go outside to use her own separate bathroom, rain or shine. She wasn't sure she would ever truly understand the people in the South.

"And listen, dear," Miss Myrtle said, "I nearly forgot. A reporter stopped by to talk to you. He'll be coming back tomorrow afternoon. Said he wants to talk to the lady who's making a painting for the post office."

"A reporter!" Anna said. The word alone made her nervous. "I don't have anything to say to a reporter. At least not yet."

"Oh, sure you do," Miss Myrtle said. "Tell him you're going to paint something that will make Edenton proud."

Miss Myrtle's words still rang in her ears by the time she climbed into bed that night. Her head was so full of all she'd seen and heard and experienced over the last week, it was hard to separate one idea from another. But slowly, as she lay there sleepless, the mural began to take shape in her mind. She got out of bed around midnight, carried her sketch pad downstairs, and sat in the chilly living room to draw by lamplight. How she would include everything she wanted to without making a mess of it, she wasn't sure. The ladies at the Tea Party would be front and center, whether the gentlemen liked it or not. The ladies were a bit of a problem as she sketched, though, since she had no models to work from. She would have to use models for the full-size cartoon, that was clear. At that moment, though, she just wanted to get her ideas down so that once her art supplies arrived from Aunt Alice, she could begin working on the thirty-six-by-eighteen-inch sketch she needed to turn in to the Section for approval.

She thought of the reporter who wanted to talk to her. What could she tell him? It would be embarrassing if she described the mural taking shape in her imagination only to have the Section reject her sketch. But then she thought of Miss Myrtle's words and relaxed. She didn't need to describe her idea to him. She'd tell him the truth: all she cared about was creating a mural that would make Edenton proud.

Chapter 13

———— ❖ ————

MORGAN

June 15, 2018

I found two bare-chested men—Wyatt and Adam—and a T-shirt-clad Oliver on the wide lawn outside the gallery as they put the final touches on the largest stretcher I'd ever seen. For a moment, I stood back, watching them from the sidewalk. Wyatt and Adam seemed to be working under Oliver's supervision, because he stood at the edge of the yard in his blue T-shirt, earbuds loose around his neck, motioning to them.

"Hey, Morgan," he called, waving me over, and I walked toward him. "They have a little more work to do on the interlocking joints," he said, "and then we can tack on the mural and set it up against the wall for you to work on. You're probably champing at the bit to get started on it."

"I am." I smiled, a frisson of anxiety in my chest.

"You do want the interlocking joints, right?" he asked.

For a terrible moment, I wondered if it was a trick question. I wasn't one hundred percent sure what interlocking joints were. Maybe he was making them up to see if I knew the first thing about restoration.

"That'll be great," I said, and I was relieved when he seemed satisfied with my answer.

The stretcher was a work of art all on its own. It was huge, made of long two-by-fours with wooden braces forming a grid between them. It was an enormous, beautifully crafted thing. Oliver was right about these guys. They were fast and they knew what they were doing. If only I could say the same about myself.

"Want to take another look at the mural?" Oliver asked, and I nodded, following him inside.

The delicious woody scent of the gallery greeted me again and I could hear the buzz of saws from somewhere in the interior of the building.

I stood next to Oliver in the middle of the foyer, looking down at the mural, which was still attached to the two-by-four on the floor. "I'm trying to find material on Anna Dale," Oliver said, "and I did find something I'll show you in a bit. But for the most part, it's like she simply disappeared after she painted the mural."

"So strange," I said, but my gaze was on the many areas of the mural that were nearly bare of paint beneath the layer of grime or mildew coating the enormous canvas.

"Doesn't look any better today than it did the other day, does it?" He laughed.

"Uh-uh," I agreed.

"Where did you work before coming here?" he asked. A casual question or was he suspicious?

I hesitated, my gaze on the women and their broken teapot. Even if I wanted to make up an answer, I didn't know what it should be. I glanced at Oliver. With his tall, slender build and dark-framed glasses, he struck me as artsy and kind, a bit nerdy despite handsome features, and I opted for the truth. "I wasn't," I said.

He tilted his head. "You were between jobs?"

I drew in a breath. "I'm not actually an art restorer." I looked squarely at him. "I was a fine arts major at UNC in Chapel Hill and had to drop out in my third year."

I thought his cheeks actually blanched. "You're kidding," he said. Was there worry in his voice or was I projecting? Suddenly, though, he let out a laugh. "So, *you're* the one," he said.

"What do you mean?"

He was still chuckling to himself. He put his hands into the pockets of his jeans. "A couple of months before Jesse died, I was over at his house talking about his design for the building, and he said, 'Watch for this white girl to show up at the gallery. She's gonna need a boatload of help.' Though he didn't say 'boatload.'"

"Oh my God . . ." Oliver's words suddenly made this whole crazy experience feel real. "Do you have any idea how he decided on me?"

He shrugged. "I don't even know how he decided to help *me*."

"Help you?"

He nodded. "I was one of his charity cases," he said. "Thirteen years ago, now."

"You're kidding!" I took a step back to really look at him. "What did he do for you?"

Oliver smiled. "I was seventeen, living in Philadelphia, and about to drop out of the stifling private school my parents had me in—"

"Wait. Private school? Charity case?"

"There are different types of charity."

"Okay." I could understand that. "Continue."

"I'd gotten my girlfriend pregnant, and thought I should get a job and support her and my soon-to-be kid—"

"Whoa," I said. "You are so not at all what I imagined you to be."

"What did you imagine?"

"Just not . . . the type to get a girl pregnant at seventeen."

"Yeah, well . . . Don't judge a book, and all that." He smiled again. "So one day I get this phone call from Jesse Jameson Williams, a guy I'd never heard of. He told me I had promise and he wanted to help me."

"He called you personally?" I wished I'd had the chance to talk to him myself. How incredible that would have been.

"Uh-huh," Oliver said. "Jesse somehow got me out of my hellhole of a school and into the University of the Arts in Philly. He paid for every-thing. He even paid child support for my son, including child care, so my girlfriend could stay in school." Oliver's voice thickened and he turned his gaze away from me. Drew in a breath. "Really, he saved me," he said. "I was going down the drain."

"How did he even know about you?"

"He'd never tell me." Oliver cleared his voice, seeming to get his emo-tions back under control. "I don't think he ever told the kids he helped. But I'm pretty sure my art teacher got in touch with him. That was just the way Jesse was. He had a lot of money and he liked to spend it on people he thought were worth saving."

"I'm not sure anyone would think I'm worth saving right now," I said, the words out of my mouth before I could stop them.

Oliver nodded. "Exactly how I felt back then," he said, without prod-ding me for an explanation.

"So, did you marry your girlfriend?" I asked.

"No, though I did get a great kid out of that relationship—he's twelve—and I see him as much as I can." He studied the mural, but I had the feel-ing it was his son's image he was seeing. "We're planning a trip to Smith Mountain Lake, just the two of us," he continued. "We rent the same cabin every year. Can't go till late August when the gallery'll be up and running, though, and I can get away. He—his name is Nathan—he loves it up there."

"Where does he live?" I asked.

"He and his mother and her new husband live down here. Well, in Greenville, anyway, which is why I ended up in North Carolina. I have an apartment there and teach a couple of classes at ECU during the school year. So"—he ran a hand through his thick dark hair where it fell across his forehead—"back to you." He looked toward me again. "I owe Jesse and I think he was asking me to help you if you needed it. And it sounds like you need it, so I guess it's my turn to pay it forward."

"Thank you." I felt incredibly relieved by his story. By his offer to help. I had the feeling he had no idea how much help I was going to need, though.

"Does Lisa know you have no experience in restoration?" he asked.

"Oh, she knows, all right," I said. "Jesse Williams wrote in his will that he wanted me to do the restoration, so Lisa tracked me down and hired me. Experience be damned." I felt my cheeks color. I was leaving plenty out of the story.

We were both quiet for a moment. Oliver looked down at the mural again. "The thing is," he said slowly, "while I understand your position, it's practically . . . *criminal*, in my opinion, to have an inexperienced person work on this. It's a valuable mural. It needs a professional conservator."

"You don't need to convince me of that," I said. "I'm scared to death to even touch that thing."

"Why did you say you'd do it if you don't know how?"

I hesitated, but there was something about Oliver that made me feel safe. And anyway, I didn't think there was anything he could say to Lisa that would make her rescind her offer.

"Lisa's following her father's directions in his will," I said. "And he clearly said he wanted me to do it, even though he'd never met me and had to know I'm an artist and not a conservator. And I'm not much of an artist, either," I added. "I wish I could be, but I don't think I'm all that talented."

I felt Oliver's quiet gaze on me. "Well, ol' Jesse may have gone overboard this time," he said. "Looks like we both know that he should have found a competent conservator to take on this work and given you something less . . . challenging. You're being thrown to the wolves. Forgive me for saying this, all right? But you really shouldn't do this," he said sincerely. "I think you should just say no."

"I *can't* say no." I let out my breath and looked toward the front windows of the foyer, my cheeks hot. "There's more to it than that," I said quietly. I looked over at him. "I was in prison," I said, my voice still low, not wanting to be overheard by any of the workers in the building.

Oliver's eyebrows shot up.

"It's a long story." I felt the alcohol monitor heavy on my ankle. "I didn't shoot anyone or anything like that. But the thing is, Lisa was able to get me out on parole to do this work. If I don't do it, I'll have to go back to prison." My eyes suddenly burned, surprising me. "I can't go back." I was whispering now. "I just can't."

He nodded, very slowly, brows furrowed above those vivid blue eyes. I wished he'd say something.

"I'm trying to read about how to do it—the restoration—online, but it's overwhelming," I continued. "Do you know any conservators I could call to give me some guidance? Jesse Williams left me money I can use to pay them."

Oliver rubbed his hand across his chin, his gaze back on the mural. After a moment, he let out a long breath. "I have some experience," he said finally. "I apprenticed to a conservator for a year after college. I don't have a lot of time, with the insane deadline for this place, but I can try to give you some guidance."

"Oh my God, Oliver!" It was as though a huge knot in my chest had loosened. I felt like hugging him, but stayed where I was. "I'll . . . I'll bake you brownies or do your laundry. Whatever you need."

He half smiled, but I could see he wasn't happy. "A simple thank-you will do," he said.

"Thank you, then," I said. "Please don't tell the other guys here." I glanced toward the front yard where I could picture Wyatt and Adam working on the stretcher. "I don't want everyone to know I was in prison."

"No problem," he agreed. "It's best if they think you know what you're doing, anyway." He pointed to the mural. "So, take a look at it," he said. "What do you notice right off the bat?"

"That it smells terrible and the colors look like various shades of dirt. It's filthy."

"Yes, it's got a pretty revolting layer of grime on it, so the first thing you'll need to do is clean it, and fortunately you don't need anything fancy for that. We'll figure out what fancy supplies you *do* need for later and order them. Then you can work on an aqueous cleaning while you're waiting for them to arrive." He went on to describe how I could use a cotton-wrapped dowel and distilled water to slowly and meticulously clean the mural. "Anna Dale painted in oil, but you know about not using oil paint for inpainting, right?"

Mortified that I knew no such thing, I said nothing, thinking, *Why not?* Then I got it. "It would age at a different rate from the older paint?" I guessed.

"Smart girl." Oliver gave me a light tap on the shoulder. "There's hope for you," he said. "Anna Dale used no varnish, so you have no varnish to remove and you shouldn't varnish it when you're done restoring it, either, since you want to stay true to the artist's vision."

"This artist had a bizarre vision," I said, pointing to the motorcycle where it peeked out from behind the filthy skirts of the Tea Party ladies.

"Or maybe a sense of humor." Oliver shook his head. "I can't quite figure it out." He grinned down at the mural. "I love it, though. I've seen a million of these old government-sponsored murals and they're usually dull as dishwater. At least this one has a little spark in it. It intrigues me. So, anyway"—he shifted, hands in his pockets again—"Restoration 101: photograph everything. Every step along the way, take pictures. You want a record. Take a good distance photo of the whole mural before you start and close-ups of each scene, especially any areas of damage. Got it?"

"I do," I said. "Photograph everything." The words made me feel hopeful for some reason. For the first time in a few days, I wasn't completely lost. Here was something concrete I could do.

Oliver pulled a notepad from his back jeans pocket and began making a list of the supplies I would need to order and where to get them. "You need to get a good spray bottle. And a dowel, maybe half an inch around, from the hardware store. Then go to the beauty supply store in town and buy some cotton. Genuine cotton. It comes in long strips."

I watched him jot down the items on the list.

"And a ball of twine and some tacks, like these." Oliver leaned over and touched one of the tacks attaching the mural to the two-by-four. "Get a lot of them," he said, "and a couple of gallons of distilled water."

I tried to imagine lugging gallons of distilled water and dowels and the other supplies down the street. "I don't have a car," I said.

"You can borrow my van."

"I don't have a license."

He studied me curiously and I held his gaze. "DUI?" he asked.

I nodded.

"You went to *prison* for a DUI?"

"It . . . got complicated."

He raised his eyebrows in a gesture I was beginning to think of as uniquely his. "I'll send one of the builders to get the material," he said.

"Sorry," I said. "Really. Sorry to create more problems for you."

He touched my bare shoulder lightly again. "Did you design this tattoo?" he asked.

"I did," I said.

"It's a stunner," he said, then smiled, "and I don't want to hear you put yourself down as an artist again."

"Thank you." I smoothed my hand over the tattoo, my cheeks heating up with the compliment . . . and the reprimand.

"So." Oliver returned his attention to the mural. "There's remarkably little flaking for you to deal with. That's a miracle. So I don't think you'll have to do any consolidation, which is fortunate, because it would take me a long time to teach you how to do that." He pointed to a section of the canvas. "Your biggest job is going to be inpainting, given all the abrasions. Fortunately she—Anna Dale—painted very thinly. That's to your benefit."

I'd never heard the term "inpainting" before, but I could guess what it meant. I'd look it up to be sure. "Thank you again, Oliver," I said. "I'm sorry. I know I'm taking you away from your work."

"I want to see this done right." He motioned for me to follow him into the gallery. "Come with me," he said. "I have an office here, such as it is at the moment. Let me show you what I found out about Anna Dale."

Chapter 14

ANNA

December 14, 1939

Anna's picture and an article about her were in the *Chowan Herald* on Thursday morning, and she felt rather famous. She was glad the interview and picture-taking was over with, though. It had unnerved her, all of it. The reporter made her go to the warehouse. She'd been afraid he was going to ask her to pose inside it, and she was relieved when he said the lighting wouldn't be good for an interior photograph. She would have to get over the discomfort she felt inside the building. Those dark corners. That beamed ceiling with its hanging lights and fans. She knew why that ceiling distressed her so. She was just going to have to get past the fear. Once she filled the warehouse with her work and supplies, she hoped it would seem less ominous to her.

The reporter took the picture of her with the warehouse in the background, then asked her questions about her plans for the mural and she gave him her new pat line: "I will paint something to make Edenton proud," she said.

But the article in the *Herald* wasn't the only reason she felt famous. That morning, she'd walked downtown to buy some toiletries. She liked Edenton's compact size and how easy it was to get around. The day was quite sunny and warm for December and the Christmas decorations strung across Broad Street seemed almost out of place, or at least out of season. She was in Michener's Drug Store when she spotted the new *Life* magazine on the magazine rack, and she gasped. She'd nearly forgotten that all the winning mural sketches for the 48-States Competition were to be published in *Life*. She picked up a copy, her hands trembling as she carried it to the front of the store, and she fumbled in her purse for coins. Trying to contain her excitement, she carried the magazine to a bench on Broad Street, where she paged through it, finally finding the spread of all the winning sketches. The pictures were very small—almost postage-stamp-sized, and they were in black-and-white, but she could imagine the colors and vibrancy of them all. There was her poor old useless sketch for Bordentown—Clara Barton and her students at the brick schoolhouse. She touched it fondly with her fingertip, missing it a little. The caption stated *Anna Dale will be creating a new sketch for the Edenton, North Carolina, post office.* There were a few other sketches by artists who also received new assignments, and she was relieved to feel less alone. She wasn't the only artist scrambling to come up with new subject matter. She noticed that a couple of other artists had divided their murals into three or more parts, so she would not be alone in doing that, either.

Seeing her sketch in the magazine gave her the confidence to call the art supply store in Norfolk and order the paper she would need for the cartoon. Her new sketch was coming along beautifully. She'd barely slept for the work—which was more like pleasure to her—and she was almost ready to begin adding color.

She was reading in the living room shortly after making the call when

Miss Myrtle walked into the room. The older woman sat down in the armchair she seemed to fancy and studied Anna's face.

"You have bags under your eyes for one so young," she said.

Anna only laughed. The insult didn't bother her a whit. She was too excited to have her mood brought down by Miss Myrtle or anyone else today.

"It's just that I love what I'm doing, Miss Myrtle," she said. "I'm very happy."

"Yes, but I'm a little concerned about you." Miss Myrtle frowned. "Freda wrote me a note saying you didn't eat breakfast or lunch today. You're already thin as a rail. Promise me you'll have a snack, all right, dear?"

Anna felt her smile falter. She'd skipped both meals? She hadn't even thought about eating, and it was nearly two o'clock. She remembered chastising her mother for not eating during her "lively spells," and the memory shook her.

"I'll have that snack right now," she promised Miss Myrtle as she got to her feet, forcing a smile, and as she walked toward the kitchen, she wondered if this was how her mother had felt during those manic episodes, so full of energy and joy that she forgot to take care of herself. Ridiculous to compare what she was feeling to her mother's situation. Ridiculous!

She found a package of Nabs in the pantry and sat at the kitchen table to eat them under Freda's silent, approving smile. The maid poured her a glass of milk to go with the crackers, and Anna dutifully chewed and swallowed, but she was anxious to get back to work and annoyed with herself for letting paranoid thoughts about her mother disturb her newfound happiness. She would make sure she ate her three meals a day from now on, but she wouldn't let anything get in the way of the joy she felt as she worked on the mural for the intriguing little town of Edenton, North Carolina.

Chapter 15

———— ➤•⤜ ————

MORGAN

June 15, 2018

Following Oliver through the gallery, I was overwhelmed by how much there was left to do before the building opened to the public. The three good-size exhibition rooms still lacked drywall, much less paint, and I spotted an electrician working with a tangle of wires inside one of the open walls. The space was definitely interesting, though.

"The walls are curved," I said, stating the obvious. I ran my fingers along the wall as I followed Oliver down the hallway.

"Jesse's design," he said.

"What was he like?" I asked. "Jesse?"

"Brilliant artist, but you already know that."

"I've loved his work forever," I said.

"And a generous guy, obviously," he said over his shoulder. "Very passionate about the people he cared for. But demanding. And fussy. He knows–*knew*—what he wanted and he always found a way to get it. Like the windows in the gallery. He wanted a special type of glass that took the architect months to track down. And the tile in the restroom had to be special-ordered from Italy. He could be hard on people if they didn't measure up to his standards."

I felt a stab of sympathy for Lisa, who was apparently still trying to measure up to her father's standards.

I followed Oliver into a small office, made to feel a bit bigger by the fact that one wall was almost entirely glass. The tall window overlooked a green lawn and a hedge, the only visible buildings a good distance away. The walls hadn't yet been painted and there were no switch-plate covers in place yet. Oliver sat down at his desk, which consisted of a board spanning two sawhorses. The makeshift desk supported a computer, half a dozen towering stacks of paper, the framed photograph of a cute, dark-haired boy of eleven or twelve, and a small speaker, from which Bob Dylan's crotchety old voice tried to sing.

"Dylan?" I raised my eyebrows.

He smiled. "Not your taste?"

"Not hardly."

He motioned toward a wooden stool at the side of the desk and I sat down. "I like old folk music," he said. "Dylan, Baez, Judy Collins. Peter, Paul and Mary. As a matter of fact, when you first showed up in the gallery, I thought you were Mary Travers walking in the door."

"Who's Mary Travers?"

"Mary from Peter, Paul and Mary?"

"Sorry," she said. "You lost me after Dylan."

"'Puff the Magic Dragon'?"

I made an "I have no idea what you're talking about" face. "That might be vaguely familiar, I think," I said. "How old are you, anyway?"

"Not as ancient as you're making me feel." He smiled. "I just turned thirty. What music do you like?"

"Mostly rap. Some pop."

"Oh, man." He cringed. "I don't think we can be friends."

I laughed and he smiled. Then I pointed to the photograph of the boy. "Is that your son?" I asked as he began looking through one of the stacks of paper on his desk.

"Nathan. Yes. And he shares your musical taste, I'm afraid. He's completely into it."

"He's very cute. He has your blue eyes, doesn't he. Does he like art?"

"Not in the least." Oliver laughed. "His stepfather is a computer guru and that's become his thing. And yeah, I'm jealous." He smiled at me. He had one of those faces that lit up entirely when he smiled. His eyebrows were expressive, and his eyes crinkled behind his glasses. "But mostly I'm happy he ended up with a decent stepdad," he said.

I thought I detected pain in his voice over sharing his son with another man. There was something about Oliver that truly touched me. I felt as though I could tell him my whole miserable life story and he wouldn't flinch. It made me want to lift the little bit of sadness I saw in his face just then.

"You'll have him all to yourself at that lake in a couple of months," I said, and I was happy to see the spark return to his eyes.

"Smith Mountain Lake, yeah," he said, rifling through the stack of paper. "I've already bought us some new fishing gear. It'll be a full week of him groaning at me and saying, 'Daaaad, you're such a dork.'" He laughed, though quickly sobered. "He's the light of my life," he said.

I smiled at him. He was so sweet. I wished I'd had a father who'd felt that way about his kid.

Adam suddenly appeared in the doorway of the office. He was taller than I'd realized. Taller and broader and half naked. He pulled his T-shirt on over the glistening skin of his chest, messing up his bun.

"We're ready to start stretching the mural," he said to Oliver. "You said you wanted to help?" I wondered if he'd intentionally waited to put on his shirt until he was in front of me because when he caught my eye, he was grinning at me. I looked away. I wasn't here to find a man, especially one who reminded me of Trey.

"Be out in a sec," Oliver said, and Adam disappeared down the hallway. Oliver pulled a yellowed piece of newspaper from the pile he'd been sorting through. "So," he said, "here's what I wanted to show you. Lisa gave me a big folder of Jesse's plans for the gallery and I found this in it."

He handed me the yellowed article, folded in half. I unfolded it carefully and laid it flat on the edge of the makeshift desk. Leaning forward, I read the date at the top of the page: December 14, 1939. The headline: *New Jersey Artist to Paint Mural for Edenton Post Office.*

"It's your Anna Dale," Oliver said.

My Anna Dale. The words made me feel instantly closer to the artist. There was a photograph of a girl about my age standing a distance in front of what looked like a warehouse. She wore a light-colored, neatly tailored coat and gloves, but no hat. Her hair looked very dark—maybe even black—and it was cut in a striking chin-length bob with thick straight bangs that just grazed her eyebrows. The overall look was very dramatic and, at the same time, almost impish. She wore an engaging smile. A confident smile. She didn't look the least bit deranged.

"Wow," I said. "So this is our talented and possibly nutso Anna Dale?"

"Read it," Oliver said.

I read the article to myself.

Miss Anna Dale, 22, of Plainfield, New Jersey, is the Edenton winner of the 48-States Mural Contest sponsored by the United States Treasury Department. Upon completion, the 12×6 mural will be mounted on the post office wall above the door to the postmaster's office. Miss Dale did not get specific in discussing the subject of the mural. "Edenton has a rich history and a rich present," she said. "I hope to capture both in the mural." When asked about the concern some Edenton residents have expressed about an artist from New Jersey painting a mural for a Southern town, she replied, "It's an honor to get to live in Edenton while I work on the mural so I can get to know the residents and hopefully give them a painting they can enjoy for many years to come. I'm very excited about the opportunity. I've already begun creating the proposed sketch for the mural and will soon submit it to the Section of Fine Arts. Once I get approval from them, I can begin working in earnest. At that time, the public will be most welcome to come to the warehouse to watch me work. I hope I can create something that will make Edenton proud." Miss Dale believes she will hear from the Section of Fine Arts sometime after the New Year.

I was transfixed. By the words. By the photograph. I gently touched the old paper, soft as felt beneath my fingertips, and was surprised to feel my eyes sting.

"What happened?" I asked the air as much as Oliver. "Why did she just disappear and leave the mural behind? She sounds perfectly sane, but if she did go crazy, like Jesse told Lisa, do you think they locked her up, or . . ." My voice trailed off as I studied the photograph of the smiling young artist.

"Something clearly went wrong," Oliver said.

"How did Jesse Williams end up with the mural?" I looked at the date of the article again. December 14, 1939. "He would only have been a kid then."

Oliver shrugged. "I don't think we'll ever know," he said.

"She looks and sounds perfectly sane," I said again.

"She does."

I sat back, my gaze resting on the photograph. I touched Anna Dale's smiling face and felt something shift inside me. All I had wanted to do when I got out of bed that morning was come up with the quickest way possible through this job to get my fifty thousand dollars and stay out of prison. Lisa didn't care as long as I could hang the mural on the wall by August 5.

Anna Dale, though . . . She'd been excited about the mural. She'd wanted to do a perfect job. Her heart had been in it and then something happened. It must have been something truly terrible to turn this pretty girl into . . . what? A mentally ill artist who mysteriously vanished from the art world? I shuddered. I wanted to do right by her. This girl who was my own age. I wanted to give life to the mural that Anna Dale never had the chance to give.

⟶•⟨⟨

The mural had been cut from its former stretcher so sloppily that it was a challenge to get it square on the new stretcher. It took a couple of hours for Adam, Wyatt, Oliver, and me, along with a few of the other construction workers, to stretch the mural into place and secure it with dozens of thumbtacks. I watched from a distance as the men attached the mural very low on the wall, helping them get it straight and square, ready for me to work on. Done with their job, the men returned to their work inside the gallery, but I stayed in the foyer a while longer. Now that the mural was on the wall, facing me head-on, the bare spots and the filth that seemed to coat every inch of the painting were more apparent, and yet the art behind the grime seemed to pop out at me. Those women and their broken teapot. They looked angry, didn't they? The black woman in the upper right-hand corner seemed to grin around the stick she held in her teeth. The motorcycle looked ready to race from the mural into the foyer.

I thought of the newspaper article again and its photograph of the optimistic young woman with her short black bob. I shuddered. It was like seeing the photograph of someone in an obituary. You could see the ignorance in their faces. Their blindness to what was coming. Anna Dale had looked that way in the photograph. She'd been at the beginning of her adventure—the beginning that had somehow become an ending.

For the first time, I noticed the artist's signature in the lower right corner of the mural and I walked forward to crouch in front of it. *Anna Dale.* Gently, I touched the filthy letters, but drew my fingers away quickly, startled by the roughness of the painting's surface. Anna's writing was vertical and round, painted in a grime-covered gold. I stared at the signature a while longer, wondering how a life that had started with so much promise could now be shrouded in such mystery.

Chapter 16

ANNA

December 25, 1939

Y ou must be Anna!" Pauline Maguire handed the grocery bag she was carrying to her husband and reached for Anna's hands. "Mama's told me so much about you!"

"You, too," Anna said, pleased by the woman's friendliness. Anna had met no one so close to her age in Edenton, and she felt an instant bond with the young woman whose room she was inhabiting.

"This is my husband, Karl," Pauline said.

Karl, his arms weighed down with bags and a large rectangular wrapped gift, only nodded with a smile. He looked quite a bit older than Pauline. A few gray strands silvered his brown hair.

"So happy to meet you," Anna said, taking one of the bags from his arms. "Miss Myrtle is in the kitchen."

Miss Myrtle had given Freda the day off to be with her own family for the holiday, so the three women set about cooking. They made a turkey, mashed potatoes, giblet gravy, and butter beans, which Anna had never heard of but which were the same as the lima beans she'd grown up with in New Jersey. Karl donned an apron and made some of the best biscuits Anna had ever tasted. She'd never known a man to willingly cook.

"I only like baking," Karl said with a wink. Anna liked him right away. He was so easygoing and friendly and it was clear that he adored Pauline. She remembered Miss Myrtle telling her that he was a policeman and so he'd been able to keep a good steady job all through the Depression when so many men went without work. He was also undeniably handsome, with blue eyes and that silver-laced hair that kept falling across his forehead in a way that Anna found winsome. She imagined he would look like heaven in his police uniform and she thought he and Pauline made a striking couple, despite the age difference.

Pauline exuded warmth. Anna remembered that she worked part-time as a nurse in a doctor's office. Her patients probably adored her. Anna could see Pauline's resemblance to Miss Myrtle in her full lips, large bosom, and dark blue eyes, but Pauline was probably half her mother's weight and the hair that spilled in waves around her shoulders was light brown instead of Miss Myrtle's dull gray. Watching mother and daughter work together and chat together and laugh together set up a dull ache in Anna's chest that she was determined to keep at bay for the afternoon. This was her first Christmas without her mother. If she thought about it, she would break down in tears, and she didn't want to put her hosts—or herself—through that. She focused on her tasks and the conversation and the Christmas carols spilling from the radio on the counter. She would get through this day, one way or another.

All afternoon, as the four of them moved around the kitchen, and later, as they ate in the dining room, Anna watched the way Pauline and Karl smiled at each other. The way they lightly touched each other's hands as they passed a plate of turkey or the gravy boat. They were such a lovely couple, and Anna worked hard not to be jealous of the clear adoration they shared. Someday, she told herself, she would find a man who cared

as much for her as Karl seemed to care for Pauline. So far, most of her potential beaus had turned out to be little more than friends. Anna's mother
used to tell her that friends were more important than boyfriends, but
watching Pauline and Karl together set up a longing inside her for something more.

Over dinner, the three of them told Anna more about everyone she'd
met in town, cutting through outside appearances to the real people inside. Mr. Arndt was as good and kind as he appeared, they said. Mr. Fiering at the cotton mill liked to dress in ladies' undies, Pauline added.

"How on earth would you know that?" Anna laughed.

"Just a nasty rumor," Karl said, with a grin that belied his words.

"Mayor Sykes is a blustering fool, but he gets the job done," Miss Myrtle
said. Pauline made a disparaging sound with her tongue. "His wife covers
up bruises and everyone knows he has a lady friend on the side."

"Pauline!" scolded her mother. "No one knows that for sure at all."

Anna thought she might have been right to feel uncomfortable with
the mayor in the warehouse. She would keep her distance from him from
now on.

Once dinner was over and the kitchen clean, Anna mustered up her
courage to show Miss Myrtle, Pauline, and Karl her sketch. She'd sent
the original to the Section the week before, but she'd created an identical
sketch to work from when she was ready to start the cartoon—assuming,
of course, that the Section gave her the go-ahead. The cartoon paper she'd
ordered had already arrived and she hoped she'd have the chance to use it.

"You're so talented!" Pauline actually gasped, as though she hadn't expected Anna to be so skilled.

"Very impressive," Karl said.

"I told you," Miss Myrtle chided them. "She's a genuine artist, our
Anna." *Our Anna.* The words touched her. Made her eyes sting.

"I was worried about making the Tea Party the main subject," she said,
"but—"

"Oh, it *must* be the main subject!" Pauline said. "Of course it has to be."

BIG LIES *in a* SMALL TOWN

"Look at how well she drew the women's faces," Miss Myrtle said.

"They'll be better when I can work from models," Anna said. She personally thought the dresses were the most beautiful part of the painting. So colorful, and she thought she had a talent for painting fabric that looked so realistic you wanted to run your fingers over it. In the lower right-hand corner, she'd painted a line of homes from the Cotton Mill Village, with the mill itself behind them, and the wispy cotton caught in the branches of the trees. On the upper right-hand side, she'd sketched a colored woman holding up her apron full of peanuts. On the upper left, a fishing boat, the fishermen quite indistinct as they hauled in nets of herring. And in the lower left-hand corner stood a lumberman, ax in hand, green trees behind him.

"The peanut lady is my favorite," Karl said.

"Well, I like the handsome lumberjack," Pauline teased him.

Karl didn't rise to her bait. "It's all quite wonderful, Anna," he said instead. "That is the bottom line."

Anna glowed. She could imagine the final painting filling the post office wall.

"When you go to Norfolk to pick up your supplies," Pauline said, "I'd be happy to go with you, if you'd like some company."

"That would be lovely," Anna said, pleased by the offer. It had been a long time since she'd had a girlfriend to chat with.

They finished the evening with tea and slices of fruitcake that Freda had made, and as they ate together, Anna felt contentment wash over her. Such a rare emotion for her these days. She would be on pins and needles for the next couple of weeks as she waited to hear from the Section, but for tonight, she would bask in the joy of having new friends, a lovely place to live, and the sense of accomplishment that came with knowing she'd created something "quite wonderful."

Chapter 17

MORGAN

June 16, 2018

At Oliver's direction and with some help from Wyatt, I hung lengths of twine both horizontally and vertically across the stretcher to divide the mural into roughly seventy-two one-square-foot segments. "So you'll know where you cleaned," Oliver said. I balanced on a ladder and started in the upper left-hand corner using the cotton-wrapped dowel Wyatt had whittled to a point for me. "If you come to any flaking, clean around it and mark where it is," Oliver added. "Take your time."

Time, I thought. The one thing I didn't have.

From the other rooms of the gallery came the sounds of hammering and buzzing saws, and I put in my earbuds, turned my phone to the Spotify Top Hits playlist, and lost myself in the music as I worked. People didn't appreciate how lucky they were to be able to listen to music any time they wanted. I felt nearly overcome by the thought. People didn't appreciate their freedom, that was all there was to it. I was never going back in that hellhole.

Cleaning the paint with the cotton-wrapped dowel was slow going, but I discovered I liked the work. Nodding my head to the music in my ears, I cleaned the squares, inch by inch. I was cautious not to disturb any paint that might be loose, and I could instantly see the difference I was making. When I finished the first square, I climbed down the ladder, my shoulders already aching, and was stunned to look up and see the vibrancy I'd revealed, despite the fact that there wasn't much going on in that corner of the painting. The ship Anna had painted there was still covered with grime, but the sky above it was now a pretty—though mildly abraded in spots—gray-blue. I smiled to myself. When was the last time I'd felt satisfaction in something I'd done? When was the last time I'd felt that shudder of genuine joy? Crazy that one square foot of a clean painting could make me feel that way. Then my gaze traveled to the grungy seventy-one square feet I had left to clean and I groaned, rubbing my shoulder. This would take me forever, and it was only the first step in the restoration. I would have to pick up the pace.

—➤•◄—

I didn't eat lunch with Adam and Wyatt and the other construction workers on the front lawn, despite their invitation to join them. I wasn't ready to make idle conversation with anyone—did I still know how? I noticed Oliver didn't eat with them, either. He stayed in his office, the door closed. So I walked to a nearby café called Nothing Fancy, savoring the music of Post Malone and Maroon 5 in my ears. I ordered a takeout chicken-salad sandwich and sat on a bench outside to eat it. I thought about the AA meeting I'd attended the night before. It had felt strange, being at an AA meeting with a group of nonprisoners, not to mention being in a meeting with mostly men. I hadn't shared. Hadn't uttered a word except when I asked the guy leading the meeting if he'd sign the form proving I'd attended. I was done with drinking, and listening to everyone's sad stories only irritated me. I hadn't had a drink in fourteen months. Even without the monitor on my ankle, I knew I was finished with it.

By four o'clock, I'd cleaned twelve of the squares and my work had given definition to part of a fishing vessel in the upper left of the painting as well as to the right arm of the hunky blond guy in the lower portion. Slowly, I came to realize the man was not holding a length of wood as I'd originally thought, but rather an ax, and something was dripping from the blade. Sap? I gently moved my cotton-tipped dowel over the lowest corner of the blade and gasped. The glistening drops were bright red. They could only represent one thing: blood. I stood back from the mural, clutching the dowel in my hand. Only a third of the man's face had been cleaned and the paint was partly abraded, but I could see that he smiled. That he was handsome. That he seemed completely oblivious to the blood dripping from his ax. I felt a little sick. I thought of the newspaper image of Anna Dale. What had gone on in that strange head of hers?

I was dying to show what I'd uncovered to Oliver, but he was shopping for supplies, so I continued working. An hour later, I realized that I was no longer hearing the background sounds of hammers and saws and the pop of nail guns. I pulled out my earbuds and could tell that the guys were finishing up in the rear of the gallery. I would keep going, though. I had plenty more to do and nothing waiting for me back at Lisa's.

Wyatt came into the foyer as I wound a fresh piece of cotton on the pointed end of the dowel. His dreadlocks were loose now, hanging long over his shoulders.

"Damn, girl, that's rad," he said, checking out the cleaned portion of the mural. "I had no clue that thing was so trashed."

I felt myself beam. "Totally changes it," I said.

His grin turned to a frown and he moved nearer to the painting. "Is that blood on his ax?"

I nodded. "I think our artist was a little whacked."

"Ya think?" he said, then looked at me. "We're all goin' over to Water-man's for a drink. Come with us?"

Oh, hell no, I thought. I could imagine the seductive smell of the place. The beer cold and foamy in tall glasses. Watching everybody drink while I nursed a Coke. Not a good idea.

"I can't," I said. A guy at the AA meeting had talked about focusing on his accounting business to keep from drinking. "I'm going to do some more work here."

"All work and no play . . ." Wyatt teased.

"I know." I smiled. "Have a good time."

Another half hour passed before Oliver walked into the gallery, a soft leather briefcase in his hand. He stopped in the middle of the foyer to look at what I'd accomplished.

"That . . . is . . . awesome," he said, loudly enough for me to hear with my earbuds in. "What do you think?"

I pulled out my earbuds. "I think I need to find a massage place," I said with a laugh.

"You deserve it," he said. "Seriously, great work today. Have you found any flaking paint?"

"I found something much more interesting than flaking paint."

I moved the ladder aside to give him a clear view of the lumberjack's ax blade, and I watched Oliver's smile fade.

"Is that . . . ?" He set down his briefcase and moved closer to the mural, studying the drops of blood. He turned to look at me. "What the hell?" he asked.

"I know. I thought it was tree sap or something when I first saw it, but once I cleaned it off, I realized what it was."

"This makes no sense at all," he said, hands on his hips as he stared at the painting. He was close enough that I was suddenly aware of his scent. Leather? Although the only leather in the entire foyer was in his briefcase yards away from us. It was a good scent—a delicious, heady scent, actually—and for a moment I had trouble remembering what we were talking about as I breathed him in. "Blood and a motorcycle," he said, bringing my attention back to the mural.

"This must have to do with why Jesse told Lisa the artist went crazy," I said.

Oliver nodded. "Well, it explains why they never installed it in the post office, that's for sure." He pulled his phone from his jeans pocket and checked the time. "I just stopped in to see how you're doing before I head home with a night full of work." He nodded toward the briefcase behind us. "You ready to call it quits for the day?"

"Not yet," I said.

Heading toward the front door, he bent over to pick up his briefcase before looking back at me. "You'll lock up when you leave?"

"I will." Lisa had given me a key to the gallery that morning.

"See you tomorrow, then," he said.

He left the gallery and I popped my earbuds back in, surprised by the sudden feeling of loneliness that slipped over me as I climbed the ladder again. Everyone was getting on with their lives this evening and I had no life to get on with. It would be worse if I went back to Lisa's, though. I'd get on Instagram. I'd check out what Trey and my old friends were doing right now. I'd search for Emily Maxwell and stew in my guilt. Better to lose myself in the mural. I was curious to see if Anna Dale had left any other surprises for me to find.

—※·※—

I'd cleaned three more squares when I heard someone call my name from behind me. I turned to see Rebecca Sanders standing there, arms folded across her chest, an actual smile on her face. I guessed this was one of those surprise visits she'd warned me about. Thank God I hadn't gone to the bar with the guys! I climbed down the ladder.

"So this is where you work," Rebecca said. She pointed to the mural. "Are you cleaning that painting?" she asked. "That's quite a difference."

"Yes." I set the dowel on one of the steps of the ladder and wiped my damp hands on my jeans. I motioned to the cleaned portion of the mural. "It's taken me all day to do this much." I didn't think Rebecca was into art. She noticed clean and she noticed dirty, but she seemed uninterested in the images on the mural.

"I went to the address where you're staying but the woman there—Lisa Williams?—told me you were probably still at work, so I'm glad to find you here."

I nodded, glad she had found me there as well. "Everyone went out drinking, but I thought I should stay here." I winced. I sounded as though I expected a medal for not going with the guys.

"Have you made it to a meeting yet?"

"Last night. I have the signed paper but it's at Lisa's."

"Mail it to me," Rebecca said. "You have the address on my card."

"Okay."

We were both quiet for a moment. "It must have been hard, saying no to going out for drinks with your coworkers," Rebecca said finally.

I shrugged. "Not really." I didn't want to get sucked into counselor talk. I didn't want to give Rebecca any more power over me than she already had.

"You're doing well so far, Morgan," Rebecca said.

I nodded. "I'm okay."

"What's been hardest for you?"

I remembered my visit to Instagram. Seeing everyone moving on with their lives. Feeling alone. "Nothing," I lied.

"Come on," Rebecca said. "I'm here to help. I'm on your side."

"Nothing. Really. I'm happy to be out and I have plenty of work to keep me busy and everything's cool."

Rebecca looked doubtful, but she finally nodded. "What'll you do when you leave here tonight?"

"Go back to Lisa's. Go to bed. Sleep. Come back here in the morning and start all over again."

Rebecca hesitated as though there were something more she wanted to say, but she simply nodded toward the mural. "All right, then," she said. "Keep up the good work."

Rebecca left and I stood in the middle of the foyer trying to decide what to do. Work or go back to Lisa's? Rebecca had disrupted my flow. I carried the container of water and the cotton-wrapped dowel to the small kitchenette at the rear of the building. Opening the cupboard beneath the sink to throw away the cotton, I was greeted by the yeasty smell of beer from a few crushed cans in the recycling bin. One or more of the guys were drinking on the job, I guessed. The scent took me back to my party days at UNC, only a little more than a year ago, a year that felt like a lifetime. I suddenly yearned for something I couldn't name. Not the beer. Not my old friends. Trey? The perfect Trey I'd thought him to be? Maybe. But I knew it was something bigger that I longed for. My innocence, maybe. I wasn't sure, but I stood in the small kitchen, my hands across my chest in a sad little hug. Whatever it was I wanted, I knew I could never get it back. I thought again of Emily Maxwell and imagined that she, too, yearned for her life before the accident. Before so much had been stolen from her. *Oh God*, how I hated thinking about her! Surprising tears burned my eyes and I was suddenly back in my car on that hideous night, remembering what we'd done to her. Yes, *we*, because even though Trey had been driving, it could just as easily have been me behind the wheel. It could have been me who T-boned Emily's little Nissan at that dark, wet intersection. I'd been as toasted as Trey when we left the party and it was only at the last second that I turned my keys over to him. I would always remember the awful moment when I realized what we'd done, the sickening image of the totaled car in front of us, its headlights still piercing the darkness, the deafening, continuous sound of the car horn that filled the air after the crunch of steel against steel. The instant sobriety. *Omigod, did we kill someone?* The shock when Trey flung open the driver's side door and said, "I wasn't here! Got it?" I watched him leap from the car and take off into the dark woods. Even through my shock, I understood what he meant.

His scholarship. Georgetown Law. He was brilliant, and he'd worked so hard. He had everything to lose. I loved him. I'd protect him.

I'd sat there numb and paralyzed for a few seconds before I'd climbed out of the car myself. Slowly, heart pounding, I'd walked toward the Nissan, its horn still blaring. The darkness of the night stole my breath. There was just enough light for me to see that my car had impaled the driver's side of the Nissan. I couldn't see inside the car. Couldn't possibly get to the driver through that door. Battling nausea, I climbed through brush and leaves around the front of the Nissan and mustered my courage to force open the passenger side door. The overhead light came on and I knew in that moment that the image in front of me would haunt my dreams forever: long black hair and blood, twisted limbs and bones. I screamed and screamed and screamed until someone showed up next to me and someone else called the police. Even when I was surrounded by sirens and flashing lights, wrapped in a blanket, and being treated for a cut on my forehead I hadn't known I had—even through all of that, I screamed.

"Is she *dead*?" I kept shouting, my arms wrapped across my chest, my whole body tightened into a ball of horror. "Is she dead? Is she *dead*?"

I remembered, with painful clarity, the words of the cop standing next to me. "You didn't kill her," he said, "but you sure as hell ruined her life."

"I'm sorry," I whispered now, standing in the gallery's kitchenette. I pressed my fingers against my eyes as if I could block out the images of that night. The memories. I thought briefly of finding Adam and Wyatt. I imagined having a couple of beers with them to wipe out the horror. *Dangerous thinking.* I was going to have to find a way to live, sober, with the memories of all that had happened. *You are alive*, I thought to myself. *Healthy and whole.* Emily never would be. I had to appreciate my second chance. That's what I had to remember.

Chapter 18

---※◆※---

ANNA

January 2, 1940

Anna had thought of Plainfield as a small town, but she'd had no idea what a real small town was like until now. She'd barely been in Edenton for a month and people already knew who she was, no matter where she went. She discovered that could be both good and bad.

When she walked into Michener's Drug Store that early January morning, the man behind the counter said, "Why, you're that mural gal, ain't you?" Then when she stopped for a sandwich in the Albemarle Restaurant, the white-uniformed waitress asked, "Aren't you that post office artist?" And when she visited the library after lunch to get something to read while waiting to hear from the Section, the librarian said, "You must be that artist from up north!" It seemed that just about everyone in town had read that little article about her in the *Herald*. And everyone treated her with kindness and an open sort of friendliness she was coming to love.

But all that came to an end late that afternoon as she was leaving the library.

She'd walked out the front door and was heading down the steps just as a woman began climbing them. The woman's hair was blond beneath a blue scarf and she was flanked by sullen identical twin daughters. The girls were about eleven or twelve years old with curly strawberry-blond hair. Anna smiled at the threesome, but the woman suddenly grabbed her arm.

"You're that artist from New Jersey, right?" she asked.

"Yes," Anna said, still smiling, though the woman wasn't smiling back and her fingers dug into the woolen sleeve of Anna's coat.

"I'm Mrs. Drapple," the woman said. "My *husband* should be the one paintin' that mural!"

"Oh!" Anna said, taken aback.

"You're nothing but an amateur," Mrs. Drapple went on. "Your drawin' in that *Life* magazine looks like a ten-year-old did it. My girls could have did it!"

Anna twisted her arm from the woman's grasp, stunned. She wasn't sure what to say. She wasn't going to apologize for winning the competition. Why should she?

One of the woman's daughters spoke up before Anna could.

"Mama," she said, trying to tug her mother toward the library door. "Let's just go inside." But the woman stood rooted to the steps.

"I wish everyone who entered could have won," Anna said, lamely. "But I won the competition, fair and square. The entries were anonymous and—"

"Well, they *shouldn't* have been anonymous!" The woman yelled so loudly that a man walking down the street turned to look at them. "The people runnin' it should have taken *experience* into account, not to mention knowin' somethin' about Edenton! And they should have taken into account that a *man* would have a family to support. We could have used the money."

The twin who hadn't spoken studied Anna hard from beneath her furrowed brow, but the other one tugged again at her mother's arm. "Mama," she said, "it's freezing out here!"

"I'm very sorry," Anna said, annoyed at herself as the apology left her lips. She had nothing to apologize for. "It's out of my control," she added. She moved past the threesome and down the steps, clutching the railing, her knees shaking.

She walked briskly away from the library, looking over her shoulder every minute or so as if worried that Mrs. Drapple might be following her, ready to grab her arm again. Ready to sling more insults. Anna felt as though she'd stolen something from someone. She pictured Martin Drapple, whom she hoped never to meet, in a deep depression, penniless, struggling to figure out how to support his family. It wasn't her fault, and yet she felt guilty. She was an interloper. An outsider. A female. Had she taken food from those little girls' mouths?

Chapter 19

———— ✦ ————

MORGAN

June 18, 2018

It was dusk when I reached Lisa's house after my third full—*very* full—day of cleaning the mural. Sharp pains pierced my shoulder blades and I thought I could already see and feel a new firmness in my right bicep. I let myself in the front door with the key Lisa had given me, pulled out my earbuds, and headed through the living room for the kitchen. I was starving. I'd again skipped going out with the guys in favor of working on the mural. Safer and smarter that way. While I was cleaning the mural today, Adam began a conversation about music with me. I could tell he was just trying to find something to talk to me about. I felt torn around him. He was my type, or at least the type I used to be drawn to. Very male, very good-looking. The sane part of me said I should run in the opposite direction, and I was glad when Wyatt came into the foyer to drag Adam back to work.

As I neared the rear of the living room, I could see through the hallway into the kitchen. Lisa sat at the table, her back to me, a glass of wine at her side. Was she on the phone, as usual? Something in her posture—the way she was a little slumped, her shoulders drooping—caused me to stop. Should I go in?

She must have heard me. She suddenly spun around, getting to her feet so quickly she knocked over the wine. The glass rolled from the table and fell to the tiled floor, splintering into pieces.

"You surprised me!" she said, hand to her throat, and I knew she'd been crying. Her eyes were red, her cheeks damp. I caught a glimpse of a photograph on her phone before the screen suddenly went dark: Lisa, her arm around an elderly man. Her father, no doubt. I was touched by her grief.

"I'm sorry," I said. I grabbed a handful of paper towels and began cleaning up the mess. The air filled with the scent of wine. Lisa seemed almost paralyzed. She stood in the middle of the floor, not trying to help, not doing anything, really. She just watched me work. "Move back," I said. "Let me get the glass up."

Lisa backed up woodenly against the far counter, her hand still at her throat, while I picked up the shards of glass with the damp paper towel.

"Thank you," she said quietly.

"I think I got it all," I said, straightening up. A pinprick of pain pierced my right shoulder. I threw the paper towels and shards of glass into the trash and washed my hands, then turned to face Lisa, who looked away from me, one hand wiping away tears on the side of her face. She wasn't wearing her Michelle Obama hair. Her natural hair, with its short curls and coils in a halo around her face, made her look younger and more vulnerable, and for the first time since meeting her, I felt sympathy for her. For the first time since meeting her, I felt as though *I* was the one with the power.

"Are you okay?" I asked. The words came out more gently than I'd anticipated.

Lisa drew in a shaky breath. "Just . . ." She glanced at her phone, as if remembering the picture of her father, but she didn't mention it. "Nothing's going very smoothly," she said instead. She moved to the cabinet over the dishwasher and took out another glass, then poured herself more wine. She looked at me. "I'm sorry," she said. "It's rude of me to drink in front of you."

"It's fine," I said. It was.

"Are you hungry?" she asked.

"I am." I walked to the refrigerator, opened it, and took out a yogurt. I was more interested in learning what was going on with Lisa than I was in fixing myself something to eat. I got a spoon and sat down at the table across from her. "What's not going smoothly?" I asked.

Lisa drew in a breath. "One of Judith Shipley's paintings and two of Ernie Barnes's that my father loaned out to another gallery have been delayed and might not make it here in time for the opening," she said. "And the roofer had an accident and is now backed up. The workers lost half a day when they built your stretcher . . . which I know is not your fault," she added hurriedly. "But still, they're behind. And you're . . ." She offered me a sad, apologetic smile. "You're a novice in an unfair position. I know that. I want you to know that I understand that. That my expectations of you are completely unreasonable. We're both in an untenable position. And we both stand to lose so much."

I was stunned by her sudden show of empathy. "Then . . . why are you killing yourself to get everything done by some arbitrary date?" I asked. "Why don't you just change the date of the gallery opening? It's a pretty simple solution."

Lisa looked away then let out a long, frustrated-sounding breath. She was not at all the woman I'd come to know over the last few days. She took a swallow of her wine, and her hand trembled when she set the glass down again. "I can't," she said simply.

"What is so magical about August fifth?" I asked. "If it's causing you this much . . . agony, why not just say, hey, we need to move it to September fifth. Or October, even. I could really use the extra time, believe me."

Lisa looked across the table at me. "My father put several conditions in his will." She held up a hand as if to prevent an argument. "Don't get me wrong," she said. "He was a kind man. A very loving man. I always felt his love. *Always*. But he was also very controlling. And I guess his will was his final attempt to control me."

"I don't get it," I said.

"He had the idea for the gallery for years and years—it was his dream—but when he neared the end . . . well, he thought if he left it in my hands, it would fizzle out. And he was probably right. I'm not an artist." She shrugged. "I'm not even particularly interested in art, except for my father's, which I love. But the gallery is not my dream. It was his. I guess he figured he had to come up with a way to force my hand. To make the gallery happen. So he tied my inheritance—specifically, this house—to the opening date of the gallery. Andrea Fuller—remember her? The attorney who came with me to the prison?"

I nodded.

"Andrea's his executrix. If the gallery isn't open by August fifth—with the mural restored and hanging in the foyer—the house will be donated to some indigent-artist fund or whatever." Lisa waved a dismissive hand through the air. Then she swallowed hard, studying the wine in her glass. When she looked up at me again, tears brimmed in her eyes. "I can't lose this house, Morgan."

I frowned. "You can put something like that in a will?" I asked.

Lisa nodded. "It's a conditional will. You can't force someone to do something . . . he can't force you to restore that mural, for example . . . but he can tie your doing so to his bequest. And he's tied you and me together, for some bizarre reason known only to him, and he's not around to explain it. I can't open the gallery until you finish the mural and if I don't open the gallery by August fifth, I lose the thing that's most precious to me."

"Wow," I said. "That sounds . . . extreme. Why didn't he at least give you more time?"

"I told you he was manipulative," Lisa said. "I suppose he figured the more time he gave me, the more I'd dawdle. And don't get me wrong. He's not leaving me destitute. He left me cash—I won't starve—but it's the house I want." She gave a sorrowful shake of her head. "He had faith that I'd move heaven and earth to keep it."

"Still, it's only a house, Lisa," I said. "I mean, I get that it's beautiful and everything, but if he left you some money, too, couldn't you just buy another? You're only one person. You don't need this much space."

"You *don't* get it," she snapped, the prickly, dry-eyed woman I'd come to know suddenly back. "Don't you have strong feelings about your childhood home?"

I pressed my lips together, remembering the chaos of the house I grew up in. The shouting and fighting between my parents, while I hid out in my room. The haphazard meals, bags of cheap burgers or fried chicken tossed on the kitchen table for dinner most nights. Staying home alone and scared at night when I was as young as five or six because they were out drinking. Spending as much time as I could at my friends' houses, afraid to go home to my unpredictable parents. I'd felt safer and more cared about in my friends' homes than I had in the house where my parents lived.

I thought of the height chart in Lisa's pantry, the handprints on the front walk, and my heart contracted with envy.

"I never really felt attached to the house I grew up in," I said, not wanting to get into all of my crazy history with her.

"Then you can't understand why this house is so precious to me." She took another swallow of wine. "Do you know how rare it was for a black family to have a house like this when Daddy bought it in 1980?" she asked. "Or even today, for that matter? How hard my father had to work to make that happen? And I came up here—was raised here. I had a swing hanging from that big oak out back." She motioned through the window toward the dark backyard. "In the summers, I sat reading in the corner of Daddy's studio, while he created glorious art that now hangs in museums. This is the house where I did my homework, and baked with my mama, and got picked up for my first date. That garden out front? I still think of it as my mother's garden. Bulbs she planted when I was a kid are still blooming in it. I don't ever want to lose this house, and my father knew I'd do everything in my power to hold on to it. And I *will* hang on to it." Her eyes blazed. "It won't be easy with people taking their good ol' time getting work to me, and the roofer dragging his feet, and this being my busy time at the office. *You*, though." She gave me a steely-eyed look. "You're my real loose end. I can't control you. *You're* the only person who can control you. You can cost me this house, not that I think you have a reason to care. But at least you should care about yourself. About the fact that this job got you out of prison and that it can make you a lot of money."

I thought of the meticulous cleaning I'd done the last three days. "I'm doing my best, but from everything I've read, a job like this usually takes weeks or even months of work by a whole team of trained people."

"I'll tell you the truth, Morgan." The dry-eyed Lisa was back. "I don't care how it turns out. It's so weird." She shuddered. "That bloody ax? Just weird. All I care about is that it's clean and has those bare spots covered over. No one's going to be looking at it close-up."

I felt a surprising flash of anger. The sympathy I'd had for Lisa only moments ago began to evaporate. She was nothing more than a wealthy woman so desperate to keep her family home that she'd ruin a piece of valuable art to hold on to it.

"I don't think I can go into it with that attitude," I said. "I don't want to do a half-assed job."

"Well, whatever your *attitude*," Lisa said, "you have to finish the mural in time for the opening. All right? That, I'm afraid, is the bottom line."

Chapter 20

ANNA

January 4, 1940

Anna, who had been brought up on *The New York Times*, had to admit that the small, provincial *Chowan Herald* fascinated her. She read the paper that morning while sitting in Miss Myrtle's little sunroom, which had a view of the backyard, the trees bare, the birdbath water crusty with ice. Billy Calhoun, the paper's editor whom Anna had met at lunch and who didn't want to be "above his raisin'," had written a beautifully crafted wrap-up of 1939 for the paper's front page. *We live in a safe haven, free from the scorching breath of war,* he'd written. Anna nodded in agreement. Americans were very lucky, she thought, when so much of the world was not. She needed to remember that and count her blessings.

Then she read that Edenton's first white baby of the new year had been born at 2:15 a.m. on January 1. She wondered if a colored baby had come earlier, but if so, the paper didn't mention it. And then she learned how to rid cattle of lice and where she could buy hog-killing supplies.

Her mother would have gotten such a kick out of this paper.

From the time Anna was twelve or thirteen, she and her mother would devour the *Times* over coffee every morning—at least during her mother's lively spells. They'd read the news to each other, argue mildly over politics, and daydream about attending shows on Broadway. More than anything, Anna missed those mornings with her mother, though if she was being honest with herself, she had to admit that her mother hadn't gotten up early enough to make it to the breakfast table since late summer. Still, as Anna read the *Herald*, she remembered those mornings with her mother with a wistful tenderness.

What would her mother have thought of the Bible lesson that was always on the front page of the *Chowan Herald*? Anna couldn't imagine seeing a Bible lesson on the front page of a Northern paper. Miss Myrtle was after Anna to go to her Baptist church with her, but so far, she'd resisted, although she was beginning to think maybe she should go. Church was important here, and she wanted to stay on people's good side. She and her mother had been Episcopalian, but they only went to church on Christmas and Easter, and sometimes not even then, depending on her mother's mood. These days, though, Anna was fed up with God. Why had he made her mother's life so unbearable? Why had he taken such a wonderful woman so young? She hadn't forgiven him for that and wasn't sure she could sit through a service that praised him.

She was lifted out of her thoughts by the sound of footsteps heading toward the sunroom, and in a moment, Miss Myrtle appeared in the doorway.

"You have a gentleman caller, dear," she said. "He's waiting for you in the front yard."

A gentleman caller? The only gentlemen she knew were the so-called movers and shakers in town. She knew they were anxious to see what she'd come up with for the mural, but she didn't think Miss Myrtle would leave one of them standing out in the cold, despite her house rules.

"Who is it?" she asked, setting down the paper and getting to her feet.

"You'll see," she said cryptically.

Anna smoothed her skirt and headed through the living room toward the foyer. She opened the front door to see a man leaning against the lamppost, smoking a pipe. He wore a brown suede jacket with a leather collar and a rust-colored woolen scarf. He was a good-looking older man, perhaps late thirties or early forties, and when he tipped his brown cap to her, she was startled by his mop of thick red hair. She didn't think she'd ever seen such a vivid color on a man's head. She stepped onto the porch and he smiled up at her. He had a dramatically crooked front tooth, but even that couldn't detract from his handsomeness.

"I'm Martin Drapple," he said, standing up straight now. "And you're the little lady who stole the mural competition out from under me." He never did lose his smile, but Anna feared she lost hers rather quickly.

"I'm sorry," she said. She remembered his wife's fingertips digging into her arm through her coat sleeve. "I know that must have been terribly disappointing."

"I'm only teasing you." He grinned, slipping his pipe into his jacket pocket. "I'm actually here to apologize for my wife's behavior. She told me about bumping into you at the library. I'm afraid she had a frightful headache and took it out on you."

"Oh, that's all right," she said. Her mind scrambled to connect that nasty woman to this charming man. "I'm sorry she wasn't feeling well."

"So," he said, dragging out the word, "have you ever painted a mural before?"

She felt immediately on guard and shivered in the cold, wrapping her arms across her chest. "Yes, in art school," she said, hoping he didn't ask the size of the painting. She didn't want to lie, but there was a huge difference between painting a five-by-four mural and a twelve-by-six.

"I just wanted to let you know that I'd be happy to help you in any way I can," he said. "No compensation," he added quickly, his hand in the air in front of him. "As long as I have free time, it'd be my honor to help you with the stretcher or anything else you might need. It's a huge job. You can't possibly do it all on your own."

She was stunned by his generosity. "Thank you," she said, "but I couldn't possibly ask you. I'm looking into having a few students help me." Her fingers were already starting to ache with the cold and she rubbed her hands together. "It's very kind of you, though. I'll certainly contact you if I need help."

Mr. Drapple tilted his head, seeming to appraise her. "My cousin's taken a shine to you," he said, in a rapid change of topic.

It took her a moment to remember that Mayor Sykes was his cousin. They certainly looked nothing alike.

"Mayor Sykes has been very helpful," she said, trying not to think about the rumors of the mayor harming his wife and having an affair. She added with a smile, "Even though he doesn't approve of me having the Tea Party front and center in the mural." The mayor had grimaced when she told him her plan. "I hope you'll reconsider," he'd said.

"Ah well, that's why he's a mayor and not an artist, right?" Mr. Drapple smiled up at her.

Would you have put the Tea Party in the mural? she wanted to ask, but of course, she didn't. What had *his* sketch been like? What had he painted to represent Edenton? She wished she could know.

"I saw the *Life* magazine spread of the sketches," he said. "Your Bordentown design was quite nice. You have a lovely style."

His wife certainly hadn't thought so, and Anna wondered if he was teasing her. She felt young and inexperienced—and also a bit as if she were on stage, up there on the porch while he stood below. She thought he sounded sincere, though. She would treat the compliment as such.

"Thank you," she said.

He looked as though he wanted to say more, but then tipped his hat again. "Good day, then," he said. "My phone number is 47, if you change your mind." Anna watched him turn and walk toward the street before she stepped inside to warm up. She stood inside the front door, her back against it, thinking about what had just happened. She was touched by Martin Drapple's generosity and warmth. She hoped she would have been as kind as he was if their fortunes had been reversed.

Chapter 21

———— ✺ ————

MORGAN

June 19, 2018

I was alone in the foyer of the gallery, balancing on the ladder as I cleaned the top square of the fourth row. After my conversation with Lisa, I started timing myself. The twelve-by-six-foot mural was divided by twine into seventy-two squares and it was taking me about forty-five minutes to clean one square. I had to work slowly, nearly holding my breath each time I set the cotton-tipped dowel to the surface of the painting, afraid of missing a speck of flaking paint and scraping it off by accident. To clean the entire mural should take me approximately fifty-four hours. I could only do so many hours at a time, though, before my shoulders and back began to seize up on me. I figured it would take me ten days to do the cleaning alone. Lisa would not be happy about that.

I gave myself a fifteen-minute break between each square, so I was sitting on the bottom rung of the ladder drinking a bottle of water and listening to Post Malone sing "Congratulations" when Oliver walked into the foyer. His mouth moved but I had no idea what he was saying.

I pulled out my earbuds and gave him an apologetic smile. "What did you say?" I asked.

"The conservation paints and other supplies I ordered for you are here," he said. His own earbuds hung around his neck.

"Oh, cool." I pointed up at the mural. "It'll be a while before I need them, though."

"Well, you're making progress. It's looking good." He stood away from the mural to study it, hands on his hips.

"How well do you know Lisa?" I asked.

"Lisa?" He looked surprised by the question. "Not well at all. I'd been to Jesse's house a few times over the years, and I knew she lived with him and was his primary caretaker toward the end, but I never actually saw her there. She was—and I guess still is—a workaholic real estate agent. She called me when he died and said he wanted me to curate the gallery, which wasn't a surprise. He'd told me as much. And I know she's in a time crunch to get this place up and running."

I looked down at the bottle in my hand, remembering back to the night before when I'd caught Lisa in tears. I didn't think I should share that with Oliver.

"I think she's a challenge, Morgan," Oliver continued, "but she also gets things done, so hang in there. I just do what she tells me to do unless I think she's completely off the wall. She's leaving the placement of art entirely up to me—with the exception of having the mural in the foyer, which was Jesse's wish." He nodded toward the mural. "I think between the gallery and her job, she's extremely stressed."

"Do you know anything about the will?" I asked.

"The will?"

"If the gallery doesn't open by August fifth, she loses her house. Jesse's house."

Oliver's jaw dropped, and I could tell I'd left him speechless.

"She won't inherit it," I said. "Not only that, but if I don't have the mural done by then, I don't get paid and I'll end up back in prison."

"What? That's insane."

"Jesse Williams specified that the mural had to be done in order for the gallery to open, so—"

"Did Lisa tell you all this?"

I nodded.

He looked away from me, out toward the glass wall of the foyer. "She did tell me—several times—that everything has to be up and running by our opening date, but nothing about her house. Could she be making that up for some reason? To put pressure on you, maybe? Jesse was a real character, but I can't imagine him disinheriting his daughter just because she can't get the gallery ready by an arbitrary date."

"I don't think she was lying. I caught her crying and then she told me."

Oliver grimaced. "Wow," he said. "Well, I guess if I were in danger of losing something precious to me, I'd be a nasty SOB myself."

"You'd always be nice," I blurted out, then felt myself blush. Oliver struck me as perpetually calm, perpetually kind. "Seriously," I said. "Thank you for helping me so much."

He smiled, and I wondered if he knew I was developing the teensiest crush on him. "We'd better get back to work," he said. "Let's stay one step ahead of the boss lady."

>—•≡←

Adam and Wyatt came into the gallery around four and began taking measurements for the long "information counter" that would run parallel to the wall where the mural would be displayed. My ladder and supplies were in their way and after dozens of "can I move this?" and "excuse us" and a few other comments that let me know they thought their work was more important than mine, I called it quits. The air-conditioning wasn't working properly, either, and being up on the ladder only added to my misery. I'd finished my quota of squares for the day, anyhow, and I left the gallery and headed back to Lisa's.

"Done for the day?" Lisa asked when I walked in the front door, and I explained about Adam and Wyatt taking measurements in the foyer. For the first time since I'd met her, Lisa was dressed in jeans. They were dressy jeans, but still. She wore a loose embroidered yellow blouse and her hair was pulled back in a small ponytail at the nape of her neck. She looked very pretty and the closest to relaxed I'd seen her.

"Hmm," she said. "Those guys are going to have to stay out of your way as they build that thing." Then she looked into the air above my head as if pondering something. "Well, listen," she said. "Would you like to see where my father grew up?"

The invitation was so out of character that it took me a moment to understand it. "Tonight?" I asked.

"Uh-huh. It's my aunt's birthday. Mama Nelle. My father's baby sister."

"Wow," I said. Did I want to spend a whole evening with Lisa? But the thought of seeing where Jesse Williams grew up was enticing. "All right," I said. "Give me a minute to change?"

Lisa looked at her phone. "Hurry up," she said. "I want to leave in five."

I raced to the sunroom. I had little in the way of nice clothes. Everything I'd bought after being sprung from prison had been with the idea that I'd spend the bulk of my time working on the mural. But I put on a pair of clean jeans and the only decent top I owned—the blue sleeveless blouse I'd worn the day I left prison. I ran a comb through my hair and hurried out front, where Lisa was already waiting in her car.

"How far is it?" I asked as Lisa began driving.

"Just a little ways outside town."

"So, this 'Mama Nelle' is Jesse's sister?"

"Yes."

"How come you call her 'Mama' then?"

"Everybody does. Don't know when that started, but everybody treats her like she's their mama. She's eighty-seven and has a serious heart condition and some of that come-and-go type of dementia, so we're all thinkin' this may be her last birthday."

Lisa sounded different. The change in her voice was fascinating, actually. Her tone was more casual, her language looser. She was definitely off duty tonight.

"He grew up out in the country?" I asked as the town gave way to fields that stretched far into the distance.

Lisa nodded. "The Williams farm's been in our extended family one way or 'nother pretty much since the end of slavery."

"Were Jesse's ancestors slaves?" I asked.

"What d'you think?" Lisa smirked as though it were a stupid question. "Mine, too. Remember? My ancestors are Jesse's."

Okay, I thought. So Lisa's language might be looser but her personality was as prickly as ever.

"Right," I said. "So, your . . . great-great-grandparents were slaves?"

"Exactly. On both sides of the family. Nearly all my people still live near the farm, except for a few who moved away. But people who move away tend to come back. Edenton's got a magnetic pull on folks who were born here."

"Have you ever thought of leaving?"

Lisa was quiet for a moment. "I only left for college," she said. "And I don't plan to leave ever again."

After a while, she pulled into the driveway of an old white farmhouse set back from the road by a deep lawn. There was a cornfield to the left, and a few more houses scattered to the right. Kids, a couple of them white, were taking turns on a tire swing that hung from a big tree in the front yard. Some older men were playing horseshoes near the side of the house. And even before I opened the car door, I felt the thrum of music in the air. Chance the Rapper. I smiled, already moving my head to the beat. I had the feeling I was going to like it here.

Lisa and I began walking across the lawn to the house. The day was finally beginning to cool off a bit, but I was still perspiring after a few steps.

"Are the white kids from the neighborhood?" I asked.

Lisa laughed and I was stunned when she put an arm around my shoulders. "Honey," she said in a voice I hadn't heard her use before, "I'm related to every one of these folks, one way or another. Our history goes back a long way. There were white big shots who had black women on the side, or forbidden love that couldn't be out in the open, or rape, maybe. Who knows? A lot of powerful men and powerless women over the generations. It all adds up to a rainbow of hues in a black family." She dropped her arm from my shoulder and immediately seemed to shift back to the distant Lisa I had come to know.

The outside of the house had a choppy appearance, as though it had been added onto time and time again over the course of many years, but when Lisa and I walked inside, the warmth of the smooth wood floors, the low ceiling, and the chintz curtains gave me a homey feeling, as if we were stepping back in time. The rap music faded into the distance, and inside, the main noise came from the chatter of aproned women preparing huge trays of food and the hum of a window air conditioner.

Lisa walked with me from room to room, introducing me to what seemed like an endless series of cousins and aunts. One of the gray-haired women hugged Lisa and said, "How're you doing, darlin'? I know you missin' your daddy."

"Fine, Auntie," Lisa said. Returning to my side, she led me into a sitting room where several women sat close together on a sofa on either side of a small, shriveled woman with nearly white hair and coffee-colored skin. The little woman looked up when we entered the room.

"Dodie!" she exclaimed to Lisa, reaching toward her with frail-looking arms that protruded from the ruffled, loose-fitting sleeves of her pink blouse.

Lisa moved forward, taking the old woman's hands.

"No, Mama Nelle," she said, bending low. "It's Lisa, remember? Dodie was your big sister."

"Lisa! 'Course! Jesse's little girl." The woman's gaze went past Lisa to me. "And who's this?" she asked, her large dark eyes intent on me from behind tortoiseshell glasses.

"This is Morgan Christopher," Lisa said. "She's stayin' with me for a while. She's an artist like Daddy—like Jesse—and I thought she might enjoy meetin' Jesse's family and seein' where he grew up."

Mama Nelle reached for my hand. Hers was cool, the skin as soft as the cotton I used on the mural.

"Hi, Mrs. . . ." I said.

"Mama Nelle," Lisa said.

"Mama Nelle." I smiled at the old woman who seemed reluctant as she let go of my hand. She turned her gaze again to Lisa.

"Did Jesse come with you?" she asked.

Lisa pulled up a straight-backed chair for me in front of the woman, then another for herself. "No, honey," she said, sitting down, patient sadness in her voice. "Jesse passed a few months ago, darlin'. Remember?"

"Oh, yes, I recall." Mama Nelle looked at me again as I sat down. "You knew Jesse?" she asked.

I shook my head. "I wish I had," I said. "I knew his work. His paintings. They're amazing."

"How you know Lisa?"

"I'm working on restoring a mural in the art gallery . . ." My voice trailed off, unsure how much Mama Nelle would know or understand of what I was saying, and the old woman frowned as if trying hard to follow me.

"Mama Nelle," Lisa said loudly, "remember Jesse wanted to have an art gallery built in town?"

"Yes, I 'member." Mama Nelle nodded. "He talked 'bout it for years and years."

"Well, Morgan is in town to restore an old mural Jesse wanted in the gallery. It has views of old Edenton in it."

Mama Nelle looked toward the window, her brow furrowed in concentration. "Miss Anna's mural?" she asked the air.

I caught my breath. In the chair beside me, I thought Lisa did the same. "Anna Dale's mural," I said. "Is that who you mean? An artist named Anna Dale painted it in 1940."

"I loved Miss Anna," Mama Nelle said. Her face had broken into a smile. She turned to the woman next to her. "Do you 'member her?"

The woman shook her head. "I wasn't born till 1950, Mama," she said with a laugh. "Don't go makin' me older than I already am."

"How amazing," Lisa said under her breath to me. "I had no idea she might know the artist." Lisa raised her voice again. "You'll have to come see it when it's finished, Mama," she said to the old woman. Then she nudged me. "Let's go and—"

"Can I stay and talk with her a while longer?" I asked.

Lisa looked at her watch. "For a while," she said. "We can't stay too long. I have a world of calls to make yet tonight."

"Okay," I said, and as Lisa headed back toward the kitchen, I turned my attention once more to Mama Nelle. The women on either side of the old woman gave me looks of caution.

"She don't remember much of anything, honey," one of them said quietly. "Don't put much stock in what she say."

I gave them an "okay, fine" smile before riveting my gaze on Mama Nelle.

"How did you know Anna Dale?" I asked.

"Who?" Mama Nelle responded.

"You were just saying you remembered Anna . . . Miss Anna. The mural painter?"

"The mural, yes. In the big barn."

"Big barn?"

"Where she done paint it." Mama Nelle lifted her trembling arms into the air again, wide apart. "Was like a . . . a big white garage wit' big ol' doors," she said.

"The warehouse!" I said, remembering the photograph and article Oliver had shown me from the paper. "You're right. She painted in a big warehouse. Can you tell me what she was like? Miss Anna?" I didn't feel as though I could come right out and ask the old woman if Anna had been crazy.

"We had to be very quiet," Mama Nelle said. She lifted a shivering finger to her lips. "Shh."

"You had to be quiet while she painted?" I asked. "So she could concentrate?"

"No, not then," Mama Nelle said. "We couldn't let nobody know nothin' 'bout her."

I frowned. "I don't understand."

"I tol' you, honey," the woman born in 1950 said. "Half of what she say these days don't make no sense, so don't worry 'bout it."

I barely heard her, my attention on Mama Nelle. "Would you like to see a picture of the mural?" I asked her, leaning to the side so I could pull my phone from my jeans pocket.

"Her eyes ain't so good," another of the women warned me.

I swiped the screen of my phone until I reached one of my first pictures of the entire mural. I held it up in front of Mama Nelle.

"What's that?" Mama Nelle asked.

"A picture of the mural Anna Dale—Miss Anna—painted," I said. "Though it's been in storage and is very dirty. Probably very different from when you last saw it."

Mama Nelle frowned. "Jes' a big ol' blur to me," she said.

"Let me see it," the 1950 woman said, and I held the phone in front of her.

The woman laughed. "That's a big mess, that's what that is. How you expect her to make anythin' out of that?"

I looked at the picture myself. I supposed to someone not accustomed to seeing the damaged mural every day, it did look a mess. To me, though, it was becoming a source of fascination.

I sat with Mama Nelle a while longer, asking her questions about her and Jesse's childhoods, and that seemed to be where the old woman's dementia had not yet taken its toll and her memories were the happiest. At one point, Mama Nelle took my hand and held it on her bony knee, and

I felt touched by the gesture. I liked sitting there, talking to her. Even though she didn't mention Anna again, it didn't matter. She had known the living, breathing Anna. *We couldn't let nobody know nothin' 'bout her.* Why not? I wondered. What was that all about?

By the time Lisa came to hustle me out of the sitting room, I found it hard to tear myself away.

In the kitchen, Lisa introduced me to a stunning woman who was setting candles into a large chocolate-iced sheet cake. *Happy Birthday, Mama Nelle* was written in yellow icing on top.

"This is my cousin Saundra, Mama Nelle's daughter," Lisa said. "And Saundra, this is Morgan Christopher who's helping out in the gallery."

Saundra set the last candle into the cake, then smiled at me. Everything about her face was symmetrical, from her perfect eyebrows, to her high cheekbones, to her straight white smile. "Lisa tells me you're restoring a huge, musty ol' mural for Uncle Jesse's gallery," she said.

"Yes, and Mama—your mother—remembers the artist, which is so cool." I heard the enthusiasm in my voice. It felt good to be excited about something. "We know next to nothing about her," I added.

"She does?" Saundra shook her head with a chuckle. "That woman. You never know what she's going to pull out of that memory bank of hers."

"Don't make so much out of it," Lisa said in the cool voice she often used with me. "Mama tends to make things up these days."

"Oh, I think a lot of what she remembers is at least partially true." Saundra stood back to admire her handiwork with the candles. "But oh Lord, I'm such a bad daughter!" She laughed. "I wish I'd written down everything she's said over my fifty-five years. She has all the family history locked in that brain of hers and we've lost it because I'm lazy."

"You're the least lazy person I know," Lisa said, patting her cousin's arm. She looked at me. "Saundra is superintendent of schools in Elizabeth City."

"Wow," I said, trying to sound polite, but I wished I was back in the sitting room, picking Mama Nelle's brain.

"Mama is the repository for the family history," Saundra said. "She has land deeds and letters and all sorts of what-not from ancient times tucked here and there in her bedroom, and I know I'm going to have to be the one to sort through all of it when she passes."

"You could just toss it," Lisa suggested.

"You're evil," Saundra said, then she looked at me. "She was always the evil cousin."

I can believe it, I thought, but I only smiled.

An older, gray-haired woman suddenly blew into the room. She was big boned and smelled strongly of some sweet perfume and she swept Lisa into her arms. *"Baby,"* she said. "How are you, honey? Come talk to me!"

I watched Lisa get pulled away by the woman as if she were a small child obeying an elder, and Saundra turned to busy herself with a tray of small pastries. I thought I should offer to help, but instead I excused myself. I wanted to go back to the sunroom and Mama Nelle, where I'd felt a strange comfort. Even if the old woman could remember very little of the past, we shared an interest in the dusty old mural. For Mama Nelle, it was a memory. For me, the here and now. Yet we did have one thing in common, I thought, and that was Anna Dale.

Chapter 22

———— ->≫•≪- ————

ANNA

January 8, 1940

From the United States Treasury Department, Section of Fine Arts

Special 48-States Mural Competition

January 3, 1940

Dear Miss Anna Dale,

Thank you for sending your sketch for the Edenton, North Carolina, mural. You mentioned that you will be using models for the cartoon and I implore you to do so. While the figures in your sketch were competent, they lacked a realism that can only come through the use of live models. Similarly, I'd reconsider the color choices of the frocks on the women in the central portion of the sketch. To my eye, those particular shades of purple and blue clash against one another. Also, I would not have known the Negro woman was holding peanuts in her apron had you not told me, but I'm sure you'll take care of adding more detail in your cartoon. I do applaud your liberal use of reds. Few of the artists have been so bold with color.

    With these slight changes, the Section believes your final mural will be a success and we are enclosing a check for your first payment of $240. Please send a photograph of the full-scale black-and-white cartoon as soon as possible.

    Sincerely, Edward Rowan, Art Administrator, Section of Fine Arts

Anna read the letter three times to be sure she understood. Her sketch had been accepted, and she'd actually been paid for her work. She could barely believe that doing something she loved could result in so much money. Mr. Rowan hadn't found the sketch perfect, but perfect enough, and that was what counted at this stage. Anna had been told that he was persnickety and always had to find something he wanted corrected. That was fine. She would happily address his concerns. She already had the roll of cartoon paper. Now she could move forward.

    She needed to find her models, though. Three women for the Tea Party. A Negro woman for the peanut factory. A white man for the lumber yard. There were no people in the painting of the Cotton Mill Village, and the men in the fishing boat were at such a distance that she didn't plan to paint them in detail. So she needed five models in all. She hoped she wasn't biting off more than she could chew.

    On Friday, she'd spoken by phone with the art teacher Mayor Sykes referred her to at Edenton High School and asked if she might have a couple of art students willing to help her in the warehouse.

    "I won't be able to pay them," she'd explained, "but the experience should be illuminating to them as future artists."

    The teacher called her back to say there were two students, a boy and a girl, who would work for her a couple of hours every afternoon for school credit. Anna was relieved. Not only did she need the help, she would also be glad to have some company in the spooky warehouse. She called the mayor's office to give him the news and asked if he'd had that key made yet, but he said he'd thought it over and a key didn't make sense, since the large garage doors had no locks.

"Why bother to lock the door, then?" he'd asked. He assured her that her supplies would be perfectly safe. She was disappointed, but she had to trust that he knew his town better than she did.

As soon as she set down the letter from the Section, she called the art store in Norfolk and ordered her canvas and paints, both in tubes and cans. She would have a great deal of canvas to cover. She hoped Pauline had been serious about going to Norfolk with her to pick up the supplies. Then she called the lumber company and ordered the wood she'd need for the stretcher. So much wood! It made her nervous to imagine the work she had ahead of her, building that stretcher, and she hoped and prayed she had the measurements right.

She took a photograph of the approved sketch to the post office to show Mr. Arndt. She was nervous, of course, knowing her plans for the mural didn't line up precisely with the suggestions of the "movers and shakers" in town, but Mr. Arndt studied the photograph with a smile on his face.

"What a masterful job you've done," he said finally, looking up at her from his desk chair. "I wish I could see the colors."

"It *is* quite colorful," Anna said, glowing from his compliment. "You're all right with the Tea Party being so central to the composition?"

He laughed. "Oh, I knew you were going to get those ladies in there one way or another!" he said. "Can I keep this?" He lifted the photograph. "Hang it up on the post office wall? That okay with you?"

"Of course," she said, relieved that he liked it well enough to show it off.

She celebrated by taking Miss Myrtle to dinner at the Albemarle Restaurant that evening. Miss Myrtle laughed when Anna ordered the Yankee Pot Roast.

"Well, that figures!" the older woman said.

Everyone in the restaurant seemed to know who Anna was and several people approached their table to talk to her about the mural.

"I can't believe you're paintin' somethin' that'll take up that whole wall in there!" one of the women said. Another told her she'd seen the photograph of the sketch hanging on the post office wall just that afternoon and couldn't wait to see it in color. But then, a woman with angry eyes and a permanent-looking sneer on her face walked over to their table.

"Wipe that smug look off your face," she said to Anna. "It's very unbecoming." The woman turned and marched through the restaurant and out the door, while Anna sat stock-still with her mouth open, utterly speechless.

"Ignore her," Miss Myrtle said. "Don't let small-minded people ruin your good fortune."

Anna pressed her lips together, looking down at her plate. She felt both embarrassed and misunderstood.

"Come on, now." Miss Myrtle tapped the back of her hand. "That gal is no doubt friends with Mrs. Drapple and she had to say her little piece and now you have to just forget all about it."

Anna let out her breath and offered Miss Myrtle a stoic smile. She would change the subject. "Will you be one of my Tea Party models?" she asked.

"Me?" Miss Myrtle looked flustered, a blush coming to her cheeks. "Don't you think I'm a bit too long in the tooth?"

Yes, she was, and she and Anna both knew it, but Anna could take some of the gray out of the older woman's hair and soften the lines around her mouth. She loved the idea of having her landlady in the mural.

"I think you'll be perfect," Anna said. "Maybe Pauline will agree to be another."

They talked about the people they knew who might be willing to model for the mural. Miss Myrtle thought the mayor's wife was a good choice, but the idea made Anna cringe as she remembered Pauline's comments about Mayor Sykes's treatment of his wife. She felt as if she knew far more than she should about the poor woman and her life.

"Or perhaps Ellen Harper," Miss Myrtle said. "She's a salesgirl at the Patsy Department Store."

"Could you ask her for me?" Anna said. "And what about Freda for my peanut factory worker?" She would have to darken the gray in Freda's hair, as well, but Freda otherwise had a pretty, youthful face that Anna would love to capture in the painting.

Miss Myrtle chuckled. "I bet Freda would get a real kick out of that," she said.

"Then I just need to find a willing gentleman for the lumberman and I'll have my four women and one man."

Miss Myrtle laughed again. "It's going to look as though Edenton is run by women," she said.

"Yes, I suppose it will." Anna smiled to herself, wondering again what Mr. Drapple had proposed in *his* sketch.

Chapter 23

———— ✦ ————

MORGAN

June 23, 2018

More and more, I welcomed the daytime hours when I could lose myself in cleaning the mural. I was working faster now that I had faith the paint wouldn't flake from my touch. It was incredibly satisfying to see colors and details emerge from beneath the grime. Today, one week into the cleaning, I finally reached the central figures of the mural: the three Tea Party women. Their dresses were beautiful once they were freed from the muck that had coated them. Anna Dale had had no fear of color and it excited me to see the vibrancy of the mural emerge with each square I uncovered.

The first square I worked on after lunch showed a small mirror in the hand of one of the ladies. The woman held the mirror up to her face as if to powder her nose, but now that I'd cleaned the grime from the mirror's glasslike surface, I could see that the reflection was not of the woman's face at all, but rather the tiny image of a man. The figure was so small against the shimmery gray background of the mirror that I'd thought it was a crack in the paint at first. But no. It was definitely a man—a red-haired man wearing a brown jacket and cap, leaning against a lamppost. Another one of Anna's bizarre anomalies. I couldn't wait to show it to Oliver. I'd gotten into the habit of zipping through the gallery to his office after every square and dragging him back to show off my handiwork—or Anna's handiwork, at least.

"Here she comes again," one of the construction guys would say.

"Another hundred and forty-four square inches down!" another would add.

Oliver seemed to get a kick out of my enthusiasm, too, stopping whatever he was in the middle of doing to join me in the foyer and stare at the newly revealed block of color.

I found him in his office, hunched over a spreadsheet on his computer. He held up a hand to keep me quiet as he moved figures from an invoice to the spreadsheet and I stood patiently, waiting for him to finish his task before I disturbed him. From the speaker on his desk, a sweet-voiced woman sang a song about paving over parking lots. Watching him, I couldn't help but smile. Intense blue eyes focused on his task. That faint, perpetually rosy look to his cheeks as though he'd been outside in the cold. I felt like bending over to give him an affectionate hug. I'd known him all of ten days, but I already had tender feelings toward him. He seemed like the sanest person in my life, which, I had to admit, wasn't saying that much.

He finished at the computer, then swiveled his chair to look at me. "Whatcha got?" he asked.

"Something intriguing." I nodded in the direction of the foyer.

He followed me back to the mural and I showed him the mirror with its little red-haired man. He climbed onto the ladder for a closer look.

"Wow," he said, a sparkle in his eyes as he looked down at me. "So now we have a motorcycle. A bloody ax. And a dapper-looking fellow in a mirror. We've got a real puzzle here, don't we?"

"Maybe," I said. "Unless Jesse was right and she was simply out of her mind. But she looked and sounded so sane in that old newspaper article you have."

"She did," he agreed. He pulled out his phone and snapped a couple of close-up pictures of the mirror.

I had a sudden idea. "Would that newspaper be online?" I asked. "The one that article was from? Maybe there were more articles about her."

"Tiny, small-town paper?" Oliver shook his head as he climbed down the ladder to the floor. "I doubt it. You could try the library, though. I bet they have old copies."

"Maybe." I looked toward the mural, nearly half clean now, and felt a smile cross my face. "I like this part of restoration," I said. "The cleaning part."

"The easy part, you mean." He grinned at me.

I sighed, my smile gone. "Everything I read about how to inpaint and . . . all of it . . . makes me feel so ignorant. It's overwhelming."

"Step by step," he said patiently, motioning to the mural as he headed back to the hallway. "Let me know what other bizarre stuff you find in the next square."

—※·※—

Instead of walking to Lisa's house when I left the gallery that evening, I headed to the Edenton library to see what I could find in the local paper from 1940.

The old editions of the *Chowan Herald*, all on microfilm, were located in the small, cramped, and quiet second story of the library. I was the only person up there, and it took me thirty minutes to figure out how to operate the microfilm machine. I was frustrated by the time I loaded the reel for 1940 and even more frustrated when I realized there was no in-dexing—no way to search for Anna's name. I began running through the papers week by week, studying the crude images with the dodgy machine, finally finding a photograph in the February 15 edition. The large but grainy picture appeared to have been taken inside the warehouse—Mama

Nelle's "big barn," I felt sure. Anna and her very cool haircut stood next to an empty canvas . . . or at least, it appeared empty until I enlarged the shot and saw the faint but clear pounce lines that covered the surface. I understood immediately what I was looking at. Anna Dale had created a cartoon of the mural and pounced the image onto the canvas. A thrill ran up my spine, knowing that the canvas I was looking at was the very canvas I was working on, and I had the out-of-body feeling that I was there, with her, in that warehouse. I squinted at the faint, grainy image. I could see no pounce marks for the motorcycle, although it was hard to make out much of anything on the canvas.

The photograph was interesting in other ways, too. Anna stood to one side, pointing to the canvas, a wide smile on her face. She wore wide-legged pants and a smudged white smock. I thought she was beautiful. I smoothed my hand over my own shoulder-length pale hair, wondering how it would look in that bob. Flat as a pancake, most likely. My hair didn't have the body hers did.

Next to Anna, a young black man held a long roll of paper—probably the used cartoon. On the opposite side of the canvas, a towheaded boy stood with his hands in his pockets. Both the man's and the boy's gazes were riveted on whatever Anna was illustrating on the canvas. There was just one line beneath the picture: *Artist Anna Dale discusses the drawing for the mural, which will reside in the Edenton Post Office.*

Anna was in command in this photograph, I thought, and I was surprised to feel a strong wave of caring for her. She looked healthy. Smiling. Engaged. This wasn't a mentally ill woman. But then I remembered the blood dripping from the ax blade. Something must have gone terribly wrong for her, or *with* her. I wondered for the first time if whatever mental illness had brought Anna down might have also taken her life. Was that why no other information existed about her? She'd been a talented artist. Talented artists didn't just disappear. If she died—or killed herself—that would explain why no one had ever heard of her again.

It was nearly closing time in the library. I found the librarian, who helped me get a copy of the photograph from the obstinate microfilm reader, then gathered up my things and headed to an AA meeting, where the main topic was making amends for however we screwed up while drinking. I found my palms sweating during the discussion. If I could manage to track down Emily Maxwell, would I ever have the courage to actually speak to her? The thought absolutely terrified me. I wanted to know how she was. I wanted to find her through the impersonal vehicle of my computer. But communicate with her? I didn't think I had the guts.

She was still on my mind when I crawled into bed that night. I stared at the dark ceiling, wondering if Emily might be awake as well, and if she was, was she in terrible pain? Was she cursing my name?

I was free, my biggest physical complaint my aching shoulders from my fifty-thousand-dollar job. I doubted that Emily Maxwell would ever again know such physical freedom.

I curled up in a ball on my bed, remembering how I'd gotten into my car with Trey. We'd been laughing hard, at what, I couldn't remember. I'd been so drunk I'd caught my scarf in the door and had trouble remembering how to open the door to free it. I didn't deserve to be out of prison. I didn't deserve fifty thousand dollars. I didn't think I'd ever be able to forgive myself for what we'd done to that innocent girl.

Chapter 24

———— ⋟⋞ ————

ANNA

January 10, 1940

Anna arrived alone and nervous at the warehouse that morning. She hadn't been there since her initial visit with Mayor Sykes a month ago, and she was stunned by what she found. The floor—concrete—had been swept clean and sun gleamed through the tall, sparkling windows. Two space heaters sat in front of one of the closed garage doors along with two tall floor lamps, two stepladders, and several extension cords. The three long tables and four wooden chairs were still in place, and a few of the crates remained, piled up beneath one of the windows on the side wall. She truly owed the mayor for his help. Or, at least, she owed Benny, his custodian. She would have to bake them something.

She carried the rolls of cartoon paper into the warehouse along with a big metal bucket filled with most of the tools she'd need for the creation of the cartoon. She wouldn't be able to do much with her supplies until her helpers arrived from Edenton High School that afternoon, but she felt a sense of satisfaction as she began to fill her new workspace. She was wearing her beloved slacks once again, and the freedom of them felt wonderful, although Miss Myrtle had gasped when she saw Anna in them that morning.

"You can't go out of the house in those!" she'd said, pointing to the slacks.

"Well, I can't wear a dress in the warehouse," Anna'd responded. "Impossible to work in."

Miss Myrtle had shaken her head, a look of worry on her face. "Well, don't go anywhere else in them," she'd said. It had sounded like a warning. Anna thought she and Miss Myrtle saw eye to eye on most things in life, but every once in a while, it was clear they were a hefty generation apart.

Anna plugged in the space heaters, setting them on either side of the area in front of the windowless wall at the front end of the building, nearest the door. They didn't exactly make the space toasty, but the temperature was quite tolerable. Tolerable enough that she could take off her coat. Her heavy sweater beneath her smock was plenty warm enough.

Around noon, she ate the ham sandwich Freda had made for her, and as she was cleaning up after herself, the lumber arrived for the stretcher. She'd never seen so much wood in an art studio and felt instantly intimidated at the thought of putting the massive stretcher together. She eyed the man who stacked the wood in the center of the warehouse for her. He was a rugged, Nordic-looking blue-eyed blond who would be perfect for the lumberman in the mural.

"How would you feel about being the model for the lumberman in the mural I'm painting for the post office?" she asked as she stood near the growing stack of wood

He looked up at her with those crystal-blue eyes and laughed.

"You're kidding," he said. "You want me on the post office wall?"

"Absolutely! You'd make a perfect lumberjack."

He offered a good-natured shrug. "Sure," he said. "What would I have to do?"

"You'd just be standing with an ax in your hands, facing forward, I think." She tried to picture the scene. She would paint trees behind him. A forest.

He laughed again, and his eyes nearly disappeared into the planes of his face with his amusement. "I've never used an ax in my job," he admitted. "I'm actually just a grader. All day long, I grade the quality of the wood. It's about time I got to hold an ax in my hands."

After he left, Anna sat down near one of the heaters and breathed in the clean scent of the wood. Now she had all five of her models lined up. Miss Myrtle, Madge Sykes—the mayor's jolly and agreeable wife, who did not at all strike Anna as a woman who suffered at the mercy of a brutish, cheating husband—and Ellen Harper, the salesgirl from the Patsy store, would be the Tea Party ladies. Freda, who finally nodded her assent after Anna talked her into it, would be the peanut factory worker. And now handsome Frank from the lumber mill would be the lumberman. Anna was disappointed that Pauline had turned her down. "Karl doesn't like the idea of me being up there on the post office wall," she'd said. Anna had wanted to ask why, but decided to just accept her—or his—decision. Maybe it had to do with him being a policeman with a reputation to protect, or maybe he didn't want his wife participating in something that seemed so frivolous. Whatever the reason for his decision, Pauline seemed content to go along with it.

⟶•≪⟶

Anna's two helpers, Theresa Wayman and Peter Thomas, arrived at two fifteen.

"You have on pants!" Theresa exclaimed before even saying hello.

"I do," Anna said, "and you should also bring some pants to wear because you'll be climbing ladders and doing some messy work."

"My parents would never let me," she said.

Anna fought the urge to roll her eyes. Theresa struck her as a very feminine girl, her pretty, shoulder-length blond hair held away from her face with tortoiseshell barrettes and her lips painted with coral lipstick. She wore a blue plaid A-line skirt and ruffled white blouse. Anna considered suggesting that she keep a pair of pants in the warehouse to change into and out of when she worked. Her parents would never need to know. But the rigid look of the girl told her to hold her words. She didn't know her well enough yet to make such a suggestion.

Peter was a slight, affable boy, small and thin but wiry, and in very good shape. He, too, was very blond. In fact, he and Theresa looked quite alike.

"Are the two of you related?" Anna asked.

They both laughed. "Heck, no!" Peter said, taking a step away from the girl. Then he looked at the stack of lumber in the middle of the floor. "So what are you doin' here, ma'am?" he asked. He actually rubbed his hands together as if anxious to get started. "How're we gonna help you?"

The three of them sat down at one of the tables and Anna showed them her sketch as she described her plans for the cartoon and mural. They'd never heard of a cartoon and both of them asked intelligent questions about the process of creating it, but it was clear to Anna that Peter was the more invested of the two.

"I want to be a serious artist someday, ma'am," he said.

"Peter *is* really good," Theresa said, rather begrudgingly. "He drew a picture of a tractor and it looked almost like a photograph."

"How about you, Theresa?" Anna asked. "Do you hope to be an artist?"

Theresa shrugged. "I hope to get out of school and get married and have five children," she admitted.

Anna laughed, thinking that marriage and motherhood were probably more realistic goals for this girl.

"Well, you only have, what? A year and a half till graduation?"

"We graduate this spring, ma'am," Peter said.

"You do? Aren't you eleventh graders?"

"That's the last year of high school, ma'am," Theresa said. "Thank the Lord for that."

"Really?" Anna asked. "Schools where I'm from go to the twelfth grade."

"Not here," said Peter.

"Thank heavens we don't," Theresa said.

"Well, I tell you what," Anna said. "I'm going to be asking some hard work of you two that might not feel as though it has much to do with actual drawing or painting, so to be fair, why don't you bring in some projects you're working on and I can give you my critique and perhaps help you make them better."

"That sounds good, ma'am," Peter said. He had a good-natured glow about him. A sunniness that drew Anna to him. She was curious to see his work.

"I don't really have nothin' I'm working on," Theresa said.

"Well, then, you can come up with something new to work on during any free time you have here," Anna said. "I won't need you to help me every single minute."

A short time later, the three of them got down to business. They unrolled the cartoon paper on the floor, cut it into twelve-foot lengths, and taped enough of it together to form a twelve-by-six-foot rectangle. Theresa refused to climb the ladder because of her skirt, so Peter climbed one and Anna the other and they nailed the paper to the wall, laughing the whole time because the paper wanted to slip back into its tight little roll and they had quite a time getting it to lie flat. By the time they'd won the war against the paper, two hours were up and Theresa and Peter were ready to go home for their dinners. Anna was disappointed to realize she wouldn't be able to add the grid lines to the cartoon until tomorrow.

After her student helpers left, she sat down at one of the tables under the floor lamp and began to measure out the grid on her sketch, but daylight was beginning to fade outside the warehouse windows, and she felt that creepy sensation come over her again as the big space filled with shadows and silence. The sheer breadth of the warehouse, the impenetrable dark spaces around the creepy beams high above, made her shudder. She couldn't look up at those beams, afraid of what she might see. Something other than lights and fans hanging from them, maybe. She didn't dare look.

Putting on her coat, she packed up her sketch and pencils and straight-edge, and was about to turn out the lights when she heard the slam of a car door outside. She froze, for what reason she couldn't say except that the darkening warehouse had simply unnerved her. A knock came at the door and she hesitated, then opened it to find a colored woman standing in the dusky light. She was dressed in a black wool coat and a smart white wool hat and Anna knew she was no one's servant.

"Oh, it looks like you're getting ready to leave," the woman said, motioning to Anna's own coat.

"Yes, in a moment, but can I help you?" Anna stepped back to let the woman walk into the warehouse.

"Oh, my," the woman said, looking around at the dimly lit space. "You've got quite the studio."

"Yes, I'm very fortunate," Anna said, thinking of how terrified she'd been of her "studio" only moments earlier. "My name is Anna Dale," she added, prompting her visitor to identify herself.

"Oh, I know who you are," the woman said. "Everyone does. I'm Tilda Furman." The woman studied the cartoon paper tacked to the wall. "You'll be sketching the mural on this paper, then transferring it to canvas?" she asked.

"Exactly." Anna smiled. "Are you an artist?"

Tilda Furman nodded. "Though I've never done a mural the likes of which you're proposing."

"Well, feel free to stop in anytime to watch," Anna said.

"Actually, I'm here for another reason." The woman suddenly sounded almost shy. "I teach art and music at the colored high school," she said. "I heard you were taking on students to help you, and I have a talented boy in my eleventh-grade class who is so good an artist that he needs more than I can give him. He could use this exposure." She gestured toward the cartoon paper. "He's smart, but a terrible student because he spends every class drawing instead of working on his history or English or what have you. Recess comes, he sits by himself with his sketch pad. All he cares about is art. He'd drop out if it didn't mean losing his art class."

Anna nodded. She could relate well to what the woman was telling her. She recalled her own high school years when she'd doodle all over the sides of her paper instead of taking notes in class.

"Would you consider taking him on to help you?" the woman asked.

Anna hesitated. "I'm not sure I'll have enough for three students to do," she said.

"Even if he just watches you, it would be a help," she said. "He should see what a real-world artist does."

"And I'm not paying the students," Anna said. "They're getting credit for—"

"Yes, I already spoke to the principal about that," she said. "We could work that out for him, too. Might help him graduate, because if he keeps going the way he is, he won't make it."

"All right," Anna said. "Have him come tomorrow."

"Thank you, miss," she said. "You might be saving this boy's life."

So dramatic, Anna thought, but she smiled. "What's his name?" she asked as she walked the woman to the door.

"Jesse Williams," the woman said. "And I don't think you'll regret this."

Chapter 25

MORGAN

June 27, 2018

Y ou look like you could use a massage," Adam said, as he walked into the foyer from the rear of the building. I stood on the lowest rung of the ladder as I cleaned the image of the broken teapot one of the Tea Party women was holding. I supposed Adam had caught me rubbing my shoulder. "I'm a pretty awesome masseur," he added.

I held on to the ladder and looked at him. He was almost too much, this guy, trying too hard, with the snake on his arm and the bun in his hair, yet I couldn't help that my stomach occasionally flipped when he was around. It was only that he reminded me of Trey—the old Trey. The Trey I thought was so phenomenal. I was not the least bit interested in Adam, and I decided against any clever comeback that could be perceived as flirtatious.

"Thanks." I smiled. "I'm fine."

"Wise answer." Oliver was crouched on the floor near the front door, uncrating a large painting, and he didn't even look up from the task when he spoke.

Adam grinned. "Well, if you change your mind, you know where to find me," he said, and he continued walking through the foyer and out the front door of the gallery.

Oliver and I were quiet for a moment as I worked on the mural and he pulled the well-padded painting from the box. Finally, he spoke. "Adam's got a girlfriend," he said.

I smiled to myself. "Like I care."

He chuckled. "Just sayin' . . ."

"I think I've just been without for too long." I felt embarrassed that any attraction I felt for Adam might be obvious.

"No guy in your life?" Oliver asked.

It took me a minute to answer. "I think it's best if I just focus on myself for a while," I said, meaning it. I stopped cleaning for a moment, resting my hands on a rung of the ladder as I thought about Trey. "I had a boyfriend," I said. "I thought he was really pretty awesome, but it turned out he wasn't."

"Ah," Oliver said, his focus still on freeing the painting from the thick padding that surrounded it. "You got a wake-up call, huh?"

That was one way to put it. "It's complicated," I said, not wanting to get into everything about the accident. "So how about you?" I asked. "Do you have a girlfriend?"

"I lived with a woman for five years. Till last year," he said. He held the painting—sunflowers on a blue background—upright in front of him to study. I knew it was one of the student pieces. The more valuable art would be brought in by escorts and packed in heavy wooden crates. We would see none of it until the gallery's security system was in place. "She wanted to move to California, pretty desperately," Oliver continued. "And I wanted to stay close to my son, also desperately."

"Are you sad you couldn't make it work?"

"There were other problems, more minor, but taken all together, it was time to end it."

"Her loss," I said, and I meant it.

He smiled across the room at me. "Thank you," he said. He leaned the painting against the wall near some of the other student work that had come in.

I returned his smile, then popped in my earbuds and went back to cleaning the mural. The spot I'd just worked on revealed drops of tea flying through the air. They were perfect, glistening, a catch light in each one. Not for the first time, I admired Anna Dale's exquisite work.

"Come look at this, Oliver," I said, taking my earbuds out again.

Oliver was opening another package, which he set down on the floor before crossing the foyer to the mural.

I pointed to the droplets. "Can you see this?" I asked. "She was so detailed. A huge painting like this and she still paid attention to every little thing. Even the catch lights in the drops of tea."

I looked down at Oliver to see him craning his neck, studying the image hard, eyes narrowed in concentration.

"Better tea drops than blood, right?" I smiled.

"Move the ladder for a sec," he said.

I climbed down to the floor and pulled the ladder aside as Oliver stepped closer to the mural. "I think you spoke too soon," he said, reaching up to touch one of the drops I hadn't yet cleaned. "Hand me the dowel."

I gave him the dowel and watched as he carefully smoothed the cotton tip over the spot.

"Oh, no," I said. The droplet was the same size and shape as the tea drops, but this one was most definitely red. Bloodred. I looked at Oliver in silence, and he met my eyes.

"This woman was not well," he said quietly.

I thought of the photograph I'd copied from the microfilm machine. The smiling, confident-looking girl standing in front of the huge canvas. "I'm starting to feel sorry for her," I said. "I think maybe she really *was* losing her mind and there was probably no treatment for her back then."

"I wish she hadn't fallen off the face of the earth," he said, handing me the dowel again. "I would love to see more of what she could do."

"I worry she killed herself," I said. "That's the only explanation I can think of. Obviously she was messed up."

Oliver nodded. "Yet for the most part, she still managed to produce a pretty phenomenal mural."

"I want to find out what really happened to her," I said. "Why did she turn a perfectly normal painting into a house of horrors?"

He looked at me with amusement. "How do you plan to do that?" he asked. "Find out what really happened to her?"

"I don't know, but I have to." I studied the bloody ax blade. The little red-haired man in the mirror. The drops of blood. The motorcycle. "I think Anna Dale is starting to haunt me."

Chapter 26

———— ✤•❦ ————

ANNA

January 11, 1940

There was a dusting of snow on the ground late that morning, and Anna's car slid a bit as she turned onto the long dirt road leading to the warehouse. Once inside the warehouse, she turned on the space heaters and pulled them close to her workspace. She was carefully laying out the wood she'd need for the stretcher when Martin Drapple suddenly cracked open the door and shouted, "All right if I come in?"

She jumped, startled. She'd been so engrossed in her work that she hadn't heard his car.

"Of course," she said, although he was probably the last person she wanted to see in her private space. She'd won the contest, so she knew she shouldn't feel intimidated by him, but she did.

Martin stomped off the snow before stepping into the warehouse, where he took off his hat and ran a hand through his thick red hair.

"I just wanted to see if you need any help," he said. His hands were in his jacket pockets as he took in every inch of the warehouse as though he'd be tested on it later. "A lot more space than I have in my little attic hovel," he said, good-naturedly, she thought.

"I was fortunate the mayor . . . your cousin . . . suggested it," Anna said, trying to forget how she'd felt the evening before when dark shadows filled the space.

Martin pulled his pipe from an inside pocket of his jacket and lit it, the sweet scent of the tobacco rising into the air. "Ah," he said, walking toward the wall with the cartoon paper. "You have the paper up."

"The students who are working with me helped me," Anna said. "We did that yesterday."

"Will you make a grid?"

"Yes, I've got it on my sketch and when the students arrive, we can—"

"Let me help you with it," he said. "We can get it done in no time at all."

Anna's insides coiled. She couldn't accept help from him. It felt wrong. Plus the thought of him seeing her sketch made her nervous.

"Oh, no," she said, before she could stop to think. "I'd feel unfair accepting your help."

His eyes narrowed and his expression seemed to darken as he held his pipe away from his face. "Don't patronize me," he said. "I genuinely would like to help you."

They were off and running on the wrong foot, Anna thought.

"I apologize," she said, giving in. "I would love some help with the grid."

He took off his jacket and they began to work together. It was clear Martin had done this before at some time. He cut plumb lines of twine and they hung them twelve inches apart from the top of the paper to the bottom. They coated them with charcoal and snapped the vertical grid lines into place. In short order, they'd completed the vertical lines, and Anna stepped back to study their work. It would have taken Theresa, Peter, and her at least an hour to accomplish what she and Martin had done in twenty minutes.

"Voilà," Martin said, lighting his pipe again. "Shall we leave the horizontal lines for your young charges to handle?" he asked, and she agreed.

She offered him one of the butter cookies she'd brought with her. She'd made a huge batch of them the evening before and dropped a tin of them off at Mayor Sykes's office on her way to the warehouse this morning. Martin declined the offer in favor of his pipe.

"So," he said, pulling one of the chairs out from under the table and sitting down as if she'd invited him to stay. "I saw your sketch hanging in the post office."

So he'd already seen it. "And . . . ?" She stood a distance away, her arms folded across her chest.

He nodded. "Quite impressive for someone your age."

"Only for someone my age?" She attempted a genuine smile, but it felt forced.

"Perhaps you're trying to please too many people by having such a conglomeration of ideas."

That had been her fear as well, but she wasn't about to tell him that. "The Section approved it and you know they can be notoriously difficult."

"Also, notoriously wrong at times." Was he teasing her or deadly serious? She couldn't tell.

"What would you have painted?" she asked.

He looked into the distance as if imagining his mural. "I left people out of my sketch altogether," he said. "I had more of an aerial scene. Broad Street with all the shops leading down to the waterfront, and in the distance, farmland that stretched on forever." He sounded a bit dreamy, describing it.

"That would have been a wise choice," she said. "Much simpler than what I'm attempting to do, throwing all those challenging-to-paint human beings into my mural."

He gave her a sharp look, then laughed. "All right, Miss Dale, I see you can hold your own."

Suddenly, the warehouse door opened and in walked a young colored man, his hair and coat dusted with snow. He carried a sketchbook beneath his arm, and he grinned at Anna. "I'm Jesse, ma'am," he said. "Miss Furman sent me here."

It took her a moment to understand. "I thought Miss Furman was sending one of her students," she said. "An eleventh-grader."

"I *am* an eleventh-grader," he said.

He must have stayed back two or three years at least, Anna thought. "How old are you?" she asked.

"Seventeen."

He was only seventeen? He was definitely more man than child, although she thought she detected a gentle innocence in his round doe eyes.

"You're not supposed to arrive until after school," she said.

"I don't need to go to my last two classes," he said, in what she guessed was a lie.

He glanced from her to Martin and back again, and Anna wondered if he thought he'd walked in on a romantic liaison by arriving early.

"Mr. Drapple was helping me with the car . . . with the paper." She pointed toward the cartoon. "He was just leaving."

Martin got to his feet. "Can I speak to you for a moment?" he asked Anna, nodding toward the far end of the warehouse.

"Jesse, please have a seat here and I'll be right with you," she said. "You can look at my sketch for the mural."

She walked with Martin nearly to the end of the warehouse.

"I'm not leaving you here alone with him," he said quietly.

"Why? Do you know something about him?"

"No, but you can't stay here alone with that boy."

"And why on earth not? Plus my other helpers will be here in an hour or so."

"It's not right and it's not safe."

"Ridiculous," she said.

"I'm not leaving until your other students come."

"Yes," she said. "You are." Who did he think he was? Her father? This close to him, she thought she could smell alcohol on his breath. It was not even one in the afternoon. "This is my space and I make the rules." She couldn't believe she was speaking to him that way, but she liked the strength in her voice. "I appreciate your help and your concern, but I really do insist you leave." She worried their voices had gotten too loud and the boy might hear them. She glanced toward him. He seemed engrossed in studying her sketch.

"It's your neck on the line," Martin Drapple said. "Not mine."

He walked the length of the warehouse, flung his jacket over his shoulder, and left without saying good-bye. Jesse never even looked up from the sketch.

Anna walked over to the table.

"So," she said, sitting down across from him. She was trembling slightly after the altercation with Martin, but pleased she'd held her own. "What do you think of the sketch?" she asked.

"You like red a lot."

"I guess I do." She smiled. "Do you think I've used it too much? The red?"

He smiled too, his gaze still on the sketch. His teeth showed. White, straight, with a slight space between his front teeth, and Anna realized who he reminded her of: Dabney Johnson from her high school in Plainfield. A big, shy, unassuming boy who did little to impress until you saw him play basketball.

"I think you ain't used it enough," Jesse said, his tone teasing, and she laughed.

"How about the composition?" she asked, wondering if he even knew what the word meant. He did.

"My aunt Jewel saw the picture . . . the photograph of this in the post office," he said, nodding respectfully toward the sketch rather than touching it. "She told me all the bits and pieces you got here and I thought, that gonna look like a big ol' bowl of Brunswick stew for sure. But it don't. The way you spread it all out, and how you made this part—the trawler and the Mill Village—how you made them smaller but they still stand out. It looks right good."

"Thank you, Jesse," she said. "I think you have a real artist's eye. Can

I see some of *your* drawings?" She carefully moved her sketch aside so he could put his sketchbook on the table, facing her. He handled the book with a delicacy she understood. It was precious to him, and she was touched. She would handle the pages with the same care as she turned them.

To say she was astonished by his skill would have been an understatement. She had to keep reminding herself that he was an untrained seventeen-year-old. The sketch pad contained portrait after portrait of his family members. "This my little sister, Nellie. This my aunt Jewel. She the midwife 'round where I live. This my mama. My other sister Dodie. This my cousin Chee." And on and on. Then there were cows and pigs and chickens.

"You have to go to art school, Jesse." The way Anna said it, it sounded like a foregone conclusion. That's how she felt at that moment. There was no other path for this young man. He *must* go to art school. "You have to hone your talent."

"What that mean? Hone?"

"You're extremely talented," she said. "You're a natural. To 'hone' it would be to learn all the technical aspects of art to bring your talent to full fruition . . . your full potential."

He shook his head. Leaned away from the table. "I'm done with school, ma'am," he said. "I jest want to sit on a stack of hay and draw."

"Please don't be done with school!" she practically begged him, and he drew back slightly. She thought she'd momentarily scared him with her intensity. "Please don't hide this talent in your . . . your family barn or wherever."

He laughed. "You sound jest like Miss Furman." He looked toward the wall where the cartoon paper was still draped with twine. "What that for?" he asked.

She stood up, and it took her a moment to shake off the surprise of what she'd seen in his sketchbook before she walked toward the cartoon paper. "Well, let me tell you what's happening here," she said. She explained about the cartoon and that she would be working on it while he and Theresa and Peter built a stretcher for the canvas, which she hoped would arrive in the Norfolk art supply store shortly. "The stretcher is very exacting work," she said, thinking that she really should have accepted Martin Drapple's offer to help with it. It had to be accurate to the inch.

"I done door framin'," Jesse said, only his accent was such that it took her a minute to understand what he meant. "My aunties and uncles and everybody call me to do it 'cause I know how to miter them corners right. Miss Furman give me some canvas and I made frames to stretch them over, even with bevel edges and all. I'm good at it."

"This'll be a bigger project than any you've done," Anna said. "Way bigger even than a door frame."

"Jes' leave it to me," he said, and Anna began to worry that he would boss Theresa and Peter around. She shouldn't have, though.

When Theresa and Peter arrived, Jesse changed into a different boy. His bravado and self-confidence seemed to disappear, and it took Anna a while to realize that he felt the need to defer to them. That deference was expected of him. She didn't like seeing the change in him. He communicated with the two of them in grunts, acquiescing to Peter's directions, which were, fortunately, excellent. She had to admit that these boys who grew up on self-sufficient farms were good with their hands. She didn't think the Plainfield boys she'd gone to high school with would have known what to do with all that wood.

Gradually, though, the awkwardness between the boys seemed to ease up. Anna had bought some cotton work gloves for all of them to use to protect their hands, but the boys just laughed at her.

"Miss Anna," Peter said, "we don't need no gloves! We build fences with our bare hands!" He looked at Jesse as if for corroboration, and Jesse picked it right up.

"An' butcher hogs with our bare hands, too!" he said.

"An' muck out the stables!" Peter said. "An'—"

"All right, all right!" Anna laughed.

Theresa rolled her eyes in annoyance at the boys and held out her hand for a pair of the gloves. It looked like she and Anna would be the only ones wearing them.

Anna gave directions and watched the three of them work. Peter was her surprise. He was so slight and blond, such a wisp of a boy, yet he was strong and very smart. Theresa didn't want to get down on the floor. Rather, she attempted to give orders from above.

"I told you, you need to wear pants in here," Anna said, and the girl turned away from her in a huff.

The boys, though, worked well together. Anna realized they were missing a couple of tools they needed to work with the wood, and Jesse promised to bring them the following day. Despite Theresa's prissy attitude, Anna thought they were off to a good start, and with the three of them there, the warehouse felt cheerful and alive and not the least bit threatening. The beams high above their heads were just beams, the huge hanging pendant lights, just lights, and she watched her young students with a sense of delight she hoped would never leave her.

Chapter 27

———— ✺ ————

MORGAN

July 3, 2018

I t was dusk by the time the Uber dropped me off at the end of the long driveway to the Williams farm. I paid the driver, climbed out of the car, and began walking toward the house, batting away the mosquitoes that instantly descended on me. I was here to talk to Mama Nelle again, the only person alive who had known Anna Dale. The only person besides me who might care about the artist who filled my days.

Lisa had all but forbidden my visit to her aunt. "Don't complain to me about how little time you have to get your work done if you're going to waste it with an old woman who can barely remember her own name," she said, when I told her my plans that afternoon.

"All right," I said. "I won't complain." I'd called Mama Nelle's daughter Saundra to arrange a time I could come over. Unlike Lisa, Saundra seemed to welcome the idea.

"Mama loves having people to talk to," she said. "And not too many actually listen to what she says anymore. Come on over!"

Saundra greeted me at the front door dressed in yoga pants and a gray tank top. Inside the house, she offered me a glass of wine, which I turned down, of course, accepting a bottle of water instead.

"Listen," she said, before taking me to see her mother. "How is Lisa doing? I worry about her."

I was surprised by the question, surprised she asked for my opinion when, truth be told, I was really a stranger to the family. I hesitated long enough that she filled the silence.

"I know she's under the gun with the gallery and work," she said. "And still grieving over Uncle Jesse. She adored her daddy and took such good care of him. When I get frustrated taking care of my mother"—she nodded toward the hall, toward Mama Nelle, I supposed—"I remember how devoted Lisa was to Uncle Jesse and it keeps me going."

"Hopefully everything will work out all right with the gallery and she can relax," I said. I hoped that for both of us.

"I'm sure it will." Saundra nodded in the direction of the hall again. "Let's go see Mama," she said, and I followed her out of the kitchen, down the hall, and into the small den where I'd visited with Mama Nelle on her birthday. The old woman sat on the sofa in the same spot I'd found her that day, although now that she was alone, no longer flanked by her relatives, she looked unbelievably tiny and inconsequential, swallowed up by the sofa's fat cushions. Across the room from her, a talk show blared loudly from the TV.

I could have sworn the old woman's face lit up when she spotted me. Her eyes shone behind her glasses and her lips curled into a smile.

"Do you remember Morgan?" Saundra asked her mother as she turned off the television. "She came to your birthday party?"

"I 'member." Mama Nelle patted the sofa next to her. "Set down, girl," she said.

As Lisa had done the night of Mama's birthday party, I opted to move a straight-backed chair in front of the old woman so that we could easily see each other, and Saundra winked at me.

"Have a good visit," she said. "You holler if you need anything."

"Mama Nelle," I began once she and I were alone, "when I was here the other day, we talked about an artist you remembered from when you were a little girl. Anna Dale. Do you remember talking with me about her?"

"Miss Anna." The old woman lifted a finger to her wrinkled lips. "Sh. Have to be quiet about her," she said.

"Why is that?" I asked, softening my voice. "Why do we have to whisper about her?"

"Everybody'd get hurt. Even me."

"Even you?" I frowned. She was losing me. Or maybe I was losing her. She nodded.

"How will you get hurt if we don't whisper?" I wondered if there was something she didn't want Saundra to hear.

"The po-lice might come," she said.

"Oh." I sat back. Lisa had been right. I was wasting my time.

I'd brought two pictures with me in a manila folder, and with a less than hopeful sigh, I took them out now. Leaning forward, I handed the old woman the first picture, and adjusted the lamp on the nearby table so that the light fell in a circle on the grainy image from the newspaper.

"Can you see this picture?" I asked. "Do you recognize—"

"Jesse!" she said, her gnarled finger touching the image of the black man.

"I don't think so, dear," I said, shocking myself when the word "dear" came out of my mouth. I'd never used it before in my life. "Jesse would only have been a boy back then. This is from 1940."

"It's Jesse," she said stubbornly. "Seventeen. Eighteen. My big brother."

I took the picture back from her and looked hard at it. Could she be right? The black man *could* possibly have been a teenager. The thought excited me. That might explain how the mural came to be in Jesse's possession. He was somehow connected to it. Somehow involved in its creation. I set the photograph on her lap again. "Do you know who the white boy is?" I asked, wondering if by some miracle that boy was still alive and clearheaded.

She looked at the photograph again, but her focus was on Anna. "She so pretty," she said, then pressed her finger to her lips again as if to shut herself up. "That white boy," she said suddenly. "He had somethin' to do with the po-lice. But later. Not . . ." She tapped the print. "Not back then." She was losing me again.

"I have another picture," I said, pulling the large print I'd made of the half-cleaned mural from the manila folder. "I'm restoring Anna Dale's mural," I said, "and I know a lot of it still needs cleaning and inpainting . . . the paint restored . . . but is this familiar?"

She was already grinning as I set the photograph in her lap. "Ain't seen this thing in forever," she said. "Where's the black lady? She was my fav'rite."

I smiled, excited that she recognized the mural. "She's up here in the corner," I said, pointing to the upper right-hand corner of the print. "I haven't cleaned her off yet, so she's hard to see."

Mama Nelle squinted behind her glasses. "What you done to her mouth?" she asked.

"I'm not sure what's going on with her mouth," I admitted. "It looks like she has something in it, or she's biting a stick or something. I'll know once I clean that part off."

Mama Nelle frowned at the picture. I could see her gaze shifting from one bit of the painting to another.

"There are some odd things here," I said, pointing. "Do you see the ax? Those little red spots are blood drops coming off it. I don't know what that—"

"Weren't no ax." Mama Nelle shook her head. "'Twas a hammer."

It was my turn to frown. "What do you mean, 'a hammer'?"

She quickly turned her face away from me, tightening her lips as if she'd said too much.

"Can you tell me what you mean by a hammer?" I tried again.

She looked back at the photograph and another smile came to her face. She laughed, tapping a long finger on the motorcycle, which was still grimy but identifiable. "I 'member that!" she said. "Jesse done cover it over. Miss Anna, she paint it again. Jesse cover it again."

I was lost. "What do you mean?" I asked.

She lifted her watery gaze to my face. "You know you got to be quiet about her, right?" she asked me in a hushed voice.

"*Why?*" I asked, wishing I had the key to unlock this old woman's skittering brain. "Why do I need to be quiet about her?"

She only pressed a finger to her lips again, and I sighed.

"All right, yes, I'll be very quiet about her." I looked at the grainy newspaper photograph, which now rested on my knees, and ventured the question that disturbed me the most. "Mama Nelle," I said. "Do you know if Miss Anna killed herself?"

Behind her glasses, Mama Nelle's dark eyes widened in surprise. "Oh no, child!" she said. "Why, that girl? She couldn't even kill a chicken."

Chapter 28

———— ✦ ————

ANNA

January 12–15, 1940

The morning started out very well, the day full of promise. Miss Myrtle, Ellen Harper—the salesgirl from the Patsy Department Store—Freda, and Mayor Syke's wife, Madge, all came to the warehouse to pose for the cartoon. Anna had borrowed dresses for Miss Myrtle, Ellen, and Miss Madge from a local historian Mr. Arndt had put her in touch with. The women changed their clothes one by one in the revolting warehouse bathroom, laughing over too tight bodices and scratchy petticoats. Then Anna sat the three Tea Party ladies around a crate they pretended was a table. The ladies giggled too much for grown women, but all in all, Anna was happy with the way her drawing turned out on the cartoon paper.

Freda was the real star in the modeling department, though. Because she never spoke, Anna had never really seen her teeth. When Freda smiled, as Anna asked her to do for the portrait, the woman displayed beautiful white teeth and a fetching smile. Anna's plan was for Freda to hold out her apron full of peanuts. Anna had the apron, but no peanuts, so she would have to add them to the drawing later.

Jesse arrived before Anna was even finished sketching the women. She wasn't surprised by his early, enthusiastic arrival, and without a word, he began cutting wood for the braces on the stretcher as she continued working with the women.

She was both exhausted and elated by the time the models left. Then Theresa and Peter arrived. Peter joined Jesse at work on the stretcher, but Theresa took Anna aside.

"My daddy won't let me work here if *he's* here," she whispered, nodding in Jesse's direction.

Anna was momentarily confused. "Why not?" she asked. "Do you know something about him I should know?" She recalled asking Martin the same question.

Theresa shook her head. "I ain't never even seen him before yesterday," she said, "but I can't work with no colored boy."

"Oh, for pity's sake," Anna said. "He hopes to be an artist, just like you. The three of you are here to learn."

"My daddy—"

"Why did your daddy even need to know?" Anna said, aware she was crossing a line. Theresa stared at her with disbelief at the idea that Anna would suggest she withhold such significant—to her—news from her father. Across the warehouse, Anna heard a burst of laughter from the boys. It warmed her. At least the two of them were getting along well.

"You don't understand," Theresa said.

"No, I guess I don't," Anna said wearily. "It's up to you, Theresa. Jesse is working here. I'd like you to also work here. The choice is yours."

"It ain't right, what you're asking." She looked away from Anna, her coral-colored mouth set. "I got to leave." And with that she stomped across the concrete floor, grabbed her coat from a hook on the wall, and headed out the door.

The boys looked up from their work.

"Theresa's decided she doesn't want to work here," Anna said simply.

"What the—" Peter said, wrinkling his brow in confusion, but Anna watched Jesse go right back to work, measuring and hammering. He knew. She had the feeling that beneath his dark skin, his cheeks were burning.

⊰⊱

Anna found Pauline to be a delightful traveling companion on their drive north to Norfolk, at least for the most part. They talked about what it was like growing up in Edenton and how Karl proposed to her (on a small boat while paddling through one of the many creeks in the area) and then Pauline shared all the gossip she could possibly remember about people in town. There was certainly plenty of it. She didn't ask Anna much about herself, and that was fine. Anna still didn't feel ready to talk about her mother with anyone.

"How many teenagers are working with you?" Pauline asked when she'd exhausted every salacious story she could think of about her fellow Edentonians.

"Just two," Anna said. "Two boys. The girl quit because one of the boys is colored. She said her father wouldn't approve."

Pauline laughed. "I'm sure she's right," she said. "Who's her father?"

Anna shrugged. "I haven't met him. Her name is Theresa Wayman."

"Oh, good heavens," Pauline said. "Do you know who her father is?"

"I have no idea," Anna said.

"Riley Wayman is president of the bank. A real bigwig in town."

His name suddenly sounded familiar. Someone at that first meeting she'd had with the "movers and shakers" must have mentioned him.

"Well, is he that much of a jackass that he'd make his daughter quit working with me because of Jesse?"

"That and more," Pauline said.

"I haven't heard a peep out of her father, so I think everything is all right," Anna said. "Of course Theresa only walked out on me Friday, so who knows, but I'm not worried about it."

Pauline didn't respond for a moment. From the corner of Anna's eye, she saw her staring straight ahead through the window, blue eyes catching the sunlight. Finally, she took in a breath and turned to Anna. "I guess you have to ask yourself if having this Jesse helping you is going to create more trouble than it's worth."

"Of the three of them he's by far the most talented," Anna said. "And he's passionate about art. He really needs more exposure to it, though. He needs the chance to visit museums. To get to study other artists. I wish I had my art books here to share with him." She heard the rise in her voice. The enthusiasm. And she felt Pauline's eyes on her.

"Are you . . . Do you have inappropriate feelings for this boy?" Pauline asked, ever so delicately. "You sound rather smitten with him."

Anna laughed. "No!" she reassured her. "Not at all. Not the way you mean, anyhow. What I do have is a fear that his talent will go to waste. That he'll end up working on his family's farm instead of doing what he's meant to be doing."

"You can't save him, you know," Pauline said. "We're all born with limitations of one sort or another. A family that needs us or a bum leg or the wrong skin color. We just have to make do."

Anna didn't answer. She didn't want to *save* him. She just wanted him to have the same chance as everyone else.

"What about the other boy?" Pauline asked. "The white boy?"

"Very nice young man," Anna said. "He could be an architect, his sketches are so technically perfect. He wants to be an artist, but his drawings have no passion in them."

"Like Jesse's," Pauline said.

Anna nodded. "Like Jesse's."

—※•※—

They found the shop without too much trouble and they were both astonished by the enormous roll of canvas. Fortunately Karl had thought to give them a good length of rope before they left his and Pauline's house, so with the help of the salesman in the shop, they were able to tie the roll securely to the roof of Anna's Ford. She picked up the paints she'd ordered as well as some brushes and charcoal and other supplies. She felt that thrill of excitement she always got when she had new tools in her possession. On a whim, she also bought two stretched canvases as gifts for Peter and Jesse.

She drove well under the speed limit back to Edenton, and Pauline helped her carry the roll of canvas into the warehouse, where they set it down by one of the garage doors. A little breathless, Pauline stood with her hands on her hips and looked around at Anna's vast working space, with its beamed ceiling, dusty skylights, and dark corners. "This is a . . . I don't know . . . a bit of a strange place to work," she said.

Anna laughed. "You should have seen it before it was cleaned out," she said. "I hated it. But now it feels like home. Almost."

"Oh my, look at this!" Pauline exclaimed, walking toward the cartoon paper where Anna had drawn her three Tea Party ladies plus Freda. "I recognize each one of them." She turned to Anna. "You really are very good," she said.

"Thank you." Anna carried the sketch across the room to show her how the drawing would look in color.

"I wish I had some artistic talent," Pauline said.

"Well, I don't know the first thing about nursing, so we're even," Anna countered.

Pauline stayed a while longer, but Anna was glad when she left. Pauline was becoming a good friend, but Anna's work felt like a greater calling at that moment than friendship. Was that a terrible thing? It was the truth, and once Pauline left, Anna happily organized her new paints and brushes and palette, feeling the thrill of excitement at the thought that she would soon be using all of them.

Chapter 29

————— ✦ —————

MORGAN

July 7, 2018

The mural was entirely clean. Abraded, scratched, and worn, but clean. And extraordinarily, nightmare-inducingly weird.

That stick in the black woman's mouth? Once clean, it became a knife. But the weirdest discovery of all—the discovery that made me gasp out loud and had me running to Oliver's office to drag him back to the foyer—was that one of the Tea Party ladies dangled a hammer from her hand. Like the ax, the hammer dripped blood, which stained the hem of the woman's dress and pooled on the floor near the ladies' feet. Anna Dale might have been crazy, I thought, but Mama Nelle appeared to have most of her marbles still intact.

Once I'd finished cleaning the lower right-hand corner of the mural where Anna had placed her rounded and oddly distorted-looking signature, I called everyone into the foyer for a viewing. I moved the ladder and my supplies table out of the way and all of us stood in the

middle of the room. Lisa, Adam, and Wyatt on my left. Oliver and his visiting twelve-year-old son Nathan on my right. All I could see was the work
that was still waiting for me to do, but everyone else seemed impressed.

"Awesome colors," Adam said. He lightly punched my bare arm. "Nice
work, Christopher."

"Thank you." I *had* done nice work. The colors popped. Not the way
they would have with a coat of varnish, but still. Compared to the way
the mural had looked when we'd first stretched it? A completely different
animal.

"It looks pretty messed up to me," Nathan said, and everyone laughed.
I'd met Oliver's cute son only a couple of hours earlier—he was spending
a few days with his dad—but already I'd learned that this was a boy un-
afraid to speak his mind. I liked that about him.

"It has a way to go," Oliver agreed with his son.

I looked at Nathan. "If you'd seen it before I started cleaning it," I said,
"you'd realize how much better it looks now. I'll show you a 'before' picture later."

"I like all the blood," Nathan said. "It's so sick."

Everyone except Lisa laughed.

"If you say so, Nathan," Lisa said, then let out a sigh. "Well"—she
peeked at the phone in her hand—"I'm not happy it took two weeks just
to clean this thing, but it obviously needed it. Quite a difference. And I
have to say I have no idea what to make of it."

"That Indian." Adam shook his head. "So crazy."

"What Indian?" Nathan asked, most likely scanning the mural for a
warrior in headdress.

"He means the brand of the motorcycle," I explained. "See the motorcycle tire and red fender poking out from between the women's dresses?"

"Why is it there?" Nathan asked.

"Wish we knew the answer to that," Oliver said.

As soon as I'd started working on the motorcycle, I'd understood what
Mama Nelle had meant about Jesse covering it over. Anna had painted the

mural thinly, but in the area of the motorcycle, the paint was extremely thick as though the cycle had been painted over and then repainted, maybe more than once. Maybe even more than twice. I couldn't explain why, but Anna and Jesse seemed to have some sort of duel going on there.

"We should make a list of all the strange things the artist put into the mural, so we can add them to your wall text about it, Oliver," Lisa said. "Make it sound mysterious. Make gallery visitors try to guess what message the artist was trying to convey."

"If they figure it out, I hope they'll tell me," I said, shaking my head. I looked at Nathan. "Want to see what else we uncovered?" I asked him as I walked toward the painting. "You have to come closer to see." I had a funny feeling as I moved toward the mural with the boy at my side. A sense of intimacy and ownership of the painting. It was more mine than anyone else's in this room. "There's also this little skull peeking out of a window." I pointed to one of the little Mill Village houses where Anna had painted a small, hollow-eyed skull in one of the windows. "And there's a little man in the reflection of that mirror the woman's holding, right where you'd expect to see a reflection of her face. And there are not only drops of tea coming from the shattered teapot but drops of—"

"Is that blood, too?" Lisa moved near us, hand on her chest. "Oh my God. I wonder if my father remembered how disturbing this thing is when he thought of hanging it in the foyer?"

"There *is* a lot of blood," I said, almost apologetically.

"She was, like, possessed." Nathan sounded frankly delighted. "The artist."

"She may have been," Oliver said.

"It's a mess," Nathan said. "All those places where the paint's, like, worn away?"

Lisa let out a pained sigh. "It is indeed still a mess." She knotted her hands together around her phone. "But you have a whole month left." She gave me a hopeful look. "I'm sure you can do it."

I glanced at Oliver, whose expression told me he doubted *anyone* could do all the necessary work—and do it well—in a month. Then I nodded at Lisa.

"I'll do my best," I said.

-≫•≪-

Lisa left, and Adam and Wyatt went back to work in the rear rooms of the gallery. I looked at the box of inpainting supplies waiting for me on the floor by the ladder.

"You look nervous." Oliver smiled at me.

"Can you help me after lunch?" I asked. "Just to get me started?"

"Of course." He turned to his son. "You hungry, Nate?" he asked.

"Starving!"

Oliver pulled his wallet from the back pocket of his jeans and handed me a twenty. "You and Nathan get lunch for the three of us while I move my computer out here to the foyer. That way, I can supervise you for a few days," he said. "Chicken wrap for me."

"Thank you," I said, happy to know he'd be close by. I'd pictured myself running back and forth to his office, dragging him to the foyer to advise me on every brushstroke.

Nathan and I set out for Nothing Fancy, talking about what we'd order for lunch: a BLT for him, chef's salad for me. Then Nathan pointed to my ankle.

"Is that one of those exercise things?" he asked. "Like, it tells you how far you walk every day?"

I'd thought my jeans had been long enough to mask the monitor, but apparently not. I could lie, but decided against it. "Actually, no," I said. "It's an alcohol monitor. I had a problem with drinking." I surprised myself with the admission. It was the first time those words had come out of my mouth. I'd never uttered "problem" and "drinking" in the same sentence before. About my parents, yes. About myself, never. At the AA meetings, I had yet to stand up and proclaim I was an alcoholic. "A problem with drinking" didn't sound quite so ominous, and yet the words made me wince. It was the truth, though, wasn't it? I had to own up to it. I wouldn't be in the mess I was in if I didn't have a problem with drinking. If I'd been sober the night of the accident, I would have been driving and my life—and Emily Maxwell's life—would be completely different now.

"So this keeps me from drinking," I continued, "because when you drink, the alcohol comes out in your sweat and the monitor would know and would tell . . ." My parole officer? I really didn't want to go into all that with this boy. "It would tell my doctor I had a drink. So this helps me to not drink."

"You're an alcoholic?" he asked, cutting to the chase.

I hesitated. "I guess you could say that," I said finally. "And I drank too much and got into a car accident, so I can't—I don't want to—drink anymore."

"Oh," Nathan said. "Do you always wear it? Like do you have to wear it for the rest of your life?"

"No. Just for now."

"What happens when you take it off? Then you'll need willpower, right? To not drink?"

"Exactly." I smiled, impressed that he'd made that leap in his thinking. He was so cute. Such a miniature Oliver. I wanted to put an arm around his shoulders. Give him a squeeze. "But by then I'll have made a new habit. A new nondrinking habit. So I won't drink once I take it off, either." We'd reached the corner and started across the street. I needed to get the conversation off myself. "Your dad is really looking forward to going to Smith Mountain Lake with you," I said as we stepped up the curb at the other side of the street.

"Mmm," he said. "I don't know if I can go."

"Really? Why not?"

"My stepdad is getting us tickets to Disney World and he thinks that's the only time he can get off before school starts up."

"Does your dad know?"

He shook his head. "It's not for sure yet, so I won't tell him till it is. I've been to Smith Mountain Lake like a million times, but I've never been to Disney World and it'll be so cool."

I was surprised how much my heart ached for Oliver. Truly ached. I rubbed my chest, thinking of how Oliver's eyes lit up when he talked about having a whole week with his son. It had been a while since I'd felt such concern for someone, but then it had been a while since I'd had a friend who didn't want something from me. A friend who only wanted to help me.

"Your dad would be really disappointed," I said.

"I don't think so," Nathan said. "He actually hates how sticky hot it gets at the lake in the summer and all the mosquitoes and everything, so maybe he won't care. And I really want to go to Disney World."

Stay out of it, I told myself. *This is not your problem.* Yet a million responses ran through my mind. *Don't be so selfish!* I wanted to say. *You are so lucky to have a father who loves you and wants to do things with you and isn't drunk all the time. Please don't break his heart.*

"I hope they have lots of mayo for the BLT," Nathan said, and only then did I realize we'd reached the door of the café.

"I'm sure they do," I said, and I followed him inside, vowing to keep my mouth shut. This was not my problem to solve. I had plenty of my own.

--->=■=<---

Oliver had set up a new workspace for himself in the foyer by the time Nathan and I returned with lunch. The folding table now held his computer, several of his towering stacks of paper, and the photograph of his son.

"All set here," he said.

The three of us ate together sitting on the cool tiled floor. Then Oliver spent the afternoon teaching me about the conservation paints and how to use the annoying magnification visor, while Nathan played games on his dad's computer.

"You have to forget you're an artist," Oliver said, as he demonstrated brushing the paint onto an abraded area. "Think more like a technician.

You not only want to match the color of the area where you're painting, you need to match the texture of the paint as well. The level of the gloss, too." He showed me how to reduce the gloss of the paint by mixing it with a little silica, fine-tuning the result until it matched Anna's oils.

"Got it," I said. I watched Oliver use short pointillist strokes with a tiny brush, touching the canvas with the gentlest care, but I was remembering what Nathan had said about not going to Smith Mountain Lake with him and felt like putting a comforting arm across his shoulders. I glanced at Nathan where he was engrossed in the computer. *Spoiled little guy.* I supposed most twelve-year-olds were just like him, only thinking of their own needs. Their own wants. I hadn't been that way, though. No one could ever have accused me of being spoiled.

"If you want me to check your work the first few times, just ask," Oliver said, bringing me back to the here and now. "Might be a good idea."

I smiled at him from under the visor. "You worried I can't do it?"

"The paint's just different than what you're used to," he said. "But I have confidence in you."

—⧭•⧭—

By the end of the day, I'd inpainted one tiny square inch near the upper left-hand corner of the mural. It was only background, only blue sky, nothing like what I'd be dealing with later—one of the Tea Party ladies' missing eyelashes, for example—things that would truly matter, but Oliver declared my work competent. His faint praise told me it was quitting time for the day and I was relieved to slip the visor from my head.

Standing back, I looked up at the speck of paint that had taken me so long to apply. *August fifth,* I thought. *One short month away.* Slowly, I shook my head. This was going to be impossible.

Chapter 30

———— ➤•➤ ————

ANNA

January 17, 1940

Anna stopped in the library on her way to the warehouse, hoping to pick up some art books for Jesse. Peter had borrowed some of the library's books on drawing, and when Anna suggested to Jesse that he do the same, he replied, "Ain't no colored library here, Miss Anna." She'd been more frustrated than surprised at that news. So she checked out some books for him herself, wondering what the librarian would say or do if she told her she planned to put them into the hands of a colored boy. But she behaved herself, quietly checking out the books without comment. She thought people talked about her quite enough already.

She'd been working on the cartoon alone in the warehouse for a few hours when an unfamiliar man suddenly pushed open the door and strutted into the space as though he owned it. Anna stepped back from the cartoon, charcoal pencil in hand, unsure if she should be frightened or angered by the intrusion.

"You're Anna Dale?" the man asked, his voice deep and gruff.

"Yes, and you're . . . ?"

"I'm Riley Wayman," he said. "Theresa Wayman's father."

Oh, she thought. *Theresa Wayman's father and president of the bank.* She set down her pencil and walked toward him, dusting her hand off on her smock before holding it out to him. "How do you do?" she asked, but he seemed to want nothing to do with her hand. She felt him eye her up and down, taking in her slacks, her charcoal-smeared smock, her oxfords. A cold wind had blown into the warehouse with him and Anna shivered despite the warmth her two space heaters were putting out.

"I want to know why you brought in this colored boy and kicked my daughter out," he said.

"I didn't kick her out," Anna said. "Theresa told me you wouldn't allow her to work with me if Jesse stayed. She chose to leave."

"She was with you first."

"But I have room for three students to work with me and Jesse was referred to me by his art teacher," Anna said. "I would have loved to have Theresa stay. She's quite talented." Was she? Anna hadn't actually seen any of her work. "It was her choice to leave."

Riley Wayman folded his arms across his big barrel chest and looked at the cartoon, frowning. He studied the drawing for so long and so silently that Anna said, "I'm happy to take her back if she chooses to come," simply for something to break the silence.

He turned back to her. "You don't belong here, little lady," he said. "You know that, don't you? You don't fit in; you could live here twenty years and you still wouldn't fit in. People here like you right now because you're a novelty and they're excited our post office was chosen for one of the paintings, but they'll get past that pretty soon and realize it was a mistake bringing you here."

"I'm doing fine in Edenton." Anna stood her ground. She *was* doing fine in Edenton, but she knew what he meant. She knew *exactly* what he meant. She'd been in Edenton nearly a month and a half and there were some things she would never understand. She would always be thought of as a *furriner*, no matter how long she lived in the town.

She knew arguing with Mr. Wayman would get her nowhere, so she took on a different tack.

"Please let Theresa come back," she said. "She's interested in art and this could be a very good experience for her."

He was shaking his head before she'd even finished her sentence. "I'm not going to open my door to all sorts of talk and innuendo," he said. His eyes traveled down her body again, which was masked quite thoroughly by her smock. He shook his head in what she took to be disgust. "She said she had to wear pants to work here." He nodded toward Anna's dusty slacks. "That it was a rule you made."

"There's no such rule." She was annoyed that Theresa would fib that way. "It's just easier to move around in pants. To work on the stretcher, she'd have to be on the floor. Don't you think pants of some sort would make a lot more sense?"

He glanced at the stretcher taking shape on the concrete floor, then looked around the warehouse as if noticing its vast size, its dark corners, and its spooky beamed ceiling for the first time. He was making her increasingly nervous. She wanted him to leave.

"Never mind," he said finally. "I don't want her working here with you anyway." He turned on his heel and walked out of the warehouse, his footsteps echoing behind him.

Lovely man, Anna thought, and she felt some sympathy for Theresa as she watched him go.

⟶•⟵

She had plenty of other visitors to the warehouse that day. Her lumberman, Frank, came to pose for her. He was an excellent model, keeping perfectly still, even though he had to hold a long-handled ax steady the whole time. Anna could tell he got a kick out of posing and having some time off from his real job grading wood. About half an hour after he left,

Jesse and Peter arrived and started working on the stretcher, and a short time later, Martin Drapple showed up again.

"I had some spare time," he said. "Thought I'd come see if I could help out with the— Hey!" He noticed the cartoon. "You're making great progress!" He stood back to admire—she hoped—her drawing. "You're quick," he added, and Anna wondered if he thought she was working *too* quickly to do a good job. Why did she doubt herself so? She would accept his words as a compliment. Still, she was annoyed he was there. Was he keeping an eye on her?

"Thank you," she said. "It's going well so far."

He turned toward Peter and Jesse where they grappled with the stretcher on the floor.

"Hey, fellas," he said. "Looks like you could use another pair of hands."

"Sure could, sir!" Peter said. Jesse kept his head down, focusing on the screw he was turning into place. Martin lowered himself to the floor and held the two lengths of wood steady for him. Anna watched for a moment as the three of them worked together and she gradually shifted from annoyance at Martin's arrival to gratitude. The boys could not easily manage the stretcher alone. She turned back to the cartoon and let the boys and Martin work on their own.

Did Martin's wife know he was at the warehouse? she wondered. Did she know he'd stopped in last week as well? Did he go home and tell her he'd helped Anna Dale make the grid lines on the cartoon? She doubted that very much. They'd be divorced by now if he had. She remembered the angry woman on the library steps, how she'd clutched Anna's arm. How afraid she'd seemed over the family finances, with Martin's design for the post office not being accepted. He shouldn't be here in the warehouse, Anna thought, working for free. He especially shouldn't be here with *her*.

It would be best if he didn't come again, but as she watched him working side by side with the boys, giving directions she might not have known to give, she was very glad that he had come.

Chapter 31

---◆◆◆---

MORGAN

July 9, 2018

I heard sirens the moment I stepped out of Lisa's house for my walk to the gallery. The sound didn't slow or stop; instead, it built on itself, one siren on top of another on top of another. The sounds alone were enough to take me back to the accident and set my heart racing. I stood paralyzed on the sidewalk in front of the house, trying to decide if I should go back inside and wait it out or start walking toward the gallery. *Get a grip*, I told myself, beginning to walk again. I was not going to live the rest of my life in fear.

The sound had settled down by the time I turned onto Broad Street, but then I found myself less than half a block from the clot of ambulances, police cars, and a fire truck. I froze. From where I stood, it looked like a horrific accident between a minivan and a delivery truck. I saw a stretcher and although I couldn't see the person it carried, in my mind it was Emily Maxwell's bloody body being loaded into the ambulance. I backtracked and took a cross street to avoid walking past the wreck, but it was really too late. The damage was done. My knees threatened to buckle. The whole world spun and I had to stop walking, pressing my body against the wall of a building to stay upright. I looked around for a bench I could sink onto, but there were none. Instead, I stood there, eyes closed, waiting for the worst of the dizziness to pass.

I thought I had myself under control by the time I reached the gallery, but as soon as I entered the foyer, Oliver looked up from his computer, eyes wide.

"What's wrong?" he asked, pulling out his earbuds.

I shook my head. "Nothing."

"Bull," he said. "Are you sick? Your face is white."

I sat down next to the table that held my paints and brushes. My palms were damp and I wiped them on my jeans. "I just saw an accident," I said. "The aftermath, anyhow. It shook me up."

"I heard the sirens," he said. "Where was it?"

"Broad Street. I didn't really look. I . . . accidents . . . I . . ." I looked away from him. I wasn't sure what I'd intended to say.

He bent forward, elbows on his knees, searching my face. "You what?" he prompted. "Were you in an accident?" I could see the concern in his eyes.

I nodded.

"When . . . oh. The DUI?"

I nodded again. "It was so terrible, Oliver," I said. "We almost killed someone."

"What happened?" He straightened up again, all of his attention still on me.

Before I could stop myself, I began talking. "I'd been at a party with my boyfriend, and . . . we'd both had too much to drink." I twisted my hands together in my lap. "I turned my car keys over to him. I thought maybe he was more sober than I was. Neither of us should have been driving. I was so stupid."

Oliver frowned. *"He* was driving?"

"Yes, he was driving." My voice sounded bitter. "And he drove too fast. About sixty miles per hour in a thirty-five-mile-per-hour zone. He went right through a stop sign at this intersection, and he crashed into a car. We nearly killed the girl who was driving it. She was in a coma for two months and now she's paralyzed from the waist down. For life." I looked over at him. "For ever and ever," I added quietly.

Oliver's frown was deep and troubled. "What about you and the boy-friend?" he asked. "Were you hurt? And why did you go to prison if he was driving?" Was he suspicious of my story? Who could blame him?

"We were completely okay," I said. "Physically, anyway." I thought of the inconsequential scar on my forehead beneath my bangs, then looked down at my hands where they rested in tight fists on my thighs. "But Trey—my boyfriend—ran off. He wanted me to say I was the driver."

"What the *hell?"*

"I was an idiot." I looked up at him. "I was so wasted, Oliver. I knew he was afraid of losing his scholarship to Georgetown Law. And I loved him. And I wasn't thinking clearly and . . . it made sense to me in that crazy mo-ment. I could protect him. Protect his future. I thought it was *our* future. Together. It didn't seem like such a big deal. So I let the police think I was driving." I shut my eyes, the miserable scene coming back to me again. "I got out of the car to try to help the driver—the girl—but I was so messed up, I didn't know what to do. I was screaming my lungs out. Shouting for help. The girl—her name is Emily—she was crunched up against the horn and it was blowing in a steady stream. This horrible sound."

"You didn't tell the police your boyfriend had been driving?"

I shook my head. "I thought I was being a good girlfriend. I would have done anything for him. I never in a million years thought I'd end up in prison. When I finally told the truth about what happened, no one be-lieved me. They talked to Trey and he had a friend lie for him. His friend said he was with him at the time of the accident."

"What a prick."

"Yes," I agreed. "What a prick."

"So nothing happened to him?"

"Nothing. He's in law school now. At least, I suppose he is. I've had no contact with him."

Oliver rubbed his temple. There was such kindness in his face. I wished he'd say something.

"I have nightmares," I added.

"I bet you do."

"The whole time I was in prison, I blocked out thoughts of the girl we hurt."

"You keep saying 'we.'"

"I blame myself almost as much as I blame him."

"You didn't leave the scene."

I said nothing. Looked down at my hands.

"Have you had any contact with the girl?"

"No. Though . . . I've tried to find her online, but if she has any social media stuff she's hidden it." I looked up at him. "I think about her all the time," I said. "I worry about her. I hope somehow she's found some peace."

He stared at me, his beautiful blue eyes so serious behind his glasses. So pained.

"And how about Morgan?" he asked.

I looked at him, perplexed. "How about Morgan?"

"How are *you* doing with finding some peace?"

I shook my head. "Not so well," I said. "I'm . . ." I searched for the right word. "I'm ashamed of who I was."

"'Was' is the definitive word in that sentence, Morgan." He nodded toward the mural. "And I think you're the perfect person to work on this mural," he said, with a small smile.

"You do? Why?"

"You and Anna," he said. "I think it's safe to say that, for whatever reason, she had her own share of nightmares. I know you already care about her, don't you?"

I nodded. He was right. I did.

"I have the feeling that if anyone is going to do right by her," he said, "it's you."

Chapter 32

———— ✦ ————

ANNA

January 24, 1940

Jesse was lying to her. She'd wanted to believe him when he said he had all those extra periods at school and that was why he was able to spend so much time in the warehouse, coming a couple of hours earlier than Peter each day. She'd wanted it to be the truth. But she'd received a letter from Mrs. Furman, his art teacher, the day before, telling her that Jesse was failing every subject except art. *He's skipping most of his classes,* Mrs. Furman wrote. *Perhaps I made a mistake, sending him to work with you.*

Anna read and reread the short letter, her heart sinking. Yesterday, Jesse's eyes had been bloodshot from lack of sleep because he'd stayed up late to devour the latest library book she'd brought him.

"I want to learn *everythin',*" he'd told her when he arrived in the warehouse. He'd set the heavy book on the Old Masters down on one of the warehouse tables, his hand resting on top of it as if he could soak up everything in its pages through his skin.

She'd been delighted as usual by his enthusiasm. "Which of the artists were you most drawn to?" she'd asked.

"I got a favorite," he said. "That Vermer fella."

"Vermeer." She corrected him with a smile. "And which Vermeer do you like best?" She fully expected him to pick nearly everyone's favorite, *The Girl with the Pearl Earring*, but he surprised her.

"I like that *Geographer* one," he said. "I like how the light is comin' through the window with all them little panes." He glanced down at the book. "I looked at it for a hour last night," he said. "I wanna know how to paint like that."

She was surprised to feel tears burn her eyes. *The Geographer*, with its complex composition and intriguing use of light, was one of her favorite Vermeers as well, and the fact that Jesse saw the beauty in the painting both touched and pained her. He needed a chance to learn all there was to learn about his craft. How he was ever going to get that chance, she didn't know. Now, with the arrival of Mrs. Furman's letter, she knew his chances were slimmer than ever.

-->≫•≪--

When Jesse arrived at the warehouse early that afternoon, Anna was ready for him. He was grinning, sketch pad in hand, anxious to show her a portrait he was working on, and she felt almost guilty for putting a damper on his excitement.

"I heard from Mrs. Furman," she said, before he had a chance to open the cover of the sketch pad, and she watched his smile fade.

He looked away from her, then lowered himself to the chair by his easel in a silent slump, sketch pad askew on his lap.

"I know you're neglecting your other subjects and responsibilities, Jesse." She stood above him, arms folded, voice stern. She felt like an old schoolmarm. "It's so important that you keep up with your schoolwork. I don't want you to help me here if it's interfering with your regular studies." This was not quite the truth. Yes, she wanted him to do well, but she would miss his help—she'd miss *him*—if he no longer came to the warehouse each day. She would miss his passion.

"Don' care 'bout school," he muttered, then raised his gaze to her. "I'm gonna drop out and I'll jest help you here ever' day."

"Oh, no you won't," she said, lowering her arms to her sides. "You can't drop out. You have too much promise, Jesse. You need to finish high school and graduate and then go to college where you can study art." Even as she said the words, she knew what she was describing was a pipe dream. First, according to Mrs. Furman, his grades in all his other subjects would never get him into college. Second, he surely came from a poor family. How could they afford to send him away to school? Third, where could a colored boy go to study art?

Jesse said nothing, just sat there staring at the unopened sketchbook on his knees.

"I'd like to come by your house and speak to your parents about this," Anna said. His parents needed to know that their son was shirking his responsibilities at school and that, if he'd only apply himself, he might have a future in art. "When would be a good time for me to stop by?"

She expected the proposal to alarm him, but it had the opposite effect. He lifted his face to hers with a grin. "Mama wants to meet you, actu'lly," he said. "She said to ask you to come to Sunday dinner, but I didn't think you'd wanna do that so I didn't say nothin'."

She was surprised. "Well, then, that's perfect," she said after a moment. "Please tell your mother thank you, and I'd be delighted to come."

Chapter 33

———— ❧ ————

MORGAN

July 10, 2018

I stared at the scarred section of the mural near the lumberjack's cheek, uncertain what color Anna Dale had intended to paint the forested background in that area. The paint was horribly abraded in the trees, and there were hundreds of places just like it throughout the mural. Thousands, probably. Places where I'd have to guess. To rely on my best judgment. The realization made me anxious. I didn't know what I was doing, and I didn't want to bother Oliver before every single brushstroke I had to make.

He was still working near me in the foyer and I was glad, and not just because I still needed his guidance. I liked his calm, quiet company. Crates of artwork for the gallery arrived daily now, and he'd carefully open each one, peel back layer after layer of protective padding, and check the contents over with a fine-tooth comb while making notes about it on the clipboard he carried around with him. Then he'd package the painting up again to take it to the temperature-controlled storage building where he was keeping the work until the gallery was ready. The elaborate security system was now in place and it wouldn't be long before the display rooms were painted, the humidification system up and running, and the rooms ready to be filled with art.

When he wasn't dealing with the art, Oliver was busy writing the wall texts that would go beside each piece. I knew he was particularly stewing over what he'd write for Anna's mural. What could you say about a puzzle that had no answers?

Just like the blank spot near the lumberjack's cheek. I stared at it a while longer as though the answer might magically come to me. Finally I gave in and turned to Oliver.

"I can't figure out what should go here," I said.

Without a word, he set down the box he was opening, stood up, and joined me in front of the mural. He chewed his lip as he appraised the abraded area. Then he pointed to another spot in the lumberjack's section of the mural.

"Look at the way she treated similar areas," he said. "That'll help you figure out what she intended."

I studied the way Anna had used color to bring out the depth of the forest. She really had been a staggeringly good artist. "She always goes dark," I said. "She always goes for red. That deep blackish red, wherever she can. Even here in the trees."

"That 'dried-blood' red." Oliver smirked. "Her signature color."

I elbowed him, laughing. "Exactly," I said.

I expected him to walk back to his folding table, but he stood still, and I felt his gaze on me. I turned to look at him, breathing in that enticing leathery scent he seemed to carry with him.

"You have such a good eye, Morgan," he said. "Trust yourself a bit more."

He did return to his worktable then, and I began mixing paint, but my mind was still on him. I thought I was sort of falling in love with him. He seemed so much older than me, and so different. Bob Dylan? Really? But where I'd seen a nerdiness in him only a few weeks ago, I now saw an intelligence. Where I'd seen a straight-arrow rule follower, now I saw a maturity I wished I could emulate. And where I saw the smooth, slightly pink skin of his cheeks . . . well, there were moments when I wanted to press my lips against that skin, just to see what it would feel like. The thought sent a surprising jolt to the pit of my stomach, and I returned my attention to my work, smiling to myself as I carefully brushed Anna's "signature color" into the trees.

It was dark by the time I walked home that evening. I felt no fear walking through Edenton's downtown at night. The town seemed idyllic to me, a charming water-bound haven that was easing the hypervigilance that had been my companion in prison. I no longer looked over my shoulder as I walked. I no longer tightened my fists when I was out in the open, ready to defend myself.

Lisa's car was gone when I reached the house. I took a bath in the walk-in bathtub that had been installed for Jesse, then headed for the sunroom. In the hall, I passed a small framed medallion I had never truly noticed before. I stopped to look at it, gasping when I realized what it was. The National Medal of Arts. I knew Jesse had been awarded the medal at some time, but it never occurred to me that the actual bronze medallion was here, just a few yards from where I slept each night. I read the inscription on the plaque beneath it.

**Presented by President Barack Obama to Jesse Jameson Williams
on this day, August 5, 2012**

Oh my God. *August 5?* Was this the reason Jesse wanted the gallery to open on that date? To commemorate his receiving the National Medal of Arts? If that was the case, the medal was more important to him than it appeared to be, hanging in the hallway here between the sunroom and bathroom. We needed to move it to the gallery.

We.

I stunned myself as the pronoun passed through my mind. *We.* Not *they.* The gallery was no longer simply my job. My mere ticket out of prison. It had become more to me than that.

Carefully, I lifted the framed medallion from the wall and carried it into the kitchen. I propped it up against the fruit bowl on the island, then wrote a note for Lisa. *Check out the date! We need to hang it in the gallery.*

Then, with a smile on my face, I went to bed.

Chapter 34

ANNA

January 28, 1940

Following the directions Jesse had given her, Anna drove into the countryside, imagining what her afternoon with the Williams family would
be like. Sunday dinner would be at three o'clock because they apparently
spent the entire morning and early afternoon at church. Anna hoped they
didn't ask her about her own churchgoing habits—or lack thereof. She
felt nervous about this visit. What right did she have to tell a mother and
father how they should handle their son?

She expected that they would be very poor, like so many colored families. She pictured their farm on a small plot of land. Perhaps they were
sharecroppers and their home little more than a rundown shack. She
needed to prepare herself to feel even more like a fish out of water than
she already did in Edenton.

As soon as she pulled into the long driveway of the white, two-story
farmhouse, she knew her expectations had been wrong. She had faulty

preconceived notions about people, just like everyone else, she thought. She had prejudgments. She had prejudices.

The house was not huge by any means, but it was not a shack, either. On either side of it stretched fields, fallow now for the winter. A truck and a wagon were parked on one side of the house, a dusty black sedan on the other. She stopped her Ford in the driveway and dogs appeared from no-where to greet her as she got out of the car. Four of them clustered around her, barking, tails wagging. They seemed friendly enough and she held out her hand for them to sniff. Jesse came out of the house, screen door slapping closed behind him, and told the dogs to hush.

"Dinner's near ready," he said in greeting. "Come on inside."

She followed him up the steps to the front porch. This close, Anna could see that the house needed painting and some of the railings on the porch were splintering, but she would have to say that Jesse's house was in no worse shape than Miss Myrtle's for having gone through some rough economic years.

The front door led almost immediately into the kitchen, where three women bustled around the stove and the counters, and the air seemed thick with cooking smells both savory and pungent. Anna's mouth in-stantly watered.

One of the women worked over a frying pan filled with something that popped and sizzled on the stove. She lifted her head in Anna's direction with a half smile. "I'm Jesse's mama, ma'am," she said. Anna was surprised by the woman's light skin and silky black hair tucked behind her ears in waves. The woman could probably pass for white if she chose to. She was definitely Jesse's mother, though, no doubt about it. Her eyes were like his: round, dark, and beautiful. "We about to put dinner on the table," she said. "Glad you could join us. Jesse, you git washed up now."

"Yes, Mama," Jesse said, and he disappeared from the kitchen.

"Thank you for inviting me." Anna felt awkward standing there empty-handed while the three women worked. One of them set down the knife she was using, wiped her hands on her apron, and took a few steps toward her.

"I'm Jesse's aunt Jewel," she said. She was a pretty woman with skin the same rich shade as Jesse's, almond-shaped eyes, and coarse hair smoothed back into a bun. The woman's smile struck Anna as serene, as though nothing in the world could fluster her, and she liked her instantly. "Jesse's told us about what y'all are working on," Aunt Jewel continued. "It's all he talks about these days. And he loves those books you got for him to borrow." Aunt Jewel looked at the third woman in the kitchen who was whipping something in a large beige crock. "Dodie?" she prompted. "Say hello to our guest?"

The woman stilled her hands and looked up from the bowl, and Anna saw that she was really a girl, no more than eighteen or nineteen. She had a boxy build, a narrow dark face, and an expression that was either tired or bored.

"Hey," the girl said.

"Hi, Dodie," Anna said, but Dodie had already returned her attention to her task.

"Jesse's sister," Aunt Jewel said.

"Ah," Anna said.

"We're ready." Jesse's mother lifted a platter of fried chicken from the counter and walked past Anna into the next room.

Soon, Anna was sitting with the entire family at a large table in a spacious dining room. The table looked hundreds of years old with wood so dark and silky that Anna couldn't resist running her fingers over it. She was seated between Jesse's mother and Aunt Jewel, while across from her, Jesse's eight-year-old sister Nellie sat flanked by Jesse and Dodie. The little girl shared those round doe eyes with her mother and Jesse.

Mr. Williams sat at the table's head. A bespectacled man with black hair salted with gray, he hadn't yet offered her more than a grunt in greeting. Was he the sort of man who never smiled, or did his grim expression have to do with her presence? She hoped none of the Williams family had read Thursday's paper, which had printed a letter to the editor from Theresa's father, Riley Wayman. The letter was about Anna and was quite bitter. Riley Wayman said that Anna Dale didn't understand Edenton's "mores," and what was she thinking, having a young male colored student working with his daughter in a "seedy, decrepit warehouse"? He went on to blame the government for "hiring this outsider" when Edenton already had a "perfectly fine and willing painter" right in town. Et cetera, et cetera. If anyone in the Williams family had seen the letter, no one was mentioning it.

The meal began with a lengthy grace, perhaps inspired, Anna thought, by the family's very long morning at church. Jesse's father had some of the preacher in him. He sat at the head of the table and thanked the Lord for everything under the sun, including Anna, which surprised and touched her. Then they began passing the food. Fried chicken, whipped potatoes, a bowl of some sort of greens, corn, and canned tomatoes. Every bit of it came right from the farm, Jesse told her.

"Really!" Anna said. She wondered if the chicken she was eating had been running around the Williams's yard a few hours earlier. "That's amazing."

"What's so 'mazin' 'bout that?" Nellie asked, looking up from her plate where she'd been playing with her food more than she'd been eating it. She was a tiny, adorable child who looked closer to six than eight. Her hair was in short braids, so many of them that they nearly formed a halo around her head. She had absolutely no knowledge of how to behave with company, which led her to say funny and inappropriate things that made Anna laugh. Except for Jesse, Anna felt more at ease with the little girl than with anyone else at the table.

"Don't be so rude," Dodie said to the child in response to her question. Dodie struck Anna as sullen and quiet, and Anna wondered if she was always that way or if it was her presence that brought out that side of the girl. Was it as odd for them to have a white woman at their table as it was for her to be there? It felt strange to be the different one in the group, she thought. Being different could lead to paranoia. She kept wondering, *Are they saying that or acting that way because I'm white or is this the way they always are?* Silly thinking, she decided, and not very useful.

"Not many farms up north, I guess?" Jesse's mother asked.

"Oh, yes, there are plenty of farms up north," Anna said. "As a matter of fact, New Jersey, where I live, is called the 'Garden State.' But I live in a town not too far from New York City. We get our food from the grocery store."

"You're a city girl for sure," Aunt Jewel said with a smile. She struck Anna as the sharp blade in the family. The smart one. Well, perhaps they were all smart, but Anna thought Jewel must be better educated than Jesse's parents. She spoke better English and there was something more worldly about her. Anna remembered Jesse telling her that his aunt was a midwife for the colored community. She'd probably been educated as a nurse, then. Maybe Aunt Jewel would be the one to understand why Jesse's talent needed to be nurtured.

Anna felt Nellie's gaze riveted on her and she caught the girl's eye and smiled.

"You so pretty," Nellie said. "I wish I had hair like that. And your eyelashes." She touched her own lashes. "Yours is so thick."

"Well, I think your hair is adorable in all those little braids," Anna said.

"You got a piece of collard in your teeth," Nellie said, pointing to her own two front teeth.

"Don't be so rude!" Dodie said again.

"No, that's fine." Anna laughed, then worked the offending piece of collard free with her tongue. She regretted taking so many collards onto her plate. She'd never eaten them before and hoped never to eat them again. "Thank you for telling me, Nellie," she said.

"And you know what else?" Nellie asked.

"Nellie . . ." her mother warned.

Nellie ignored her. "Dodie stole some of Mama's toilet water when she went out last night."

"Did not," Dodie said. "I *borrowed* it."

"How you gonna give it back?" Nellie sniped.

Jesse put his arm around his little sister. "Why you wanna stir things up?" he asked her, his voice soft, and the little girl's eyes instantly filled.

"I dunno." She sounded suddenly remorseful, and Jesse gave her shoulders a squeeze. The tenderness in his gesture moved Anna. She had the feeling Jesse looked out for this little girl who didn't seem to have the self-control to look out for herself.

Anna decided to shift the conversation with what she hoped was a neutral question. "How long has this land been in your family?" she asked, which set Mrs. Williams and Aunt Jewel off on a long story of the family's history. For the most part, Mr. Williams stayed out of it, continuing his quiet observation of the goings-on, even though it was his lineage being discussed. Anna learned that Mr. Williams's grandfather had been promised land when he was freed from slavery, but that land had been taken away from him, and he and his family had had to work as sharecroppers for many years before they could afford to buy a small parcel of land for themselves. They faced all kinds of hardships—some of them the same sort that white farmers would face, like drought, but they also faced hatred and prejudice that made it hard for them to hang on to the farm. Now, though, Mr. Williams and his whole extended family—sisters and brothers and cousins and the list of relatives went on and on—all owned bits and pieces of the fields surrounding the house. Jesse pointed this way and that as they described land belonging to their many cousins. It sounded like holding on to the land was an ongoing battle for all of them. Anna got the feeling that while Jesse's family was not poor, they had to work very hard to hang on to everything they had.

"I'm sorry it's been such a rough road for your families," she said.

"Oh, we fine now," Jesse's mother said. She looked at Anna and drew in a long breath that signaled a serious change of topic. "Jesse tol' us you was a old lady," she said. "He say we don't have nothin' to worry about, him workin' with you, but you ain't no ol' lady."

Mr. Williams tilted his head in his wife's direction at the change of topic, but still said nothing, and Anna tried to set her mind at ease. "I'm twenty-two," she said. "Jesse is very talented and I want to help him grow to be a good artist. But I'm concerned—"

"Don't matter what your intent or his intent be," his mother said. "People see things where there ain't nothin' to see."

Maybe Mrs. Williams *had* seen Mr. Wayman's letter, after all. Anna understood her worry. Miss Myrtle told her colored men—and boys—had been beaten and even lynched for getting a bit too close to white women. "That's all in the past, though," Miss Myrtle had said. "That hardly ever happens at all anymore, and certainly not in Edenton."

Anna imagined Jesse's parents didn't want their son to be Edenton's first.

⋙·⋘

After dinner, Nellie wanted to show Anna around the farm. They put on their coats and walked together—Anna being careful where she stepped—and Nellie held her hand the whole time. They visited the barn and the mules and the kittens—all of whom Nellie had named—and the chicken coop. As they headed back to the house, Nellie said, "Can you come every Sunday?" endearing her to Anna forever. She was a lovable child.

When they returned to the house, they were greeted by Jesse, his parents, and Aunt Jewel, who asked Anna to join them in the living room.

Finally! They would get down to the business of her visit.

The living room was large and homey, filled with handmade quilts folded neatly on the arm of nearly every chair, a braided rug in the center of the floor, and a large gray sofa. A fire crackled in the fireplace, and photographs of Jesse and his sisters, as well as children Anna didn't recognize, covered one of the walls. She took a seat on the sofa, the cushion nearly swallowing her, it was so soft. She could tell from the atmosphere in the room that they were about to get down to brass tacks.

Jesse's father finally spoke, taking the lead. "Jesse says you worried about him not stayin' in school," he said, "but I tell you, ain't nobody gone all the way through high school in this family."

Without thinking, Anna glanced at Aunt Jewel, who smiled.

"Not even me," Aunt Jewel said, surprising her.

"Jesse got farther'n anybody," his father said, "and we're right proud of him. But we can use him on the farm, so if he's ready to leave school, that's fine by us."

"But I'd like to see him go to art school somewhere," Anna said, keeping her voice even. "And it will be easier for him to get in if he has a high school diploma."

"Art school?" Mr. Williams smiled as though she'd amused him. "That's some mighty high thinkin' for a farm boy. The farm's where he belong."

"I don't want to see his talent—" She was about to say "wasted," but caught herself. It would be the same as telling this family their farmwork had no value. "I want him to be able to develop his artistic skills," she said instead. The thought of Jesse being stuck on the farm for the rest of his life distressed her terribly. "He's immensely talented," she said. "Far more talented than I am." She looked across the room to see Jesse studying his hands in his lap. She knew him well enough, though, that she could tell he was holding back a smile at her words.

"We know he's talented." Jesse's mother spoke up. "But Daddy's right. We need him at home. He the only boy. And if he ain't in school, he should be here helpin' and not workin' on that picture of yours, either."

Oh, dear, Anna thought. Not only was Jesse going to quit school but she was about to lose him in the warehouse as well.

"Let the boy keep workin' with Miz Anna on the picture." Aunt Jewel spoke up, and she said it forcefully, as if she were the one to have the final say on the subject. "It's not doing any harm and it'll come to an end soon enough, right?" She looked at Anna for confirmation.

"In a few months, yes," Anna said, relieved by her support.

So, that was that. Thanks to Aunt Jewel, Jesse would continue working with her, but he was finished with school.

That night, Anna got down on her knees to pray, the first prayer she could remember uttering in a long time.

Dear Lord, she said, *don't let this young man's talent go to waste.*

Chapter 35

———— ❦ ————

MORGAN

July 11, 2018

I t's a stretch." Oliver frowned as he studied the framed medallion in my hands. "Why would Jesse tie the opening of the gallery to the date he received the National Medal of Arts? I mean, why tie it so . . . *obstinately* to that date?"

"That's what Lisa said," I admitted, setting the frame down on Oliver's table in the foyer. Lisa had been unimpressed with my discovery. "Do you think the date is just a coincidence, then?" I asked Oliver. "Do you think he just pulled August fifth out of the air?"

"That's as good a guess as any."

I looked down at the medallion. "I guess it doesn't matter," I said. "We're stuck with August fifth, one way or another. Lisa already sent out the invitations, so that's that."

I looked over at the mural, wondering how far I'd be able to get on it today. One thing was certain: I wasn't getting anywhere on it by standing there talking to Oliver, so I gave up thinking about the medallion and walked toward the mural, my gaze on the lumberjack's wrinkled pants, my task for the day.

⇒✦⇐

I was working alone in the foyer shortly after lunch when Oliver came into the room from the hallway, lowering his phone from his ear. I could tell with one glance at his face that something was wrong. His jaw was tight, his eyes staring unseeing into the distance.

I set down my palette. "What's the matter?" I asked.

He looked over at me, a surprised expression on his face as though he'd forgotten I was there. "Nothing," he said. "Why do you ask?"

"Your face," I said. "You look . . . worried. Upset."

He took in a breath and blew it out, no longer looking at me. "Just my son," he said finally, holding up his phone as if Nathan were inside it.

"What about him?" I asked, although I was afraid I knew.

He hesitated. Looked at his phone. Then he leaned back against the folding table, arms folded across his chest.

"He just told me he doesn't want to go to Smith Mountain Lake with me this year," he said. "He'd rather spend the time with his mother and stepfather in Disney World."

I heard the hurt in his voice. "Oh, I'm sorry," I said, surprised by the twist of pain I felt in my own chest, seeing his disappointment. He'd been so looking forward to the time with his son. "But I don't think you have it exactly right," I added.

He raised his eyebrows. "No?"

"Nathan talked to me about it that day you sent us to get lunch."

"He did?" He looked puzzled. Maybe a little hurt. "Why didn't you tell me?"

I sat down on the chair next to the mural. I felt guilty. Maybe I should have told him. "He wasn't sure of his decision then," I said. "I was hoping he'd end up going with you. And it didn't feel like my place to say anything. I thought he needed to tell you himself."

Oliver hesitated, then nodded. "True," he finally agreed. "So how don't I have it exactly right?"

"Because you think he's picking his mother and stepfather over you, but that's not it at all, Oliver. He's picking Disney World over the lake." I smiled at him with sympathy. "Any kid would. I would have given anything to go to Disney World when I was Nathan's age."

Oliver unfolded his arms and looked down at the phone in his hand as if he could see Nathan's image there. He let out a heavy sigh. "You know, I'm glad for Stephanie. Nathan's mother," he said. "She deserves a happy marriage. But . . . and I feel small about this . . . her husband makes about ten times what I make, and Nathan's at an age where that matters. His stepdad can give him anything he wants." He gave me a weak smile. "I know on the deepest level that shouldn't matter, but it does."

I was touched that he was confiding in me and I hurt for him. "I think he's so lucky to have you as a dad," I said.

He let out a small laugh. "Well, thanks for saying that," he said. "And I'm sorry to lay my problems on you," he said. "You just caught me at a weak moment."

"A *human* moment," I said. "You seem so perfect all the time that I'm glad to see you're mortal like everybody else."

"Oh, I'm mortal all right." He slipped his phone into the pocket of his jeans and stepped away from the table. "And I guess we'd better get back to work."

I nodded, but as I stood up to reach for my palette, he spoke again.

"Were your parents divorced, Morgan?" he asked.

I looked at my palette but didn't pick it up. "No," I said, raising my gaze to him again. He looked sincerely interested in my answer, blue eyes serious. "But they should have been."

"That bad, huh?"

I let out a breath. "You have no idea." I felt danger creeping in. A tight-
ness in my throat that told me I was going to fall apart if I talked about
the past. I was too tired. Too vulnerable. And yet, Oliver stood there with
those kind blue eyes, and he looked so ready to listen. "My parents were
alcoholics," I said.

"Ah," he said. "You learned from the masters?"

I nodded. "Not just that. They . . . I was their only child and they didn't
know how to be parents. They sucked at it, frankly. They were madly,
sloppily, drunkenly, disgustingly in love with each other and had nothing
left over for—" *Oh, shit.* I was going to lose it.

"Hey," he said, a worried expression on his face. "I'm sorry. I didn't realize it was such a touchy subject."

I sat down again, the muscles in my legs starting to quiver. I was surprised I was telling him about my growing-up years. I rarely spoke to
anyone about my family. "The only attention I ever got from them was
negative attention," I said. "'You want to be an artist? You don't have the
talent to be any good at it, and you'll never make any money at it, and
don't come running to us when you're broke and living on the street.'" I
looked down at my hands where they were locked together in my lap, my
knuckles white. "They'd forget to pick me up after school sometimes, and
they'd have these screaming, crying fights with each other. When I was
little, I tried to get between them. Get them to stop fighting. When I
was older, I just hid in my room." I shivered with the memory. Sometimes
I thought one of them might kill the other. Sometimes I actually wished
that would happen. "They'd have friends over and everyone would get
puking drunk and they'd expect me to clean up after them," I said. I remembered my mother calling to me from her bedroom, asking me in her
fake sweet voice to bring her the basin. I couldn't have been any older
than Nathan. I pretended not to hear her, burying my head beneath my
pillow. "My parents never told me they loved me, Oliver," I said. "Not *ever.*
Not once. You tell Nathan, don't you?"

"Of course. All the time."

"He's a lucky kid," I said. "He's surrounded by grown-ups who love him."

Oliver stood up and walked over to me, pulling a handkerchief from his pants pocket. He handed it to me, and I burst out laughing as I got to my feet.

"What's so funny?" he asked.

"You actually carry a handkerchief?" I asked. "I think you're the only guy I know under fifty who carries a handkerchief." I blotted my eyes, and when I handed the handkerchief back to him, he was smiling at me.

"Aren't you glad I had it?" he asked.

I nodded. Rubbed my nose with the back of my hand. "You know," I said, "Nathan's a kid. Maybe he shouldn't get to make this sort of decision on his own."

Oliver shrugged. "It's not a big deal," he said. "I get him for Christmas this year. He and I can take a trip somewhere then. It was just the . . . the kick in the gut that got to me."

Impulsively, I reached out to hug him. "I would have given anything to have a dad like you," I said softly, my lips against his shoulder. The muscle and bone of his back felt good beneath my arms. I hadn't touched another person this way in well over a year.

He squeezed me gently, then let go. "Thanks for putting everything into perspective for me," he said. "And I'm sorry for what you dealt with as a kid. You act tough, but you're pretty soft inside, aren't you." It wasn't a question.

"I'm fine," I said, and at that moment, I *did* feel fine. Fine, and something more. I was standing so close to Oliver, and I had a sudden urge to run the back of my finger over his cheek, the place that was always a little pink. When I first met him, I thought those pink cheeks gave him a boyish look. This close, though, I could see the gray shadow of his beard beneath his skin, the cut of his cheekbones, the sharp angle of his chin. He seemed anything but boyish at that moment, and as I turned back to my mural, I was surprised by a sudden pang of desire.

Chapter 36

———— ✦ ————

ANNA

February 1, 1940

Today was the day they would stretch the canvas, the chore more intimidating than Anna had imagined. Fortunately, she thought, she had lots of help. Jesse and Peter, of course. Then Pauline arrived with Karl in tow, dressed in his police uniform and carrying a toolbox that she knew would prove invaluable. He looked so handsome. Anna hated to see him get the knees of his pants covered in sawdust from the warehouse floor, but he got down on the filthy floor, seemingly without a care. Anna felt some envy of Pauline as she watched Karl set to work with her young helpers. Someday she'd find a man with whom she wanted to build a future, she thought. For now, though, she was married to her mural.

Pauline wore her usual skirt, blouse, and hose, so Anna knew she wouldn't be much help with the stretcher, but she cheered everyone on from one of the chairs near the paint table. Anna, Karl, and the boys ignored the cold of the concrete floor as they knelt and sat and twisted to tack the canvas to the frame. Anna used the hammer a bit, but was careful not to place the tacks too deeply. The tacks would have to be removed when the mural was complete, and the thought of digging those tacks out again with the claw end of the hammer wasn't pleasant.

They were about a third of the way through the task when a knock came on the warehouse door.

"Come in!" Anna called from the floor, but the door was already opening and in a second, Martin Drapple stood grinning inside the warehouse.

"How can I help?" he asked.

Anna sat back on her heels, frankly relieved to see him. She could tell that even with four of them, it was going to be a chore to properly get the canvas on the stretcher. Besides, Martin would know what he was doing better than any of them. She thought it was very generous of him to come.

"Thank you!" she called across the space, her voice echoing against the walls and the beams of the ceiling. "Do you know Pauline and Karl, Martin?"

Martin walked toward them, nodding at Pauline as he passed her. "Nice to meet you," he said. "And I've met Karl a time or two."

Karl looked up from the stretcher. "Grab a handful of tacks," he said in greeting, and Anna thought there was an uncharacteristic cool edge to his voice. She wondered exactly where the men had met "a time or two."

—⫸•⫷—

An hour later, they had nearly finished tacking the canvas in place when the door to the warehouse suddenly flew open. Anna looked up to see Mrs. Drapple practically fly into the room, the skirt of her green dress whipping behind her. She wore a pink apron over the dress and no coat, although it had to be thirty-five degrees outside. Her blond hair was loose around her shoulders. Anna had only seen her once before—during that nasty altercation on the library steps, when Mrs. Drapple wore a scarf and gave her a terrible chewing-out. She'd looked old and haggard that day, but now, as she blew into the warehouse with high color in her cheeks and her hair wind tossed, she looked quite beautiful. And quite furious.

"I thought I'd find you here!" she shouted at Martin. She stood near the stretcher, hands in fists at her sides, and all five of them looked up at her in shock. At least, *Anna* was in shock. She was also a little afraid. She felt protective of Jesse and Peter. They were her charges and she simply didn't know what this deranged woman might do. She was aware of Pauline hopping off her chair and backing up against the warehouse wall, out of harm's way. For no good reason whatsoever, Mrs. Drapple's presence made Anna feel guilty, as though she *had* stolen Martin away from her. Or at least, she'd stolen his *time* from her and his family.

Martin stood up from the floor where he'd been working with the canvas. He dusted off his hands and moved toward his wife, almost casually, as though he were not terribly concerned about her intrusion. "What are you doing here?" he asked, quite unkindly.

"What do you think?" she yelled, arms flailing in the air. "I'm looking for my husband, who people tell me is spending his days with *her*!" She pointed in Anna's direction. Anna's hands froze on the stretcher.

Martin laughed, and the sound was mocking. "I'm not spending my days with *anyone*," he said. "I merely stopped in to help out with this canvas."

Karl got to his feet then, looking powerful in his uniform. Authoritarian. Anna was glad he was there. He took a step toward Martin and his wife. "How about the two of you go out—"

"You lost out to her!" Mrs. Drapple jerked her chin toward Anna, who didn't think the woman had heard a word Karl said. "You lost out to a *girl* artist. You ain't near as good as a *girl*, that's what the judges said, and—"

"Shut up!" Martin bellowed, and Anna's heart began to pound. "This isn't your business!"

Anna hadn't seen this side of Martin. He'd been kind to her. Good-natured. She hadn't known this angry side existed, but his wife had clearly hit his tender spot. How galling it must have been for him to lose the contest to a female!

"How is this not my business when you're here with this tramp instead of trying to find work to feed your children?" Mrs. Drapple yelled.

He slapped her. *Hard.* It happened so fast that it took a moment for it to register in Anna's mind. She heard Pauline gasp and knew her friend was as horrified as she was.

"You fucking bastard!" Mrs. Drapple kicked Martin in the leg. He grabbed her by the shoulders and started shaking her, her hair flying through the air like a spray of golden glitter.

"Hey, hey!" Karl said. He was next to them in a flash.

Instinctively, Anna got to her feet and stood protectively in front of Jesse and Peter where they remained on the floor, stunned, their hands still on the stretcher.

Karl's air of authority seemed to wake the Drapples up from their personal battle, and Martin withdrew his hands from his wife's shoulders.

"Go home," Karl said, his voice quiet but commanding. "Both of you. Go home. Make up."

Martin and his wife were already moving toward the door, red faced and shouting at each other as though no one else were there. Anna could imagine what their home life was like. Their poor daughters! Martin slammed the door behind them as they left, and a hush fell over the warehouse. All of their gazes were on the door, and Anna's heart still pounded out of proportion to what had just happened.

"Oh my," Pauline said finally as she dropped back into her chair.

"She call you a *tramp?*" Jesse said, looking up at Anna from the floor with a sort of disbelief in his brown doe eyes. "She sure 'nough got that wrong."

She was touched by his defense. *You're a love,* she thought, but did not say. "Sticks and stones may hurt my bones," she said instead, not bothering to finish the rhyme.

"Well." Karl knelt at the side of the stretcher again, his complexion ruddy but his hands steady. "Let's get back to work here."

Anna wanted to thank him. She considered giving him a quick hug, but thought it inappropriate. She felt that little bit of envy creeping in again. Pauline had a man who was not only handsome and kind, but protective as well. She shook off the emotions—or at least most of them—and lowered herself to the floor again.

She thought about Mrs. Drapple's words as she worked, how Martin had lost out to a girl. It was tough for a girl to even be *considered* an artist much less to win a competition against a man. She felt sorry for him, then, but she thought the sound of that slap was going to echo in the warehouse for a long, long time.

Chapter 37

———— ✦ ————

MORGAN

July 11, 2018

Oliver and I were still at work at nine o'clock when Adam and Wyatt walked through the foyer to the front door. Wyatt stopped and looked over at me.

"We're gonna grab something at the pub down the street," he said. "You two wanna come?"

"No, thanks," I said automatically, but Oliver stood up from his desk and stretched.

"Let's do it," he said across the foyer to me. "I don't know about you, but I've reached the point of diminishing returns here."

I hesitated. The idea of being with Oliver made me feel safe. He knew I couldn't drink. He'd keep the guys from pressuring me. Not that I was worried I'd give in to them or be unable to handle them myself. I just didn't want the hassle.

"Okay," I said, getting up from my chair. Only then did I realize how exhausted I felt, my back and shoulders seizing up on me. "Let me clean up my mess."

Oliver helped me carry my paints and brushes into the kitchen.

"Will this be hard for you?" he asked quietly as we cleaned the brushes.

I shook my head. "No." I smiled at him. "I'll be fine." Would it be hard for me if I didn't have the monitor on my ankle? I hoped not.

We left the gallery, Oliver locking the door behind us. I walked between him and Wyatt. I was the first to speak. "I don't drink," I said, for Adam's and Wyatt's sake. Then I was annoyed with myself. Why did I say that? My whole life had been ruled by alcohol in one way or another. Was I going to let it continue to rule me, even in its absence? I felt Oliver's hand gentle on my back, and I tried to interpret what that meant. *You don't need to explain yourself,* I thought he was saying. Or maybe he just wanted to touch me. I liked that idea better.

"That's cool," Wyatt said, like my admission was no big thing. "They got club soda and whatever."

"Yeah, but they've also got Moscow mules," Adam said. "You at least have to have a sip of mine."

"No, thanks," I said.

"And mojitos," Adam added.

"You're an asshole," Wyatt said to Adam, who only laughed at the insult. He was an imbecile.

Oliver dropped his hand from my back. I missed its warmth.

The pub was crowded and smelled strongly of beer and lime and the mouthwatering scent of grilled beef. There were no empty tables but a few people were leaving the bar and we were able to grab four stools in a row. I made sure to sit next to Oliver, my safety blanket. I'd had nothing to eat since lunch and quickly ordered a burger, as did Oliver, and Adam and Wyatt ordered Moscow mules, which arrived in copper mugs. Oliver ordered a beer and I asked for a Coke. Above the bar, TV screens were showing a repeat of today's World Cup game, which apparently had taken place in Moscow, and the crowd in the pub seemed to find that fact uproariously funny as they toasted with their copper mugs.

The place was too loud for conversation, and that was fine with me. Adam and Wyatt seemed to know nearly everyone. I felt uncomfortable with the noise and the crush of people, many of them banging into us as they walked past. Even when I drank, it hadn't been in a place like this. First of all, I'd been barely old enough to go to a bar by the time I was locked up, so when I drank, it had been at parties with people I knew, people I'd cared about. People I would probably never, ever see again.

I kept my gaze on the TV as I ate. Trey had loved soccer and I followed the game easily. I felt proud of myself: I was watching a game that made me think of Trey and it wasn't bothering me, and although I was surrounded by booze, I was happy to simply enjoy my burger and Coke. It felt like a test, sitting there at the bar, and I was acing it.

Oliver and I had a shouted discussion about what was happening on the soccer field—it was clear he wasn't much of a fan—but we soon gave up and focused on our food. On my other side, a couple of women stood talking to Adam and Wyatt. I couldn't understand a word they said, but I could easily make out the conversation's flirtatious tone.

I'd nearly finished my burger when there was a sudden escalation in the noise behind me. Then male voices, shouting. I looked at the TV. Nothing special happening in the game to merit the clamor.

"Oh, shit, here they go again," Adam shouted in my ear as he pointed over his shoulder.

I turned around to see a couple of men exchanging blows directly behind us. I rolled my eyes. Idiots. The two women standing next to Adam and Wyatt started yelling, holding their drinks in the air to ward off any wild blows from the dueling men. I wanted to leave. I reached into my purse and took a twenty from my wallet. Placed it on the counter next to my plate.

Oliver set his own bills on the bar and leaned toward my ear. "We're

out of here," he said, starting to get up. Just then, the idiotic man closest
to me tossed his drink at one of the others, and I jumped from my stool,
trying to get my ankle and its monitor out of harm's way. I moved too
quickly. The stool toppled over behind me, catching my right ankle—the
one without the monitor—in one of the rungs, twisting it hard enough
to make me scream as I fell to the floor. The men never stopped fighting.
They were so damn drunk. *God, I hate drunks,* I thought. Wyatt and Oliver
were instantly next to me on the floor, helping me up, while Adam ex-
tracted my foot from the rungs of the stool. All three of them were talking
to me, but I couldn't hear a word they said for the cacophony.

Once I was on my feet, Oliver took my hand and cleared a path for us
through the sea of revelers, leaving Adam and Wyatt behind. I kept up
with him, hoping against hope that my monitor was clean and dry.

Outside, I felt a welcome blanket of thick midsummer-night air wrap
around me, the craziness inside the bar nothing more than a hum now.

"What a zoo!" Oliver said, and I could see him shake his head in the
light from the streetlamp. "Are you okay?"

"I'm fine." I bent over and lifted the leg of my jeans to see if my monitor was unscathed, but it was too dark to tell. Bending like that, though, I
suddenly became aware of pain in my right ankle, the one that had been
caught in the rungs of the barstool. It was just enough of a twinge to make
me yelp.

"What's wrong?" Oliver asked.

"Caught my ankle in the bar stool when I fell," I said. "It's okay, I think."

"Can you walk? We can head back to the gallery and I'll give you a ride
to Lisa's."

I nodded and we started walking. We talked about how the inpainting
was going on the mural and the challenge Oliver was having as he wrote
the text for it, since Anna Dale's reasons for adding her oddities to the
painting were unknown. I could barely concentrate on the conversation,
though. Every time I put my weight on my right foot, I winced, and by the
time we reached the corner, I could go no farther.

"Sorry," I said, coming to a stop. I leaned against a lamppost, balancing on my left foot and right toe. "I don't think I can make it to the gallery."

He looked down as if he could see my ankle beneath the leg of my jeans. "Wait here and I'll get my van." He touched my bare arm. The softest, quickest of touches, yet it made my knees turn to mush and I held on to the lamppost to keep myself upright. And as I watched him break into a jog as he headed up the dark sidewalk toward the gallery, I felt the slightest twinge of danger. I'd given my heart to one man and look how that had turned out. Right now, I needed a friend more than a lover. I would have to keep that in mind.

Chapter 38

———— ✦ ————

ANNA

February 13–17, 1940

Anna received a letter from the Section very quickly after she sent them the photographs of the cartoon. They seemed to be in as big a rush as she was. Mr. Rowan shared a few complaints about how fat one of her Tea Party ladies was (Miss Myrtle), and the too-slender build of her lumberman, as well as a few other minor things she could easily fix to his liking. She immediately set about trimming Miss Myrtle down and beefing lumberman Frank up on the cartoon until she thought she'd reached perfection.

Along with the letter from Mr. Rowan came Anna's second payment, which she took immediately to the bank. She loved looking in her little bankbook to see the money she'd earned all on her own. Fortunately, she made it in and out of the bank without bumping into Theresa's father and bank president Riley Wayman. That had been a relief.

She spent most of the day carefully pricking the holes along the outline of her cartoon drawing with a dressmaker's wheel she borrowed from Miss Myrtle, while Jesse and Peter watched in fascination until boredom set in and they resumed work on their own paintings. They had each painted twice over the canvases she'd given them, and she'd ordered them a couple more now that she had a little pocket money to spend. They would be able to start fresh once those canvases arrived, and keep the work they liked.

Once she'd finished with the dressmaker's wheel, the boys helped her tack the cartoon over the canvas. Trying to get it square was a challenge, but the three of them finally succeeded. A few townspeople stopped by to see how things were coming along, including Mayor Sykes and Mr. Fiering from the cotton mill. Anna was excited and nervous; tomorrow she would pounce the design directly onto the canvas, and once that was done, she'd finally start painting. She felt as though she'd been in Edenton for a year rather than two and a half months. She couldn't wait to see her design come to life.

⇒•⇐

The following day—and despite the date on the calendar—the weather was springlike and Anna and the boys opened three of the garage doors, the fourth being stuck beyond use. People seemed to have gotten the word and began showing up at the warehouse, parking cars and bicycles on the weedy earth next to the dirt road. They were shy at first, milling around outside the big garage doors, but once Anna welcomed them, they entered in a rush.

Anna had sewn a little cheesecloth bag and filled it with charcoal dust. She held it up in front of the cartoon and explained to her visitors what she was about to do with it. She was giving them a little art lesson, she thought, and she had her guests' rapt attention. There were perhaps eighteen or twenty people in the warehouse, watching and listening. She recognized several of them. Miss Myrtle, of course, and one of her friends. A clerk from the market. A couple of men she didn't know. The photographer from the paper. He stood front and center, his camera flashing in her face every few minutes.

She began pouncing the cheesecloth bag over the cartoon, climbing up and down the ladder to reach the various parts of the design. She knew it was difficult for some of the people to really see the cartoon and what she was doing, but they stood riveted, patiently waiting for the end result.

Jesse's aunt Jewel and little Nellie arrived when Anna was about halfway through. They stood in the back, but Anna insisted they come up front next to Jesse so Nellie would be able to see, and no one made a fuss. This was Anna's space and she could have whoever she wanted in her audience. She let Nellie do some of the low pouncing herself, hoping Mrs. Williams wouldn't be annoyed that her daughter's fingers and pinafore got a bit of charcoal dust on them. Nellie seemed to enjoy performing in front of the crowd, even taking a cute curtsy once she was finished. Maybe there would end up being *two* artists in the Williams family.

When Anna finally completed the pouncing, Jesse and Peter helped her remove the cartoon and everyone cheered when they saw the outline of the drawing on the canvas. The photographer had Anna and the boys pose with the canvas for the newspaper. Then the crowd slowly trickled out of the warehouse, Jesse and Peter along with them.

"It's Valentine's Day, Miz Dale," Peter informed her with a wink as they sauntered out, and she guessed both boys had special girls they wanted to see. She watched them leave with a smile, and although she was left alone in the warehouse, sweeping up charcoal dust like Cinderella, she felt as content as she'd ever felt in her life.

⇥•⇤

Anna arrived at the warehouse Saturday morning to find that someone had painted the words NIGGER LOVER in huge red letters on the side of the building by the door. A wave of nausea moved through her and she pressed her hands to her mouth. Who had done it? Had it been someone from the crowd who'd watched her pounce the cartoon on Wednesday? Someone who stood there with ugliness in his heart while she'd giddily, naïvely, happily gone about her tasks with Peter and Jesse helping her?

She hated the thought of Jesse arriving that morning and seeing those words in a place he'd come to feel comfortable and important. She wished she could snap her fingers and make them go away.

As she stood there trying to figure out what to do, she spotted Peter riding his bike up the dirt road toward the warehouse. Then suddenly, a good distance before he reached her, he turned around and headed back the way he'd come.

"Peter!" she called after him, her hands a megaphone around her mouth. She suddenly felt spooked being there alone and wanted someone— anyone but Jesse—with her. She couldn't imagine why Peter was riding away like that. Surely he'd seen the words, though. They were big enough to see from a distance. Maybe he felt the way she did: neither of them wanted to be there when Jesse arrived.

She thought of leaving, nervous about being there by herself, but she wouldn't let whoever had done this frighten her away, especially not today—the day she would begin painting. Steeling herself, she opened the warehouse door, walked inside, and turned on all the lights to illumi-nate every inch of the space.

She was mixing paint a short time later when Jesse showed up. He walked into the warehouse as though he carried the weight of the world on his shoulders. Stopping right inside the door, he slumped heavily against the wall.

"I'm so sorry, Jesse," Anna said.

"Maybe I shouldn't come here," he said. "Daddy says no good can come of it. Maybe he's right."

Anna hesitated. She wanted to say, *No he's not right! You deserve to be here every bit as much as Peter,* but she was worried. A person who wrote such ugly words in the middle of the night might be capable of doing even ug-lier deeds. In that moment, she felt afraid, both for Jesse and herself. She thought back to Wednesday. What must the crowd have thought when Jesse and Peter and Anna displayed such a casual and easy camaraderie between them? Had it been misinterpreted? Did the "lover" on the wall of her warehouse imply something more than the fact that she treated Jesse the way she treated everyone else?

All those thoughts ran through her mind in the seconds after Jesse spoke. Finally, she found her voice.

"Nonsense!" she said. "Let's not let some small-minded fool ruin what we've accomplished here."

They heard the sound of a car on the dirt road and both of them froze, their eyes on the door. Anna's heart climbed into her throat. In a moment, the door opened and Mr. Arndt and Peter stood in the doorway. A can of paint hung from the postmaster's hand, while Peter held two brushes, and Anna let out her breath in relief. She'd thought Peter had been a coward, but he'd only gone to get help. She sent him a look of gratitude.

"You two all right?" Mr. Arndt asked her and Jesse. Anna nodded. Jesse seemed frozen, perhaps still stuck in the moment before as he and Anna imagined who might be driving up the road. Mr. Arndt looked at him. "You stay inside, son," he said. "Me and Peter'll fix this right up." He started to head back out the door, but took a moment to look toward Anna again. "This ain't the real Edenton, Miss Dale," he said, cocking his head in the direction of the exterior wall with its hateful lettering. "I hope you know that."

Anna thought of the lovely people she'd met in Edenton. Jesse and Peter. Miss Myrtle and her maid Freda. Pauline and Karl, and so very many others.

"I do know that," she said.

Jesse helped her mix paint and clean brushes, while Peter and Mr. Arndt undid the damage outside, but there was no denying that they all worked in a wounded silence. Even when the painting outside was finished and Peter joined her and Jesse in the warehouse, they were quiet, and she believed their hearts were still heavy when the three of them finally headed home that night.

Chapter 39

─────※◦※─────

MORGAN

July 11, 2018

Oliver talked me into going to the ER that night, the last place I wanted to be. Emergency rooms would forever remind me of the night of the accident. Plus, I thought he was overreacting, but once we were sitting in the crowded waiting room where I could finally pry my purplish foot out of my blue Birkenstock, I knew he'd been right. My ankle was positively bulbous by then. We were surrounded by people who looked worse off than I did, though, with their bloody bandages and faces contorted with pain, and I knew we were in for a long wait.

Oliver managed to get an ice pack from a nurse, and I sat with my legs across his lap as he held the pack to my bloated ankle. If I held my foot perfectly still, the pain was bearable, but the second I moved it a millimeter left or right, I had to bite my tongue to keep from whimpering.

"I hope it's not broken," I said.

"I think your pain would be even worse," he said. He leaned over my ankles and sniffed.

"What the hell are you doing?" I asked. I would have pulled my feet away from him if the pain wouldn't have killed me.

"Don't smell any booze." He smiled at me. "I think your monitor was spared."

I laughed. "You're crazy," I said. It was a lucky miracle that nothing had spilled on the monitor during the melee. I had an appointment with Rebecca in the morning and didn't know how I'd explain myself if the monitor had gone off.

We were quiet for a moment and I realized I was shivering, though I didn't feel the least bit cold. "I hate this place," I said.

"I doubt there's anyone who actually likes it," he said. "I've spent too much time in emergency rooms myself."

"When did you need the ER?" I'd get him talking about his own experience and skip right over mine.

"I've never needed one for myself, but Nathan was another matter," he said. "Asthma attacks as a little kid, too many times to count. When he was two he ate a bunch of glass beads Stephanie was using to make a necklace. At four, he fell trying to climb over a fence. At six, he was scratched by a neighbor's cat and the scratch got infected. When he was eight, he broke his arm playing soccer, and when he was ten he got whacked in the head by a softball."

I watched his face as he spoke. The way his eyes lit up. The way the corners of his lips lifted into a half smile. "You sparkle when you talk about Nathan," I said.

"I sparkle?" He laughed. His cheeks grew even pinker than usual.

"You do." I smiled in spite of my painful ankle.

"Well, I guess that's not surprising, since he means everything to me." His voice was thick. I knew how much he wished he could have more time with his son. I touched his shoulder. "Such a good father," I said quietly, and his smile turned a little sad. "Every two years," I added.

He frowned at me. "Every two years?" he asked.

"Nathan's been in the ER every two years."

He stared at me. "I honestly hadn't thought of that," he said, then groaned. "And he's only a few months into twelve. I guess I should expect the call any day now."

"Hope not." I smiled.

"So how about you?" he asked. "What's your ER history?"

"Well," I said slowly, remembering. "Just twice. When I was nine, I broke my arm. I fell on a neighbor's brick steps. The neighbor took me home—I was screaming and crying. My mother was three sheets to the wind and she said, 'Oh, she's okay. She'll be fine.' And the neighbor said I should be taken to the ER and my mother said *she* could take me if she was so worried about me."

"You're kidding."

"I wish. So the neighbor took me and they set my arm, and then they sent protective services out to my house the next day, but my mother explained the situation away, and that was that."

Oliver shook his head. "I don't understand parents like that," he said.

"Neither do I." I looked across the waiting room without really seeing anything. "That's one of the reasons I was so hooked on Trey," I said. "His family. I loved them. They were normal." I shook my head at how pathetic that must sound. "They were very kind and loving. I hated losing them."

"Do they know their son lied about driving the night of the accident?" Oliver asked.

I loved hearing those words from his mouth. I loved that he'd believed me about Trey driving. He was the only person who did.

"His parents were really . . . compassionate to me after the accident," I said. His father had said "Anyone can make a mistake" to me as I sat numbly in their living room two days after it happened, the stitches on my forehead burning. "It's what you do about that mistake that matters."

"Eventually, though, I started telling the truth," I said. "That their son had been driving. And of course, like everybody else, they thought I was lying." I'd lost them then. Lost their sympathy. Their love. I lost my place in their hearts, which I'd believed to be so secure. "I'll never know if they actually believed Trey over me," I said. "They acted as though they did. I guess they *had* to. He was their son, and I was not their daughter, much as I wanted to be. I'd become a liability."

Oliver's hands rested on my shins, and he squeezed my left leg through my jeans. "I'm sorry," he said. Then, "So I guess that was your other time in the ER? The accident?"

I hesitated. "Yes," I said.

"You told me you weren't injured."

"Just a scratch." I lifted my bangs to show him the scar. "Five stitches. I got off easy," I said. "But I'd rather not talk about it."

"Gotcha," he said.

We waited another ten minutes in silence before we were finally called back to the treatment area and set up in a curtained cubicle. Oliver stayed there while I was wheeled down the hall for X-rays. When I returned to the cubicle, I was transferred to the examining table while he sat in a chair next to me. A nurse gave me a pill for the pain. We had another long wait, and I became aware of something dire happening in the cubicle next to mine. Doctors and nurses rushed back and forth. Female yelps of pain pierced the air. The sounds took me back to the accident. They took me back to Emily Maxwell's broken body. I pictured a twisted, ruined, bloody body on the other side of the curtain next to me, and I pressed my hands over my ears.

"I think I'm going to be sick," I said. I was shaking convulsively.

Oliver found a basin and a blanket. He spread the blanket over me and put the basin on my lap.

"You *are* a little green," he said.

"I can't stop shaking," I said, my hands on my thighs now.

"It's probably from the medication they gave you."

I shook my head. I knew what was freaking me out. I wished we were in a different cubicle, and I wished they could help that poor woman who was in agony on the other side of the curtain.

"I just need to know how the girl we hurt is doing," I blurted out, surprising myself. I looked at Oliver.

His eyes were serious behind his glasses. "There must be a way to find out," he said.

"I'm sort of afraid to."

"But it sounds like you can't really rest easy until you know. You said you can't find her online?"

I shook my head. "She's not on social media," I said. "Or maybe she is and keeps it all private. Or maybe she's in such bad shape, social media is the last thing on her mind. Or maybe she *has* no mind. Maybe she ended up with brain damage." I squeezed my trembling hands together. "I know she was paralyzed, but who knows what else is wrong with her?" I said. "When I Google her name, I just get the newspaper report of the accident. That's it."

He pressed his lips together as I rambled on, sympathy in his face. Then he reached over and wrapped his hand around both of mine where they were locked together on my lap next to the basin. "I'm so sorry, Morgan," he said.

I looked at him. "Do you know about the ninth step in AA?" I asked.

He hesitated. "Something about forgiveness?"

"Not exactly. It's about making amends." I shuddered. "I think about it a lot, but I don't think I could do it. I don't think I could ever face her."

Oliver let go of my hands as the doctor interrupted us, pulling open the curtain to my cubicle. She greeted us with a smile. "Good news," she said. "No break. Just a grade one sprain. The nurse will be in with a compression bandage and walking boot for you. Ice it. Keep it elevated. Should be good as new in a week or two. I'll write a prescription for the pain."

I shook my head. "I don't want anything for the pain," I said. I wasn't going to trade alcohol for opioids. No, thank you.

She hesitated, her quizzical look giving way to understanding. "Are you in recovery?" she asked.

I nodded. I felt myself blush that Oliver was hearing this, not that it was news to him.

"See how you do with acetaminophen or ibuprofen," she said. "I'll give you the scrip, just in case, and you can talk to your regular doctor about it." She held the slip of paper out to me, but I didn't reach for it. Oliver finally took it and slid it into his jeans pocket.

We were quiet as we waited for someone to bring me the walking boot, but after a while, Oliver broke the silence.

"What's her name?" he asked. "The girl you . . . your boyfriend . . . hurt? Where does she live?"

"Emily Maxwell," I said. "Somewhere . . . I don't know. The accident happened in Raleigh. Why?"

He shrugged. "Maybe I can track her down," he said. "I have friends in high places." He winked at me and a lightning bolt of panic pierced my chest.

"I don't want to talk to her," I said quickly. "I can't. But I really wish I could just know how she's doing." I bit my lip. "You wouldn't try to contact her or anything, would you?"

"Of course not," he said. Then he smiled at me. Squeezed my hands again. "That, Morgan Christopher, would be your job."

Chapter 40

———— ✦ ————

ANNA

February 28, 1940

Anna awakened with a weight on her chest that made it hard to breathe. She knew that weight. It had been with her off and on since her mother's death in November, and she knew why it was so heavy and breath-stealing this morning: today was February 28. Her mother would have turned forty-four today.

"*Why, Mom?*" she whispered into the air above her bed. She wished she could wind back time and do everything differently. It seemed she should be able to do that somehow, if she could only figure out the secret. If only she could go back to that argument with Aunt Alice, she could turn the horror of what happened on its head. She would still have her mother with her.

It took her nearly an hour to shift the weight off her chest long enough to get up, shower, and put on her pants and blouse. She had no appetite, and she was glad Miss Myrtle wasn't home so she didn't have to make idle chatter over a breakfast she didn't want to eat. Freda, always easygoing, didn't bat an eye when Anna said she wasn't hungry, and for once, Anna was glad for the housekeeper's muteness.

She drove to the warehouse and wasn't surprised to find Jesse already inside at his easel, intently working on an overly ambitious painting of a woman staring out a window. Anna had bought him three more canvases as well as a couple of sketchbooks, and his paintings and sketches were now strewn all over the walls of the warehouse. He'd taken to arriving very early in the morning. Sometimes he would get there before sunup. He wanted to get as much time in the warehouse as he could before he had to go home to the farm.

On the table next to the easel, she could see that he had the Old Masters library book open, probably to one of the Vermeers, since it was clear he was experimenting with evening light in the painting. It did something to her heart, seeing this young boy's attempt to emulate his idol, and she smiled for the first time that morning. There was so much she wanted to teach him. So much she wanted him to have the chance to learn. She wished she could take him to New York. She'd told him about the Metropolitan Museum of Art and the new Whitney Museum, but telling him about them was no substitute for actually being there. For seeing the art up close. She'd told him, too, that he would be allowed into any museum he wanted to visit in New York City. "The color of your skin wouldn't matter up there," she'd said. She knew that was a lie, but at the moment she said it, she felt giddy with the thought of all he could do and see in the city. But then she snapped back to reality. They were trapped in a warehouse in Edenton, and she was filled with sadness again.

"Do you want some help?" she asked, trading her sweater for the smock that hung over the back of her chair.

"Not yet," he said. "I wanna figger this out by myself." He stood back and studied the painting on the easel. "Can you tell who this is?" he asked.

Anna came to stand next to him, buttoning her smock over her blouse.

The woman was looking out the window, and her large eyes, so much like Jesse's, gave her identity away. Slowly, she nodded. "Your mother," she said. "Without a doubt." The angle of the fading daylight on the woman's bare arms was not quite right, but she thought it best to let him see that on his own. "Did she model for you?"

"I sketched it while she was washin' dishes," he said, chuckling. "Then she hollered at me for jest sittin' around, doin' nothin' worthwhile."

"Did you show her the sketch?"

"Nah, it's gonna be a surprise, this paintin'." He nodded toward the easel. "Next week's her birthday so this'll be her present."

"Oh, she'll love it," Anna said, hoping that was the truth. A beat of silence followed, then without thinking, she said, "Today would have been *my* mother's birthday."

She felt Jesse's eyes on her but kept her own gaze on his painting, her hands resting on the back of the chair in front of the easel.

"Would've been?" he asked.

"She died in November," she said. "Just a couple of weeks before I came here." She glanced at him. "She killed herself." It was the first time she'd said those words out loud. Why she said them to Jesse but not Miss Myrtle, not Pauline, she had no idea. But there they were, a burden of syllables dumped on the shoulders of a seventeen-year-old boy.

"Damn," he said. "How . . . I mean . . . why she do that?"

Anna returned her gaze to the woman in the painting. "She had an illness called manic-depressive psychosis," she said. "That means she would be very happy and energetic—*extremely* energetic—for a while—sometimes months—and then she'd be very sad for just as long. Her sadness this time lasted and lasted and . . . it just didn't let up. My aunt Alice thought she needed to go into the hospital where they'd . . ." She didn't want to have to explain the electroshock treatments and all of that with him. "I didn't think she needed to go and she didn't want to go. My aunt tried to insist, but I finally won the argument." Anna felt her lower lip start to tremble and she bit down on it to stop the quiver. Jesse was so still and quiet that she barely knew he was next to her. "I came home from job hunting one day," she said, "and I couldn't find her. I knew she was home because I could see her car through the windows in the garage door. I called for her. Walked around the house. Finally I went out to the garage." Anna shut her eyes, her hands locked tight on the back of the chair. Jesse waited, still as stone next to her. "She'd hung herself from the beams in the garage ceiling." She lifted a hand to her mouth, pressing her fist against her lips, wishing she could block out the image she would never forget. Her mother's grotesque, almost unrecognizable face. Eyes wide open, features twisted, her skin gray. She had suffered; that much was clear. Anna could feel the beams of the warehouse high above her. She did not look up. "Aunt Alice had been right," she said to Jesse. "She needed to go to the hospital, but I was too—"

"Weren't your fault," Jesse said, force in his voice. "Not no way."

His words jerked her out of the memory, and for a moment neither of them spoke.

"I'm sorry I told you all that," she said finally. "It's just . . . I'm not myself today. It's all I can think about. Her birthday. And that she's not here."

"Maybe don't work today?" he suggested softly. "Go someplace quiet."

She looked at him. "Have you ever lost someone special?" she asked.

"Ever'one of my grandparents," he said.

She moved toward the mural and leaned against her paint table, arms folded across her chest. "Were you close to them?" she asked.

"Only really my granny. My mother's mama. Two year ago, she left us. There was a big funeral and lots of food and talkin' and you know what I did?" He widened his gentle doe eyes, waiting for her response.

"What did you do?"

"It was August and the south field was chock full o' corn. I jest went out there and set down in the middle of all them cornstalks where no one could see me except the worms and sap beetles and thought on the things Granny used to do . . . like how she'd drag me around by the ear when she was mad at me." He laughed. "But she'd play horseshoes with me and she'd smoke a pipe and give it to me when Mama wasn't lookin'. Them kind of things."

Anna smiled at him. He was such a tender soul. "You're very wise, Jesse Williams," she said. "But actually, I don't want to go someplace quiet. I think it would be best for me to stay here and focus on my work today."

He nodded. "That's jest like you, Miss Anna," he said. "But you change your mind, I can point you to some good places for hidin' out by yourself."

"I'll let you know," she said, still smiling as she turned around, reaching for her palette. She didn't say what she truly wanted to say: *This was the first time I've said it all out loud. It feels good to tell someone what happened. Thank you for listening.* Perhaps now that she'd told the story, it would lose its power over her. She hoped she would never have to repeat it to anyone ever again.

Chapter 41

———— ✦ ————

MORGAN

July 12, 2018

I t was nearly three in the morning by the time an orderly wheeled me out of the emergency room toward Oliver's van. I was wearing the awkward walking boot, and it took some careful maneuvering for me to stretch out on the van's second-row seat, my back against the side door. Finally, we were off.

"How're you doing back there?" Oliver asked once we'd put a few miles between us and the hospital.

I watched my walking boot glow each time we passed beneath a street-light. "I'm okay," I said. "It's not too bad." The van's radio was on, playing softly. A guy was singing about Vietnam, and I smiled. "We have to do something about your music, though," I added, and Oliver laughed.

"You mean right now, or in general?" he asked.

"In general. It's old-people music. Vietnam protests are ancient history."

"My parents were old folkies and I grew up on this stuff," he said. "It's deeper than today's music. Has more of a message than 'oh, I wanna get laid tonight' or whatever."

I laughed. *I love you*, I thought, but of course I kept my mouth shut. Dangerous thinking. The last man I'd fallen in love with screwed me over royally. Instead, I said, "It'll be easier to relate to Nathan if you listen to the music he listens to. Music's a bridge between people."

In the rearview mirror, I saw his face, caught in the headlights of an oncoming car. His look was sober, and he nodded.

"Point taken," he said.

In another few minutes, he turned the van into Lisa's driveway. I drew in a long breath. What a terrible night it had been, and yet I felt oddly happy. Happier than I'd felt in a long time.

Oliver helped me hop my way to the front door. I opened it with my key and quickly turned off the alarm system once we were inside, not wanting to awaken Lisa. The house was dark and silent.

"Where's your room?" Oliver asked quietly.

"At the back of the house. The sunroom."

"Jesse's old room?"

"Yes."

He put his arm around my waist and helped me maneuver through the dark living room and dining room. Instead of the pain, I focused on how wonderful his hand felt against my side, but he let go of me as soon as we reached the sunroom. I turned on the light, glad I'd made my bed that morning. I sat down on it and looked up at him.

"How am I going to work?" I asked.

He put his hands on his hips and looked down at me. "We'll figure out a way," he said. "For right now, what can I get you? Water? Snack? Can you take off the boot by yourself? Can you get to the bathroom?"

Oh God, I didn't want to be this needy around him! I could feel the pain beginning to throb in my ankle now that the medication they'd given me in the ER was wearing off.

"Just one thing," I said. "Lisa has Tylenol in the kitchen cabinet by the sink. Could you bring me a couple and a glass of water, please?"

"You've got it," he said, and he disappeared into the hallway.

He returned a moment later with the Tylenol, water, and an ice pack. "Look what I found in the freezer," he said, holding up the ice pack.

I took the ice pack from him and set it on the bed, then looked up at him. He was eyeing me with worry. The night table lamp caught the blue of his eyes. The straight line of his nose.

"What else can I do?" he asked.

You can lie here next to me until I fall asleep, I thought. It would be so comforting to curl up against him all night long, breathing in the leathery scent of his aftershave or whatever it was. Instead, I smiled up at him.

"You've done a lot," I said quickly, before I said anything I'd regret later. "And I'm fine, really. I'll see you tomorrow—after my appointment with my PO—and we can figure out how the hell I'm going to work with a screwed-up foot."

"Okay," he said. "Call if you need me." Then he leaned over to give me a hug I could only describe as brotherly. It was all I could do to let go.

Chapter 42

---※•※---

ANNA

March 6, 1940

Ever since the anniversary of her mother's death, Anna had been staying late in the warehouse each day, unable to tear herself away from the mural. At first, she thought she was focusing on her painting as a way to stop the memories, but now she knew she was painting simply for the joy of it, the way she had as a student. There was nothing she would rather do. This was her passion. Her calling. She wondered if she would ever have time for a husband and children. She doubted she could attract a man at the moment, anyway. She always seemed to have paint in her hair and she'd stopped trying to get all of it out from under her fingernails. Looking pretty wasn't her priority, and she believed Miss Myrtle had completely given up on turning her into a lady.

So, she had no man in her life, but she did have a best friend—Jesse Jameson Williams—and she thought that was even better. What would she do without him? It wasn't so much that Jesse seemed to know what she needed in the warehouse even before she did—moving the ladder a few feet to the left, or adding a bit of Prussian blue to her palette—but that he was a hungry student and she enjoyed teaching him. He devoured every art book she brought him from the library, giving them back to her when they were due and asking her to check them out again a few days later. She let him read the books in the warehouse, because when he was at home on the farm, he was expected to work—work he loathed.

Peter was no longer helping in the warehouse. Baseball season had begun in the high school, and Anna was surprised to learn that Peter, despite being small and slender, was the star catcher on Edenton High School's baseball team. That meant he had practice after school every day. Anna missed his industriousness, but she had little work for two boys now that the heavy lifting was over, and to be truthful, Peter was never going to be an artist. He was technically competent and created detailed renderings of car engines and tractors, but he lacked Jesse's passion and creativity. Anna thought Peter would make a fine engineer someday.

She was rarely alone in the warehouse these days, whether Jesse was there or not. People stopped in during the day to watch her progress. Teenagers came by after school. Housewives running errands stopped in to watch and chat. And the men. The tiresome men. They stopped in during their lunch hours or after work, and they were curious and often critical. The women were kind, accepting of anything Anna chose to do in her painting, but the men all had opinions. They seemed to enjoy telling Anna what she was doing wrong, as if they could possibly know. She ignored them. The movers and shakers—Mayor Sykes, Mr. Fiering, and Billy Calhoun—were still distressed about having the Tea Party front and center, but they complained about it less now, at least to her, so she guessed they'd come to realize it was out of their hands.

Two men had not returned and for that Anna was grateful: Theresa Wayman's father and Martin Drapple, whom she hadn't seen since the day he'd slapped his wife. He was wise to stay away. She had no need of him now that the canvas was on the wall, anyhow. Some of the women asked her if she'd paint portraits of their children. She had no time for that, but she was both flattered and taken aback by the requests. Martin was the portrait artist in Edenton. Everyone knew that, and she had no desire to harm his career.

March 8–9, 1940

Anna awakened at three Friday morning, unable to go back to sleep because all she could think about was how much she wanted to go to the warehouse and get back to work. After tossing and turning for half an hour, she finally got out of bed, dressed, tiptoed out of the house, and drove herself to the warehouse in the dark. The dirt road was black and silent. It was too late for the cicadas, too early for the birds, and she fought her nerves as she drove through the trees. Walking into the suffocating pitch-blackness of the warehouse was even more of a challenge, but once she turned on the lights, her heartbeat began to settle down and the mural came to life in front of her in all its half-painted glory.

She painted until nearly nine A.M. It was as though some force were under her skin that wouldn't let her stop, and she was filled with the joy of creating. But then, suddenly, all the steam seemed to go out of her body and she was utterly exhausted. What she wouldn't give for a bed to climb into! She remembered that Jesse was working on the farm this morning, so she had the warehouse to herself. Sitting down next to her worktable, she leaned forward and rested her head on her arms, and before she even had a chance to think, she was asleep.

⤖•⤙

"Wake up sleepyhead!"

Dazed, Anna lifted her head from her worktable. It took her a moment to get her bearings. She was in the warehouse and Pauline stood in front of her, a garment bag in her arms.

"Oh, my." Anna rubbed the back of her stiff neck and looked up at Pauline. "I didn't mean to fall asleep. What time is it?"

"Nearly noon," Pauline said. "And I'm taking you to lunch at the Albemarle, though you look like you need a nap more than a meal. You work way too hard, Anna."

"I can't go to lunch." Anna pushed her chair away from her worktable and stood up. She held her arms wide to display her paint-stained pants and smock. "I'm hardly dressed for it."

"That's why I brought you one of my skirts and blouses." Pauline shoved the garment bag into Anna's arms, then looked worriedly down at her oxfords. "Your feet and bare legs will be hidden by the table, I hope," she said.

It had been a while since Anna had visited with Pauline. If her friend had gone to that much trouble to get her out of the warehouse, she should go, exhausted or not. She carried the garment bag to her small bathroom at the far end of the warehouse, where she changed into Pauline's skirt and blouse. They hung a bit loosely on her, but what did it matter? They would do.

Pauline drove them to the Albemarle Restaurant on Broad Street, where they both ordered the platter with chicken salad, tuna salad, a bit of candied apple, and a slice of American cheese. They chatted about this and that and then Pauline gave her a secret-looking smile.

"I have news," she said, her cheeks flushing. "I'm expecting a baby! Karl is over the moon about it."

"Well, my goodness!" Anna said. "How wonderful!" She was surprised by the confusion of feelings that came over her. Joy for her friend's happiness. Excitement at the thought of a new baby in their midst . . . although she would certainly be back in New Jersey by the time the child was born. And envy. That surprised her. Did she want to have a baby? Or was she just concerned about losing Pauline's friendship as her priorities changed? It made Anna glad she'd decided to join Pauline for lunch today. She had to nurture her friendships. They were too easy to lose. "Your mother must be thrilled," she said.

"Oh, she is! And Karl and I are coming over to dinner tonight to cel-ebrate, so I wanted you to know ahead of time. You'll join us, of course."

"I'd love to." She always enjoyed it when Karl and Pauline came to din-ner, although she was so sleepy today she wasn't sure she'd be able to stay up for much merriment.

Pauline chatted for a while about her plans for a nursery, but then abruptly changed topics, leaning across the table toward Anna.

"People are talking about you and the colored boy, honey," she said quietly. "You need to be careful."

"Pauline!" Anna was stunned. She felt sorely disappointed. "First of all, I consider Jesse an art student who has also become a friend." She remem-bered telling Jesse about her mother. How he'd listened. How he'd truly heard her. "And second," she said, "I don't care what people say."

"Well, you *should* care," Pauline said. "Karl told me how someone painted"—she leaned forward to whisper—"those words on the warehouse."

"That was weeks ago. Nothing's happened since then. Probably just some hoodlums out causing trouble. I don't want to live my life in fear."

"It's different here than where you came from." Pauline's voice was quiet but earnest. Her dark blue eyes held such grave concern that Anna felt taken aback. She could tell that her friend was sincerely worried about her.

She let out a long sigh. "People keep telling me that," she said. "But I can't change who I am, and I think you're silly to worry. I'm five years older than Jesse, for heaven's sake. I adore him like a little brother. He may not look like a kid, but he *is* a kid and he acts like one." She sat up very straight. "I plan to continue ignoring such catty talk."

"Your intentions may be pure," Pauline said, "and *his* may be pure. But it doesn't matter. People still believe what they want to believe and you're only inviting their criticism." She cut a corner of her slice of cheese and lifted it to her lips without taking a bite. "And it can get worse, dear."

"What do you mean?"

"I mean, it's against the law. Colored and white . . . you know."

Anna laughed. "You have nothing to worry about there," she said. "I have no interest in—"

"That may be the truth." Pauline set down her fork without eating the cheese. "But it's not what people believe, and that's what matters."

"No, Pauline, what matters is the reality," Anna said, getting angry now. At the sound of her raised voice, a few people turned to look at them. "I don't care what people think." She leaned closer. "Can we close this subject please? Let's talk about your baby again. Have you thought about names?"

⸻ ❈ ⸻

Baby names were definitely the topic of conversation over dinner that evening. Even Karl seemed to have an excited glow about him, only letting go of Pauline's hand when he needed his own to eat the chicken and dumplings Freda had made. They talked about names for most of an hour before Karl politely changed the subject, asking Anna how the mural was coming along.

"It's all I think about," she admitted. "I even got up in the middle of the night last night and went over there to paint." She knew as soon as the words left her mouth that she should have kept her nighttime foray to herself. She was too tired to think clearly, and the three of them stared at her as if they'd misheard.

"You *did?*" Miss Myrtle said finally. "When was this?"

"Oh, around three this morning." She shrugged as though it had been nothing. "I was just itching to paint."

"Women can't stay out all night unchaperoned like that," Miss Myrtle said. "Maybe up north they do, but it's not the way we do things here, dear."

Anna was so tired of hearing that sentiment. "It wasn't 'all night,'" she said, carefully holding on to her smile. "Think of it as early morning."

"People will talk if they know you're out at all hours like that," Pauline said.

Pauline and her talkative people, Anna thought. But even Freda disapproved. The maid had brought another basket of her biscuits into the room, and she caught Anna's eye as she set them on the table and shook her head. Her silent two cents.

"Seriously, Anna," Karl said. "You could have an accident driving late at night and no one would know. It's not a good idea. At the very least, you need to let folks know your whereabouts."

"All right." Anna gave in with a sigh. She was sorry she'd brought it up. "It probably was silly of me, anyway. I ended up so tired this afternoon I fell asleep with my head on my worktable. I often wish I had a little settee or something like it at the warehouse. All I needed was half an hour's shut-eye and I was ready to go again."

"You artistic types are so intense!" Pauline said. "I wish I had some of your drive."

Karl rested his hand on hers. "You're perfect just the way you are, dear," he said.

Pauline glowed at the compliment and Anna felt that niggling bit of envy again. Pauline was so lucky to have him.

"You know, we actually have a cot you could borrow," Pauline said. "You could keep it at the warehouse and take a catnap in the afternoon any time you like."

"It's hardly a settee." Karl chuckled at his wife's suggestion.

"True," Pauline said, "but better than your worktable."

"I suppose," Karl said. He looked at Anna. "It's just an old army cot," he said. "It was my father's and we use it for camping, though I doubt I'll be able to get this one camping again any time soon." He smiled at his wife.

Anna imagined having the cot in the warehouse. She could take a little snooze whenever she liked, then get up and go back to work. "That would be wonderful," she said. "Thank you for the offer."

"What about William?" Miss Myrtle said, and it took them all a moment to realize she was returning the conversation to baby names. Miss

Myrtle looked at her daughter. "That's a good strong name, don't you think?"

-->>-•-<<--

The following day, Anna stopped by Pauline's to pick up the cot where they'd left it for her on their front porch, since neither Pauline nor Karl were at home. The cot was compactly folded and Anna set it on the backseat of the Ford, then turned the car around in the wide driveway. She'd nearly reached the street again when one of those red Indian motorcycles sped around the corner and whizzed past the front of her car at breakneck speed. Startled, Anna pressed hard on the brake, the cot whacking into the back of her seat, sending her heart into her throat. Her leg trembled on the brake as she stared after the motorcycle and its rider: *Martin Drapple*, his red hair far too long and wild from the wind, speeding down the road like a maniac on a mission. She'd heard rumors that his wife had kicked him out of the house, so perhaps Mrs. Drapple had kept the car and this was Martin's new transportation. Anna didn't know. All she knew was that she was glad he no longer came around the warehouse. That slap he'd given his wife still rang in her ears.

Chapter 43

MORGAN

July 12, 2018

Rebecca's gaze dropped to my walking boot as I limped into her office that morning.

"I already heard about this," she said, gesturing toward the boot.

I dropped into the chair next to her desk, my guard suddenly up. "How could you have already heard about it?" I asked.

"Your supervisor-slash-landlady called me."

I groaned. Lisa had been angry that morning when I told her how I ended up with the sprained ankle. I hadn't expected sympathy from her, exactly, but I didn't expect her to go ballistic.

"I'm not paying you to hang out in a bar," she'd said, her brown eyes blazing. "I would have thought you'd learned your lesson about that sort of thing."

"I was only there to get dinner," I'd argued back. I should have backed down, but I'd been exhausted after so little sleep, plus my ankle was killing me and my patience was thin. "And as soon as the fight broke out, I left. At least, I tried to leave. But that's when my foot got caught in the rungs of the barstool."

Lisa had only stared. "You're scaring me," she said finally. "Don't let it happen again."

Now I looked at Rebecca. "Does she have a right to do that?" I asked. "Is she allowed to talk to you about me?"

"She can *tell* me anything she likes," Rebecca said. "But I won't share anything about you in response, so you don't need to be concerned about that. I'd like to hear your side of the story, though. What happened last night?"

I shut my eyes, remembering back to the night before. It was all still very, very sharp in my mind. *This is what happens when you don't drink,* I thought. Things stayed sharp and crisp. Not like after the accident, when everything had been a cloud of blood and fear in my memory. I told Rebecca the whole story. The only thing I left out was that I was falling in love with Oliver. At least, I was pretty sure I was. I didn't completely trust myself when it came to love. Did I even know what it was? I didn't think I'd ever felt love from another human being. Not the real thing, anyway. Not from Trey, no matter how many times he'd said those words to me. Certainly not from my parents. Sitting there, I could actually picture the huge empty space in my heart where love was supposed to be. The only person I could see in that space was Oliver—a little image of him tucked down in a corner.

"That was very risky for you, going there." Rebecca brought my mind back to her office.

My eyes suddenly burned, surprising me. I was so tired after last night, and so tried of feeling criticized. "Everyone from the gallery was going," I said. "I knew I could go and not drink. I didn't think it was a big deal. I still don't."

Rebecca looked down at my ankle in its walking boot. "What did they say at the ER?" she asked.

"A mild sprain, though it doesn't feel very mild. They said to ice it. Elevate it. But I have to work."

"Lisa is worried you might backslide."

I was angry, but tried not to show it. "I'm not going to backslide," I said.

"And she's worried about how your ankle will affect your work," Rebecca said. "She told me that if you can't work, she'll have to fire you and hire someone else, though she sounded so—"

"*What?*" Fear rose in my chest. "No! I have to do it. I *will* do it!" The thought of returning to prison was only part of my sudden panic. The mural was *mine*. The sudden sense of ownership I felt over it stunned me. It was *my* handsome lumberjack and *my* old Tea Party ladies and *my* little skull in the window and *my* bloody hammer and motorcycle fender. I wasn't letting anyone else work on it.

"I was going to say she—Lisa Williams—sounded . . ." She seemed to hunt for a word. "She sounded *frantic* about you not being able to work on the mural. Something about going against her father's will, and—"

"I *love* it, Rebecca," I interrupted her. "I love what I'm doing with the mural. Restoring it. It's challenging, and when you see what you've done, and you see a bit of the picture go back to the way Anna—the artist— intended . . . It's so rewarding."

"How will you be able to work with your ankle like this?" Rebecca pointed toward the walking boot.

"I don't know, but I'll find a way," I said. "Seriously, I will. My ankle is going to heal one way or another. Maybe it'll take a week longer if I don't keep it elevated every minute, but I don't care. It'll heal eventually. I cannot lose this job!"

Rebecca hesitated, looking at the papers on her desk. "I believe you," she said. "I guess you just need to convince Lisa you can keep at it." She looked up at me. "And how about an AA meeting tonight?"

"Fine," I said, shoulders slumping. I felt overwhelmed. I needed sleep tonight more than I needed a meeting, but I would agree to anything at that moment to be able to get back to work and keep Lisa happy. "Can I go now?" I asked, wincing as I got to my feet.

She nodded. Gave me a half smile. "No more bars, all right?"

"No more bars," I agreed, and I half hopped, half walked out of the room.

※

I'd taken an Uber to Rebecca's office and now I called another to drive me to the gallery. I wouldn't be walking anywhere for a while. When I arrived at the gallery, Oliver, Adam, and Wyatt were in the foyer, crouched on the floor as they examined a cracked tile near the folding table, and it was clear to me that Adam and Wyatt knew what had happened. The smell of the white wall paint that was being used throughout the gallery seared my nostrils.

"Here she is!" Adam looked up from the floor. "How're you doin'? Oliver said you spent the night in the ER."

"I'm fine," I said, as I hobbled over to the mural. Damn, my ankle hurt! I could barely read the labels on my paint bottles for the pain.

"Looks like you haven't slept in a week," Wyatt said.

Great, I thought.

"How're you going to climb the ladder with that boot on?" Adam asked.

"Leave her alone, guys." Oliver got to his feet with the broken tile in his hands. "Let's focus on replacing this tile, all right?" He handed the pieces to Wyatt, then walked over to me and spoke to me in a whisper. "How're you doing?"

I nodded. "All right," I said, whispering back. "Lisa's angry with me, though. She called my PO. Even talked about firing me."

"That's crazy," he said. "None of it was your fault. And we'll find a way for you to keep working. I'll talk to her."

"No, don't," I said, my hand on his arm. I loved having an excuse to touch him. "Might make things worse."

He hesitated, then nodded. He gestured toward the mural. "Why don't you focus on everything that's at chair level for a while," he said. "It might be awkward, but maybe you can keep your ankle elevated that way. There's a stool in my other office . . . my real office down the hall . . . It should be the right height for you to rest your foot on. What do you think?"

I looked at the mural. The lumberjack's perfect arm I'd created—or at least, the perfect arm Anna Dale had created and I'd re-created—gave me enormous pleasure, so much so that it nearly erased the misery of the night before. Lisa would consider replacing me? I couldn't imagine losing this. This work. This *joy*. And if I lost my work on the mural, I'd also lose my freedom.

"Good idea," I said to Oliver. "Thanks."

Oliver disappeared into the interior of the building and returned a moment later with a short stool I recognized from his makeshift office. He set it down for me, then gave me a quick, gentle hug I wished would last longer.

"I would have missed you if Lisa let you go," he said, and that tiny image of him grew a little bigger in the empty space of my heart.

Chapter 44

---※·≪---

ANNA

March 14, 1940

Although there were still some very nippy days, spring definitely began early in Edenton. Quite suddenly, the little town felt like a different place. The waterfront was alive with fishing boats that glittered with herring, and the air near the wharf reeked quite nauseatingly of fish.

"You won't even notice the smell in a couple of days," Miss Myrtle assured Anna, who found that impossible to imagine.

Away from the water, gardens bloomed with color, and only then did Anna realize how badly she needed spring and growing things and all those vibrant colors surrounding her. The more color there was in her world, the happier she was, and she thought she now understood her mother's passion for photographing flowers, preserving them in pictures she could enjoy when the cold weather set in.

Yet Anna wasn't getting to see—or smell—too much of Edenton's springtime: she was practically living in the warehouse these days.

Her borrowed cot seemed to worry everyone. Now that she had the cot, she painted well into the evening, refreshed from the nap she often took after Jesse went home to help on the farm. She'd hang a DO NOT DISTURB sign on the door, turn out the lights, and sleep deeply for twenty or thirty minutes in the shadowy light that slipped in through the big windows. She'd bring a sandwich with her for dinner, and Miss Myrtle complained that she was staying out after dark, which wasn't "fitting for a single girl."

The cot was just a simple old khaki-colored thing. It was low to the ground and more comfortable than it looked. Anna covered it with a thin quilt she'd borrowed from her bedroom closet at Miss Myrtle's house, and she'd nap on a small pillow she'd picked up from Holmes Department Store. The funny thing was, a couple of months ago she never would have considered taking a nap in the warehouse. The creepiness of the place had been too much for her then, even when she was wide awake with her eyes open. She still didn't like the long walk from her comfortable "studio" end where she had her work and lights and heaters, to the dark and dismal end when she needed to use the lavatory, but she no longer felt afraid. The warehouse was her home away from home now.

Mayor Sykes stopped by one evening after leaving his office and he, too, seemed concerned at realizing how late she was working in spite of the fact that he was the person who told her she didn't need a lock on the warehouse door in the first place. Even Jesse gave her a talking-to about it.

"You shouldn't stay here after dark," he said. "Remember them words on the side of the warehouse? You don't wanna be here at night when someone's out there paintin' on your buildin', do you?"

No, she certainly did not, but a full month had passed since hooligans defaced the warehouse and nothing had happened since. The only reminder of the deed was that the paint Mr. Arndt and Peter used to cover up the words was much brighter and whiter than the old paint on the warehouse exterior. Anna didn't look at the paint when she walked from her car to the door. That was the way she dealt with it.

"You know," Jesse said one afternoon, "you sound like your mama." He kept his eyes on his work at the easel as he spoke, as if he knew he was treading into dangerous territory.

Anna looked at him sharply, her guard up at the mention of her mother. "What are you talking about?"

He glanced at her. "You said how she had all that energy sometime," he said. "That's how you sound now."

Anna bristled. "This is completely different," she said, although his words shook her, ever so slightly. She thought of her mother's "lively spells," remembering how she would scour the house from top to bottom or race through the neighborhood with her camera, trotting up strangers' driveways to take pictures of their gardens. "Really, Jesse. You didn't know her. I'm nothing like her."

It annoyed her—perhaps even angered her—that he would mention her mother at all and particularly in that context. Her mother's manic spells had been like a living, breathing thing, a third being in the house with them. Jesse was completely wrong. Yet as Anna returned to her own work after their conversation, she was aware that her heart was thudding like a drum in her chest.

Chapter 45

———⯈•⯇———

MORGAN

July 16, 2018

Five days had passed since I sprained my ankle, and although I still couldn't walk more than half a block without grinding pain, I barely felt a twinge when I focused on the mural. I was working faster and more confidently now. I understood what I was doing. I knew exactly how to mix the conservation paints with silica to match the sheen in Anna's oils. I knew how much pressure to apply to my brush to match Anna's strokes. Only when I came to an unusual abrasion in a delicate area did I need to turn to Oliver for advice.

"You know as much as I do now," he told me. I knew that was a lie, but it pleased me nevertheless.

Still, there were only three weeks left before the gallery was to open, and I figured I had five weeks' worth of work left to do. Adam and most of the other workers were now gone, having taken other jobs, but Wyatt stayed behind to hammer molding into place and help Oliver frame any artwork that was coming in unframed.

Late that morning, Lisa blew into the gallery carrying a large flat package wrapped in brown paper and taped together with crisp, yellowed, ancient-looking tape.

"Wait till you see what I stumbled across in my father's studio closet!" she said, motioning Oliver and me to come close to her at the folding table.

I set down my brush and stood next to Oliver as Lisa untaped the brown paper to reveal a plain white board about three feet by one and a half. She turned the board over and I gasped. In front of us was a full color sketch of the mural.

"Too cool!" Oliver said, grinning. "What a find! You know what this is, Morgan?"

"Other than the obvious?" I asked.

"This is what Anna Dale would have turned in to the Section of Fine Arts to get her commission to move forward with the mural," he said. "This would have been her first interpretation of what the mural would look like."

I quickly scanned the sketch, looking for the aberrations that were so apparent in the mural. "Look." I pointed to the circle of women at the mural's heart. "No motorcycle."

Lisa looked from the sketch to the mural. "No knife in the peanut lady's teeth," she said.

"And no hammer," Oliver added.

"No skull," I said. "No little man in the compact mirror." The list went on and on. Anna Dale had created the sketch, it seemed, before she'd lost her mind.

"We have to frame this," Oliver said. I could tell he was excited. It made me smile to see how enthusiastic he became about all things artistic. "We'll hang it here in the foyer along with the mural."

Once Lisa left, Oliver and I shared a container of pad Thai for lunch, sitting across from each other at his table, both of us eating quickly so we could get back to work. Oliver could have returned to his office now that I didn't need his help all that much, but he seemed content to continue working in the foyer and I was glad. We worked mostly in silence, listening to our wildly different music, but occasionally we pulled out our earbuds to talk. That afternoon, Oliver talked about Nathan, telling me all sorts of funny and touching anecdotes about the son he loved. It warmed me, listening to him.

I worked until five thirty, then took an Uber to the library. Seeing Anna's sketch made me want to dig deeper into her time in Edenton, and I hoped I could find more articles about her in the old *Chowan Herald*. I had to know how she came to fall off the face of the earth. If only the newspapers were indexed! Then I would know in two seconds if there was any other information about her.

I was soon back in that cramped atticlike space in the library, fighting with the microfilm machine as I worked my way through the blurry print of the newspapers from early 1940.

I nearly missed the article in the February 22 edition, since it had no picture with it and Anna's name was buried in the text. *Mural Artist's Warehouse Defaced*, the headline read.

> Policeman Karl Maguire stated that the former Blayton Company warehouse, where New Jersey artist Anna Dale is painting the government-sponsored mural that will hang in the Edenton Post Office, was reportedly defaced with a racial epithet over the weekend. Maguire learned of the event only after the offending words had been painted over. The identity of the culprit remains unknown.

I read the article a few times, trying to imagine what the racial epithet might have been. I remembered the picture of Anna standing in front of the canvas with the young white boy Peter somebody and the boy-who-could-pass-as-a-man, Jesse Williams, and I thought I could guess. Had there been more between Anna and Jesse than a work relationship? There was only one person alive who might know. I thought of how Mama Nelle pressed a finger to her lips when I talked to her about Anna. "You know you got to be quiet about her, right?" she'd asked me. Was this why? Were Anna and Jesse closer than artist and apprentice? I would invite Mama Nelle to the gallery, I decided. I'd show her the mural up close and personal, and pick her brain at the same time.

Chapter 46

—❖—

ANNA

March 21, 1940

Anna awakened in the darkness of the warehouse, confused. Was she in Pauline's bedroom? No. Her hand felt the rough fabric of the cot beneath her. She squeezed her eyes closed, concentrating, trying to remember. She'd eaten a bowl of cold leftover stew she'd brought with her from Miss Myrtle's. Yes. And then she'd gone back to the mural. So close to being done, yet as driven as ever. She'd painted the fine lines of the netting on the fishing vessel. Made a mistake. Painted them over. And over. She'd pulled the lamp closer. Stood on the third rung of the ladder to reach the upper left corner of the mural. She hadn't been able to space the lines of the netting evenly. No one would notice, but she would know. She'd been working too long. She'd had no nap today and she'd noticed that her hand had a little tremor. She'd decided to lie down for a few minutes. Yes, it was all coming back to her. She'd stretched out on the cot. Pulled the quilt over her. Now she had no idea what time it was.

She should get up. Work on the ship's netting some more, or better yet, go back to Miss Myrtle's for a good night's sleep and return in the morning when her mind would be fresh.

She heard the sound. Was that what had awakened her? A scuffling sound. She lay still, listening. *Scuff. Scuff.* Suddenly the floor lamp clicked on and she sat up, the cot creaking beneath her.

Martin. Walking toward her.

"What are you doing here?" she asked.

He didn't answer. She didn't feel fear. Not exactly. Not yet. She was more angry over his brazenness. The lamplight caught the greasy tangles of his red hair. His eyes were circled by darkness. "Martin?" She lifted the edge of the quilt to her chest, as if she'd forgotten she was still fully dressed in blouse and slacks. "Why are you here?" she asked again.

She could smell his whiskey breath as he moved closer, yet she still didn't feel afraid. Not until she saw what he was doing: unbuckling his pants. *Oh God.*

Suddenly, before she had a chance to get to her feet, he was on her. She screamed. She felt the cot give way and heard the splintering of one of the legs echo through the building. She was tilted toward the ground, headfirst, Martin's weight on her. He smelled of sweat and booze and dirty hair. Anna tried to scramble out from under him, but he held her pinned beneath him. He was a thousand times stronger than she was.

She clutched his arms. Dug her fingernails into the skin through his shirt. "Think of your wife," she pleaded. "Think of your daughters." *Please don't do this. Please don't hurt me.* Was she begging him out loud? What did it matter? Her words were useless. The smell of him was all over her. Up inside her head. She felt the hardness of him press against her. He got to his knees and started yanking off her pants, and she took that chance to fight him. She tried to kick him, but by then, her pants were halfway down her legs, trapping her. "*Stop it stop it stop it!*" she screamed. She clawed his face and he slapped her, *hard,* harder than he'd slapped his wife.

"Shut the hell up!" he shouted. "You fucking wrecked my life! Shut up!"

He yanked off her pants. She yelped, trying to sit up, trying to grab his hands, but he pushed her down again, his own hand at her throat, tight, pressing, making her struggle for air. His strength overwhelmed her, his body no longer flesh and blood but concrete and steel, and she knew he was going to kill her.

"Think you're so special 'cause you won a fucking contest!" His spit sprayed against her cheeks. "A fucking imbecilic painting of old ladies and trite crap! It's gone to your *head*, you bitch!" He kneed her in the belly, making her cry out. "You wrecked my career!" he shouted. "You wrecked my marriage!"

Both his hands were around her throat now, tightening as she struggled against him. She stopped fighting. She would let him do what he was there to do while she thought how to save herself. How to survive. He tore into her. Plowed into her. She felt herself split open and she gasped. *Too numb.* Her mind was too numb to think of a way to save herself. A way to live. She lay there limp and weak, her head turned away from his face and his stench, while he ruined her.

And then she saw, lying on the floor only inches from the broken cot, the hammer. She focused on it. Forgot about what he was doing. Forgot he was ruining her.

She was going to ruin *him*.

Chapter 47

———— ➤•◄ ————

MORGAN

July 18, 2018

Looking from Anna's sketch to the mural was making me crazy. Several times that morning, I took a break from my work to stand at a distance with the sketch in my hands, studying the differences between it and the mural. Oliver shared my fascination. He got close to the mural with a magnifying glass, hunting for pounce marks beneath the hammer or the knife in the black woman's teeth, but he could find none.

"It's got to be one of two explanations," he said, coming to stand next to me as we gazed at the painting. "Either she always knew she was going to add the unusual objects, but she guessed the Section of Fine Arts would never approve her sketch if she included them, so she left them off. Or, she truly did lose her mind while she was painting it."

"Or she just had a bizarre sense of humor," I suggested. I looked toward the front door of the foyer and he followed my gaze.

"What time do you expect her?" he asked.

"Any minute." Saundra had promised to bring Mama Nelle to the gallery before noon, and it was now after eleven. I wasn't one hundred percent sure they would show. Saundra had been reluctant.

"She's frailer every day," she'd said to me on the phone. "But I suppose at this point it can't hurt and she'd enjoy the visit. She likes you. She can't remember your name but she calls you 'the girl with the yellow hair.'"

I heard the slamming of a car door and walked to the foyer entrance where I could see Mama Nelle struggling to get out of the car. Saundra nearly had to lift her from the front seat, and I suddenly felt guilty for asking them to come. But as soon as the two of them reached the front of the gallery and I opened the door, Mama Nelle's eyes lit up behind her glasses. "The girl with the yella hair," she said, smiling.

"I'm so glad you could come," I said, trying to figure out if I'd be more help or hindrance if I took Mama Nelle's free arm to lead her into the foyer. I opted to hold her arm lightly by the elbow while Saundra guided her into the room.

Oliver had pulled the two chairs a few yards from the mural, and I nodded toward them. "Come sit down," I said, but before the words were out of my mouth, Mama Nelle had stopped in her tracks, her gaze fixed on the mural.

"Is she here?" she whispered to me. "Is Miss Anna here?"

"No, she's not," I said, glancing at Saundra, "but her *mural* is here and I wanted you to see it."

"Please sit down." Oliver sounded as worried as I felt. The old woman had lost her smile. Her body felt limp where I held her arm.

"Yes, come sit," I said. "This is Oliver. He's the curator of the gallery."

"Mama, this is Uncle Jesse's gallery," Saundra said loudly as she helped her mother onto the chair, then sat down next to her. "He planned it before he passed."

Mama Nelle didn't hear a word her daughter said, I was sure. Her gaze was riveted on the mural, and now that I had her in the gallery, I wasn't quite sure what to say to her.

I glanced at Oliver, who gave me a nod that said, *You brought her here, now ask her your questions.*

"Does the mural look like you remember it?" I began, thinking that was a safer question than the one I really wanted to ask: *Had Miss Anna and Jesse been lovers?*

Mama Nelle lifted one tremulous hand to her lips, then shook her head. "Where you get this?" she asked, nodding toward the mural.

"Jesse had it in his studio for many, many years," I said. "I'm restoring it. Cleaning it up. Fixing the paint."

"Is Jesse the one what ruint it?" she asked.

"Ruined it?"

She pointed, her arm trembling. It looked like she was pointing to the peanut lady, the woman with the knife between her teeth. "What'd he do to it?"

It hadn't occurred to me that in all the years the mural had been in Jesse's possession, *he* might have been the one to tamper with it. That didn't fit the story, though. The "Anna Dale lost her mind" story.

"There are strange things about the mural that we don't understand," I said, moving to stand in front of the painting. "The knife in her teeth. The motorcycle." I pointed out the other oddities. "But we think Anna . . . Miss Anna painted them. Not Jesse. But . . . Mama Nelle." I took a deep breath. "I was wondering if Jesse and Miss Anna were more than friends."

Saundra turned her head from the mural to me. "You think they were lovers?" she asked.

Mama Nelle didn't seem to hear either of us, her gaze still on the mural.

"I saw an article in the paper from back then," I said to Saundra. "It said there'd been a racial slur written on the outside wall of the warehouse where Anna painted and where Jesse was her . . . apprentice, or helper, or . . . I wondered if there was something more between them."

"Ah," Saundra said, understanding. "Well, if there was, it's certainly ancient history now. It hardly matters, does it?"

It didn't matter at all, actually, but it was more than prurient interest driving me. "You're right," I said. "It doesn't matter. It's just that I've come to feel . . . close to Anna Dale, working on this thing." I gestured toward the mural. "She created a perfectly nice sketch for this mural and then when she actually painted it she added all these . . . horrific details to it, and . . ." I seemed to run out of words.

"We'd just like to understand her better." Oliver stood next to me and he surprised me by cupping my elbow in his hand. The touch didn't last nearly as long as I would have liked. "And of course there are very few people alive now who were alive then," he continued, dropping his hand to his side, "and Morgan thought maybe your mother might have some—"

"They wasn't anythin' of the kind," Mama Nelle said suddenly. She looked across the room at me. "Ain't you never had a friend that was a boy but not a boyfriend?"

I felt Oliver next to me. Until recently, he'd fit that description perfectly. Was it my imagination that there was something more between us? Something growing? Something I wanted to grow.

"Yes," I said to Mama Nelle. "I know what you mean. Are you saying that's all there was between Anna and Jesse? Friendship?"

"That's 'xactly right."

I tipped my head, curious. "How do you know that for sure?"

She looked at me in silence for so long I began to wonder if she was having some sort of spell.

"Mama?" Saundra prodded.

"We ain't talkin' 'bout Miss Anna no more," Mama Nelle said in a near whisper. "Come here." She motioned me to come closer. I walked the five or six steps to her chair and she reached out to take my hand. I bent low until her lips were next to my ear. "You'll keep her secrets, right?" she whispered to me. "Me 'n' you? We the only ones that know."

Know what? I wanted to ask her. Her cool dry fingers grasped mine in a plea or a promise. I wasn't sure which, but I knew it wasn't the time to press for more. That would have to wait. "Yes," I whispered back. "I'll keep her secrets."

Chapter 48

————— ⋙●⋘ —————

ANNA

March 22, 1940

Jesse arrived before dawn. Anna sat, half naked, on the broken cot. All the way broken now, its legs splayed and splintered on the concrete. She followed Jesse's gaze to where Martin lay on the floor. She followed his gaze to the bloody hammer. His eyes grew wide. He raised a trembling hand to his mouth.

Anna thought of how the hammer actually belonged to Miss Myrtle, who'd said she could keep it as long as she needed it. She'd liked the feel of the smooth wood in her hand when she pounded nails into the walls of the warehouse. She'd liked the solid head of it.

At midnight, though, she'd liked the claw end.

"What happened?" Jesse lowered his hand from his mouth, his voice a husky whisper.

Anna couldn't speak. It would have taken effort she didn't have.

Jesse walked toward her. He pried the journal from her fingers where she held it on her bare thighs and read what she'd written earlier that morning when she was sick to her stomach. So, so sick. She didn't even remember what words she'd used.

"Oh, *shit*, Anna," Jesse said. He stood above her, reading. It was the first time she'd heard him swear. The first time he'd said her name without "Miss" in front of it.

She started to cry. Again. She'd thought she was out of tears.

Jesse made her stand up. She started to fall, but he caught her. He helped her put on her underwear. Her pants. She felt no modesty. She didn't care. Then he helped her walk around the other side of the cot so she wouldn't step through the blood. So much of it! It had soaked into the concrete floor. Already dark, ruby red for all time. She thought she would get sick again, but the feeling passed. Jesse had her sit in the chair by his easel.

"Are you all right?" he asked, though it would be clear to anyone that she was not all right. Not in the least. She couldn't speak, but she didn't need to explain what had happened. He'd read it all. She watched him look around the room—the broken cot, the bloodstained hammer, the red concrete, Martin's skull split open like a bloody egg.

"I'll take care of it," he said.

How? she wanted to ask, but the effort it would take to produce that word was more than she could summon.

She turned her gaze away from Martin. She wouldn't look at him again. Did she strike him more than once? She thought she had. Once had been enough to kill him. She hit him more than once, though. Once, twice. Maybe three times. She couldn't remember. She'd used all her might, but it hadn't felt like enough for her. Was he truly going to kill her? She didn't know. He'd been turned away from her when she rose in a fury from the cot, grabbed the hammer, and struck him down with all her might. Strength she hadn't known she had. A side of herself she hadn't known existed.

She would tell the police he was going to kill her.

That was what she'd say.

"I'll take care of it," Jesse said again.

She looked up at him, vaguely aware that he was the child and she, the adult, and that this was all backwards.

"I'll have to use your car." He picked up her keys from the table where she kept her paints. Then he picked up a pair of those work gloves she'd bought for him that he never used. He studied them for a moment.

"I'm gonna wreck these."

She nodded her consent and he put the gloves on.

Maybe there will be no police, she thought.

Jesse opened the warehouse door and she turned away as he dragged Martin's body outside. Although it was very early morning and few people would be out, she was glad the warehouse was nearly surrounded by trees and at the end of a long road cut off from the rest of the world. Jesse came back inside. He picked up the hammer, walked over to her paint table. He opened a can of paint with the bloody claw of the hammer. Then he walked over to the bloodstained concrete. Anna watched in shock as he poured red paint over the blood. He dropped the can on top of the mess.

"Anyone ask, you accidentally dropped the paint," he said, so calmly. "You gonna have to git more."

From the front corner of the warehouse, he picked up the huge piece of cheesecloth that had lined the canvas when Anna bought it. "For your car," he said. He walked to the door. "I'll shut this after me." He looked past her toward the wall of the warehouse, staring hard as if he could see through it to the dirt road. "I ain't never rode one of them motorcycles," he said, "but when I come back I'll do my mighty best to git it gone." He looked at her then, still sitting there cold and dumb as a rock, and told her, "You got to git rid of that book, Anna," he said pointing to the journal in her hands. "That there diary. You done wrote too much in it."

She clutched the journal to her chest. Nodded. But she knew she would never get rid of it, this last gift from her mother. Never.

⟶•⟝⟞•

Jesse turned people away from the warehouse all that afternoon, while Anna sat numbly in the chair by his easel. He stood at the door. "She ain't feelin' well today," he said to anyone who wanted to come in and watch her paint. She was glad he was there. She was afraid one of the men would come in and she'd be alone with him. The mayor, or Mr. Fiering, or some other man from town. She suddenly feared all of them and how they had the power to hurt her. Or maybe they would realize that the red paint on the floor covered blood. Or maybe the police might come. Maybe they found Martin's motorcycle? Jesse didn't tell her what he'd done with it—or with Martin's body—and she didn't ask. He told her only that he'd burned the gloves.

Pauline came to the warehouse sometime that afternoon. Anna wasn't sure when, exactly. Time was falling apart for her. She was still sitting on Jesse's chair when Pauline arrived, while Jesse painted some of the border of the mural. He'd asked her if he could, and she'd nodded yes. She wasn't sure she'd be able to paint any of the mural ever again.

Jesse quickly walked to the door when Pauline stepped inside.

"Miss Anna ain't feelin' well," he said, trying to block her entry, but Pauline pushed him aside with a hand on his chest.

"I'm a nurse," she said, marching toward Anna across the warehouse. Anna knew she should do all she could to appear like her normal self, but the effort seemed too much for her. She gave in to the catatonia that had taken hold of her, staring into space as Pauline crossed the room.

"My God!" Pauline stopped suddenly. "What happened here?"

Anna followed Pauline's gaze to the spilled paint, the broken cot. For the first time, she noticed the blood in the exact center of the cot's khaki body. It was *her* blood there, not Martin's. She let out a sob before she could stop it.

Pauline squatted in front of her, the skirt of her white nurse's uniform fanning out around her. She rested her hands on Anna's knees. "What happened, Anna?" she asked, her voice gentle but firm. Then more softly in a whisper. "Did the boy . . . Jesse . . . did he . . . hurt you?"

Across the warehouse from them, Jesse stood against the wall by the door. Anna felt his fear from where she sat.

"No." It was the first word she'd spoken aloud since Pauline's arrival and it came out as a croak, but she couldn't allow Jesse to be blamed for any of what happened. "Jesse," she said to him. "Go. Go home."

"No, Miss An—"

"Yes," she said with as much authority as she could muster. Jesse was keeping her safe. She needed to do the same for him.

He hesitated, then finally picked up his sketch pad and left the warehouse. Pauline watched him go, then turned back to Anna.

"What did he do to you?" she asked her.

"Pauline!" She tried to put a playful note in her voice. She was certain she failed. "You're jumping to silly conclusions," she said. "I'm sorry about your cot. I got my period earlier than I expected and—" She glanced at the bloodstain and nearly gagged. It took every bit of strength she had in her body and mind to speak to Pauline normally. "When I realized I had my monthly, I got up so quickly that I must have . . . somehow the legs broke. I'll replace it for you."

Pauline stared at her and Anna knew she didn't believe her. She could feel her words twisting in her mouth. In her head.

"I'm taking you to the hospital," Pauline said, reaching for her hand, but Anna pushed her hand away.

"I'm all *right*," she insisted. "I don't need the hospital."

Pauline got to her feet and looked down at her. Anna could tell she was trying to figure out what to do. She knew she should get up. Go to her paints. Act as if nothing at all was wrong. She thought of Jesse, riding home on his bike, and how frightened he must be. She looked at her friend and could see the wheels turning in Pauline's head, jumping to the wrong conclusion. What if she shared her suspicions with Karl?

"Jesse and I are not lovers," she said firmly. "That's what you're thinking, isn't it?"

Pauline glanced at the blood on the cot again, as if she could assess whether it was menstrual blood or not.

"I'm worried about you," she said. "I think you're playing with fire and are too naïve to know it."

"Nonsense." Anna forced herself to stand up and walk toward the mural. Her knees were rubber. "I really need to get back to work," she said, a tremulous hand reaching for her palette.

Pauline stood there another moment or two. Then she said something kind or worried or . . . Anna wasn't sure what words came out of her friend's mouth. She was thinking of how Pauline said she was playing with fire. Pauline had no idea the magnitude of the fire Anna was playing with.

—➤•◄—

"I'm glad you're staying home tonight," Miss Myrtle said when Anna returned to the house that evening. The landlady sat at her drop-down desk in the living room, writing something. A letter. Something. Anna didn't know or care. "You spend far too much time in that horrid warehouse," Miss Myrtle continued. "I was mortified to discover you weren't in your bed last night. I hope no one knows you were there all night. I don't ever want you to stay out like that again. Do you hear me?"

"Uh-huh." *I killed someone,* Anna thought. *Not even twenty-four hours ago, I took a life.* She remembered Martin's fatherless daughters. She rested her fingertips on the back of an upholstered chair to keep herself upright.

Miss Myrtle frowned. "Are you ill?" she asked.

"I'm all right." Anna's voice sounded husky. She'd used it very little that day.

"Are you sure?" Miss Myrtle stood up and came forward to rest the back of her cool fingers on Anna's forehead. "You're not warm, but you look . . . quite pale." She seemed concerned now rather than angry. "Can I make you some tea?"

Anna shook her head. "I'm fine," she said. She needed to get away from Miss Myrtle's scrutiny. She couldn't carry on a normal conversation for one more minute. "Just tired." If Miss Myrtle studied her face any longer, Anna was certain she'd know what she'd done. She turned toward the stairs. "I'm going to bed," she said.

In her room, she shut the door, then leaned her back against it.

You took a life, a voice accused her.

He was a beast, another voice answered.

"Stop!" she pleaded out loud, then whispered, "Please stop. *Please please please. He was going to kill me!*"

She crawled into her bed, still fully clothed, face unwashed, teeth unbrushed. She hugged her arms around her body. She ached all over. She had bruises on her arms, her shoulders, her throat. The inside of her thighs were turning black with them. She was so sore between her legs. Torn up. She knew her body would heal. Her mind, her heart, her soul, though—she wasn't so sure.

Chapter 49

———— ✦ ————

MORGAN

July 20, 2018

O liver pointed to the wall adjacent to the mural. "I think we should hang Anna's original sketch there," he said. "That's where I envision the wall text for the mural, so the sketch will be a cool addition. What do you think?"

I liked knowing that Oliver valued my opinion. "I think that's perfect," I said. "What are you going to say in the wall text?

He shrugged. "I think we admit that we don't understand why Anna Dale added the objects and—as Lisa suggested—we invite the viewer to examine both the sketch and the mural and draw his or her own conclusions," he said. "Then a biographical text will tell what we know—or rather, what we don't know—about the reclusive artist."

"'Reclusive' isn't really the right word, though, is it?" I asked. "I mean, we don't know if she was a recluse. We don't even know if she was crazy. We only know that she did some things we don't understand. Maybe 'mysterious' is a better word." I looked at Oliver to see an amused expression on his face.

"You trying to take over my job?" he teased.

"No, thank you," I said. "I have enough on my plate already. And I need to get back to work."

"Me, too," he said. "But first"—he pulled his phone from his pocket and held it out to me—"let's exchange music for half an hour."

I looked at his phone as if he'd lost his mind.

"C'mon," he said. "You said I need to listen to Nathan's music. Just thirty minutes. It's an experiment."

I smiled, then pulled my phone from my pocket and handed it over. I attached my earbuds to his phone as he did the same with mine. I slipped the earbuds into my ears. A guy was singing something mellow. Very mellow.

"This might put me to sleep," I said. I watched Oliver wince at whatever it was he heard on my Spotify playlist. I laughed.

"Good luck," I said.

"Same to you."

He walked back to his table and I returned my attention to the mural and the delicate, half-missing eyelashes of one of the Tea Party ladies. Some of Oliver's music was pretty, actually. I had to admit it. But it would never keep me awake for long.

When twenty-five minutes had passed, I turned to look at Oliver. He appeared to be deep in concentration, studying something on his computer, but his head was gently bopping to a beat I couldn't hear. I laughed.

"Rock it, homeboy!" I called across the room, loud enough for him to hear.

He looked up and gave me a sheepish smile that made him look boyishly handsome. Pulling my phone from his pocket, he stood up and walked across the foyer to me and we exchanged phones again.

"Pretty music," I said, "but a little too tame for my taste." I nodded toward my phone. "And what did you think?"

"I get the attraction," he said. "The beat. The rhythm. The . . . um . . .

power in it. And some of the women—their lyrics are moving. But I couldn't take a steady diet of it the way you and Nathan can."

"We'll have to toughen you up," I teased.

Lisa suddenly walked into the room from the hall. "What are you two doing, just standing here shooting the breeze?" She gestured toward the mural. She sounded more tired than angry. "C'mon, Morgan," she said. "Start slapping some paint on those bare spots."

"We were just discussing the wall text," Oliver said smoothly.

"Crazy white woman painted ridiculous mural," Lisa said. "What more do you need?"

Oliver laughed, but I could tell something was going on with Lisa. Her eyes were red, the way they'd been the day I caught her crying in the kitchen.

"What's wrong?" I asked.

She sighed. Folded her arms across her chest, tightly, as if she were hugging herself. "Mama Nelle died during the night," she said.

"Oh, no!" I filled with sudden guilt, wondering if bringing Mama Nelle to the gallery, taxing her and her fading memory with my questions . . . I wondered if it had all been too much for the old woman.

"I'm sorry, Lisa," Oliver said.

"Me, too," I said. "I really liked her. And she seemed to know Anna well. She was probably the last person who did." I looked at the mural without really seeing it. "I felt like we really connected," I said.

Lisa studied me curiously. Lowered her arms from across her chest. "The funeral's Monday," she said, turning toward the hallway again. "Make some good progress here and you can go with me to pay your respects."

Chapter 50

———— →•←← ————

ANNA

March 28–29, 1940

That morning's *Chowan Herald* reported that Martin Drapple had gone missing, although there'd been plenty of gossip of his disappearance for nearly a week now. The rumors were that he had marital troubles and money troubles and was deeply depressed over not winning the mural contest. A woman—a friend of his wife's, perhaps—had come to the warehouse to tell Anna that his depression was her fault.

"Martin's a local artist who knows this town like the back of his hand, dear," the woman said, in that kindly Southern voice that could mask daggers. "As soon as you learned that he'd also entered the contest, perhaps you should have gracefully withdrawn and turned the painting of the mural over to him."

Anna wished she had done exactly that. She wished she'd never set foot in Edenton.

Maybe Martin killed himself, people speculated. Or maybe he ran off with another woman. Most likely, the majority seemed to think, he was simply taking some time alone to nurse his emotional wounds. Sometimes, Anna thought that, too. *Oh, Martin Drapple is simply away on a trip*, she fantasized. She frightened herself when she imagined such things. Was she losing her mind? She'd see the red stain on the floor of the warehouse and think, *Oh, I remember the day I dropped the can of paint. How clumsy of me!*

-->=•=<--

"You gonna need to buck up, Anna," Jesse told her later that morning as she stood helplessly in front of the mural, useless brush in her hand. He'd been doing some of the painting for her this week, always the background, leaving the more intricate work for her. But most days, she'd simply sit on one of the chairs and turn her head away from the mural.

"It makes me sick to look at," she told him.

The cot and its telltale stain were gone. Jesse had gotten rid of them and Anna didn't ask what he'd done with them. She didn't care. All that remained of that night in the warehouse was the revolting splash of red paint on the floor. Bile rose in her throat every time she saw it. Guilt and anger took turns toying with her and there was rarely a moment that she wasn't suffering from one or the other. She barely slept, and when she did, she had frightening nightmares that left her confused about what was real and what was not. When she remembered what *was* real, she would break down sobbing whether she was alone in her room at Miss Myrtle's or in an aisle of the pharmacy or sitting numbly in the warehouse.

Once, during the week after it happened, Pauline stopped by the warehouse to ask her to go to lunch. At the sound of Pauline's car outside the warehouse, Jesse put the brush and palette in Anna's hands and pulled her to her feet, his hand on her elbow.

"'Least *pretend* like you workin'," he whispered.

Anna turned down Pauline's invitation, too afraid of what she might say if she spent more than a few minutes with her friend. She didn't want to hear any more of Pauline's questions and suspicions. She was afraid of saying the wrong thing. Giving herself—and Jesse—away. Anna could no longer trust her mind or her tongue. Her brain felt soft, her thoughts jumbled.

If Miss Myrtle wondered why Anna was so quiet at breakfast time, and why she was now home for supper each evening instead of working late into the night, she didn't say, but the landlady *was* clearly worried about her.

"You should see a doctor," she told her Thursday morning. "You're usually so happy-go-lucky. Most likely, you just need some iron."

It took Anna a moment to smile in response, as though Miss Myrtle's words had to fight their way into her brain. If only the cure for what ailed her could be so simple, she thought. But iron wouldn't help her. There was nothing that would ease her guilt and fear.

⇒•≪

When Anna dragged herself to the warehouse Friday morning, she found Jesse already there. He stood in front of the mural and looked over at her, his eyes dark with worry.

"Anna," he said quietly. "What did you do?"

She followed his gaze to the mural. There, jutting out from between the skirts of the Tea Party ladies, was the red fender and black tire of Martin's motorcycle. Anna gasped, her hand to her mouth. Why was she surprised? She'd painted it. She knew she had. Yet her memory of painting it was hazy and dreamlike.

"I'll fix it," Jesse said. "You rest."

"I'll only put it back," she told him.

He frowned at her. "*Why?*" he asked. She heard panic in his voice. "You gotta forget what happened!"

She didn't *know* why. All she knew was that the motorcycle had to be there.

But Jesse painted over it. Anna watched him add the ladies' skirts back where they had been. He was a good artist, but he was only learning how to work in oil and Anna could see him struggle to imitate her style of painting. Anyone with even a slightly discerning eye would know she hadn't painted those skirts. Yet she felt indifferent, watching him. She would come back later tonight, after he was gone. Even though the warehouse haunted her at night, she'd return. She needed to put that motorcycle back where it belonged.

Chapter 51

MORGAN

July 20, 2018

I thought about Mama Nelle as I sat in front of the library's microfilm reader that evening, hunting for more articles about Anna. I wished I'd had the key to unlock Mama Nelle's memory, and now it was too late. I felt saddened by her death. I hoped she'd died peacefully. Painlessly.

I'd just about mastered the microfilm reader now, yet it took forever to hunt for articles that mentioned Anna, especially since they were few and far between. But an article suddenly jumped out at me. An odd one. I noticed it only because of the word "artist" in the headline.

Local Portrait Artist Goes Missing

Anna? I wondered, though it seemed odd they'd call her a portrait artist.

I began to read.

Well-known Edenton portrait artist Martin Drapple disappeared sometime
Friday, according to his wife. Friends reported that Mr. Drapple had been
despondent over losing the government-sponsored post office mural competition to New Jersey artist Anna Dale. Mrs. Drapple stated that her husband had helped Miss Dale work on the mural and that "it was humiliating
for him to lose out to a girl artist." She said that his new motorcycle is
also missing. Anyone with information to the whereabouts of Mr. Drapple is
asked to contact the Edenton police department.

I sat back in the chair and frowned at the microfilm screen. Who the hell
was Martin Drapple? He'd helped Anna? Was there some sort of love triangle going on with him, his wife, and Anna? Or with him, Anna, and Jesse?

It took a minute for that one statement to register: his new motorcycle
is also missing! I thought of the motorcycle poking out from the Tea Party
ladies' skirts. A coincidence or something else?

I paged through the following week's paper, hunting for more news and
found this:

Post Office Artist Anna Dale Closes Warehouse to Visitors

For a number of weeks now, artist Anna Dale has had an open-door policy
in the former Blayton warehouse where she's been busily painting the mural that will hang in the Edenton Post Office. Abruptly this week, she shut
her doors to the public, stating she wanted the completed mural to be more
of a surprise when people finally see it.

Postmaster Clayton Arndt is unconcerned. "Artists are mercurial," he
said when asked for comment. "We're giving Miss Anna the privacy she
needs to concentrate on her work right now." Mr. Arndt thinks the mural will
be completed by the end of April.

Others were not so certain that all is well with the artist. "I think she
must be ill," said Mrs. Oscar Grant who lives on North Granville Street.

"I'd stop in most days to watch her paint and she'd say we were welcome to visit any time we wanted, and now suddenly we can't. Doesn't make sense."

I made copies of the articles, then took an Uber back to the gallery, hoping Oliver would still be there. He was. It seemed he lived there these days. I found him in the empty rear gallery, measuring one of the walls.

"Oh, good," he said when I walked into the room. "I can use a second pair of hands. Hold this?" He handed me the end of the tape measure and motioned for me to walk to the far end of the room. "What are you doing here?" he asked. "I thought you were done for the day?"

"I found some articles I wanted to show you." I walked the end of the tape measure back to him and watched him jot something down in his notebook.

He slipped the tape measure into his jeans pocket and held out his hand. "Let's see," he said.

I handed him the two sheets of paper, then stood next to him as he read. His scent was ever so slightly earthy, as though he'd worked hard all day, and we were close enough that our shoulders touched. He wore a black T-shirt and I wore a blue top—sleeveless, of course—and I liked the feeling of his skin against mine. I liked it more than I ever could have imagined, and I didn't move away. Neither did he.

"Hmm," he said, when he finished reading, his gaze still on the articles in front of him. "What do you make of the motorcycle?"

"I have no idea. It's crazy, isn't it? And then the speculations that she's sick. Maybe she was dying of natural causes. I don't . . ." My voice trailed off. I'd lost my train of thought as I breathed in Oliver's scent. I wished he'd put his arm around me. I wanted to feel his fingers press against my shoulder. Were my feelings toward him completely one-sided? I was eight years his junior. I'd thought that was a lifetime when I first met him. Now I didn't care. *Please touch me before I go out of my mind.*

But he stepped away so he could look at me. "We're never going to know the answers to all this," he said, nodding toward the articles in his hand.

I felt suddenly despondent. "I know," I said. "But at least we can speculate, just for the fun of it."

He smiled at me, and maybe he even said something more to me, but the gallery lights all settled in the blue of his eyes and I seemed to momentarily lose my hearing.

He was, suddenly, extraordinarily beautiful.

Chapter 52

———— ⇒•⇐ ————

ANNA

April 2, 1940

At breakfast that morning, Anna prepared her own plate so that there was not as much food on it as Freda would dish out. She'd taken to doing that lately, the only way to keep Miss Myrtle's questions about her withered appetite at bay. This morning, though, Miss Myrtle must have noticed, for she wrote down the name of her doctor on a piece of paper and set it next to Anna's coffee cup. Then she lifted her own cup to her lips and took a sip.

"The police found Martin Drapple's body on the banks of Queen Anne Creek," she said, setting her cup down again. "Some children stumbled across it and they were acting funny and their mama finally got it out of them. She went down to the station and . . ."

Anna didn't hear the rest of the sentence. Her hand was frozen around her fork.

"Pauline told me last night," Miss Myrtle continued. She picked up her knife to crack the top of her soft-boiled egg. Anna turned her head away from the sight.

What questions would an innocent person ask? she wondered, though her foggy brain would not cooperate. Miss Myrtle saved her the effort.

"His head was bashed in, poor troubled soul," she said. "I thought he was such a lovely man and gifted artist, but something was terribly wrong with him. Pauline said that Karl told her he beat his wife and the children sometimes. Can you imagine? I'm guessing she did it. The wife. But if he beat her, who could blame her? I hope she gets away with it."

Anna's breathing came in quick little gasps and spots dotted the air in front of her eyes. Miss Myrtle seemed too lost in her blather to notice that she was falling apart on the other side of the table, and when Anna stood up so quickly that she nearly took the tablecloth with her, Miss Myrtle looked up in surprise.

"What is it, Anna?" she asked.

"I just remembered . . . something I n-need to do." She stumbled over her words. "Excuse me." She lifted her plate quickly, shakily, hoping Miss Myrtle didn't see that she'd eaten nothing from it, and carried it to the sink. Then she rushed from the house, gulping in lungful after lungful of clean air. Weeping, she walked toward the water in the hope no one would see her tears, her sobs growing stronger with each step. She sat on the sea wall, the stench of fish overwhelming, until she had control over her tears, but they were replaced by the horrid image of Martin's body when the police discovered it. What did he look like after a week and a half? Face eaten away by animals. Brains oozing onto the earth. She still could not believe what she'd done. Leaning over, she vomited into the water.

Getting to her feet again, she began walking, aimlessly, pressing her handkerchief to her mouth. She should go to the police. She could call Karl. Explain what happened. But she would get Jesse in terrible trouble. She would no doubt cost Jesse his life.

She found herself near the Mill Village, which was quiet. Eerily quiet. The only sign of life seemed to be the occasional housewife hanging laundry in her yard. And then Anna spotted it: the face of a skeleton in the front window of one of the small Mill Village houses. She stared at the bony skull. It stared back at her. She walked on and saw that the next house also had a skull in the window. And the next. And the next. They didn't frighten her. She was curious, standing still to observe each one. She thought of the Mill Village homes in her painting, then raced back to Miss Myrtle's, holding the image of the skulls in her memory. She got into her car and drove quickly to the warehouse, where she found Jesse mixing paint. He might have spoken to her; she wasn't listening. She quickly grabbed her palette, mixed a little Cremnitz white with a touch of lampblack and a smidgen of Antwerp blue. She pulled a crate in front of the mural, sat down on it, and painted the small delicate skull in the window of the first Mill Village house.

"Oh, no," Jesse said from behind her. *"Anna."*

She sat back to admire her rendering of the skull. It was absolutely perfect.

Chapter 53

———— ✦ ————

MORGAN

July 23, 2018

Mama Nelle's funeral went on and on and I thought I'd made a big mistake, agreeing to be there when I should have been working on the mural. My ankle twinged as I listened to Saundra and a few of Mama Nelle's other children and relatives tell the tales of the old woman's life. There were funny stories and poignant stories, but I felt little connection to the woman her family described. My relationship to Mama Nelle had been different. We'd shared secrets about Anna. The only problem was, I didn't have a clue what those secrets were.

When the service was over and we were walking up the aisle of the church, Lisa said, "People will get together at the farm but *you* need to go back to work, so I'll drop you at the gallery before I head out there."

"All right." There was no point in me returning to the farm for food and conversation when the person I most wanted to talk with was gone.

"You wait here," Lisa said when we had nearly reached the front door of the church. "I'll bring the car around so you don't need to walk that far." My ankle was much better and I was out of the boot, but walking a distance was still hard for me.

Lisa disappeared into the crush of people filling the vestibule and I pressed myself against the wall to keep out of the way. I felt a tap on my shoulder and turned to see Saundra at my side.

"It was very sweet of you to come," she said.

"I wanted to," I said. "I really liked your mom."

"She liked you, too," Saundra said, then added with a smile, "Even more than I knew."

"What do you mean?"

"Well, I don't know what to make of this, but Mama has . . . had . . . this big old chest in her bedroom. She kept all sorts of things in there." Saundra rolled her beautiful dark eyes. "Papers and receipts and clothes and moth-eaten quilts. Anyway, the strangest thing . . . when I went in her room the morning she died . . . I found her . . ." Saundra seemed to choke up a little and I lightly touched her arm.

"I'm sorry," I said.

"Well"—she pulled herself together—"that morning, I went into her room and the floor and dresser were littered with everything she'd had in the chest. She'd emptied it out, tossed things around the room like she'd gone a little mad. But there was one thing . . . it must have been at the very bottom of the chest and she was driven to find it . . . a diary of some sort. At least I think that's what it is. It has a lock on it, but no key that I could see among her things. I never even knew she kept one. She was not what you would call a writer."

I wasn't sure why Saundra was telling me all this, and my confusion must have shown in my face.

"She wrote a note and put it on the cover of the diary," Saundra said. "She wrote, *Give to the girl with the yellow hair.*"

I was stunned. "Why would she do that?" I asked, but my mind was racing. How far back did the diary go? Was there a chance Mama Nelle had revealed something about Anna in it? Something she thought I should know?

"I have no idea," Saundra said.

I looked down at her empty hands. "Did you bring the diary with you?" I asked.

"Well, I hope you don't mind," she said, an apology in her voice. "I'll definitely turn it over to you, since that's what she wanted me to do, but I would really like to read it first myself. I had no idea she kept it and I really—"

"Of course." I could imagine how hungry the daughter of a loving mother would be to read about her life, although I couldn't care less what stories my own mother might tell. I wanted to ask Saundra, *When can I get it?*, but managed to hold my tongue.

"I'll have to break the lock." Saundra looked apologetic.

"Of course," I said again. "I wonder if there's something in it about Anna Dale and that's why she's leaving it to me."

"I'll let you know if I come across anything like that," Saundra said, "but honestly, Morgan? You shouldn't get your hopes up. She wasn't thinking clearly at all the last couple of days. It doesn't make any sense she'd leave her diary to you. I think she was simply not herself that night."

I nodded. "I understand," I said. "And I'd like to read it, but I'll give it back to you afterward. It should stay in your family."

"Thanks for understanding that," Saundra said. "Oh, and I also found some old sketches of family members that Uncle Jesse drew when he was a boy. Do you think Lisa might want them for the gallery?"

"Maybe," I said. "I'll ask her." But my words came out woodenly, mechanically. All I could think about was getting my hands on Mama Nelle's diary.

Chapter 54

—➤•⊰—

ANNA

April 5, 1940

Anna wasn't sure if Jesse was angry at her or maybe just worried. She didn't really care which. He was wisely keeping people away from the warehouse and they didn't understand why they couldn't come inside to watch her paint, as they had in the past. She didn't know what he told them or why they obeyed him, either. She heard someone muttering about the "uppity colored boy" giving them orders, but she shut out the words. They had to stay away.

Martin's spirit was in the warehouse. Jesse didn't believe Anna when she told him, but two of the lights that hung from the ceiling beams blew out during the week and Anna was certain Martin had made it happen. She'd never believed in spirits before, but now she did, utterly and completely. The lights were up too high for her and Jesse to fix, but she didn't care. She didn't care about anything. She didn't even care about painting the mural . . . except that she'd added a hammer to the painting before

Jesse's arrival the day before. He hadn't even noticed, which had struck her as amusing for some reason.

"Why you laughin'?" Jesse had looked suspicious. "That ain't no real laugh."

Anna'd tightened her lips to hold back her laughter. The hammer was practically right in front of him and he didn't see it. It didn't seem all that funny to her later, but at that moment, she'd nearly been in hysterics. She'd thought she should add some drops of blood dripping from the hammer's claw.

"You done lost your marbles," Jesse had said, worry in his dark eyes.

She knew she'd lost her marbles. Every once in a while she thought she found them again, and in those moments she knew clearly that her mind was going downhill, but it was easier to just keep plowing forward than to find a way to fix the mess she'd made.

-->=-=<--

The doctor came to the house on Friday afternoon. Miss Myrtle insisted that Anna see him, and he came upstairs to her room and listened to her heart and her lungs and looked into her throat and her ears.

"You are very slender for your height," he announced, tweaking the end of his waxy mustache, "and Miss Myrtle is afraid you're not getting enough to eat."

"I don't have much of an appetite lately," Anna said. "It must be the weather."

"Try to eat more," he said. "You need to put some meat on your bones."

The word "bones" made Anna think of the skull in the window of the Mill Village house and she thought she was going to start laughing right then and there. It was a monumental struggle to prevent the burst of laughter from leaving her mouth, but she succeeded.

"Do you sleep well?" the doctor asked.

"Perfectly," she said, but in her mind she added, *Except for the nightmares.*

They were wretched things, the nightmares. If she thought the doctor had a pill to make them go away, she would have told him about them.

"Do you feel melancholy?" he asked.

"No!" She spoke sharply. Melancholia had been her mother's diagnosis during her dark spells. Anna resisted the word. She was not like her mother. "Melancholy" didn't capture how she felt. She was *angry* about what Martin had done to her. What he'd taken from her. And she felt sick to her stomach with guilt, and scared to death. But the doctor didn't ask her about any of that.

"Miss Myrtle thinks you might be working too hard," the doctor said.

"I'll slow down," she said, thinking, *If I got any slower, I'd be dead.* She was now spending her time in the warehouse either staring into space, thinking of nothing, really, or telling Jesse how to do what still needed to be done on the mural. Jesse kept trying to get her to pick up a brush and work on it herself, but she had no interest.

"When was your last menstrual period?" the doctor asked.

She was surprised by the question, and she didn't know the answer. She'd never kept good track.

"Three weeks ago," she said, but she started thinking about the sanitary belt in her lingerie drawer. When was the last time she'd had to wear that wretched thing? When did she last reach into the box of sanitary pads?

She made herself think about something else. The way the doctor's mustache was uneven, one side higher than the other. That made her smile.

"Why are you smiling?" He smiled warmly back at her.

"I don't know," she said. "I guess I'm happy."

She waited until he'd left her room before she burst into tears.

Chapter 55

MORGAN

July 27, 2018

I handed my signed AA attendance form to Rebecca as I took my seat next to her desk.

"Sorry I'm late," I said. I was only late by five or six minutes, but the last thing I wanted to do was irk Rebecca. I'd lost myself in the mural that morning. Absolutely lost myself. I'd been working on the silver handle of the knife in the peanut factory worker's mouth. It took me hours to do the inpainting. I did it perfectly, though. I was tempted to call Oliver over to have him tell me how awesome it was, but I didn't need his approval anymore. I knew it was awesome. Even sitting there next to Rebecca's desk, I could still see the sheen of the silver blade and the line of shadow where no light hit the handle.

"You look like the cat that swallowed the canary today," Rebecca said, looking up from the AA form. "What's up with you?"

"I did amazing work today," I said. "Amazing work all week, actually. It feels good."

Rebecca raised her eyebrows, then smiled. "That's nice to hear," she said.

"I didn't think I was going to be able to finish the mural in time for the gallery opening and then I'd end up back in prison, but now I think maybe I can."

Rebecca cocked her head to one side. "Why would you end up back in prison?"

"Because I didn't finish on time."

Rebecca took off her black-framed glasses. "Morgan, you are *out*," she said. "Out on parole. You were released on parole with the understanding that you'll work and pay restitution, but that has nothing to do with some arbitrary deadline."

"No." I frowned at her. "I have to finish the mural by the time the gallery opens or I go back to—"

"No." Rebecca spoke firmly. "Who told you that?"

"Lisa and the lawyer, Andrea Fuller." Had they ever actually said those words? I couldn't remember. "Though maybe . . . maybe I just assumed from what they were saying . . ." My voice trailed off as I tried to piece together the long-ago conversation I'd had with the two women.

"I'm sorry you've misunderstood all this time," Rebecca said. "You can relax. You know my requirements for you and none of them has to do with when you finish restoring that mural."

I should have felt angry. I'd had the threat of prison hanging over my head all this time. Yet a strange indifference came over me. A strange peace. I was going to finish that mural on time, not because I had to but because I wanted to. I'd finish it for Lisa and her house. I'd finish it because that's what Jesse'd wanted. I'd finish it for Anna.

Most of all, I thought, I'd finish it for myself.

Chapter 56

———— ✦ ————

ANNA

April 8, 1940

T he police found Martin's motorcycle in the woods by the Mill Vil-
     lage," Miss Myrtle said over breakfast Monday morning.

"Oh?" Anna aimed for boredom in her voice as if the news were of no
consequence. As if it had nothing whatsoever to do with her.

"Pauline said that Karl was actually the one who found it," Miss Myrtle
continued. "He was on a call over there about something or other and
spotted the red fender tucked in some shrubbery."

Anna tried to lift her coffee cup to her lips, but it shivered so violently
in her hand that she quickly returned it to its saucer.

"I think you should know, dear," Miss Myrtle said, "that Mrs. Drapple
told Karl she thinks Jesse Williams killed him."

"That's ridiculous," Anna said. "Jesse wouldn't hurt a fly."

"Well, Mrs. Drapple thinks Martin might have been going to the warehouse to see *you* the night they suspect he got killed, and that Jesse was there and murdered him."

Anna focused on cutting a piece of the sausage patty she wasn't interested in eating, but she felt Miss Myrtle's eyes boring into her face.

"I hope you don't believe that for an instant," she said, before slipping the sausage into her mouth. She couldn't seem to make eye contact with her landlady. She moved the sausage around with her tongue, unsure she'd be able to get it down.

"I don't know Jesse Williams well," Miss Myrtle said, her eyes gazing into space as though deep in thought. "I know he comes from a good, hardworking colored family, though. I just don't like people thinking that way about you. You never should have gotten into the habit of staying after dark in that place. It gave people the wrong idea."

Anna nodded, still moving the sausage from one side of her mouth to the other. She wished she hadn't gotten into that habit herself. She thought of how the warehouse lights kept blinking out. Martin, working his evil magic from the grave.

"They don't think Mrs. Drapple killed him, at any rate," Miss Myrtle said. "That was my hunch, but I guess they've been able to rule her out for some reason."

Anna finally swallowed the sausage, then looked across the table at Miss Myrtle's kind face with its plump pale cheeks. She had the strongest urge to confess: *It was me,* she wanted to say. *Me, me, me!*

But before she could open her mouth, Freda walked into the room carrying the silver coffeepot. She held it in the air in the gesture that meant *Who'd like more?,* and Miss Myrtle held up her cup, while Anna covered hers with her hand.

——⋙•⋘——

Later that morning, Jesse and Anna were in the warehouse when they heard a car driving up the dirt road. They looked at each other. Anna was sitting on the chair by Jesse's easel; he was on the crate in front of the mural, adding some fine detailing to a clothesline in the yard of one of the Mill Village houses. Anna figured they both knew who it was. She raced to the window and peered out to see Karl and another policeman getting out of the big black Ford V8.

"The police," she said.

In an instant, Jesse opened the can of blue paint and used a wide brush to slap some of it over the tire and red fender of the motorcycle that— thanks to Anna—kept emerging no matter how many times he scraped it off or painted over it. His hands shook as he set down the paint can, resting the brush across the top of it.

Anna opened the door and drew in a tremulous breath. She needed to keep her wits about her. Not say anything crazy. Although the truth was, she no longer trusted herself to know crazy from sane.

"Hi, Karl!" she called as the two men neared the doorway. Karl wore his uniform and had one of those blackjacks attached to his belt. The sight of it made Anna's heart pound. She imagined him using it on Jesse.

"Hey, Anna." Karl and the other man, a rotund little fellow in a too-tight uniform, stepped inside the warehouse. "This is Officer Charles," Karl said.

Anna nodded to the young officer. He looked about her age. "And you remember Jesse Williams, Karl," she said, nodding toward Jesse. Her voice seemed to boomerang in her ears. She sent it out and it tore right around and back into her head again. Did she sound strange to Karl, too?

Jesse walked toward them, wiping his hands on his dungarees. He didn't reach out to shake the men's hands, though, and they didn't reach out to shake his.

"We'd just like to ask the two of you a few questions, given as you knew Martin Drapple," Karl said.

"Not very well," Anna said, then added, "Hey! I haven't seen Pauline in ages. How is she?" She remembered how her mother used to say, *Hay is for horses!*, and the thought made her chuckle out loud. Even she could hear the anxiety in the sound, so inappropriate to the conversation. All three of them stared at her. She only wanted to remind Karl that they were friends. Him. Pauline. Her. "How is she doing?" Anna had the feeling Pauline had cut her from her social life after the day she'd jumped to conclusions about her and Jesse. *That terrible day.* Anna couldn't let herself remember it right now or she would fall apart. How much had Pauline told Karl about that morning? The blood on the ruined cot? Pauline would have had to tell him they weren't getting their cot back. What else had she said?

"She's fine," Karl said finally, his voice businesslike. "Now, when is the last time you two saw Mr. Drapple?

Oh God. She wasn't ready for questions about Martin. She should have thought about what she might be asked and rehearsed her answers. She looked at Jesse. "When was it, Jess?" she asked him, but she could tell by the look of stark terror on Jesse's usually calm face that he was going to be no help. She'd grown accustomed to him taking the lead these days. Accustomed to him saving her, really. Right now, he was paralyzed with fear. She was a white woman; he was a colored man. Even though she'd been the one to kill Martin Drapple, Jesse was undoubtedly in far more danger than she was.

She turned back to Karl. "I think it was the day you were here," she said, scrambling to get it right. "Remember? All of us stretched the canvas? And Martin's wife showed up?" She looked at Jesse again. "Right, Jesse?" she asked. "Was that the last time?"

Jesse tried to speak but nothing came out. He cleared his throat. "Yes, Miss Anna." He spoke in the most subservient voice she'd ever heard come out of his mouth. "Pretty sure you got it right."

"That was the last time?" Karl asked. His buddy was wandering around the warehouse, making Anna nervous. She tried to follow him out of the corner of her eye. Was there anything incriminating for him to find?

"What happened here?" the man asked, pointing to the red paint stain on the floor.

"Oh, I was clumsy when I opened a can." She smiled at the little man.

He was so round, the way he was packed in his uniform, that he looked like he should roll instead of walk. "I tried to open it too quickly," she added. "Dropped the whole thing."

"You opened the can way over here?" Officer Charles asked. "Why not over there?" He pointed to the table where all the paints were neatly lined up.

"I had a crate over there at the time, and I . . . it was too low." She shrugged. "I should have opened it by the paint table. You're right." *Brilliant*, she thought, pleased she'd come up with an explanation, weak though it may have been. She smiled at him again. She needed him on her side.

"Why don't you open the warehouse up to the public anymore?" Karl asked. "Folks were enjoyin' it, watchin' you paint."

"Oh, I thought it would be more fun for them to see the finished product, you know, all at once. As a surprise. More dramatic that way. Weather hasn't been too good for having the garage doors open, either." Did that make sense? She couldn't remember how the weather had been lately. It was the last thing on her mind.

Karl gave her a look that raised the hairs on the back of her neck. She had to turn away. She glanced at Jesse, but he was staring into space. His body might have been in the warehouse, but Anna had the feeling his mind was on the banks of Queen Anne Creek.

Karl walked over to the mural and pointed to the fresh blue paint Jesse had hastily slapped over the motorcycle. "What's going on here?" he asked.

Anna scrambled to find an answer in her untrustworthy brain, but Jesse cleared his throat. "Miss Anna, she don't like how it was and is doin' that part over again," he said.

"I wasn't addressin' you, boy," Karl snarled at him

"Don't talk to him that way!" Anna said. She knew instantly that she'd spoken too quickly and too sharply, but she'd never heard Karl talk like that. "You know his name." She tried to speak more calmly. Softly. "It's 'Jesse.' You worked side by side with him to get this canvas on the wall, so please don't act like you never saw him before."

Karl glared at her and she knew she'd said way too much. She knew it before half those words were out of her mouth. One of the big burned-out ceiling lights suddenly flickered back to life and she let out a yelp.

"You're wound up mighty tight, aren't you?" Karl said. He nodded toward the door. "Come outside with me, Anna."

Reluctantly, she followed him outside. He shut the door behind them and she hoped Jesse could handle Officer Charles on his own.

Outside, she turned to face Karl. "Why are you here?" she asked. "We don't know anything about Martin Drapple."

"So you and the boy are a 'we'?" he asked.

"What? No! Not the way you mean. For heaven's sake, he and Peter . . . I couldn't have gotten the mural as far along as it is without them. You saw how hard they worked to help me."

"Why is he still here, though? Where *is* Peter Thomas, by the way? Why isn't he here, too?"

"He's on the baseball team at the high school. But Jesse's—" She didn't want to say that Jesse had dropped out. "Jesse's finished with school, so that's why he's still here. He helps me, and in return, I'm teaching him how to be a better artist." She thought of Jesse dragging Martin's body out of the warehouse. She would be in jail right now if not for his help.

"Pauline thinks you've gotten a bit too familiar with him," Karl said.

"Pauline is wrong." She folded her arms across her chest, proud of how firm her voice sounded.

"Is he harming you?"

She laughed. "Of course not."

"You can tell me." Karl tried to soften his voice, but it sounded false. She'd liked Karl so much, but at that moment, she didn't like him at all.

"Karl, no, he's not harming me," she said. "Quite the opposite. He's a big help to me. How many different ways do I need to say it?"

It seemed to take forever, but the men finally left. Anna worried they were listening outside the windows of the warehouse, even though she'd heard their car head back up the dirt road. She held her finger to her lips after they left and then went outside to walk the perimeter of the ware-house, knowing she was acting crazy again. But before she and Jesse spoke to each other, she needed to be absolutely certain they were alone.

By the time she was in the warehouse again, she'd started to cry. She stood in front of the mural, tears running down her cheeks, and Jesse sat on the crate just watching her go to pieces. Finally she was able to speak.

"I'm so sorry I got you involved in this."

"My choice to git rid of him," he said. "Only thing is, I believe I made it worse for you. Made you have to lie. Made you go plumb off your rocker."

"I didn't tell Karl anything about you," she said.

"I knew you wouldn't." He let out a small laugh. "No matter how nuts you gonna git, I know you won't never do nothin' to make trouble for me."

"We've got to think of ourselves as innocent," she said. "We have to think as though we have nothing to hide. Nothing to be afraid of." Her gaze fell on the mural, on the big blue smudge Jesse had painted over the motorcycle. She would put the motorcycle back in the picture. Tonight, maybe, or tomorrow. It would be her punishment for taking a man's life, having to look at that thing every time she saw her painting.

Chapter 57

———— ✦ ————

MORGAN

August 2, 2018

I was alone in the foyer at six o'clock Thursday evening, sitting cross-legged in front of the mural, when Saundra walked into the gallery carrying a large, rectangular box. I started to set down my palette, but she stopped me.

"Don't get up," she said. "I just wanted to drop these things off. Those sketches of Jesse's I told you about and the diary." She set the box down on one end of Oliver's folding table.

"Mama Nelle's diary!" I couldn't mask my excitement at the thought of seeing what was in that book. I set my palette down and got to my feet, brushing the dust from the back of my jeans.

"Well, guess what?" Saundra said, lifting a thin, ancient-looking leather-bound book from the box.

"What?" As I moved closer, I could see that the book's small gold lock had been pried open. I reached out to take the book from her hands. The leather felt like butter beneath my fingers.

"It's not Mama's after all," Saundra said. "I believe it might be your artist's."

I simply stared at her, speechless. "Anna Dale's?" I finally managed to say, as if there could possibly be another artist she would refer to as mine.

Saundra nodded. "The inscription in the front reads *To Anna* and it's from her mother. When I realized it wasn't Mama's, I felt like I'd be intrusive reading it—not to mention I have zero time—so you'll just have to tell me if it says anything exciting."

I looked down at the book in my hands and gently lifted the leather cover. There, in slightly blurry, slanted blue handwriting, were the words:

> *My darling Anna, share your deepest thoughts here in this journal,*
> *my love, and know that I will always be with you, forever and ever.*
> *Mom*

I could barely tear my eyes away from the words to look back at Saundra. "Oh my *God*, Saundra!" I said. "This could tell us so much." I opened the book at random. The pages felt crinkly and brittle, and they were covered with a rounded vertical script—a miniature example of the distinctive vertical loops so evident in Anna's signature on the mural. "This is so cool!" I looked up at Saundra again. "I spend half my day wondering what was going through Anna's mind while she painted this thing." I nodded toward the mural. "Maybe this will tell me."

"Why on earth my mother would have it, I don't know," Saundra said.

"It doesn't make sense," I agreed. "Mama Nelle would have been a little girl when Anna painted the mural, right? Nineteen-forty?"

"Right." Saundra nodded. "But however it came to be in her hands, I'm just happy you want it, and that Mama was able to let me know I should give it to you."

"Me, too." I hugged the journal to my chest. I felt ridiculously happy, holding something that had spent so much time in Anna's hands.

"Would you like to see the sketches?" Saundra asked.

"Yes, sure," I said, although I was answering more to be polite than anything else. What I really wanted was to dig into the diary. The *journal*.

Saundra pulled a sheaf of sketch paper from the box and began spreading the portraits out on the table. There were six of them and the subjects all looked like African Americans.

"I'm pretty sure this one was my mother when she was a little girl," Saundra said, pointing to one of the drawings. "It looks like a photograph I have of her. And this one might be my aunt Dodie, Mama and Uncle Jesse's older sister. I can make some educated guesses as to the others, but I really don't know for sure."

"These really don't look like Jesse Williams's work," I said, frowning at the sketches. "I'll have to show them to Oliver—the curator—and see what he thinks."

Saundra pulled out her phone to check the time. "Well," she said, slipping her purse over her shoulder, "do what you want with them. They have to be from when he was a kid, given the age of my mother in the drawing, so probably not as polished an artist as he was later. And I've got to run." She nodded toward the journal I still held against my chest like a treasure. "You be sure to tell me what you learn, all right?"

Chapter 58

——— ✦ ———

ANNA

Wednesday, May 22, 1940

I'm pregnant with Martin Drapple's child.

Those words make my skin crawl.

I haven't written anything here in so long because . . . I don't know. I guess because I didn't want to see the truth in writing. I've been sick, but it seems the sicker I've felt physically, the stronger I've felt mentally, and the sickness is finally waning. I'm thinking clearly these days. I paint constantly and well. The mural is once again my friend.

Jesse doesn't agree. He tells me I'm still not myself. "You ain't a right-thinkin' woman, Anna," he says. He bases this on the fact that I have left the motorcycle and the skeleton head and the hammer and a few other odds and ends in the painting. I've come to see beauty in them, which worries him and sometimes makes me think he's right. I don't think I'm crazy, but I have changed. Of course I have. Martin no longer haunts me in the warehouse, turning out the lights, turning them on again. No, Martin now haunts me from inside. His spirit grows in my belly and I can't get away from it. There is no question which haunting is worse.

Miss Myrtle asked the doctor to come see me again, but I refused to let him into my room. Miss Myrtle commented on how little I eat. "Yet you seem to be putting on weight," she said. Oh, she must know, but how? I certainly am not yet showing. Has she heard me getting sick in the early mornings? Does she think I'm carrying Jesse's child? If she thinks I'm expecting, who else could she possibly imagine to be the father? And what exactly am I going to do? I will be able to camouflage my growing belly with my smock when I'm in the warehouse, but out in the world it will be another story. I must finish the mural and install it on the post office wall very soon before everyone in Edenton guesses my secret. I've already ordered the lead white that I'll use for the installation. Jesse will help, and Peter and Mr. Arndt, and I'll have to find one or two other people. It's going to be quite a job. Jesse says I have to take out the motorcycle and other things before it's installed. I know he's right, but for now, they remain. That's my Edenton in the mural right now. My personal Edenton. Beauty and the beast.

This morning, I finally told Jesse about the baby. I think he'd guessed, because I've been so sick. His aunt Jewel, who lives with his family, is a midwife full of stories. He knows more about these things than most ~~seventeen~~ eighteen- (he just had a birthday) year-old boys.

He flat-out told me I have to get rid of it. "Aunt Jewel might could help," he said.

I don't think I could do that. The baby was fathered by a monster, yes, but it is half mine. And yet . . . I can't possibly have a baby! Where would I go? I can't return to Plainfield with a child. I have no one there to help me and I'd be ostracized by my neighbors and bring shame to my mother's memory. But I can't stay in Edenton, either. I would be more of an outcast than I already am. Jesse said people will think the baby is his, and he's probably right. "Who else you been spendin' every day with?" he asked me. If people believe the baby is his . . . I can't bear to think about it, and I'm sure it's on his mind. Negro men have been hung for less.

I told him I'd protect him. If anyone questions me, I'll make up a lover. I won't let him be hurt by what's happened.

Jesse is with me in the warehouse only in the afternoons now, as his family needs him on the farm for planting in the mornings. He still comes nearly every day though, and I look forward to the sound of his bicycle tires on the dirt road. No one else comes to the warehouse these days, and that is fine. Karl and Pauline rarely come to Miss Myrtle's for Sunday dinner any longer, either. The couple of times they came were nothing like our chatty festive Christmas meal. Conversation was stilted. Karl was stiff and quiet. Pauline was distant, although she does talk rather incessantly about the curtains and blankets and things she's making for the nursery. Miss Myrtle chatters throughout the meal, seemingly ignorant of the chill in the room. I liked Pauline and I'm sad to lose her, but I have no time for her, really, now. I must finish the mural and then figure out what to do about this child I'm carrying.

Thursday, May 23, 1940

Odd that just yesterday I wrote about my sadness over losing Pauline's friendship and then today she showed up at the warehouse! Her smile seemed sheepish, and I guess she felt embarrassed about letting our friendship fall to the wayside. She'd brought along a small box of ginger cookies and she set them on the table where I keep the paints. I think the cookies were a peace offering. Then she stood back to look at the mural. She said, "Why, it's a masterpiece!" which ordinarily would have pleased me, but I didn't want her to study it too closely. I stood in front of the Tea Party ladies where the motorcycle cut through their dresses, masking it from her eyes. Jesse'd told me I was playing with fire, leaving the motorcycle in the painting, and in that moment, I realized how right he was and how foolish I'd been. I'm not as sane as I thought.

I swept forward, slipping my arm through Pauline's as though we are still great and intimate pals, and steered her away from the mural. I asked about how she was fixing up her house for the baby, which I know is her favorite topic, and I could hear my nervousness as I spoke and my fake enthusiasm. I wondered if my question sounded as false to her ears as it did to mine.

I sat her down in the chair by Jesse's easel and moved the other chair—the one I still thought of as Peter's—close to her, picking up the box of cookies along the way. She said nothing, but simply obeyed me by taking a seat.

I told her how much I missed spending time with her, and my fingers shook as I struggled with the string on the cardboard box. My heart pounded with the lie about missing her. How could I miss a woman who had almost certainly spread a rumor about Jesse and me to her husband?

She claimed to miss me, too, but I thought her smile, too, seemed insincere.

We chatted for a bit, but it was nothing like the early days of our friendship when she shared confidences and her deepest feelings. I thought we both knew we were now playing a game.

After eating a cookie and filling the air with a mundane recitation of the curtains she was making for her living room windows, Pauline got to her feet and began strolling idly through the area of the warehouse where I work. Her belly protrudes somewhat. She is a couple of months ahead of me, I think. Looking at her, I wonder how long I'll be able to mask my own pregnancy.

She asked me what it's been like, painting in the warehouse.

It struck me as an odd question to ask after all these months and I guessed she was just making conversation. My heart pounded every time she neared the mural, but she seemed disinterested in it. Instead, she studied my paints table, peered into the metal bucket where I keep my straight-edge and tape measure and other tools, all the while asking me lackadaisical questions about the trials of working in isolation. I tried to determine what she was getting at. The only thing I could think of was Jesse. She was feeling me out to see if Jesse and I were now—or were still—more than friends. It began to irritate me, her idle chatter, and after a short time I got to my feet and told her I needed to get back to work.

She looked abashed and apologized for keeping me from my painting.

"No bother," I said. I told her it had been a delight to have her visit. I added that I didn't think I'd be in Edenton much longer, and she asked if I'd go back to New Jersey. I said I most likely would. How I wish I knew where I was going! I told her I'd have the supplies to install the mural within a couple of weeks, and then could have kicked myself for mentioning the mural, since her gaze darted toward it. I ushered her quickly to the door, thanked her for the cookies, and sent her on her way.

What an odd visit! Now, though, I feel bad about it. Maybe Pauline was lonely and I'd rushed her out, blathering on about inconsequential things, when she may have had a burning need to confide in a true friend. So now I feel guilty for treating her as less than that. Perhaps she was trying to make amends. I am ashamed that I didn't let her.

Friday, May 24, 1940

I'm terrified as I write this.

No, Pauline was not looking for genuine friendship yesterday. Pauline was a damn *spy! I thought she was behaving oddly, but it never occurred to me that she was doing her husband's dirty work. How foolish of me for not guessing!*

Jesse was at his easel this morning and I was working on my signature on the mural, when a knock came on the warehouse door. Jesse and I looked at each other. We hadn't heard a car and I had no idea who it might be. I stood up from the crate where I'd been sitting to paint my name, walked to the door and pulled it open. There stood Karl Maguire in his police uniform. I peered around the door frame to see his car parked far down the road. He'd wanted to surprise me. Or surprise us, I suppose.

I'd told Jesse I planned to paint over the motorcycle this afternoon, but now I wondered if I was too late. I'd been too eager to paint my name, to see it glowing in the corner against the deep green of the Mill Village lawn. Now I was kicking myself for my narcissism.

Karl greeted both of us, touching the brim of his policeman's hat. Then he looked past me and I saw that Jesse—my brilliant Jesse—had quickly moved his easel in front of the mural, blocking the motorcycle from Karl's view. Instead of the motorcycle, all Karl would be able to see was a detailed drawing of one of the Williams family's mules on the easel. But Karl didn't so much as glance at the mural. I didn't want to let him inside the warehouse, but he stepped past me, glanced around my studio space, then stood squarely in front of me.

"Where is your hammer, Anna?" he asked.

I played dumb, desperately trying to buy time. Finally I said, "I don't have a hammer."

Karl pointed out that I'd had one back when he was helping us stretch the canvas. He looked past me at Jesse. "Do you remember that, Jesse Williams?" he asked. "And Pauline told me she stopped by yesterday and she didn't see one, so I was wondering what happened to it?"

I was stunned, torn between my anger at Pauline and my desperate scrambling to find a way around Karl's question. I could say that the hammer he saw that day hadn't been mine. That Peter had brought one with him. But then I'd be getting Peter in trouble.

Then Karl told us that a bloody hammer had been found in the woods near Martin Drapple's motorcycle. "Just wondering if it might have been yours," he asked.

I was breathing hard and fast. Surely he noticed. I tried to figure out what an innocent person would say at that moment.

I asked him if that's what he thought killed Martin. The hammer.

"No, a person killed him with the hammer," Karl said. "And I know you had a hammer you can't seem to produce."

I said maybe someone else might have brought a hammer the day we worked on stretching the canvas. Karl had brought tools, himself.

Karl gave me a look I can only describe as disgusted and said he'd just wanted to give me a chance to show him my hammer. "I see you can't do that," he said. He touched the brim of his hat and wished Jesse and me a good day. Then he was gone.

Jesse and I turned to stare at one another.

I asked him where the hammer is, and he said he threw it in the woods by the Mill Village. He spoke quietly, one hand clutching the back of his chair. "I throwed it hard," he said, "way out into a mess o' cat claw and creeper and poison ivy." He demonstrated the pitch he used to send the hammer flying into the brush. He didn't think anyone could possibly have found it. Maybe Karl was lying? he suggested. Maybe he was trying to trick me in some way?

I don't know what to make of it all. I knotted my hands together, trying to think. I remembered Jesse'd had the wherewithal to put on a pair of the work gloves when he got rid of Martin and the hammer and the motorcycle. My fingerprints would be on the hammer, but not his. That gives me a strange sense of peace. I don't know what they would do to me, but if they found Jesse guilty of murdering a white man, I am sure that would be the end of him.

I sat down with this journal and began to recount what just happened. Writing has a way of calming me, but Jesse is angry and keeps interrupting me.

"What're you doing?" he asked. "You supposed to fix that motorcycle!"

I promised him that I would. I looked over at the mural, at my distinctive, prideful signature in the lower right-hand corner. I wonder if I'll ever get a chance to see the mural hanging in the post office? What will they do with it if I am locked away in jail?

Later on Friday

Everything changed just minutes after I wrote about Karl's visit this morning. My whole life changed.

I was mixing some of the paint I'd need to cover the motorcycle and restore the ladies' dresses when Peter burst into the warehouse. His face was red, his pale hair plastered to his forehead with sweat.

"The cops are coming to arrest you!" he said breathlessly, his eyes on me. He said that two policemen came to his house and asked him if I kept a hammer in the warehouse and he'd said yes, not knowing he was getting me in trouble. He glanced at Jesse. He said the police think both of us killed Martin. He was bent over, trying to catch his breath. "You need to run!" he said.

Run where? I stood up, my heart pounding, thinking, my baby will be born in jail. And they will kill Jesse. I had the mob scene, the brutal lynching, already running through my mind when Jesse jumped to his feet, pulled out his pocketknife, and stabbed it into one edge of the mural. Then he sawed at it, cutting the fabric free from the stretcher.

I ran toward him in shock, trying to grab his hand where he clutched the knife, but he shook me off. "We gotta go!" he said. "But we ain't leavin' this behind."

I couldn't think. My mind turned to powder. Jesse had a plan. I didn't. I would do whatever he said, but I wouldn't make Peter a party to our crime. I told him to leave and not tell a soul that he'd spoken to us.

Peter hesitated only a second before taking off. I grabbed my own utility knife from the bucket and began cutting the left side of the mural free from the stretcher as Jesse cut the right side. We finished our work in a few silent, panicked minutes. Jesse crumpled the huge mass of canvas in his arms. All my work. I felt a moment of grief, looking at the splash of colors spilling from his hands and trailing on the floor.

"Let's go!" he said.

I grabbed my purse and this journal and followed him outside, my heart drumming in my chest as I looked down the road. I expected to see Karl's car heading toward us, but as far as I could see, the road was clear.

I helped Jesse cram the canvas into the backseat, then got behind the wheel. It took a few tries to get the car to start. I turned it around and headed back up the dirt road wondering where to go. Should we just head out of town? Which direction should we drive? How long before they caught up to us?

But Jesse said to head for his house. His family's farm. I protested, but I had no better idea. Yet it seemed like a mistake. Wouldn't they look for us at the Williams farm? I didn't want to involve his family. His parents. I felt ashamed that I'd gotten their son into such a mess. But I followed his directions into the countryside and soon I was turning down the road that ran to his family's house.

His father came out of the barn, and Aunt Jewel came out of the house, little Nellie by her side. Nellie ran toward Jesse, flinging her arms around his waist. Jesse spoke to his aunt rather than his father.

"We in trouble," he said. "Anna and me."

His father's eyes widened with fear or anger, I couldn't tell which, and Jesse quickly set him straight before I had a chance to.

"Ain't what you thinkin'," Jesse said quickly. He explained that the police thought we'd killed Martin. That he had to leave. That the Williams family had to let me stay with them. Hide me. Keep me safe.

I wanted to tell him not to run away, that somehow this would all work out, but I knew he had to go. In that moment, I felt as though I might be safe, but he was in great danger. I felt the protection of the two adults standing next to me. Deep down, though, I knew a colored family was no protection at all. They couldn't even protect themselves from the danger I was bringing to them.

Jesse said he had to take my car, and I pressed the key into his hand. I wanted to say more—so much more—but he took off at a run toward my car. We watched him drive off in a cloud of dust, the bulky, crumpled mural blocking the side and rear windows. Where could he go that he would be safe?

Nowhere, I thought, and I started to cry.

Tears running down my cheeks, I looked from Mr. Williams's startled face to Aunt Jewel's. I sobbed, apologizing to them over and over again.

Mr. Williams was angry. He said something about Jesse spending too much time with me, too little time working on the farm where he belonged.

I wanted to say something about Jesse's talent. How he shouldn't be held back. But who was I to pass that sort of judgment when I'd thrown him into a mess that could hold him back for the rest of his life?

Aunt Jewel put an arm around my shoulders and told me to come with her into the house. She called me "Sugar," and I felt like a child as she led me inside. The house seemed empty and quiet and our footsteps echoed as we walked through the dining room where I'd shared a meal with the family not all that long ago, then up the stairs. I was glad no one seemed to be home.

She led me into a small bedroom. A narrow bed was against one wall, a window next to the metal headboard. There was a wooden chair near the window, but no dresser or bureau in the room. A huge old chest stood at the foot of the bed.

She told me we were in Nellie's room. There was a mattress beneath Nellie's bed that could be pulled out for me to sleep on. "The police less likely to look in a child's room for a . . . for you," she said, but added that she needed to think of a good hiding place for me in case they showed up. She asked if I thought they would, and I heard the first hint of worry in her voice.

I just nodded. I couldn't seem to find my voice.

Aunt Jewel studied my face and I didn't turn away. I needed to put my trust in her.

"How far along are you?" she asked.

Somehow she knew. I told her it wasn't Jesse's and she asked me whose it was.

I told her everything then, struggling to keep my wits about me. I told her how Martin Drapple raped me. How I killed him with a hammer. I told her that Jesse hid his body and the hammer but the police found them, so they were after both of us now. I told her how sorry I was that I'd gotten Jesse in trouble.

She pressed a hand over her mouth as I spoke, her dark eyes never leaving my face. I could tell I'd shocked her, and I didn't think she was the sort to shock easily. Finally, she let out a long breath. She said that Jesse made the decision to help me, so that wasn't my fault. Nobody made him do it, she said. That was small comfort to me, though. "And our Lord Jesus ain't never gonna forgive me for this," she said, "but I ain't got no sympathy for a man who'd rough up a woman, and what that Mr. Drapple done to you went way beyond that, didn't it?"

I nodded. I felt grateful for her words—and somewhat vindicated by them as well—but that didn't solve the predicament I was in.

She asked again how far along I was, her gaze dropping to my belly behind the smock I was still wearing, and I told her about two months. She stood up and walked to the window and I guessed she was looking out at the road, watching for the police. She had to be nervous, but she didn't show it. She was a midwife. I thought she must be used to things going terribly wrong.

She asked me if I had any place else to go where the police wouldn't be looking for me, and I shook my head. She let out a breath she must have been holding in, then said I would have to stay with them until the baby came.

I was stunned by the thought. I couldn't imagine staying with them for seven months. The police would look for me here. I'd put all of them in too much danger.

"Jesse said to take care of you, so we gonna take care of you."

I felt weak with gratitude and relief. I longed to turn myself over to someone stronger, someone smarter than I felt at that moment.

Then, Aunt Jewel told me to follow her into the hallway. She led me to a narrow closet. Pulling open the door, she revealed clothes hanging so tightly together they seemed to form a solid wall. I could smell mothballs. She told me that was where she and her cousins all hid when they were children. She reached through the wall of clothing. I heard something pop and above the hangers, I watched the rear wall give way, falling inward a few inches at an angle. Aunt Jewel told me to step into the space behind the wall to see if I would fit.

I pushed my way through the sea of clothing. The false wall had opened a bit like a door, allowing me to squeeze through the opening and into a suffocatingly narrow, dark space I imagined was teeming with spiders and who knew what else.

Aunt Jewel told me to push the wall back in place. I hesitated. I wanted to ask if she planned to leave me in the closet all the time, but thought better of expressing any doubt. Gulping, I pushed the wall back in place. Then I stood in the narrow pitch-black space, hardly able to breathe. Seconds passed and my breathing quickly grew shallow. Panicky, I tried to find a knob or something that would allow me to open the false wall again, but my hands felt only smooth wood. I called to Aunt Jewel, pounding my fist against the wall.

The wall tilted inward again and I let out my breath. "Scary in there, ain't it?" she said with a laugh. I asked if there was a way to open the wall from the inside on my own, thinking ahead. What if the police came and no one was home to let me out? They'd find my skeleton in the wall someday, generations from now.

Aunt Jewel showed me how to dig my fingers into the edge of the door to pull it open again. She helped me step through the forest of clothing. She said finding me a hiding place was the easy part and I asked her what the hard part was.

"Telling Abe and Agnes—Jesse's daddy and mama—you're stayin' here for the next seven months," she said.

At that very moment, I heard the sound of voices coming from downstairs and my heart leaped into my throat. I reached for the knob of the closet, but Aunt Jewel set her hand on my wrist. She cocked her head to listen. It was just the family, she said. She told me to go back in Nellie's room and stay there. She'd talk to them.

So that is where I am right now. In Nellie's room, sitting on her bed. From here, I can look out the window at the long straight dirt road leading up to the farm. I'm watching for a police car. Why haven't they come yet? The only reason I can think of is that they've already caught Jesse. I hope that isn't so. Would they torture him to tell them where I am? I can't bear to think of what they'd do to him if they caught him. Please, God, keep him safe!

And where are they looking for me?

I picture Karl going to Miss Myrtle's house, asking her if she's seen me. He'll tell her I'm wanted for the murder of Martin Drapple and she won't believe him. "Oh, that's nonsense!" she'll say. "Why, Anna wouldn't hurt a fly!"

And he'll say, "She killed him with the claw end of a hammer." He'll tell her that she's lucky to be rid of me. That I'm dangerous.

I feel bad about that, imagining Miss Myrtle thinking of me as a danger.

I think of my clothes and books, my perfume and rouge and everything else I left at her house. It's likely I'll never see any of it again. Other than my purse and the clothes on my back, the only thing I have with me is this journal.

4 P.M.

I guess a half hour or longer passed as I sat there alone in Nellie's room, my gaze glued to the long driveway, waiting to see Karl's car coming to take me away. I could no longer bear voices downstairs and wondered how Jesse's parents had reacted to Aunt Jewel telling them that they now had a fugitive on their hands. I heard light, rapid footsteps on the stairs, and in a moment, Nellie burst into the room, pigtails bouncing.

"We get to sleep in the same room!" she said, her huge eyes twinkling. She is so adorable. I'd felt drawn to her when I met her before and I'm even more so now. I tried to act like everything is fine as I talked to her. I didn't want to frighten her. I told her I would try not to take up too much space in her room and she said she didn't care, that she liked sharing.

She bounced a little on the bed. She pointed to my journal on my lap and asked me what it was. I explained that it's like a diary, then realized she probably had no idea what a diary was. "It's where you can write down your thoughts, just for yourself. So you can keep them to yourself," I said. "No one else should read them."

She leaned over and lifted the pages a bit, just enough to see my writing. She told me I wrote "that funny way. Where the letters get all hooked together."

I explained the difference between printing and cursive writing, and she said she was going to learn how to write that way. She said her daddy doesn't know how to read or write except for signing his name. "Mama can read good. Aunt Jewel and Dodie and Jesse . . . they can do all of it 'cause they got more learnin'."

I said something about learning being very important, but my gaze was once more out the window. Then Nellie said she would never want to have a journal, and when I asked her why not she said, "I like everybody to know what I'm thinkin'!" She hopped off the bed and twirled in a circle and I laughed, but then I felt worried that she might share my whereabouts with someone. I told her how important it was that it stay a secret that I was living with her family, and she reassured me that she understood, pressing a finger to her lips.

Just at that moment, I heard voices downstairs. Abe's. Aunt Jewel's. And Karl? I gasped. In the few seconds I'd let my guard down, he must have come up the driveway.

I whispered to Nellie that the police were downstairs and got quickly to my feet. I grabbed this journal and my purse and carefully opened Nellie's bedroom door, ready to rush to the closet and its false wall, but I could see the living room floor at the bottom of the stairs in front of me. I could see the lower legs and shiny shoes of two policemen and the dusty shoes of a man who had to be Jesse's father.

Nellie saw what I saw. She gave me one brief look of panic, those big dark eyes of hers even bigger. Then she shut the door again, quietly, and flung open the lid of the big chest at the foot of her bed. She began tossing its contents—clothing, toys, stuffed animals—on the floor, while I watched, my heart thumping. "Get in!" she commanded.

I took no time to think about it. Clutching my purse and journal, I climbed into the chest and Nellie closed the lid. I had to fold myself in two to fit. I heard muffled voices from somewhere in the house and then I heard what I was certain was Nellie's door opening.

"Hey, girlie," a male voice said. It wasn't Karl's voice. I thought of the roly-poly policeman who'd come with Karl to the warehouse that one time. Was it him? He asked Nellie if she'd seen a "white gal" around the farm. Nellie answered, oh so politely, that "no, sir, I ain't seen no white gal."

There were a few noises. The scuff of shoes on the wood floor, maybe. Inside the chest, I could hear myself breathing.

"You're a messy little child, ain't you?" the policeman said. "Your mama let you throw your clothes and such all over the room like this?"

Nellie said something about cleaning the room up real soon.

I heard heavy footsteps coming closer. I felt a pressure against the chest and pictured Nellie leaning protectively against the lid. Don't be too obvious, Nellie, I thought to myself.

"What you got on under that pretty little dress of yours?" he asked.

I was horrified! My hands tightened around my journal.

"Bloomers," Nellie said, calm as you please. "And you better git."

"Oh, I better git, huh? Or what? What do you think you could do to me?" I was certain it was Roly-Poly now. I hated him. I had my hands on the lid ready to break out of the chest if that boor laid a finger on Nellie. I could have sworn I heard her rapid breathing above me.

But just then, another male voice called out for "Barney," which I guess is Roly-Poly's first name. Was it Karl? I couldn't tell. But he said that I wasn't there and to "quit horsing around with that nigger" and come downstairs.

I heard the footsteps recede, then the bedroom door slammed shut.

"They gone, Miss Anna!" Nellie raised the lid. "They—"

I quickly hushed her, looking toward the closed bedroom door, praying they hadn't heard her.

"They gone," she whispered this time. "You safe."

I stepped out of the chest and pulled her to me. Hugged her tight. I told her what an incredibly brave girl she was. I thanked her for saving my life. I believe she truly did.

Monday, May 27, 1940

At lunch today, I asked how I could help out around the house while I'm staying on the Williams farm. They call lunch "dinner." I've come to realize that if I have a question to ask anyone in the family, "dinner" is the best time to ask it. In the three days I've been here, I've eaten breakfast alone, unable to get up at the crack of dawn like everyone else. At the first sign of light, they are up and out, gathering eggs and feeding animals and doing whatever else needs to be done out there. This was Jesse's life. There is a void here without him and no one says it to me, but I imagine everyone has to work much harder without him here. I worry they blame me. Why shouldn't they? There is no one else to blame.

The first night here, I weepily told them everything. I said how sorry I was for putting them in danger. I offered to turn myself in, and I meant it. They are taking such a risk and I wanted to give them a chance to back out of helping me. They are not happy about having me here—well, except for Nellie, whose ignorance of what is truly going on helps maintain her sunny disposition—but they all know Jesse is in grave danger and they conspire to keep me hidden in the hope I will never be questioned by the police and that will somehow keep Jesse safe. Only Jesse's father is not really in agreement, but the women—Jesse's mother and Aunt Jewel and nineteen-year-old Dodie—override him. Only Aunt Jewel treats me warmly, though. I can tell that Jesse's mother and Dodie think I'm the cause of his problems. Of course, they are right.

Aunt Jewel is very kind, but I think she sees me as a project. I am a project for her. I won't be having this baby at a hospital, that is for certain. She'll have to deliver it here. And then what? I can't live here with my baby. She says it's too early to worry about it, so I'm taking her advice and trying to put the baby at the back of my mind for now.

Mr. and Mrs. Williams exchanged a look when I asked how I could help. So far, I have done little other than clean up after myself and try to help a bit with cooking, although to be honest, I feel lost in their kitchen. I'm accustomed to getting my groceries at the market. I have never killed a chicken, butchered a hog, ground meat, canned a single vegetable, picked lettuce from a garden, and God knows, I'll never know how to cook those stinky collards that seem to be on the stove all day long.

Mr. Williams said it would be too dangerous for me to do anything outside where I could be seen, so I offered to clean the house, nearly giggling at the thought, wondering just how many colored families had a white maid. I suggested I do the sweeping and dusting and bed making. The wringer-washer is out in the open on the porch, so doing the laundry is probably unwise. I offered to wash the dishes. "Whatever needs doing, I'm happy to do it," I said.

Mrs. Williams asked me if I can stitch. I wasn't quite sure what she meant.

"Sew," she said impatiently. I'm not sure if her impatience comes from my presence or if this is the way she always is.

I told her I can sew, that I've made many of my own clothes, and she said they have plenty of mending to keep me busy.

So, this afternoon I swept the downstairs rooms and dusted furniture, waiting for my first sewing assignment. It's not much, but it feels good to be paying something back to these people.

Saturday, June 22, 1940

Four weeks have passed since Jesse and I fled the warehouse, and for the first time, there is no mention of us in the Chowan Herald. Mr. Williams picks up the newspaper each Saturday when he goes into town to sell his eggs and melons and I don't know what else, and I've gotten in the habit of reading the paper the moment he returns to the house. Since the paper comes out on Thursday, the news is always a bit stale, but it's all we have to go on. Mr. Williams doesn't read, and I feel touched when Mrs. Williams reads him the Bible lesson and the other articles that might interest him. At first I wondered what it would be like to have a husband so uneducated that he can't read, but he is such a hard worker and good provider, that I don't think Mrs. Williams cares a bit.

The first week, an article about Jesse and me was on the front page of the paper. The speculation was that we were illicit lovers who had killed Martin Drapple in a sordid triangle gone sour. (I once again had to assure Jesse's parents that this was not the truth. I've since learned that some of their church friends have turned their backs on them, but they still seem to have many people to lean on.) To escape the police, the paper said, we ran off together and haven't been found despite a multistate search. It hadn't occurred to me that the police think we are together. In a way, I wish we were. I miss Jesse and wonder if I'll ever see him again. I was very happy to learn, though, that—at least as of this past Thursday—they hadn't yet found him.

I'm hopeful that Mrs. Williams either skipped over this article when she read the paper to her husband, or that she doctored it a bit to tame it down.

According to the paper, my car was discovered a week after our disappearance on a street in Norfolk, Virginia. There was no mention of the mural being inside it and I wonder what Jesse did with it. I can't imagine him trying to travel unnoticed while carrying that enormous canvas. It hurts to think that he might have had to burn it or find some other way to get rid of it. I have to keep reminding myself that it's only an object. It's Jesse's escape that really matters.

The reporter must have interviewed half the people in Edenton that first week. Everyone had an opinion. People thought they'd spotted Jesse and me one place or another. A man thought he saw the mural in the woods, but it turned out to be an old patchwork quilt. Some people who watched me paint in the warehouse say they saw a romantic spark between Jesse and me. Others said I was envious of Martin's talent, "which Miss Dale couldn't begin to match." Mr. Arndt seemed more upset over the loss of the mural than anything else. "I hope that it can be recovered in pristine condition," he said. "We were truly looking forward to having it grace the post office wall."

And now, a month after our "disappearance," the paper seems to have run out of news on us. I think that is the best news of all.

Monday, July 22, 1940

I've been living with the Williams family for two months now. I have a routine, starting with getting up when they do. It took me a while to make that transition, but I felt selfish sleeping in while they all got up to work. I have a quiet breakfast with them in the near dark. Then they all—even little Nellie—go outside to work on the farm, rain or shine. I could never be a farmer! Only Aunt Jewel stays behind. She puts on a white pinafore, gets her medical kit, and heads out to see her patients. She has a car, a very old Buick that she worries will give out on her someday at a critical time, but for now it's working well enough to take her—or as they say here, to "carry" her—from farm to farm or into the colored neighborhoods of Edenton. She wears a serious expression when she leaves the house. Serious, with a sense of purpose and anticipation, all her focus on the patients she will see that day. On the babies she will deliver. Someday in the not too distant future, all her focus will be on me.

I spend the day cleaning and sewing and cooking (to the best of my ability). Dodie taught me how to pluck and clean a chicken and how to get the grit out of the leafy vegetables. I think she's smart and could probably go back to school and then college, but she seems content to live here and help out on the farm. I know she doesn't like me. She calls me "a right spoilt white girl" and I guess I am. She sees me as a burden, which I also am. She has friends, including a boyfriend, and it annoys her that she can't invite them into the house at any time the way she apparently used to. I'm more than happy to hide in Nellie's bedroom when the friends come over, but she gives me a sour look when she asks me to do so. I don't think very many things make Dodie happy.

Sometimes in the evening, I sketch the family members on pads that Jesse left behind. Except for Nellie, they refuse to pose, so I have to catch them on the sly. Mr. Williams falls asleep in his big rocking chair while everyone else reads, and that's when I draw them, waiting for the moment they look up so I can sketch their eyes. The whole family looks tired from working so hard. I am tired too, which is why I haven't written much in this journal of late.

I don't dare sign anything I draw here. One evening a policeman came by. Fortunately, Dodie saw the car come up the driveway and I was able to rush up the stairs and into the closet with its claustrophobia-inducing wall pocket just in the nick of time. He didn't stay long, but when I came downstairs again, Mr. Williams chastised me for leaving the sketches in plain sight on the table by the sofa. Dodie told the policeman the sketches were old, from when Jesse lived here. I hope he believed her.

Anyway, I'm doing my best as I wait nervously for my baby to come. It's the nights that are hard. I hate going to sleep because of the nightmares. They are bloody dreams about murder and childbirth. I toss and turn and wake up trying to scream but only squeaks come out. At first, I scared Nellie, but I told her I just have bad dreams sometimes, so now when I wake up that way, she comes over to my mattress on the floor and tries to comfort me. "You all right," she coos, smoothing one of her small hands over my hair. She tells me my dreams are only make-believe. "Ain't nothing to worry 'bout," she says.

I tear up when she treats me so kindly. I wonder if my own child could be like her? A funny, smart, winsome little thing with a caring heart? But then I remember my child is also Martin Drapple's child, and I feel ill.

How can this be happening to me? I lie on my mattress, Nellie often curled up next to me, asking myself that question over and over again.

I have no answer.

Wednesday, July 24, 1940

Last night, Mrs. Williams and I were sewing in the living room when she suddenly asked me if she was ever going to see her boy again.

I don't know what got into me. I broke down crying. It was her voice, so different from her usual voice. It had pain in it—the pain of a mama who knows she might never again see her child. I went over to where she sat on the sofa and put my arms around her. She didn't soften or return my embrace, but I didn't care. I know she still blames me for getting Jesse into this terrible mess. But I needed the comfort of a human touch, and I held her as long as I dared.

"I sure hope so," I said, when I finally pulled away. I told her I hoped we'd both get to see him again someday soon, but I know that will never happen. It's too dangerous for him to come home. Mrs. Williams turned away from my impossible words. Most likely, neither of us will ever see Jesse again.

Friday, July 26, 1940

I was taking my turn in the bathtub last night when I felt the baby move. At first I thought it was some odd bubbling in the bathwater, but then I realized what it was. I guess most women feel joy at that sensation, but it made me sick to my stomach. Maybe I'd been denying what was really happening in my body all this time. I don't know. What I do know is that I felt no joy, only the horrible realization that a part of Martin Drapple is still alive and, worse than that, it's alive inside me.

I rushed out of the tub, put on a robe Mrs. Williams had given me, and ran down the hall to Aunt Jewel's room.

I have been in her room several times. She checks my blood pressure there, takes my temperature. Feels my belly. Hers is the most sterile-feeling room in the house. There is nothing on the top of her bureau or vanity dresser. Her spotless yellow bedspread has sharp corners and is tucked smoothly beneath her pillow. She does have a bookshelf lined with what I assume are books about midwifery, and even the tops of the books look free from dust. I don't clean in this room—there is nothing to clean—so I know she keeps it that way on her own.

When she saw the frantic look on my face and that I was still dripping water from my bath, she took my arm and led me to the stool in front of her vanity dresser. Then she sat down on the corner of her bed. Her room is so small, so compact, that our knees were practically touching.

She asked me if I was in pain, and I told about feeling the baby move.

She smiled. Sat back. "I figured that would be comin' soon," she said. "Good. You have a healthy little one in there."

I began to sob, pressing my hands to my belly through the thin robe, saying over and over again that I don't want this baby. I looked at her imploringly. "What am I going to do?" I asked her.

She said nothing for a moment, just let me cry. Finally, she touched my knee and said she thought I'd change my mind in time.

I know I won't. This poor child would always remind me of Martin. Of that night. Of what he did. I swallowed hard, suddenly afraid I was going to be sick. I cannot stand remembering that night! The baby would always remind me of what I did, too. "This baby was conceived in a night of rape and murder," I said. I stared hard at Aunt Jewel to make my point, but lowered my voice to a hoarse whisper. "I . . . don't . . . want . . . it," I said. If I ever do have a child, I added, I want it to be conceived in love.

Aunt Jewel nodded in silence, her gaze steady on me. She nodded for so long that I began to squirm under her scrutiny. Finally she told me that there is a white family who lives not far from the farm. They aren't wealthy, she said, but they have a lot of love. It's a man and wife and the husband's parents, and they all live together. Aunt Jewel was the wife's midwife for two pregnancies, both of which ended in stillbirths.

When the woman got pregnant a third time, Aunt Jewel insisted they go to a doctor. So the woman had that baby with an obstetrician in the hospital, and that baby died, too.

I can only imagine that woman's pain. "What was wrong?" I asked Aunt Jewel.

"They don't rightly know," she said, "but the doctor told them not to try anymore. The news just about killed that woman."

I was beginning to follow her. I asked her if that family might be willing to take my baby.

Aunt Jewel thought they would. "I believe they'd be thrilled to the moon and back to have your baby," she said. But she told me I still needed to wait to decide. She is convinced I'll love the baby "more than you love your own life," she said.

I shook my head slowly. She was wrong. I know I won't. I asked her to please talk to that family for me, but she refused to talk to them yet.

I looked toward the window, thinking about handing my baby over to another woman. A woman who would never attach horror to a little innocent child, the way I always would. I looked back at Aunt Jewel and asked her if she'd tell them how the baby was conceived.

"No, Sugar," she said. "I sure won't." She said my "little one" deserves a fresh start. That nobody should hear about the sins of the father.

"Or the mother," I added wryly.

Aunt Jewel leaned forward, resting her hand on mine, and she told me that I did what anyone would have done to save her life.

"But . . . maybe he wasn't really going to kill me," I said.

"He kilt somethin' in you," she said to me. "The way I see it, that's just as bad."

Tuesday, October 29, 1940

I'm shocked to see how long it's been since I wrote in this journal. It used to be my everyday friend, but now it feels like a reminder of all the wrong turns I've made in my life.

I'm so big now, I feel like a hippopotamus moving around this house. I can't believe I still have about two months left to go, according to Aunt Jewel. My appearance has changed in other ways, too. I've always been fair, but now I'm downright paper white from being inside all this time. My black hair hangs down past my shoulders. The bangs I've worn all my life are gone and I now sweep my hair away from my face. I wanted to keep it in the style I've loved for the past few years—that little bob with short bangs—but Aunt Jewel says this is better. When I leave, I'll be far less recognizable without that distinctive haircut. I hardly recognize myself when I look in the mirror. Who is that white-skinned, long-haired, rotund woman? I don't know her.

Actually, I do know her. She looks very different than she used to and she's been through a lot, but she finally has her sanity back. I read through this journal before writing in it tonight, and I am shocked to see how thoroughly I lost my mind after what happened with M.D. (I can no longer bear to write his name.) I don't know who that woman was who painted the motorcycle in the mural. The knife in Freda's teeth. I wish I could erase those weeks and months from my history. In retrospect, Jesse was extremely tolerant of my insanity. I'm sure he'd been waiting and hoping for it to pass.

Where are you, Jesse?

I catch Mrs. Williams crying from time to time and I want to cry along with her, but I don't do it in front of her. I don't feel I have the right. I leave her alone. I just try to make her life easier by helping all I can around the house.

Meanwhile, I am getting more and more frightened of having this baby. The bigger

I get, the less I can imagine being able to push it out of me. Aunt Jewel reminds me that women tinier than me have been giving birth for all time, but that doesn't help. I keep thinking of the white woman she knows who had the stillborn babies. I've told Aunt Jewel to let that woman know she can have my baby once it comes, but she still refuses to talk to her and her husband. She still thinks I will warm to this child once it's born. Even if I did, what would I do with it? Where would I go? One thing I know for certain: I will have to leave soon after I have the baby. I can't ask the Williams family to live this way, in fear and danger, any longer.

Monday, December 16, 1940

This will be the last time I write in my journal. I'm waiting for Mr. Williams to fix a tire on his truck and then he'll drive me to the bus station in Elizabeth City. I don't dare take the journal with me. If I'm caught, the journal would lead the police right back to the Williams family and I fear every one of them would be arrested for "harboring a fugitive." I don't know what's going to happen to me but, no matter what, I'll protect Jesse's family till the day I die.

The baby was born last week. Aunt Jewel delivered him in her own bed, not wanting Nellie to be frightened by my screams of pain. I'm afraid my screams of pain probably carried through the house, out to the barn, and all the way into town! Aunt Jewel said it was actually an easy birth. I guess she should know, but it's not something I ever hope to repeat. Not under these circumstances anyway.

The baby had red hair.

I didn't name him. I didn't fall in love with him, as Aunt Jewel predicted. I did hold him long enough to feel his tenderness. His innocence. But I felt no love. Once I saw his hair, it was the end for me. I know that is small and cruel of me. He is an innocent baby. But he deserves a mother and father who will see only his pure little soul with no ugly memories attached to him. That is what he now has: he is already with his new family in his new home. Aunt Jewel said his parents already adore him. I feel numb. Dull and empty. But I know I made the right decision.

I don't know where I'll go. I have some ideas, though I won't spell them out here. I should burn this journal, yet I find I can't. It has been my trusted friend. My link to my mother. I'll tuck it deep in Nellie's chest. It will be several years before she'll be able to read what I've written here and I know that when she does, she will hold my secrets tight. There is a bond between that little girl and me. I am trusting my safety to you, dear Nellie!

I've thought of a new name I will use, and I plan to create a new future for myself. I hope Jesse is doing the same. If he is still out there, somewhere, somehow, someday, I will find him. I owe him my thanks. Perhaps I even owe him my life.

Chapter 59

———— ➤•◄ ————

MORGAN

August 3, 2018

What happened to Anna?

I read the journal cover to cover while sitting in the recliner in Jesse's sunroom, and I closed the book after midnight with that question burning in my brain. Had she been able to safely escape from the Williams's farm? And if she escaped, did the police ever catch up to her?

I felt emotionally drained after reading her story. Anna had felt real to me, increasingly so as I worked on the mural. Now, she felt like a friend. I needed to know what had become of her. I feared the ending couldn't have been good. Had Jesse Williams known how Anna's story ended? Had he wanted the mural front and center in the gallery as a tribute to his friend who had no longer been able to create art of her own?

I climbed into bed, the musty old journal on the nightstand next to me, but I knew I wouldn't fall asleep. After lying there for more than an hour, I got up, pulled on my jeans and T-shirt, and quietly left the house, not

wanting to awaken Lisa. I'd been secretive about the journal, not mentioning it to Lisa or even to Oliver. I'd needed to be the first to read it.

Edenton slept as I walked through the dark streets to the gallery, the
journal clutched to my chest. It was my first long walk since I'd hurt my
ankle, and I only started limping a bit as I neared the gallery. I punched
in the security code and let myself into the building, turning on the foyer
lights. The mural seemed to spring from the wall with the colors I'd help
bring back to life. I pushed my chair away from in front of it. Dragged my
paint table off to the side. Then I sat on the floor in the middle of the foyer,
legs crossed, my hands on my bare knees where they poked through the
holes in my jeans, and I began to cry for Anna, who had started the mural
with such hope and joy and had ended it with fear and sorrow.

"Hey, Morgan. Wake up."

I opened my eyes at the sound of Oliver's voice. The mural was side-
ways in my vision and I realized I'd fallen asleep on the cool hard floor of
the foyer. I pushed myself to a sitting position, blinking my eyes against
the light.

"Have you been here all night?" Oliver squatted next to me. I saw concern in his face.

"Oh, Oliver!" I said, grabbing the journal from the floor. I held it out to
him. "You have to read this! It's Anna's journal from when she was working
on the mural!"

"What? You're kidding." He took the journal from my hand and got to
his feet, then reached down to help me up. "Where did you get this?" he
asked.

I told him about Saundra's visit the evening before and how Anna had
left the journal behind at the Williams farm.

"Wow," he said, flipping through the pages. "What a gold mine of information this will give us."

"Read it," I said. "But it still doesn't tell us what happened to her."

"How does it end?" He flipped to the last page of the journal, and I put my hand on his to stop him.

"You have to read it from the beginning," I said.

He smiled at me, his blue eyes clear as crystal, beautiful behind his glasses. "You love her, don't you?" he said. "Anna Dale."

I turned my face away from him, afraid I was going to cry again. "I feel really close to her." I heard the huskiness in my voice. "You will, too, when you read this. She went through so much."

He nodded, still smiling. "I think you were exactly the right person for this job." He nodded toward the mural. "Somehow Jesse knew that."

"How could he?" I asked. "He never even met me. If he heard about me from one of my teachers, he didn't hear anything encouraging."

"Maybe that's how he knew you needed his help. You know how much he liked fixing people." He set the journal on the table next to his computer. "Think about it, Morgan," he said. "You came here scared and unsure of yourself, kind of angry, a little screwed up, feeling put upon, and—face it—not very interested in restoring this painting." He nodded toward the mural again. "Not interested in restoration at all. Now you're hooked, aren't you? Hooked on Anna Dale. Hooked on the whole process. And you've done an awesome job." He smiled. "The student has become the master."

I felt the blush creeping up my neck to my cheeks. I didn't buy that last compliment, but he was right about the rest of it. "Thank you," I said. I looked past him to the journal. "I just wish we knew what happened to her."

"What do you mean, what happened to her? How does the journal end?" He picked up the journal but I stopped him before he could begin flipping the pages again.

"From the beginning," I said. "You have to understand what she went through."

The sound of slamming car doors—most likely from Wyatt and Adam's truck—echoed through the foyer. They were going to help Oliver with the installation of the art today, while I continued working on the mural. I should have spent the night painting instead of reading. I glanced at Oliver. "Gotta get to work," I said, and I crossed the foyer to my paints and brushes and the strange mural I had come to love.

Chapter 60

———— ✦ ————

August 3–4, 2018

I worked on the mural all that day and into the evening while the guys hung paintings throughout the gallery. Oliver had read the journal early that morning and whenever he passed through the foyer, he and I would speculate about what might have happened to Anna. It was an intellectual exercise for Oliver, I thought, but for me, it was something more. I found myself choking up as I inpainted the scratches on the little skull in the window of the Mill Village house, thinking of the confusion and anguish Anna had experienced as she painted it.

Lisa arrived at six thirty carrying two huge boxes of pizza, designed, I was sure, to keep us all working in the gallery without a good long dinner break—not that I'd planned to break for dinner anyway. Oliver took the boxes from Lisa and set them down on the folding table, and I swiveled in my seat to face them.

"Oliver and I have something mind-blowing to show you," I said, paint-brush and palette still in my hands.

"What?" Lisa looked even more frazzled than usual. Her linen business suit was wrinkled and a lock of her hair was coming loose from the pony-tail at the nape of her neck.

Oliver handed her the journal. "You need to read this," he said.

I set down my brush and palette and got up from my chair to walk toward them. "Saundra brought it over," I said, "along with these sketches of her family that she thought were Jesse's." I handed the sheaf of sketch paper to Lisa. "But they're *not* Jesse's," I said. "They're actually Anna Dale's."

"*What?*" Lisa asked. "Why would Saundra have anything of Anna Dale's?"

"You have to read the journal," Oliver said.

Lisa looked annoyed. She glanced at her phone. "You'll just have to tell me what it says," she said, setting down the journal and the portraits. "I don't have time to read anything right now."

"The journal's incredible, Lisa," I said. "It explains all about the—"

"Not you." Lisa waved a hand toward me. "You keep working. Oliver can tell me."

"I can talk while I work." I walked back to my seat in front of the mural, and Oliver and I told Lisa the whole story of Anna Dale in Edenton.

"My God," Lisa said when we'd finished. By that time, she'd stopped looking at her phone every few seconds and was sitting in Oliver's chair, leafing through the sketches. "I wonder what ever became of her?"

"Wish we knew," Oliver said.

"Well," she said, getting to her feet. "No point in wondering about it right now. We have bigger things to deal with at the moment." She turned to Oliver. "Do you have all the . . . the write-ups about each piece ready to go?" she asked.

"They're all ready to slip into their frames and get on the walls," he said. "With the exception of Anna Dale's, which I've rewritten three times already. She's a moving target, you might say."

I felt Lisa's gaze burning into the back of my head. I kept my fingers moving, delivering the infinitesimal brushstrokes to the roof of one of the Mill Village houses.

"You know, Morgan," Lisa said, crossing the room toward me. "I know you've done a meticulous job on this thing and I appreciate it, but I personally don't care if you rush through the bit you have remaining. Who is ever going to look closely at all that grass and whatever else is down there in the corner?"

Facing the mural, I tightened my lips as I tried to pick my response. "I'll be looking closely at it," I said finally. "I have to do it right, Lisa. Don't worry. I'll have it done by Sunday morning."

"Doesn't it need to be stretched or something again?" Lisa touched the side of the mural where it was tacked onto the stretcher. "With staples instead of these tacks? How long is that going to take?"

Oliver spoke up. "If worse comes to worse, I'll add something to the wall text saying the restoration was just completed and the mural will soon be—"

"No," Lisa said. "Don't put anything in writing about it not being absolutely finished. Andrea Fuller—my father's executrix—will be here for the opening and I don't want to give her any reason to say we haven't met our requirements. You need to be finished by tomorrow night." She looked down at me. "Just get it done," she said.

"I will," I promised.

How? I wondered, and I imagined that behind me, Oliver was wondering the same thing.

—⋗•⋖—

For the rest of the evening, I kept my earbuds in, tuning out the hammering from the other rooms. I focused only on the mural, working on the gray siding of one of the Mill Village houses. I felt panicky as I watched the minutes tick by on my phone. It was nearly ten o'clock. How was I going to finish this by the deadline? I was kicking myself for every minute

I'd relaxed or eaten lunch or gone to bed early over the last few weeks . . . any minute when I could have been working. I was close to the end—so close—and yet I didn't think I could meet the deadline even if I worked twenty-four-seven for the next two nights. I suddenly understood Anna's desire to have the cot in the warehouse.

My music wasn't calming me down, either. The next time Oliver passed through the foyer I called him over.

"I'm in panic mode," I said from my seat on the floor. I detached my ear-buds from my phone and handed it to him. "Add a playlist of your calming old-people music for me, please."

It took him a minute to understand what I was asking. Then he laughed, and took my phone from my hand.

"Listen," he said as he tapped the screen on my phone. "I talked to Wyatt and Adam. They're willing to come in at six A.M. Sunday morning and staple the mural to the stretcher and hang it then. That gives you some extra time. You'll be dragging at the gallery opening, but you'll have it done."

"Thank you," I said, and I wondered if I could finish it even with those few extra hours.

"Don't cave in to Lisa," he said. "You have integrity. You won't be happy with yourself if you rush through this last section." He motioned toward the grassy corner of the mural.

I swallowed hard, suddenly emotional over his compliment, but it was more than that. "I don't want Lisa to lose her house," I said, my voice a whisper. I thought of Lisa's attachment to her mother's garden in the front yard. The handprints on the sidewalk. The height chart in the pantry. "I feel like it'll be my fault."

"It won't be your fault. It's not fair she laid that on you. Just do the best you can. It's all anyone can ask." He squeezed my shoulder lightly as he handed my phone back to me, and in a few minutes, I felt a bit of the tension leave my body as I listened to that Mary Travers woman—the one Oliver said I looked like—sing about leaving on a jet plane.

You have integrity. I thought that might have been the nicest thing any-one ever said to me. The words ran through my mind as I finished the siding on the house and began working on the sea of grass in the lower right-hand corner of the mural. I was getting closer and closer to Anna Dale's signature, which I would save for last. It was going to feel so good to work on those rounded gold-hued letters in the handwriting that was now as familiar to me as my own.

Shortly after midnight, I pulled out my earbuds to listen. Everything was still. The hammering had stopped in the back rooms. I heard truck doors slam outside and knew Adam and Wyatt had left the gallery through the rear door. In another minute, Oliver walked into the foyer.

"Time to go home," he said to me.

"I'm going to keep working."

He looked from me to the mural. "It's late. You're exhausted. Come on. You can come back early in the morning." He nodded toward the front door of the foyer. "I'll drive you back to Lisa's."

"I need the time," I said.

"You'll only start screwing it up if you keep at it tonight."

I looked at the grass of the Mill Village. It was nothing more than a blur of green to my exhausted eyes. He was right.

"Okay," I said.

He waited while I cleaned my brushes. Then we walked out to his van side by side.

"Had a long talk with my son today," he said, once we were on the road.

"About Smith Mountain Lake versus Disney World?"

He hesitated. "More about 'Dad versus John, his stepdad,'" he said, turning onto Broad Street. "It was pretty deep. He told me he feels guilty because he realized he loves John."

I reached over to touch his arm. I felt a tenderness toward him as well as sympathy for Nathan. "What did you say?" I asked.

"I told him he never has to feel guilty about loving someone."

I smiled to myself. "Great answer," I said. "Was it hard to hear, though? That he loves John?"

"Yes and no." He glanced at me as he made the turn onto Lisa's street. "For obvious reasons I wish I could be his only father figure, but I want my kid to be happy. The more good people he has in his life, the better."

"Oh, Oliver." I suddenly thought I was going to cry. God, I was tired! "He's so lucky to have you as his dad," I said. "You're so . . . tolerant and forgiving."

He gave me a rueful smile, barely visible in the dark. "Well, I don't know about that," he said. "I told him next year it's Smith Mountain Lake with his old man, or I'll disinherit him."

I smiled as he pulled the van into Lisa's driveway.

"Get a good night's sleep," he said, putting the van in park. "I'll see you bright and early in the morning."

"Okay." I leaned across the console to kiss him on the cheek. I felt his hand on my bare shoulder. Felt his fingers trail down my arm until they tightened—it was not my imagination—around my elbow. There was something more than friendship in that touch, and when I drew away, I didn't reach for the door handle, hoping against hope that he'd kiss me and feeling too uncertain to take the lead myself. But he only smiled, touching my cheek with the back of his fingers. I wondered if he knew he was driving me crazy or if I was reading him all wrong and he wasn't the least bit interested in me that way. Either way, by the time I got out of the van, I was almost dizzy with hunger for him.

Starting up the long sidewalk to the front door, I stopped to look at the only lighted window in the house: Lisa's second-story bedroom. She was usually in bed early, and I knew it was worry keeping her up.

"Hey, Morgan?" Oliver called from his van window. "You all right?"

I hadn't realized he'd been waiting for me to get safely inside. I smiled, the warmth of his touch on my cheek still with me. I waved him on. Then I walked up the steps and into the house, heading for my dark sunroom and a very short night's sleep.

Chapter 61

———— ❧ ————

August 4, 2018

Oliver sat at his folding table, slipping the various wall texts into their plastic frames, when I arrived at the gallery in the morning. I'd slept right through my alarm, but still managed to get there by seven thirty, eating a blueberry muffin along the way. I took out my earbuds to exchange a "hello" with him. I found it a little hard to hold his gaze this morning, remembering the subtle but undeniable—to me, anyway—shift in our relationship the night before. It hadn't been much at all, just a light stroke down my arm, but it had electrified me and I was certain there'd been more than friendship behind it. You didn't touch your friends that way.

"I have something for you," he said, setting down one of the wall texts.

I walked over to his table. "What?" I asked, curious.

He tore a piece of paper from the notepad on his table and held it out to me. "Emily Maxwell's address and phone number," he said.

Stunned, I kept my hands by my sides. "You're kidding."

He reached over to lift my hand, then pressed the paper into my palm. I lowered my gaze to it. *Emily Maxwell, 5278 Kellerman Road, Apex, North Carolina.* There was a phone number as well.

"How did you get this?" I asked.

"A friend who's a state employee got it for me. She said it was easy."

"I don't think I can . . ." My voice trailed off. I bit my lip and looked down at him. "Do you think I'm a coward?" I asked.

"I don't think I'm in a position to judge." His expression was sober. "I don't know how I'd feel in your shoes." He nodded toward the slip of paper in my hand. "But now there's nothing standing in your way if you decide you want to talk to her."

"Thank you," I said, then gave him a weak smile. "I think."

I buried the paper in my jeans pocket and headed for my seat on the floor in front of the mural. The scrap of paper seemed to burn through the fabric of my jeans. I could feel it there. The paper might have had Emily's address on it, but it didn't tell me what I needed to know. How was she? How horrendously had we destroyed her life?

I did my best to return my focus to my work. The gallery was utterly silent now that Adam and Wyatt had all the art installed. I knew they wouldn't be in today, and I hoped they'd remember their promise to show up early tomorrow morning to get the mural stretched and hung. I would have to work all night to have it ready for them, but then my job would be over.

Anyone else who looked at the mural this morning would probably think the restoration was complete, but in my eyes, that lower right-hand corner still screamed *"Finish me."* I had less than twenty-four hours to do so . . . and that was if I took no time out to eat or sleep.

I mixed my paint, added it to my palette, and was once again working on the grass of the Mill Village when Lisa arrived.

"Hi, you two," she said. "Oliver, I've got to get to the office, but I just stopped in to let you know I contacted the *Charlotte Observer* about the mural and Anna Dale's story. I'm hoping they'll send a reporter and we can get some word of mouth going about the gallery." She looked at her phone. "The caterer finally has his act together, as far as I can tell. But I owe the fact that we can open on Sunday to you two."

I turned to see Lisa looking directly at me, a mix of genuine gratitude and worry in her face. "It'll be finished," I said, assuring myself as much as I was her.

"Get out of here, Lisa," Oliver said. "Everything's under control."

It was nearly noon when Oliver finished hanging all the wall texts. He walked over to where I was still inpainting blades of grass. Reaching toward me, he popped out one of my earbuds. "You've been sitting here for hours," he said, bending over to pry the brush from my stiff hand. I was too tired to offer much resistance. "I'll take over while you stretch your legs. There's food in the kitchen, and the art is on the walls. Go enjoy it. The rooms look pretty incredible now that they're full."

My body seemed frozen in place in front of the mural. I looked up at him. Pointed to the brush in his hand. "That's my job," I said.

"Do you mind if I help?"

I thought about it. I was hot, tired, and hungry. Pointing to the color I'd mixed on my palette, I said, "This is what I'm using on the shaded area of the grass."

"Got it." He held his free hand out to me and I rose stiffly to my feet. "Take half an hour," he said. "Just chill."

In the kitchen, I wolfed down a rubbery piece of pizza I found in the refrigerator, then carried a Coke with me into the gallery. I was most interested in the work of the students Jesse had helped, financially or otherwise. I wished I could have had one of *my* paintings in the room with the other student art, but it didn't really matter. The work I was proudest of would hang in the foyer, the first thing anyone would see when they walked into the gallery.

Some sculptures were displayed here and there in the student room, but I was more drawn to the two-dimensional art. I moved from painting to painting, reading the wall texts Oliver had put together for each one. I stopped at the etching of a plane, a marvel in its detail. The wall text told me that Jesse had discovered the student artist when the boy was in middle school and living in foster care. Reading the texts next to each piece touched me. I could hear Oliver's voice in them as he described the artist's background and connection to Jesse, and for the hundredth time, I wondered why Jesse had zeroed in on *me* to help.

I paid attention to my own feelings as I explored the student paintings, waiting for the yearning to paint—to create—to overwhelm me, but it didn't. As a matter of fact, I felt a strange distance from the work in the room. I could appraise it, admire it, dissect it. But I didn't envy the artists for being able to create it. I knew my professor had told me the truth when he said I wasn't all that talented, and the reality was, while I loved art, I'd never truly loved creating it. It had frustrated me, never being able to translate what I could see so clearly in my mind to the canvas on my easel. I knew with a rush of surprise that what I *had* loved doing was restoring the mural. I pressed my fist to my mouth, nearly overcome by the realization. I'd spent so much of the last few weeks worrying about returning to prison or being angry with Trey or feeling guilty about Emily that I hadn't let myself recognize the joy I felt in my work.

The next room was filled entirely with Jesse's paintings, some of them familiar to me. I glanced at my phone. My half-hour break was nearly up. I would look at Jesse's work more closely later.

I walked into the third room, this one displaying paintings from Jesse's personal collection, much but not all of it from North Carolina artists. This was where I would really have liked to spend the time that I didn't have today. I stood in the center of the room and turned in a slow circle, taking in all the work from a distance. There was a wintry landscape by Francis Speight. One of Ernie Barnes's distinctive paintings, probably my favorite in the room, displayed a group of black men and women, their elongated bodies dancing against a peach-colored background. There was one of Kenneth Noland's bull's-eye paintings, and an intriguing black-and-white contemporary piece by Barbara Fisher. But the huge painting that anchored the room was Judith Shipley's *Daisy Chain*, taken from the foyer of Jesse's house. Although I'd passed by that realistic painting of four little girls sitting in a field of daisies nearly every day since my arrival in Edenton, I'd still never found the iconic iris Shipley would have hidden in it as a tribute to her mother. Here in the gallery, the painting had a perfectly lit wall all to itself, and I spotted the purple flower almost instantly. It was off to one side in the endless field of daisies, jutting above the yellow flowers, small and delicate. It made me smile. How nice to have a mother you wanted to honor that way.

⇥•≽⧏•

Back in the foyer, I found Oliver in my place on the floor, carefully inpainting the weedy grass of the Mill Village. I held out my hand for the brush.

"I'll keep helping," he said, holding the brush away from me. "You know you can't make the deadline on your own, right?"

I looked at the abraded grass, the disintegrating signature. He was right. Adam and Wyatt would have to stretch and hang the mural in the morning with the right-hand corner unfinished or poorly restored. How savvy was Andrea Fuller about art? Would she notice slipshod work in one tiny bit of the mural? Probably not, and yet it pained me to think of making a mess of that corner when I'd been so meticulous all along.

I motioned once more for him to give me the brush. "It's my job," I said, but he didn't hand the brush to me.

"My work is pretty well finished," he said. "Let me help you. I can work on the grass here." He pointed. "You can work on the signature."

Reluctantly, I sat down next to him and picked up my own brush. We worked together until five, when we stopped to order and devour Hunan chicken and egg rolls. Then we were back at it, and I began to feel hopeful. I thought Oliver's brushstrokes were not quite as clean as mine, but I kept my mouth shut. No one was going to notice, and we were getting the work done.

Oliver was talkative as we painted after dinner. "So, were you really in love with Trey?" he asked.

I was surprised by the question, and I had to think about it. "I was in love with the Trey I wanted him to be," I said. "Not the Trey he really was. And he didn't love me, either. He said he did, but he doesn't have a clue what it means to love. You don't treat someone you love the way he treated me." I touched my brush to the paint on my palette. "Same with my parents."

"Do you really believe they didn't love you?"

"I'm certain of it." I didn't look at him. "I think it's hard for you to imagine, because you probably had great parents and you're a great parent yourself. But mine didn't give a shit about me. And I don't give a shit about them." I'd reached the top of the *D* in "Dale," and held the brush away from the canvas. I was getting upset. The last thing I wanted to do was screw up Anna's golden-hued signature. I looked at Oliver. "It's a pretty crappy feeling, knowing that no one in the world has ever loved you," I said. "It makes you feel worthless." I turned back to the mural, touching my brush carefully to the abraded top of the *D*. For a moment, neither of us spoke.

Finally, Oliver broke the silence. "You deserved a lot better," he said quietly. "I'm sorry you didn't get it."

"Let's put on some music," I said. I wanted to get the conversation off myself.

"Good idea." Oliver set down his brush. "I'll get my speaker. We'll have to fight over whose music we play, though."

I smiled to myself as he left the foyer. We would listen to his music; I owed him that. He could be home resting up for the opening tomorrow. Instead he was here, helping me. I wanted to make him happy. He was one of the best people I'd ever known.

I went back to work on Anna's signature while he was gone. There was something wrong with the *D* in "Dale." The top of the rounded portion of the letter was discolored and I guessed I hadn't cleaned it well enough. I'd probably gotten pretty sloppy by the time I'd reached that section of the mural as I cleaned. I still had a bowl of distilled water and a cotton-tipped dowel on the floor near the mural. I picked up the dowel, then began to gingerly touch it to the top of the *D*. The letter would not come clean, the gold paint blocked not by some sort of grime that wouldn't budge, but by something else. Paint? Frowning, I leaned back from the mural for a better view. Only then did I understand what I was looking at, and a chill ran up my spine.

Oh my God, I thought to myself, scrambling to my feet. *Oh. My. God.*

Chapter 62

I raced from the room, down the curved hallway, and into Oliver's office where he was unplugging his speaker from the wall. I took the speaker from him and put it back on his desk. "Come with me!" I said, grabbing his hand.

"What are you doing?" He laughed, letting me nearly drag him out of the office and down the hall. In the foyer, I pointed to Anna's signature.

"Look!" I said. "Look closely at the *D* in 'Dale.' What do you see?"

Oliver squatted next to the mural. "Is it a flower? A purple . . ." He looked up at me, eyes wide behind his glasses. "It's got to be a coincidence," he said.

"It's not a coincidence!" I said, excited. "Look at Anna's signature. Then come in the other room."

Getting to his feet, Oliver followed me into the gallery where the Shipley painting hung. Standing next to him, I pointed out the iris in the sea of daisies, then watched his face as he took in the distinctive loopy handwriting in Judith Shipley's signature. It wasn't just the unusual shape of the script. "Look," I said, pointing to the name. "The small *l* and *e* in 'Shipley' are nearly identical to the same letters in 'Dale.'"

"Holy effing shit," he said.

It was the first time I'd heard him even come close to swearing, and I laughed. "Anna was never caught!" I said happily, pressing my hands together in front of me. "She went on to find fame, and somewhere along the way, she and Jesse must have reconnected and some of Anna's work came to be in his collection. She changed her name, Oliver! She reinvented herself."

"Okay, let's not jump to conclusions," Oliver said, his voice calm now. "Let's take a closer look at everything."

For the next thirty minutes—precious minutes when I knew I should be working on the mural—we hurried back and forth between the foyer and the room where *Daisy Chain* was displayed, comparing the shapes of eyes, the way fingers and nails were painted, the distinctive length and depth of the artist's brushstrokes, the thinness of the paint layer.

"This is definitely Anna's," I said with certainty as we stood once more in front of *Daisy Chain*. "I've spent the last month getting to know these brushstrokes."

Grinning to himself, Oliver put his arm around my shoulders, almost absentmindedly, I thought. "I'm not sure I would have noticed this on my own." He tightened his arm around me, and my body went soft, leaning against him. "Good sleuthing, Christopher," he said.

"It just . . ." I lost my train of thought, distracted by the weight of his arm. Distracted by the leathery scent of his aftershave. By his nearness. "It was the iris," I said weakly, because I could think of nothing else to say. My brain had suddenly turned to mush. But then I noticed the wall text Oliver had written and hung next to the painting.

"Oh, no," I said, feeling the keen sting of disappointment.

"Oh no, what?" He lowered his arm from my shoulders.

I pointed to the wall text. "Judith Shipley is still alive, but look at her birthdate. June seventh, 1922. Anna Dale was twenty-two when she painted the mural, so she was born in 1918."

Oliver laughed. "If she changed her name, she probably changed her birthdate as well, don't you think?" he said. "Took the opportunity to shave a few years off her age?"

I bit my lip, hopeful that he was right. "What do we do?" I asked, nodding toward the painting.

"I'm going to call an art authenticator I know at the museum in Greenville to see if he can take a drive up here to give us his take on this," Oliver said. "We don't dare go public with this without knowing for sure."

"Do you have any doubt?"

"I'll be shocked if it isn't," he said, "but I'm not an authenticator."

"Is there any chance Judith Shipley's coming to the opening?" I asked. My heart was in my throat at the thought of meeting her, but she was ninety-six—or one hundred—years old, and she lived in New York. Very unlikely.

"I don't think so," Oliver said. "Lisa said only a couple of the artists in Jesse's collection can make it. The majority are dead, and a lot of the others are elderly or live too far away."

I stared at the painting. "We have to get her here."

"How do you propose to do that?"

"I'll call her . . . Try to see if there's any chance . . . But I can't ask her outright if she's Anna, can I? That might scare her into a heart attack."

"And she might not *be* Anna, Morgan," Oliver said. "Let's not get our hopes up too high." He nodded toward *Daisy Chain* again. "We may just be seeing what we want to see."

Chapter 63

————— ❧✦❧ —————

From the wall text next to Judith Shipley's painting *Daisy Chain:*

Daisy Chain (mid-80s) oil
Judith Shipley
June 7, 1922–

Little is known about Judith Shipley's early life or formal art education. Her birthplace is also unknown. Although she spent her
early adulthood in New York City, Shipley was never part of the
New York school of experimental artists, preferring the dramatic
realism of other New York painters of the era such as that of her
contemporary, Jesse Jameson Williams. Shipley found her own
acclaim in the late fifties to the late eighties, and many of her
vibrant paintings from that period are displayed in museums and
galleries around the world. Her work can be a puzzle for the cu-

rious viewer, as she always hides an iris somewhere in her paintings in honor of her late mother, Iris.

Daisy Chain was a gift from the artist to Jesse Jameson Williams
in 1988.

Private life: In 1952, Shipley married her agent Max Enter-
hoff (1921–1999). They had one daughter, Debra, who died in
2014. Shipley lives in New York City, where she and her grand-
daughter maintain an atelier, training new artists.

Chapter 64

⟶•⟵

First of all," Lisa said from her seat at Oliver's folding table. "No one utters a word about this possible link between the two artists outside this room until we have more information from the . . . authenticator guy from the museum. We don't want to look like idiots."

"Right," I said. I sat on the floor in front of the mural, facing her and Oliver, who stood, arms folded, by the end of the table. We'd called Lisa to come back to the gallery as soon as she could, and while she was intrigued by the similarities between the paintings, she remained unconvinced. Oliver had been able to reach the authenticator from the Greenville museum, but he couldn't come to Edenton until late next week. We'd have to keep the secret of the mural to ourselves for now.

"Look," Lisa added. "I met Judith Shipley on numerous occasions. Like so many other artists, she floated in and out of our house over the years. She—"

"What was she like?" I interrupted.

Lisa shrugged. "You must know by now that art was my father's world, not mine. He always had his fellow artists around. I paid no attention. I just know she stayed with us a few times. I couldn't even describe what she looked like."

I pictured the short black bob, but remembered Anna had let her hair grow long before leaving Edenton. And all of that had been so long ago.

"What did she—Judith Shipley—say about the invitation to the gallery opening?" Oliver asked. "Is it certain she's not coming?"

"She sent back the response card with 'not attending' circled, which I have to say, is more than many people bothered to do," Lisa said. "Why people aren't considerate enough to return those stamped response cards is beyond me."

I wrinkled my nose at the thought of the response card with "not attending" circled. But what had I expected? A long letter from Judith, describing her secret past, her long-ago friendship with Jesse?

"Can I call her?" I asked. "Do you have her number?"

"What would you say?" Oliver asked.

"You can't come right out and ask her if she's Anna Dale," Lisa said, a warning in her voice. "If she is, she's kept that secret for a long, long time and I certainly don't want to put her on the spot."

"No, I wouldn't do that," I said. "I just want to . . . could I mention that we have an old post office mural here? Maybe I could learn something from her reaction."

They were both quiet, looking off into space as though thinking about my proposal.

"I don't see why that would hurt," Oliver said finally.

"I have no idea if the number I have for her from my father's records is still good," Lisa said. "She's probably in a nursing home by now."

"Though her biography says she still has a studio," I said. "An atelier."

Lisa got to her feet. "All right," she said. "I think Oliver should call her, though. You need to keep painting. And Oliver, remember you're a representative of this gallery."

"Got it," Oliver said, but he was looking at me where I sat with my paintbrush in hand, distressed that I'd just had the opportunity to speak with . . . Anna? Judith? . . . snatched away from me.

"You're going to fix that corner of the mural, Morgan, aren't you?" Lisa asked from behind me, and I fought the urge to roll my eyes. "You know Andrea Fuller will be here when we open in the morning to make sure my father's conditions have been—"

"Don't worry," I said. "It'll be finished by tomorrow morning, no problem." How I was going to make that happen, I didn't know.

⸻ ⋅ ⸻

Five minutes after Lisa left, I was sitting at Oliver's table as he read a New York phone number aloud to me and I punched the numbers on my cell phone. "You should be the one to make the call, not me," he'd told me once Lisa was gone. "She's *your* artist."

The number rang for a very long time, and I pictured Judith Shipley hobbling into her kitchen to pick up the receiver of an old-fashioned wall phone. Or maybe she used a wheelchair. Or maybe she *was* in a nursing home and no one was going to answer this call at all.

Finally, though, I heard a click, and a moment later a curt female voice—decidedly not elderly—said, "Shipley residence."

"Hello!" I said, quickly putting my phone on speaker so Oliver could hear. "My name is Morgan Christopher. May I speak to Ms. Shipley?"

The woman didn't respond and I had a terrible feeling that "Ms. Shipley" might be dead. Finally, she spoke.

"Ms. Shipley is unable to come to the phone," she said.

"Oh, well, I'm calling from the new Jesse Jameson Williams gallery in Edenton, North Carolina, and we'd invited her to be an honored guest at our opening tomorrow, since we have a couple of her paintings here, but—"

"I already sent our regrets," the woman said coolly.

"Yes, we received them but I was hoping I could change her mind. Could I talk to her, please?"

"Ms. Shipley no longer travels," the woman said, and I heard the click as she hung up the phone.

I made a face at Oliver. "Did I screw that up?" I asked, wondering if Oliver *should* have made the call. If he might have had some magical way of getting a different answer.

Oliver shook his head. "There was no way that icicle of a woman was going to come around," he said. "Maybe when we get a definitive answer from the authenticator, we can try writing to Judith personally."

—≫•≪—

Oliver and I returned to work on the mural. I kept looking over my shoulder, afraid Lisa would show up again and find him helping me.

"Do you really think she'll care at this point?" he asked, and I shook my head. I'd done ninety-nine-point-nine percent of the work on the mural myself. I thought that would be enough to satisfy anyone.

It was nearly three A.M. by the time we finished. I was dead tired, but I couldn't stop looking at the golden-hued signature in the lower right-hand corner of the mural and the delicate iris curled around the *D*. Oliver nearly had to drag me out of the gallery to his van.

He drove through the dark, deserted streets to Lisa's house. We were both quiet. Utterly depleted. But when he pulled into Lisa's driveway and I reached for the door handle, he said, "Morgan?"

I turned to look at him, waiting. The streetlight picked up the perfect line of his nose. His lips.

"I just want you to know . . ." He hesitated, turning toward me. "What you said tonight about never being loved? I just want you to know that you're wrong."

It took me a moment to understand. "You?" I whispered.

He nodded. "Me." He gave me a half smile. "And not as a big brother, either. You're a good person, Morgan Christopher." He reached out to brush my hair away from my throat, and the touch of his fingers . . . or maybe it was his words, or maybe just the solid, comforting presence of him . . . I couldn't have said . . . but something made my eyes sting and my throat tighten. For a moment, I was too stunned to speak.

Then I seemed to pull myself together. I leaned across the console to kiss him and felt the warmth of his hand against my cheek. The intensity of his touch as his fingers wrapped around the side of my throat. I heard him groan, ever so slightly, just enough to let me know the kiss was having the same effect on him that it was having on me.

He drew away, but didn't let go of me. "Damn console," he said with a smile.

"Damn console," I agreed. I wanted my body next to his.

"I've wanted to do that ever since the first day you walked into the gallery," he said.

"You just wanted to kiss that Mary Travers singer, and I happened to look like her," I teased.

He shook his head. "Nope. It was you I wanted. You, with this sexy tattoo"—he ran a finger over my shoulder—"and your cute knees poking out of the holes in your jeans, and your silky hair . . . and . . . I could go on and on about your . . . sexiness, but it's really the person you are that won me over, Morgan," he said. "The way you listen to me go on and on about Nathan. The way you care. Your passion about the mural. Your . . . what's the matter?"

I'd started to cry. He leaned across the console to wrap me in his arms. "What is it?" he asked, his breath warm against my temple.

It took me a moment before I could speak. "I just . . . It's been a long time since anyone said anything nice about me," I said. "It's been a long time since I deserved it."

"I don't buy that." He tightened his arms around me. "You hit a rough patch. Maybe some of it was of your own creation, but we all screw up. I had a son at seventeen, remember?"

I smiled, my chin resting against his shoulder.

"It's all behind you." Drawing away from me, he looked into my eyes. "Now you move forward."

"I love you, too," I said.

"I know."

"How did you know?"

"I've been picking up the vibes," he said. "I didn't want to act on them, though. Didn't want 'us' to get in the way of our work."

"God, you are so mature!" I laughed, giddy with a joy I couldn't remember ever feeling before. I felt safe with him.

He let go of me then. "Get a good night's sleep," he said. "Tomorrow's going to be crazy."

I instantly sobered. "Do you think Adam and Wyatt will get the mural up in time?"

He nodded. Tugged at a lock of my hair. "It's going to be fine," he said, leaning in for another kiss. "Everything's going to be fine."

Chapter 65

August 5, 2018

The gallery opening was scheduled for noon, and I intentionally took my time getting ready, aiming to be there no earlier than eleven. If Adam and Wyatt hadn't shown up at six A.M. as promised, and the mural was still resting on the foyer floor, I didn't want to know. I sped up as I walked toward the gallery, though, checking my phone with every other step. If there was a problem, surely I would have heard. So far, not a single text this morning.

Even though I'd dropped exhausted into bed at three thirty that morning, it had taken me a while to fall asleep. That last-minute surprise from Oliver? Wow. It felt real, everything he'd said. It felt genuine and it felt right. And that kiss! I smiled to myself, remembering, and a woman walking toward me on the sidewalk smiled back.

"'Morning," I said as I passed her, and then I laughed. And despite the fact that I was wearing a dress and heels for the first time in well over a year, I ran the last block to the gallery.

━━━•◆•━━━

Although Lisa's sedan and Oliver's van were parked in the small lot, and the catering company's van was parked at the curb, I found myself alone when I walked into the foyer. Winded from the run, I stood in the middle of the room and saw that the information counter, laden with brochures, had been moved into place, and above it, stapled imperceptibly to the stretcher and high on the wall, hung the mural.

Damn, I thought. *That is one beautiful, crazy painting!*

The lump in my throat surprised me. I loved the painting in front of me. I loved all I'd done to return it to the intriguing composition Anna Dale had intended.

"It's beautiful!" I yelled into the echoey air of the gallery, and soon Lisa and Oliver joined me in the foyer, along with a young guy from the catering company. To my surprise, Lisa gave me a hug—and not a baby, half-assed hug, either. She held me a long time, wrapping me in the scent of jasmine.

"Thank you," she said, drawing away, yet still holding me by the shoulders and looking intently into my eyes. "You saved my house. I know I've been a bitch to deal with." Her smile was rueful. "But I'm very, very grateful to you."

"You're welcome," I said, although I thought Lisa had it backward. Lisa had saved *me,* whether she'd meant to or not, and in more ways than one.

I saw Oliver leaning against the wall by the wall text, arms folded across his chest, a smile on his face, looking sexy as hell in a black shirt open at the collar, and I wondered how I could have ever thought of him as anything but.

"Dynamite job, Morgan," he said.

"I couldn't have done it without you," I said, remembering his help the night before, and he winked.

Lisa looked at the catering guy. "Are we squared away now?" she asked. I heard sounds coming from the small kitchen and guessed the servers were setting up for the opening.

"Good to go," the man said. He looked at me. "You paint that?" he asked, nodding in the direction of the mural.

"I restored it," I said.

"What's that mean?"

"It means she brought it back to life," Oliver said.

The man looked at the mural again, then gave me a confused-looking smile. "Cool," he said. He headed for the foyer door, speaking to Lisa over his shoulder as he left. "I'll be back to pick up the servers at five," he said.

"Fine." Lisa was already looking past him to the gallery's first visitor: Andrea Fuller.

Andrea stopped in her tracks in the middle of the foyer. "Well," she said, "that certainly looks different than the last time I saw it." She looked at me, and I was afraid she might ask if I'd done the work entirely by myself. Did I have to admit to Oliver's contribution to point one percent of the mural? But Andrea just smiled.

"Nice job, Morgan," she said. She walked toward the side wall where Anna's original sketch was displayed along with the "before" photograph of the mural and Oliver's wall text about Anna Dale. She glanced from the photograph to the mural. "Unbelievable job, actually," she said. Then she turned to Lisa. "You all set for the grand opening?"

"We are." Lisa smiled broadly, and I knew she was letting out her breath in relief at Andrea's response to the mural. Lisa was home free. "Let me show you around," she said.

The two women started down the curved hallway and Oliver looked at me. "How're you doing this morning?" he asked.

I looked again at the mural. It filled the entire foyer with color. "I think," I said, returning my gaze to Oliver, "that I want to be an art restorer."

He smiled. "And I think that's an excellent idea," he said. "Lots of schooling ahead of you, though."

"That's better than lots of jail time."

He laughed and held an arm toward me. "Come here," he said.

I walked over to him and he wrapped me in a hug. "You okay after last night?" He spoke quietly into my ear.

I knew what he meant. His loving words in the van. The kiss.

"I don't know." I pulled away with a smile. "I was really enjoying the whole 'big brother' thing."

"This'll be even better," he said, a serious expression on his face now. "I promise."

The front door opened and two women walked into the foyer, dressed in their Sunday clothes. "We're your Art Guild volunteers, ready to man the information desk," one of them said.

"Perfect," said Oliver, letting go of me. "Let me show you around."

➤✦◄

It was an extraordinary day. People came from as far away as Asheville and Washington, D.C., and the reporter from the *Charlotte Observer* stayed for two hours. She interviewed me about the mural, and toward the end of our talk, she pointed to my alcohol monitor and said, "Interesting ankle jewelry."

I told her the truth, all of it, while she scribbled her notes, and I had the feeling the whole tone of the article she would write changed in that moment.

The only negative of the day was that by five o'clock, my feet were killing me and my ankle let me know that my sprain was not completely healed. Shortly after five, once the last guests had left and the servers were cleaning up, I found Lisa sitting on the steps of the gallery's small back porch, teary with happiness, or perhaps with relief. I sat down next to her and put a tentative arm around her shoulders. We sat in silence in the hot, sticky August air as Lisa blotted her eyes with her fingertips. Finally, she spoke.

"You don't need to move out any time soon," she said. "I think you have something cooking with Oliver, and I'm guessing you don't have any place to go. Am I right?"

"Yes and yes," I said, dropping my arm from her shoulders. "And I'd really like to stay for a while. Thanks."

"You'll have to find a job," she said, sounding more like herself. "No freeloading."

I smiled. "I'll start looking right away," I promised, though I had no idea what sort of job I could find in this little town. I'd do anything to be able to stay while I figured out what I'd do about school, though. "I think I want to go back to college," I said.

"Good," Lisa said with a decisive nod. "Exactly what I was hoping to hear. I owe you the rest of that fifty thousand, plus there's something I didn't tell you."

"What?"

"My father specified that if you'd return to school, his estate would pay for your education, regardless of what you decide to study."

I was speechless, the thrill of her words sinking in. "Oh my God," I said finally. "I don't know what to say. Are you *sure* he was 'of sound mind'?"

Lisa gave me a genuine smile. "You're the last beneficiary of my crazy father's generosity. Use it well." She got to her feet, looking down at the phone in her hand. "And now I need to run to my office," she said. "I'd like you to stay and help Oliver straighten up."

"Sure." I winced as I got to my own feet. "Go do what you need to do," I said. "Oliver and I will take care of the gallery."

⟶⋇⟵

At five thirty I was helping the servers carry the last of the trays out to their van when a limousine pulled into the parking lot, the late summer sun glinting off its shiny black finish. I watched the driver get out of the car and reach for the handle of one of the rear doors, but the door flung open before he'd even touched it, and a woman nearly sprang from the car. She was about sixty, maybe older, and her gray hair was chopped short.

Ignoring the driver, she walked around the front of the limo and opened the other rear door. My heart began to pound. Somehow, I knew who was in that backseat. I *knew* it, and I handed the tray I was carrying to one of the servers and walked toward the limousine. By then, the gray-haired woman was helping a much older woman from the limo. The old woman, who was about my height but whose ramrod-straight posture made her appear taller, didn't look much like the ancient newspaper photographs of Anna Dale, yet I knew without a doubt that was who she was. Her white, chin-length hair was thin, the texture of cotton candy, and she wore small, sparkly pink-and-purple glasses. Her face was full of sharp angles—her chin, her slender nose, her high cheekbones. She wore pink lipstick that looked freshly applied.

"We're very late, I know!" she called to me in a surprisingly strong voice as I approached her. "We had quite the flight, and the drive from the airport took forever. But"—she motioned toward the gallery—"I didn't want to miss this!"

Chapter 66

———— ✤•✤ ————

I reached the old woman where she stood next to the limousine. Her right hand rested on the top of a turquoise wooden cane, so she reached for me with her left hand, which I took in mine. I squeezed her hand gently, surprised to realize that I was fighting back tears.

"Judith Shipley?" I asked, just to be certain my emotions weren't clouding my thinking.

"That's right," she said. "And this is my overprotective assistant, Gloria Hite."

Gloria Hite and I nodded at each other. I seemed unable to find my voice.

"I found the invitation to Jesse's gallery opening in a stack of papers on my desk early this morning," Judith said, cutting a glance at her assistant. "Gloria knows I don't like traveling anymore, so she took the liberty of making the decision for me not to attend. Had I known about it before this morning, we would have been here on time." She gave Gloria a look of mock annoyance.

Gloria ignored the dig. "Let's get you out of this heat," she said.

"We *are* too late, aren't we?" Judith said as we moved at a snail's pace toward the gallery entrance.

I managed to find my voice again. "The . . . festivities ended at five, but you are very, very welcome." My whole body tingled with the excitement of walking next to her. "You're one of our featured artists," I said. "I'm so happy you're here."

"That's very kind of you," she said. I could hear the Northeast in her voice. As I'd read the journal, despite knowing she was from New Jersey, I'd imagined her sounding like me. A born-and-bred Southerner. But now, her—or at least Judith's—roots were clear.

We'd reached the gallery entrance. Through the glass doors, I could see Oliver behind the information counter, the mural a wall of color and craziness behind him. Taking a deep breath, I pulled open the door and held it wide for the two women.

Oliver looked up as we walked inside, but before he had a chance to say anything, Judith dropped her cane to the floor with a clatter.

"Oh!" She raised both hands to her face. "Where . . . ? How did this . . . ?" She turned to Gloria. "I need to sit," she said.

Before Gloria could budge from Judith's side, Oliver raced across the foyer, grabbed a chair from the side wall, and slipped it behind the old woman just in time. Judith nearly fell into it. She pressed her hand to her mouth.

"Do you have some water?" Gloria asked me, and again, Oliver was quicker than I was, producing two small bottles of water from behind the information counter. I seemed to be too numb to move. Oliver unscrewed the top of one of the bottles and handed it to Judith. The second, to Gloria.

"Judith Shipley?" he asked the older woman, as I had only moments earlier.

Judith was drinking from the bottle, her hand shaking wildly, her gaze riveted on the mural.

"Yes," I answered for her. *Yes,* she was Judith Shipley, but if I'd had any doubt that she was also Anna Dale, it had been erased the moment she reacted to the mural. I walked to the side of the foyer to grab another of the chairs and carry it over to where we had gathered, and Gloria sat down on it without a word. She looked at Judith with genuine concern in her dark eyes.

"I *knew* this would be too much for you," she scolded. "You know you don't travel well any—"

Judith raised a hand to stop her. "It's not the travel," she said. "It's this mural. I . . . It's been so long since I've seen it."

I looked at Oliver to discover he already had his eyes on me. I was sure he had the same questions running through his head that I did. How should we approach this? At this point, was there any danger to Judith in revealing that we knew the truth? And how much did Gloria know?

Oliver ducked the questions by getting two more chairs for us, and we sat in a semicircle in the middle of the foyer, all of us gazing at the mural.

"I'm Oliver Jones, the curator for the gallery." Oliver finally introduced himself. He nodded in my direction. "And Morgan here is the person who restored the mural."

Judith looked at me as if seeing me for the first time. "Jesse had it?" she asked.

"Yes." I looked directly at her. "An artist named Anna Dale painted it." Almost without thinking, I reached over. Rested my hand on top of hers. Took a deep breath. "Judith . . ." I glanced at Oliver and he nodded. "We believe that you are Anna."

"*What?*" Gloria looked annoyed. "Who the hell is Anna?"

Judith didn't look at me, but to my surprise . . . and relief . . . a smile began to light her face. "I haven't heard that name in a very long time," she said.

"*Are* you Anna?" Oliver asked. The gentleness in his voice touched me.

Judith nodded. "I suppose there's no harm in saying that now," she said. "I doubt anyone's going to lock up an old woman after eighty years."

"What are you talking about?" Gloria asked.

"Oh, hush," Judith said to her. "I'll explain it all later." She looked at Oliver, then me. "How did you know? Did Jesse say something?"

"I never met Jesse," I said, "but in his will he asked that I be the one to restore the mural, and I—"

"Ah," she interrupted. "You were one of his projects?"

I smiled. "Apparently, though I have no idea how he even knew I existed," I said. "Anyway, Jesse kept the mural in his studio for many years, and—"

"*Here?* In Edenton?" Judith looked stunned, her eyes wide.

"Yes," I said.

"All those times I visited him here, and he never told me he still had it." She looked bewildered. "I knew he . . ." She seemed to catch herself, then continued. "I just didn't know he still had it," she said.

"It was in terrible shape when I started working on it," I said. "But I gradually discovered some strange things about it. A lot of . . . disturbing images, and—"

"Yes, yes." She nodded. "I was going through a . . . a rough patch when I worked on it. It was a difficult time for me."

"What are you talking about?" Gloria asked again.

"I understand that now," I said. "I understand it because I read your journal." Across from me, I could almost feel Oliver tense. We were heading into delicate territory.

Judith frowned, the paper-thin skin of her face suddenly full of new lines and her eyes cloudy with confusion behind her sparkly glasses. "My journal?" she asked.

"Do you remember keeping a leather-bound journal?" I asked. "Your mother gave it to you?"

She looked into the distance, then slowly nodded. "What did I do with it?" she asked. "How did you find it?"

"Do you remember Mama Nelle—"

"Nellie," Oliver corrected me.

"Right," I said. "Nellie. Jesse's little sister? You stayed with them when—"

"The cutest little girl." Judith smiled. "Of course I remember her."

"She passed away recently, and she and I . . . we'd gotten to know each other and she knew I was working on the mural and she left me your journal."

"Nellie had my journal?" Judith looked perplexed, and I guessed she didn't remember leaving it behind when she ran.

"Her family—Jesse's family—kept you safe," Oliver said. "Do you remember that? You stayed with them, while Jesse drove off with the mural in your—"

"Oh, yes, I remember that very well." She chuckled. "Years later, he told me he stowed it in one of his cousin's haylofts before he went in the army. He never told me he found it again, though." She looked at me. "Do you know about the . . . the man? The Edenton portrait artist?" Her expression was wary, as though she wasn't certain she wanted to go there.

I nodded. "Martin Drapple," I said. I thought the name made her wince, but I couldn't be sure. "I'm sorry all that happened to you."

"*What* happened to you?" Gloria asked.

"*Later.*" Judith held up a hand to hush her. She looked from Oliver to me. "I was scared when Jesse moved back to Edenton in . . . when was it? The late seventies. Early eighties? I didn't know who they thought killed that terrible man. I felt safe, hidden away with a new name in New York. But for Jesse to come back here then? A black man? And he kept his same name? I knew there was no . . . what do you call it? The statute . . ."

"Statute of limitations," Oliver said.

"Right," Judith said. "No statute of limitations on murder, and—"

"Murder!" Gloria exclaimed, and we all ignored her.

"And if they suspected he might have done it . . ." Judith let her voice trail off.

"We wondered about that," I said. "How could he have come back safely?"

"It was that boy . . ." Judith looked into the distance, as if trying to remember. "A boy who helped Jesse and me in the warehouse. Blond hair. I don't—"

"Peter?" I asked.

"Was that his name? I believe it was." She nodded. "By the time Jesse had some fame as a New York artist, twentysome years had passed. Peter was high up in the police force here by then. I don't know exactly how, but he swept things under the rug. And by the time Jesse actually moved back to Edenton, Peter was chief of police. Plus forty years had passed. No one remembered what had happened, and if they did, they didn't care. By then, it was 'keep your hands off Edenton's claim to fame, Jesse Jameson Williams.'"

"How did the two of you ever meet up again?" Oliver asked the question I was wondering.

Judith had her eyes on the mural, but I thought she wasn't really seeing it. She was lost in her memories. "Well," she said, "I knew the best place for me to disappear was New York City, so I went there as Judith Shipley, and—" She suddenly laughed and looked at me. "Want to hear how I got that name?" she asked.

"Yes!" I smiled, more at the enthusiasm in her face than the question. I thought I could see the younger woman—Anna—in her face when she laughed.

"Well . . . you must know from the journal that I had a baby, right?"

I nodded. "I'm so sorry you had to go through all that."

"Yes, it was a hard—"

"Was that your daughter Debra?" Gloria interrupted.

"No, no," Judith said. "Debra was born much later. No, that baby was . . . not conceived in love, shall we say. And my labor seemed to go on forever. And I was in Jesse's aunt's room, in her bed—"

"Aunt Jewel," I said.

"Yes, that's right!" She seemed delighted to be reminded of the name. "Aunt Jewel. *Saint* Jewel, I came to think of her. What I would have done without that woman, I don't know." She waved a hand through the air, brushing away the thought. "Anyhow, I knew I'd be leaving soon after the baby was born and I had to think of a new name for myself. Aunt Jewel had a bookshelf in her room, and the whole time I was in labor, I could see those books. And there was one by a Judith Somebody, and the one next to it was by a Somebody Shipley. And I just took those names and threw them together, and that's who I've been ever since."

Gloria's mouth hung open. "I've known you eight years and you never said a word about any of this!" she said. I couldn't tell if she looked more shocked or hurt.

"Because it's ancient history," Judith said. "It's as though it happened to someone else. I made peace with all of it long ago. You have to make peace with the past or you can never move into the future."

"So how did you and Jesse reconnect?" Oliver gently reminded her of the original question.

"Ah, yes," she said. "It was in the late sixties. I'd already made a bit of a name for myself, and one day a friend told me about a show in the Village by a talented black artist who'd just moved to New York from Paris. I just had a feeling it was Jesse. It was like a sixth sense. I walked in and there he was. I was forty-six . . . at least *Judith* was forty-six." She chuckled. "Anna would have been fifty. I hadn't seen him in nearly thirty years. Of course, Jesse didn't recognize me right away, but you should have seen his face when he did! I made sure he met all the right people, then, and of course we became fast friends, as equals finally. There had always been a bond between us. My husband Max was an agent and he took Jesse on as a client, and we introduced him to Bernice, who became his wife. We never lost touch, even after he moved to Edenton. But in all these years, he never mentioned that he still had . . . this." She motioned toward the mural.

"He was adamant you be invited today," Oliver said. "We thought it was because your painting—Judith's painting, *Daisy Chain*—would have a place of prominence in the main gallery. We had no idea it was because of the mural."

Judith turned toward me. "What kind of shape was it in before you restored it?" she asked.

"It was a mess," I said. "And I had such a short time to work on it because he—Jesse—insisted that it be finished by the gallery opening—today. If it wasn't finished, his daughter Lisa—do you remember Lisa?"

"Yes, yes. Of course. I saw her many times."

"If the restoration wasn't completed by today, she'd lose the house."

Judith frowned. "I'm not following you."

Oliver and I explained about Jesse's conditional will. "So I had less than two months to restore the mural and I had no idea what I was doing," I said. "Oliver had to pretty much teach me everything."

"You were a very quick learner." He smiled at me, but Judith hadn't seemed to hear me. She looked deep in thought.

"He insisted the opening be today?" she asked. "August fifth?"

"Yes," Oliver said. "He was firm about it."

Judith nodded. "Well, I can think of one reason why."

"Why?" I asked.

She smiled like the cat that swallowed the canary. "Judith turned ninety-six on June seventh," she said. "But Anna turns a hundred today."

Oliver and I sat in silence as her words registered. I pressed my hand to my mouth.

"*What?*" Gloria sounded shocked. She leaned back to look at Judith. "You're a hundred years *old?*"

"Jesse knew your real birth date?" I asked.

"Oh, yes. He'd always send me a card on that date. *This* date. Today. Not a birthday card, of course. Just a 'thinking of you' type card. I felt sad knowing I wouldn't hear from him this year. It was . . . it was our shared secret, you know? My husband and daughter were the only other people who knew everything. Well, and Jesse's Bernice, of course. But no one else."

"Well." Oliver smiled past the shock he had to be feeling. "Happy birthday!"

"Thank you." Judith returned his smile, and with some effort and a hand on her turquoise cane, she got to her feet. "Now"—she said, nodding toward the mural—"I'd like to get a closer look at that old thing, if I may."

"Of course," Oliver said. He stood up and reached for her elbow, but Gloria slipped between him and Judith to do the job herself.

All four of us stood in front of the mural, and Judith read the wall text—the wall text that was now wildly inaccurate and would have to be rewritten once again. I watched her face as she read, her pink lips moving ever so slightly. Suddenly she gasped. She turned to look at me, her eyes intent on my face.

"Oh, my dear," she said, her voice barely audible. "Oh, my goodness."

The three of us stared at her. "What?" I asked.

She licked her thin lips, her eyes riveted on mine. "I think I know why Jesse chose you to do this work," she said.

Chapter 67

J udith pointed to the last line on the wall text: *Restored by Morgan Chris-topher.* "Is this your name?" she asked. "Not your married name, or . . . is this the name you were born with? Morgan Christopher?"

"Yes," I said, frowning.

She turned back to the wall text and it was a long moment before she spoke again. "Perhaps it's just a coincidence," she said, "but . . ." She glanced toward Oliver. "May I sit down?"

"Of course," he said, and slid one of the chairs over to where she was standing. She shifted the chair slightly so she was facing us and lowered herself into it with a soft groan, her eyes on me the whole time. There was the slightest tremor to her lips.

"My daughter Debra died four years ago," she said.

"I'm sorry," I said.

"Terrible thing, to bury a child." She looked away for the first time in what felt like minutes, but quickly returned her gaze to me. "Shortly before she died, she did one of those . . . DNA tests? You know the ones I mean?"

"Yes." Oliver and I spoke at the same moment.

"Debra knew I'd given up a baby long ago and she was curious to see what might pop up on the test."

"I don't understand how those tests work," Gloria said.

"I would have preferred she not tamper with the past, but I thought she had a right to know if she had cousins or whatever out there." She pressed her lips together, her eyes on me again. She drew in a breath. "Well, what popped up was the surname 'Christopher.' Over and over and over again. Lots of second and third cousins and . . . I don't know what else, but it was clear that name had significance in her family tree."

A chill ran up my arms. I felt Oliver's hand on my back. "It's a pretty common name," I said. Was Judith thinking I was somehow related to the baby she gave away? And how would Jesse have known that? And what possible difference could it make?

Oliver rummaged around on the information counter and found a small notepad and pencil. He set it on the counter near me. Patted my hand. I was sure it felt cold to him. My blood seemed to have stopped flowing.

"Let's figure this out," he said, beginning to write on the notepad. "Anna had a baby in 1940."

"That's right," Judith said from her seat in front of the mural. Her gaze was still riveted on my face. I felt her studying me.

Anna had a baby in 1940 with Martin Drapple, I thought, repelled.

"Why haven't you told me any of this?" Gloria asked Judith, and we all ignored her.

"The baby was given to neighbors of Jesse's family," Oliver said, jotting something on the notepad. "Let's say, for the sake of argument, they had the surname Christopher." He looked at me. "What do you know about your lineage on the Christopher side?"

I thought about it. "Not much. My parents aren't exactly the type to hang on to old mementos and photographs. I know my father was born in

Cary. My grandparents on that side lived in Cary, too. They died when I was pretty young."

"Could your grandfather have been born here in Edenton?" Oliver asked.

"I don't think so . . . I never heard my parents mention anything about Edenton. I'd never even heard of Edenton myself before I met Lisa. And besides, I never met Jesse. How could he have known who I was?"

"Jesse knew who the family was that took my son," Judith said quietly. Now she was looking into the distance with an expression on her face that suggested she was lost in a memory. "He told me once . . . when was it? . . . Maybe 1980, when he moved back here? Yes." She nodded. "That makes sense. I would have been in my early sixties. He told me that his sister Nellie knew the family and where they'd moved to long ago. My son—the baby I gave away—would have been about forty years old then. Jesse said he could tell me where he was, if I wanted to know." Judith looked from me to Oliver. "I told him I didn't want to know," she said with a shake of her head. "I'd closed that chapter of my life long ago."

I frowned at her. "But even if your son was my grandfather, which just . . . I doubt very much, is it just a crazy coincidence that I ended up here? That Jesse picked me to—"

"Not a coincidence," Oliver said.

"He's right." Judith nodded toward Oliver. "I imagine Jesse kept an eye on my son. I'm guessing that he followed that family line just in case I one day said to him, *tell me about my child*. And then you came along, with an interest in restoration and—"

"No, I didn't know anything about restoration," I said. "I was an art major at UNC, and not a very good one, either."

She studied my face for a moment. Then she chuckled. "Well, there you have it," she said. "I can imagine how delighted Jesse was to stumble across someone in the Christopher line who was not only an art major but who was also having a rough time of it. No wonder you became one of his projects."

I held up my hands. "Wait," I said. "I'm still not buying that I'm one of that line of Christophers."

"Call your parents," Oliver said. "Find out where your grandfather was born. Then we'll know if there's anything to this, one way or another."

I felt my face heat up as I thought of making that call. "I can't call them," I said. "I'm not speaking to them. They don't even know I'm out of—" I cut myself off. I didn't want to get into all of that in front of Judith and Gloria. I felt suddenly self-conscious about the monitor on my ankle.

"Call them," Oliver said again. The tone of his voice left no room for argument. I knew he was right. It was the only way to find an answer to this puzzle.

I looked at him for a long moment. "My phone is in the kitchen," I said. "I'll call from there." It was going to be hard enough talking to my parents without an audience. "I'll be back." I turned toward the hallway.

"Want me to come with you?" Oliver offered from behind me, but I shook my head. I needed to do this alone.

⊰•⊱

My mother picked up even before I heard a ring. "Who is this?" she asked instead of hello. A charmer, through and through, my mother. Even with those three words—"Who is this?"—I could hear the booze in her voice.

"It's me," I said. "Morgan."

"What's this number you're calling from?" she asked. "It's not your usual number at the prison."

"I'm out. I'm just calling becau—"

"You're out?" She sounded surprised. "Are you coming home?"

"I'm not coming home," I said. "I just need to speak to Dad for a minute. Is he there?"

"Yeah, he's here, but talk to me. How come they let you out? Why aren't you coming—"

"Put him on, please." I would not get sucked into my mother's weird games and guilt-tripping. I was twenty-two years old. An adult. I could live wherever I pleased.

My mother hesitated. I heard the clink of ice in her glass. Heard her swallow.

"I need to talk to him," I said again. "Please put him on."

"Hold on," she said with a sigh.

I pictured her shuffling through the house toward my father's office. She was probably still in her robe, although it was nearly evening. I cringed at the memory of the house. The air would be filled with the scent of cigarettes and booze and whatever was crusted on last night's dishes in the sink.

"Morgan!" My father shouted in my ear and I quickly adjusted the volume on my phone. "What's this about you being a free woman?"

"I have a question for you," I said.

"What's that, honey?" He could always suck me in with that "honey" crap. Not this time.

"Where was Grampa Christopher born?"

"What?" He laughed. "You just get out of jail and that's the first thing you want to know?"

"Please just tell me."

"Edenton. Why?"

I shut my eyes, the truth dropping on me like a boulder. For a moment, I couldn't speak.

"What color was his hair when he was young?" I asked finally.

"Morgan, I don't under—"

"What color?" My thumb was already on the button that would end the call.

"Red," he said. "People called him 'Red' when he was a kid, and even—"

"Thanks, Dad." I turned off my phone so he couldn't call me back, then stood stock-still, staring out the rear door of the gallery at the lush shrubbery that lined the property.

I was Martin Drapple's great-granddaughter. The thought made me nauseous. But I was Judith's, too. I would focus on that.

"I'm Anna Dale's great-granddaughter," I whispered to myself. "I saved my great-grandmother's mural."

I turned and began walking through the curved hallway of Jesse Williams's gallery, and by the time I reached the foyer, I wore a smile on my face.

Epilogue

———— ✦ ————

MORGAN

Late October, 2018
Apex, North Carolina

Oliver brings his van to a stop in front of the yellow house with the deep green door—the Maxwells' house. The yard is a good size, maybe half an acre, and filled with trees, most of them beginning to show their fall colors. The house is nineteen-eighties vintage and looks well cared for.

"Nice neighborhood," Oliver says.

It is. It reminds me of the neighborhood I grew up in. I study the yellow house. Three steps lead to the front door, but as I look more closely, I can see that a concrete walkway cuts a winding path from the driveway to the side of the front steps. Shrubs line the walkway, making it seem like an organic part of the landscape. Seeing the walkway tightens my heart. Makes everything feel very real. I wonder what other renovations had to be made to the two-story house to accommodate Emily Maxwell and her injuries.

There's a blue van parked in the driveway. Someone is home.

"You sure you don't want me to come in with you?" Oliver asks.

"I'm sure." I think I lean on Oliver too much. He disagrees, pointing out how much he leans on me when it comes to making decisions about Nathan. Maybe it's because I'm eight years closer to twelve than Oliver is, but whatever the reason, Nathan and I click. I love that kid. I suppose Oliver and I are actually pretty even when it comes to leaning on one another. Nevertheless, seeing Emily Maxwell is one thing I need to do alone.

"So, have you decided? Are you going to tell her the truth?" he asks. "That it was Trey behind the wheel?"

I stare at the house. I don't yet know the answer. Oliver wants me to profess my innocence. He hates that I paid for what Trey did. But what is the point? It would be self-serving to tell her. I'm here to make amends, not to make excuses.

"I only want to tell her I'm sorry," I say. "I want to see if there's any way I can help her. I just hope she'll talk to me."

I didn't write to Emily. I didn't call her. I was too afraid she either wouldn't respond or would hang up on me. Of course, this way, showing up uninvited, has its own pitfalls. I fully expect the door to slam in my face. The last thing I want to do is make things worse for her.

"If someone actually lets me in, why don't you go get a coffee or something?" I say to Oliver. "I can call when I'm ready to leave. I don't want you to have to—"

"I'm waiting right here," he says. "I have a book with me. You don't need to rush."

I think he's as uptight about this as I am. "Okay." I look toward the green door. "I don't know whether to hope she's home or hope she's not."

He gives me a gentle shove. "One way to find out," he says.

I nod. Open the van door. Start walking up the driveway. I'm empty-handed and suddenly wish I could have thought of something to bring her. I considered flowers. Homemade cookies. Nothing felt right. I would have to make do with myself and my words. I tell myself I survived prison, restored a mural when I had no idea what I was doing, and haven't had a drink in a year and a half. I can do this. I'm so much stronger than I ever thought I could be.

I'm suddenly overwhelmed by the incredible power of this last year. Working together with Oliver in the gallery. Making discoveries so few people had the privilege to know about. Learning that Judith Shipley is my great-grandmother. My good fortune seems to hit me all at once. What if Jesse Williams had never even known my name? I'd still be in prison. Still spending my nights wide awake, waiting for my silent roommate to slit my throat with a dull butter knife. Still wondering what I could possibly do with my ruined life once I got out. Still with no goals, no love, no passion of any sort.

I climb the front steps, my mind suddenly on Judith. I think of how she was able to face hard truths, writing about them in her journal, painting them into the mural for all the world to see, and then setting them aside, rebuilding her life and moving on. "You have to make peace with the past or you can never move into the future," she said.

Taking a deep breath, I raise my hand to the doorbell. I hear it chime inside and I stand tall, waiting to see what my own future holds.

ACKNOWLEDGMENTS AND AUTHOR'S NOTES

———— ➤•⤜ ————

After my first visit to the charming town of Edenton, North Carolina, I knew I would someday set a book there. It wasn't until I read about the 48-State Mural Competition sponsored by the Treasury Department during the Great Depression that I could envision a story that might fit the small town. I should note that Edenton's post office was not the actual North Carolina recipient of a mural—that honor went to the post office in Boone. But to my mind, Edenton's history and industry lent itself perfectly to such a mural.

Although Edenton's population is under 5,000 people, those people are passionate about their town. As I did my research, I discovered that many, if not most, Edentonians are very tuned into their history, which made writing *Big Lies in a Small Town* a bit daunting, since I wanted to present the town as accurately as an outsider possibly could. In that regard, I had a lot of help and I'm grateful to many people for their generosity and enthusiasm.

I'm most grateful to Sally Kehayes and her husband Alex for introducing me to Edenton and being my enthusiastic guides during my first visit.

Alex's father owned the Albemarle Restaurant where Anna occasionally dines, and Sally has served for many years on Edenton's Historical Commission. She wisely knew I would find inspiration for a story in the little town she and her husband adore.

It's often extremely difficult to see a modern-day town and imagine what it was like nearly eighty years ago, but I was very lucky. The people of Edenton have long memories. I met with Edenton native Philip McMullan, an author in his own right who has written about the parts of North Carolina he loves so much. Phil helped me reconstruct much of Edenton as it was in Anna's time. He could remember every store and filling station and restaurant, helping me map out how the town would have looked—and even smelled—to Anna. He helped me figure out where Anna could stay (with the fictional Miss Myrtle) and what scenes might go into Anna's mural. Thank you, Phil, for your generous spirit.

I knew that race relations were going to play a major role in my story simply by virtue of the town's large African-American population (currently about sixty percent). Although I did my best to understand life between the races both in 1940 and today, I don't pretend to know what it is like now—or was then—for any individual to live there. It was my good fortune to stumble across the Racial Reconciliation group that has met at the United Methodist Church in Edenton for several years. The group was started by Jo Baker and several other concerned townspeople to foster communication between the races. I'm grateful to Jo for inviting me to a meeting, where I expected to find five or six dedicated folks chatting for an hour or two. Instead, I found a large circle of perhaps thirty animated people, black and white, who had clearly become important to one another. They moved me to tears as they described how they'd tiptoed around difficult topics in the beginning, afraid to say anything that might offend. But they were determined to find new ways to understand one another and it was clear to me that they were succeeding. The most obvious indicator of that success, to my eyes, was the little boy who ran from lap to lap in the room, no one a stranger to him. I think Edenton's

Racial Reconciliation group could be a model for similar groups in many other cities in the United States. Here's a link to a video about the group for anyone who might be interested: www.dailypress.com/visuals/video/84720339-157.html.

Through the Racial Reconciliation group, I met two African-American men, Norman Brinkley and Dr. Ben Speller, a historian, both of whom had been boys in Edenton in the forties. I'm grateful to each of them for spending time with me as they helped me understand what Jesse Williams's life might have been like as a teenager. It would have been close to impossible for me to write about Jesse without Norman's and Ben's valuable input.

The Shepard Pruden Memorial Library is near the lovely waterfront in Edenton. Librarian Jennifer Finlay answered my questions, and Joyce White helped me use the microfilm machine to read the 1940 *Chowan Herald*, as Morgan does in *Big Lies*.

Speaking of the *Chowan Herald*, I'm grateful to the late reporter Rebecca Bunch for accurately and generously covering my visits to Edenton. Rebecca was clearly devoted to the town. I quickly learned that I could trust her reporting, and I'm very saddened by her death.

During my visits to Edenton, I stayed at Susan Beckwith's beautiful Inner Banks Inn, where the rooms are filled with history. Thank you, Susan, for your lovely inn and the incredible breakfasts.

One more Edentonian I'd like to acknowledge is Elizabeth Berry of the Garden of Readin' Bookstore and Tea Room. Thank you for helping me with my first Edenton book event, Elizabeth, and I hope we get to work together again. Elizabeth also makes a great cup of tea!

Probably most overwhelming to me as I did my research for this book was my need to learn about mural restoration. Jan Hessling of Hessling Conservation LLC in Durham, North Carolina, spent hours with me, illustrating the tools and techniques of her trade. Thank you, Jan, for the time you took to give me so much information about your work—and the work Morgan would have to do on the mural. You were an amazing resource.

I'm also grateful to my stepdaughter, Brittany Walls, an artist by training, for helping me understand some of the artistic elements that went into
Anna's painting and Morgan's restoration.

Speaking of Morgan, I needed to learn about her crime, her punishment, and her parole. Former probation officer Jason Dzierzynski was a
wonderful resource for me, as was an old high school friend who prefers
to remain nameless. Thank you both for taking the time to answer my
many questions and for helping me make Morgan's crime and punishment
realistic and believable.

I'm grateful to my assistant Kathy Williamson for whom no task is too
challenging, and my sister Joann Scanlon for reading an early draft of *Big
Lies in a Small Town* and offering helpful feedback.

Thank you to my North Carolina writing friends, those women who
understand the joy, creativity, self-doubt, and just plain hard work that goes
into writing a novel. Special thanks to Mary Kay Andrews. We spent a
week together in her beautiful Tybee Island home, writing and researching and brainstorming our works in progress. Thank you, Mary Kay, for
sharing your home, your friendship, and your ever-inventive brain with me.

I'm convinced I have the best agent in the world in Susan Ginsburg.
Susan is perceptive, talented, and kind, but ferocious when she needs to
be on behalf of her clients. I'm so lucky to have her in my corner. Thanks
also to the rest of the staff at Writers House for their hard work on behalf
of my books, especially Catherine Bradshaw and Peggy Boulos Smith and
those folks who work behind the scene to get my books into the hands of
my readers. Thanks, too, to Lucy Stille at the Agency for Performing Arts.

Jen Enderlin, my ever-perceptive editor, can read a manuscript and
immediately see how it can be improved. Authors get so close to their
work that it's sometimes impossible for them to see the imperfections. I've
learned to trust and respect Jen's editorial superpowers and I'm grateful
that I get to work with her.

My publicist at St. Martin's, Katie Bassel, gets special thanks for setting
up my book tours—and setting them up again after my bouts of laryngitis

caused cancellations last year. Thanks, Katie, for your patience and perseverance.

I'm also grateful to the rest of the folks at St. Martin's who make my books the best they can be. Thank you, Sally Richardson, Brant Janeway, Erica Martirano, Jeff Dodes, Lisa Senz, Kim Ludlam, Malati Chavali, Jonathan Hollingsworth, Anne Marie Tallberg, Tracey Guest, Lisa Davis, Mike Storrings, and everyone in the sales department. Special thanks to Danielle Fiorella for the beautiful cover!

Thanks also to my UK editor, Wayne Brooks, and to all the people at Pan Macmillan who work hard to help my books reach my beloved UK readers.

As always, I'm grateful to my significant other, John Pagliuca, for all he does to free up my writing time, for not complaining about all the DoorDash meals, and for being ready and willing to help me escape any corner I've written myself into.

And finally, thank you to my readers around the world. You are the people who make it all worthwhile!